Kiwi Rules

ROSALIND JAMES

Kiwi Rules

Afghanistan hadn't quite killed me. Karen Sinclair just might.

You don't find many too-pretty rich boys in the New Zealand Defence Force. Turns out there's a reason for that. Fortunately, you can find your true self in the oddest places. Of course, you can lose yourself in those places, too—at least some pieces of you.

Since I was back home with a new leg, some facial alterations, and time on my hands, I might as well help out my sister. Showing a potential buyer around some of New Zealand's quirkier ecotourism sites, having a few adrenaline-fueled adventures? Fine. It wasn't like I'd never been camping, unlike the walking tornado that was Miss Karen Sinclair. Unfortunately, Karen had never heard of the phrase, "Let me get that," let alone, "We don't have time." She'd definitely never heard, "There's no more room in the car."

And then there was the sexual frustration.

A coward dies a thousand deaths before his death,
but the valiant taste of death but once.
— William Shakespeare, *Julius Caesar*

He toa taumata rao.
Courage has many resting places.
— Maori proverb

CONTENTS

AUTHOR'S NOTE

This is a work of fiction. Names, characters, places, and incidents are products of the author's imagination or are used fictitiously and are not to be construed as real. Any resemblance to actual events or persons, living or dead, is entirely coincidental.

1

WINTER CHILL

KAREN

The annoying *beep-beep-beep* of my phone alarm finally pierced my concentration.

Nine fifty-five, and five minutes until I had to be in the conference room. *Damn* it. I pulled off my headphones and shoved back from my desk, and the rolling wheels of my chair took me all the way across my work space, which was separated only by a filing cabinet from the next desk in our not-yet-gentrified loft space in Philadelphia's Brewerytown. The whole place was buzzing with the heady excitement of a company about to explode, like the moment when the booster rocket fires and the space shuttle launches into the stratosphere. Just that scary, and just that exciting.

I was so close to getting this proposal together, though, and I'd wanted to surprise Josh and the corporate reps with it in the meeting, my own "Welcome to our new incarnation!" gift. You got what you gave, I'd figured, and I had so much still to give. I'd been up until two this morning working on it, and had caught three hours of sleep on the couch in the break room before the ideas had pulled me back to my desk again. Which may have meant that I wasn't quite as put-together as a woman might want to be on the occasion of her company being bought out by one of the largest food conglomerates in the world, but I wasn't being brought on board for my glamour.

I'd *meant* to wear a red knit turtleneck dress and high boots today—the building was never quite warm enough, especially in December, and red was my celebration color—but they were at home in the closet, so there you were. I pulled my oversized gray sweater down over my skinny jeans to hide the mustard stain from where a piece of yesterday's sandwich had dropped into my lap, hoped my hair wasn't too much of a disaster, grabbed my phone, a ballpoint, and the spiral notebook I carried everywhere—glittery silver this time, because it had seemed like the right month for glittery silver—and headed across the office to the conference room.

"Hey, good luck," Jada Castor called to me from where she was lying on the floor, going from bridge pose into a backbend. "Getting my mojo back," she called it, "and the blood to my head, where it can do me some damn *good.*" I should do that, too, stretch during the day. I always forgot.

I waved at her, and at the other heads that popped up like prairie dogs to watch me. Not everybody would be moving to New York after the buyout, but at least they had the choice, and the prospect of so much more. This was the best thing that could happen for the team.

As for me, I couldn't wait, even though I'd miss the world's coolest condo. Josh and I had already given notice on our place in the brick building on Race Street, in the heart of Old City, with its art galleries and coffee shops. I'd miss running three blocks to the river, too, then starting to push it for real, getting in my workout along the Delaware. If the guy with the Saint Bernard was around, I'd get the chance to pet her while she leaned her head against my leg and waved her enormous tail. There'd be dogs in New York, of course, but where would I find one sweeter than Buttercup? I'd also miss the rowing club. I got a pang even now thinking that this spring, I wouldn't be out there helping to put the boat in the water for the first outing of the season.

On the other hand, New York meant my family. My sister, Hope, my brother-in-law, Hemi, and my three favorite kids in the world. I'd loved living there before, and I could love it again, the same way I'd come to love Philadelphia. I was good at adapting, and I'd be moving for the best of reasons. For opportunity. For progress.

The sky outside the huge windows of the freezing-cold conference room was too dark for this to be morning, though, surely, and I got one of those sideways moments where your reality tilts, when you're not sure what you're seeing or even where you are.

Never mind. Lack of sleep. Excitement. I shook reality back into place, then went to sit beside Josh, on the window side of the room, and said, "Huh. Snowing."

He looked at me oddly, and his blue-marbled, gold-nibbed fountain pen tapped against the leather-bound legal pad under his hand. Back and forth, a tattoo of nerves. "It's the biggest storm of the season," he said. "Didn't you even look out the window last night?" He looked me over, and probably saw the mustard stain, but he didn't say anything.

I should have asked him to bring my good clothes from the condo. It had never even occurred to me. He was wearing a black blazer and wool slacks that Hemi would have approved of, especially on Josh's muscular physique, with black leather sneakers and a pumpkin-colored crewneck sweater in fine wool, and he'd obviously shaved about an hour ago. He'd gotten a haircut, too, in the past couple days. Unlike me.

Oh, well. I wasn't the outward-facing part of the company. I was the idea woman.

The door opened, and Deborah Delaney came in with David Glass. The representatives from M&P, the conglomerate that was acquiring Prairie Plus. The acquisition I'd worked toward, and possibly dreaded, too, for seven years now. It meant sharing the responsibility, and it opened so many doors, but it also meant not having nearly as much say. I wasn't all that good at toeing somebody else's line. I'd been able to work with Josh because he treated me like a partner.

Witness my being part of this meeting. What would it be like when we were folded into M&P?

I stood up and shook hands, but as Deborah and David took their seats, I muttered to Josh, "We could still change our minds."

He stared at me like he didn't know me, or like he knew me too well. "No. We couldn't. It's done."

"Let's get started," Deborah said, "shall we?" She nodded at Josh, and he pulled a couple stapled sheets of paper from his leather binder as she tapped her own pen—also fancy, because being corporate obviously meant having a fancy pen—on the secondhand table we'd bought from an office-supply liquidator.

I was surprised that the document wasn't longer, and that Josh had it. I'd pictured him signing in fifty places. But then, I'd also been surprised the formal handover wasn't happening in New York. Josh had told me not to worry, so I hadn't.

Deborah said, "First order of business. We've had quite a few discussions at headquarters over how to structure Prairie Plus over the past few weeks, and, Karen, our final decision on that concerns you."

"Oh, good," I said, "because I have a new idea. A whole new product line. Sausage. Everybody loves it, but it's about the worst thing for you, and if it isn't bad for you, it doesn't taste good. I've figured out how to fix that."

Deborah had her hand up, palm out, and I stopped talking and glanced at Josh. His pen was going faster. *Taptaptaptaptap.*

Deborah said, "We've decided not to bring you on board. We have the R&D capability in-house, and it's a question of economies of scale and being free to find the most efficient processes. It was a tough decision, and I know it will be a disappointment to you, but I suggest you look at it as your next opportunity. You still have your stock options, of course, and Josh is going to take care of those now."

Josh slid the paper over to me. Silently. He also wasn't quite looking at me. I stared down at the black type. I was having trouble breathing. I was having trouble not passing out, in fact.

4

Meanwhile, Josh was pulling something else out of the folder. Another piece of paper. A green one. The exact size and shape of a corporate check, in fact. *Our* corporate check. He cleared his throat, and the blood drained from my head.

They'd planned this. They'd *rehearsed* this.

We'd ordered the first batch of checks together, choosing the cheapest option, black type on a green background, because we were going to be about the product, not the trimmings. It was one of those scary, heady days at the very beginning, soon after I'd joined the bare-bones, not-yet-profitable corporation Josh had started on the money he'd saved from five extremely well compensated years as a brilliant and ruthlessly efficient Wall Street analyst. We'd come up with our concept before we'd even finished the MBA program, when I'd woken from a dream of green grass, black-and-white cattle munching contentedly, a flock of orange chickens pecking around them, and a field of garbanzos beyond them. Who dreams about garbanzos? Me. I'd sat upright in bed and shouted, "Prairie Plus!" And here we were.

Right here.

Prairie Plus was everything we were, I'd thought on the day when the fake-leather binder full of cheap-ass green checks had arrived. It was our bodies and our minds both, and Josh's body and mind were as well trained and as intensely focused as mine. What was even better, though? They were focused on the exact same thing. I'd felt so lucky to have found that. To have found *him*.

His heart, though? His soul? Maybe not so much.

He was talking. Confidently, as always. Persuasively. He said, "You have forty thousand options. I'm calling them. At the forty-dollar strike price, and a fifty-dollar buyout price, that leaves you with four hundred thousand dollars. All you have to do is sign, and the money's yours."

He handed me his pen, and I took it without thinking as I stared at him, then at Deborah, and at David Glass beside her. They both looked absolutely calm. David's hair was parted too perfectly, and it lay too neatly. His hair annoyed me.

They weren't sweating, of course. Nobody was, because it was cold in here. Nobody was burning but me.

Four hundred thousand dollars for seven years of eighty-hour weeks, working in the test kitchen until my eyes blurred and my muscles quivered with fatigue, finalizing my notes so I wouldn't forget, and then cleaning up after myself, when all I'd wanted was to crawl onto the break-room couch and collapse? Seven years of making calls and taking flights and meeting farmers, of negotiating and persuading and listening? Of taking half of what I could have earned in a larger company, so Josh could pour back more into the business? Seven years of helping him build a national brand that was poised to take off and soar, knowing that once it did, I'd be set?

This wasn't how it was supposed to work.

Wait, though. I was *out?* I was off the team? I didn't get to do any of it with them? How could I . . . how could that . . .

I couldn't breathe. I didn't want to keep looking at Josh, but I did anyway. He said, "I'm sorry. It wasn't my idea."

"When did you . . ." I had to stop and haul some air into my lungs. "When did you know?"

"Barely more than a week ago. I couldn't tell you. It was part of the deal." I kept staring at him, and his blue eyes slid away, then back to mine. "And it's probably for the best. For you, too. It was time. You'll see that, when you've got some distance from it. I know you think you're the only one who can do this, the one who really makes it happen, but you're too idealistic. We've talked about that. It gets in your way. It got in *our* way. Anyway, now the deal can go through, which will be better for everybody else, which you care about, and you can develop some of your other ideas. You can be as idealistic as you want."

I was so hot, I wanted to pull off my sweater, and the red mist was rising into my head, behind my eyeballs. I said, "It's for the *best?* Is that why you didn't tell me before? For somebody who's supposed to love me, selling me out sure came easy, didn't it? But that's not even the worst part. You're dumping me because I keep insisting on doing it right. That's not just wrong, it's stupid. No matter what you think, you can't separate the ideals from the business. The ideals *are* the business."

I looked at Corporate Ken and Barbie. They weren't impressed. They were waiting for me to finish melting down, after which they'd start in on stripping the soul and the mission from Prairie Plus, turning our carefully sourced, sustainably produced products into more plastic-wrapped packages from the factory farm.

"I'm not dumping you," Josh said. "This isn't about us, it's about the business. Your ideals aren't realistic. They're not cost-effective, and they're holding us back. You're not living in the real world. It's a phase that you can move out of, though. You have everything it takes."

Wasn't that special? "No," I told him, "I'm living in a new world. Lots of other people want to live there, too. Like our *customers*. It's why we sell! It's what people want! And—" My brain was catching up too slowly, my thoughts too jumbled. I wasn't professional? I might as well own it. "Where's loyalty in your real world?" I asked him. "Is that idealism, too? You told me we were partners in every way that counted. That somebody had to be in charge, and the business side was the boring side. I was so *smart*, so *talented*, so I should just focus on what only I could do, and let you do the rest. I believed you. I'm sure that makes me even more stupid, but what does it make you?"

Oh, boy. I was realizing something else. Slowly, but what could you do. "And this doesn't have to do with us? What about when we made love, what, three nights ago? You already knew that you were going to stab me in the back, didn't you? You didn't have any problem with me being too generous then, either. You didn't have any problem at all asking for more. Remember how you said that next time, it was my turn? It's not my turn, is it? It's never going to be my turn, because it's always *your* turn."

Josh glanced at the others, then away, and said, "This isn't the right time or place. I'm sorry you're hurt, but this isn't personal. We'll talk about it later."

My chair made a scraping noise as I got to my feet, and I

realized I was still holding Josh's pen. What kind of Judas moment was that, having me sign the separation papers with his special pen? Who would do that? I signed my name to the paper in a looping scrawl and told him, "Give me my check."

He handed it over without a word, I folded it and stuffed it into my jeans pocket, and I could see the relief on his face. Like—"Whew! Glad that's over! Now let's get to work, shall we? Without any of that pesky emotion. Any of that troublesome passion and determination." Everything that had made me push for us to be the best, and not to settle for less. Everything I *was*.

He didn't want that? Well, I didn't want him, either. I didn't need a weasel sellout in my life. I didn't need a rat.

Behind Deborah, the conference-room door opened. A guy stood there. A driver, he looked like. A big guy.

They'd called in security. To escort me out of *my* office. *My* space. *My* company. My *brainchild*.

I was still holding that stupid pen, the one Josh had been using since we'd been at NYU together. That very first day in Firms & Markets, in the junior year of my Biochem degree and the first year of the concurrent MBA program I'd tacked onto it, he'd been sitting in the front row like nobody but me ever did, wearing a black sweater that looked like cashmere. His dark hair had fallen over his eyes as he wrote with his fountain pen, while everybody else took notes on their laptop. He'd caught me looking, had stared back at me for a long moment, and then, when I'd thought he wouldn't, he'd smiled. A knowing smile, like he knew my dirty secrets. Like he was ten years older and a hundred years more worldly, and he couldn't wait to show me how. My heart had jumped into my throat, and I'd thought, *That's my guy. Oh, baby.*

Now, he held his hand out for his pen. I ignored him, opened my dollar-ninety-eight, silver-glitter-covered spiral notebook to a new page, wrote *Josh Ranfeld is four inches. Maybe five,* in enormous sapphire-blue-ink letters, ripped it out, and slapped it onto the table.

"Karen," Deborah said, her voice pained. "That's hardly helpful."

"No?" I asked, and my voice barely shook. "And yet I find it strangely satisfying." I pressed down on the gold nib of the pen, then, like I wanted to press all the way through the notebook to the cardboard backing. I pushed with the strength of a hundred hours of running beside the river to clear my head and let the wonderful ideas come. Five hundred hours of rowing until my palms blistered, heaving air into my burning lungs. *Tens* of thousands of hours of thinking and planning and talking and testing and *working* to make all of this happen, because it was going to pay off someday. We were going to make our fortunes, and everybody else's, and do good for the planet, too.

I pressed until the ink pooled on the paper and the pen's nib snapped off, and Josh jumped up.

"Too late," I told him. "But then, you always did have trouble keeping up with me." Then I whirled toward the windows. They still opened, because we couldn't afford rent on a fancy place, not when we were saving our money for the important things. I yanked the black handle and got ready to throw.

I checked first, of course, that I wasn't going to hit somebody. I mean, however mad you got, you couldn't hurt some innocent pedestrian, or crack a motorist's windshield and make them crash. The hesitation gave Josh a chance to grab my hand, and gave the security guy a chance to head over, too.

I shoved Josh hard with my other hand, right in the stupid pumpkin sweater, and sent him crashing backward into the corner. Then I threw the paper and pen out the window.

The wind swirled and blew the paper against the glass, and it stuck there.

Josh Ranfeld is four inches. Maybe five.

The security guy smiled. I saw it. So did Josh.

The pen landed in the street, like I'd meant it to, and a UPS truck rolled over it and drove off through the slushy snow.

"Your package is busted," I told the man of my dreams. "Sorry."

☆☆

JAX

I was so cold, my teeth were chattering.

The bone-white sky above me was tinged with brown clouds. Clouds weren't meant to be brown. They should be gray, full of rain. Keeping the hills green.

I hadn't felt rain in so long. I wanted to feel it now. The cool touch of it, the wetness on your face, your tongue. The prickle of wet grass under your bare feet as you ran, and the patter of raindrops on leaves when you took shelter under the trees. Instead, the choking dust hung in the still air. There was wetness in my mouth, but I was desperately thirsty all the same. The liquid tasted metallic, like I'd drunk from an old-fashioned canteen. I could sense movement around me, but I couldn't hear a thing.

Somebody's face over mine, then. Sergeant Sharif Khan, part of the Afghan unit we'd been training. His mouth was moving, his expression urgent, but I couldn't hear. He wasn't wearing a helmet, and he needed to put it on, because the base was under attack. Wasn't it? There had been a truck. I'd seen the face in the window, the smile, and had been moving forward at a run, shouting, when the white light and the pressure wave had hit me.

I needed to get up. Right the hell now. Where there'd been one explosion, there could be more, and I needed to deal with that. The freezing cold was creeping up my legs, though, and I couldn't feel my feet.

I turned my head, because there was more movement over there. Figures coming through the brown haze, moving fast.

Taliban. Get up. My weapon was there, on the ground, my LMT MARS-L, which should be on its sling, around my neck. I could see it. Out of reach.

Not if I *moved.*

Come on, you bugger. Move. The brown haze was wavering, though, trying to go into blackness, my head was light, and the nausea was rising from my chest and into my throat.

You're not dead yet. I raised myself on my elbows and was preparing to scoot back when another shock wave hit me.

Another explosion. White-hot, blooming like a mushroom cloud.

Not an IED, I realized dimly, through the frenzy in my body. This explosion came from inside me.

You couldn't feel this much pain. It wasn't possible. It would kill you.

I kept working on dragging myself toward my weapon anyway. If I got to it, I could fight back, instead of lying here, unable to help. I set my teeth against the scream, raised my head, scooted back another few centimeters on my elbows, and saw the boot. On its side.

It wasn't empty.

Some poor bastard had lost a leg, because I hadn't been fast enough. My fault.

The pale leather had a white mark on it, a deep scratch on the heel that was cut nearly through, from where I'd slid down a gully feet-first and had cut it on a rock outcrop two days ago.

Somebody else materialized from the dust cloud. Herbie Wilson, medic, and foulest mouth in the New Zealand Defence Force. His mouth was moving, which meant he was swearing, even if I couldn't hear it. He had his hands on me, which meant I couldn't make it to my weapon, or that I could stop trying. I could feel the vibration through the ground, too, the steady *whomp-whomp-whomp* of a bird coming in.

Medevac, or air support, or both.

I needed to replace that boot, I thought as the pain took me into the fire, burned me down, and charred my bones. That boot was buggered.

There wasn't much more important than your boots.

You couldn't . . . run . . . without your . . . boots.

2

☆☆

DEFINITELY NOT A FETISH

KAREN

The man came out of the ocean like the god of the sea. Or half of him did.

At first, I thought, *Wait. How is the water that deep?* I might only have been in New Zealand for five hours this time around, but I'd spent a fair amount of time in the past on Main Beach at Mount Maunganui, and there was no way the bottom dropped out as quickly as that, even at low tide. It was a long beach. An enormously long, sheltered, peaceful, absolutely New-Zealand-y beach, which was why I'd come here straight from the airport instead of driving the forty-five minutes to Waihi Beach, where I could have—well, gone to the beach. By stepping over the wall from the patio.

It wasn't what somebody else would have done, maybe, but I didn't have to make sense or be logical. I was giving myself a pass on that for today. I might feel like a woman whose soul had been scrubbed raw, who was starting again from the bottom, but you know what they say about the bottom. The only place to go is up.

Tomorrow, I'd start answering to somebody else, being responsible for somebody else's money and somebody else's business. Tomorrow, I'd start getting my optimism back, and my drive. Tonight, I was on my own, and I was going to do what I wanted. And when I'd stepped off the plane at Tauranga Airport more than twenty-four hours after I'd stepped onto another one at New York's LaGuardia, and had been catapulted magically out of the slushy depths of winter, with icy berms of snow turned to a dirty brown by too many honking cars and too many people hustling through the whistling wind like it was a race, and into a sunny afternoon in a place where even the birds looked relaxed, what I'd wanted was to go to the beach right the hell now.

So I'd left a company I loved and had helped build from the ground up, and been beaten down in the process. So I'd lost a boyfriend, or a fiancé-without-the-ring, or an almost-partner, or whatever Josh had actually been besides "bad boy." And "rat." I was far away from all of it and ready for some Girl Time, and I'd learned something, which mattered. Or it would sometime, when it had stopped being "flayed-skin humiliation" and had become "life lesson" instead.

One of those life lessons should be that every bad boy I'd ever met had just turned out to be a bad man. Yet here I was, caught up once again in the seduction of the slow burn, the sidelong, smoldering glance, and the tantalizing suggestion of darkness inside, just from watching a man coming out of the water.

Wait, though. The beach *didn't* slope that much, because there was a toddler standing in the water not too far from him, and she looked normal. Mr. Intense was on his knees. *Walking* on his knees.

Well, *that* was weird.

He wasn't the god of the sea anyway, because that would have been Neptune. Poseidon. Whatever you wanted to call him. Old guy, white beard. This guy wasn't old, and he didn't have a beard. He did have some *very* manly shoulders, though. And not much tan at all, which was strange in a sea god. Not even a below-the-T-shirt-sleeve tan, like you'd expect from a man who spent any time at all outdoors. He did, however, have abs you could eat off of. Like a table, that is, not in a dirty way. Or possibly in a dirty way, too.

New York women of my acquaintance, especially those who'd gone to NYU, tended to be drawn to the metrosexual type. The sensitive, artistic type. Unfortunately, my preference now seemed to be muscles, non-gym levels of toughness, and men who could do things with their hands and possibly didn't smile much. See "Bad-boy obsession, unfortunate." Right this moment, I was liking dark, aggressively short hair sticking up spikily from what I guessed had been a hard swim, shoulder and arm muscles that announced they were here to work, and something about his body language that was way too purposeful for a guy hanging out at the beach.

There was something odd about his shoulder and chest, though I couldn't see quite what from here. Maybe he was a merman. That would explain the top-half deal, the no-tan, the fined-down muscle, and the intensity, if mermen were intense. I'd read a book once, as a teenager, about an intense merman. He'd stuck with me.

There were no actual mermen, though, in New Zealand or elsewhere, so . . . why was he on his knees? Had he stepped on a stingray? Been stung by a jellyfish? You'd be hopping, though, or hobbling, in that case, wouldn't you? Also, you'd be screaming. At least I had, the one time I'd been stung by a jellyfish, in Australia. I'd thought I knew all about pain, but that had *hurt*.

He looked too calm to have been stung by a jellyfish, no matter how tough he was. Just as I was thinking it, he leaned forward, set his palms on the firm sand at the water's edge, swung a foot up and between them in a sort of yoga pose that was nearly a handstand, got upright on his feet—foot—and hopped.

Oh. His left leg ended a few inches below the knee. *That* was something you didn't see every day. He hopped on the other leg up the beach, bent over and lowered himself down, and came up shoving glasses onto his face. Black-rimmed, rectangular glasses. Nerd glasses.

Nerd glasses and muscles *and* toughness? Whew.

Maybe I had a previously unrealized amputee fetish. That would be weird and uncomfortable, except that I wasn't checking out his missing leg. I was checking out the rest of him as he pulled a khaki T-shirt over his head and down a whole long stretch of torso.

No tattoos, which meant he was unlikely to be Maori or Samoan even in part, disappointing as that was. In New Zealand, tattoos were mostly tribal, and you didn't ink up with a tribal tattoo if you weren't part of the tribe. It was disrespectful, which was why I had no tattoos. Non-tribal ones seemed lame in comparison: Flowers or zodiac signs or birds, not to mention Chinese characters that turned out to mean "Terrible mistake" or "Barbecue grill" instead of "Courageous heart," like the tattoo artist had told you. My sister Hope had bought me a robe like that in college, when I'd finally moved out and gone to live in the dorms, and a classmate had had to clue me in. I'd *wondered* why the Chinese girls had giggled when I'd encountered them in the bathroom. Imagine finding out that was your tattoo. The mind boggles.

And if I felt like I was wearing that "Terrible mistake" tattoo right now—that was why I was here, wasn't it? Life reboot.

Which reminded me that I didn't want a man anyway, so the merman's ethnic background didn't matter. I was in no position to have a romance, and I was bad at hookups, since I tended to lead with my heart. At least I'd been bad at them eight or nine years ago. Call me out of practice. The very *last* thing I needed was an encounter, romantic or no, with a brooding, damaged bad boy. A fling guaranteed to leave me sobbing into my pillow and seeing a couple more ribs in the mirror? Nope. I didn't need any more drama.

That sounded breezy. Breezy was good. I'd used to be that way naturally. Right now, I was having to fake it, but it beat sobbing and collapsing again.

Meanwhile, I was noticing that my not-rebound had *really* nice thighs, thick with defined muscle. When he hopped, they had to work hard, and I could see them doing it.

Possibly, I was creepy. But I hadn't even *looked* at a man

this way for so long. Josh had been surprisingly insecure, I was realizing. I'd thought it was "sexy possessiveness," but then, I'd thought a lot of stupid things. Now, it was like being too sick to eat for months, when you hadn't been able to stand even looking at food, and then getting well and thinking, "Ooh. I want some of that. With bacon and extra cheese."

I'd stop staring at him, though. Not cool. Anyway, if I had somebody in mind to help me over my rough patch—and I might—it wasn't him.

My non-staring wasn't quite working, because I noticed when he wobbled a little on the sand, then caught his balance and looked around. He saw the kids at the same time I did, and he went—"on alert," I'd call it. Like something was going to happen, but what could happen? The teenagers were a good twenty-five yards away, and he was balanced on one foot. The guys were messing around with a pair of crutches. Laughing. Entitled. Punks.

Oh.

I knew that kind of kid. I *hated* that kind of kid.

I could do something about that, anyway.

3

☆☆

ONE LITTLE PUNCH

JAX

First time, worst time, I'd thought when I'd come out of the anonymity of the sea on my knees and prepared to face the world again.

Swimming had been better than I'd expected, once I'd adjusted for the difference in my kick that'd had me traveling persistently to one side at first, since my left leg couldn't do as much without a foot, and there were no lane markings here to keep me on course. The salt water was cooler and more buoyant than the pool at the therapy center, and the solitude, the endless, scrubbed-clean expanse of sea and sky, were exactly why I was in this spot, the thing I'd missed most during four and a half very long months.

The quiet, or not exactly, because the sea was never that. The murmur and swish of the water as you passed smoothly through it, the undulating sound that was the ocean breathing, the taste of salt water on your lips. The feeling that settled all the way into your belly. You could call it peace. Not something that had been in overlarge supply in my life in recent years. I wouldn't want it all the time, I hoped, but I could use it just now.

I'd had to use my core more during the swim to compensate for my lower legs, which was all good. I had more core strength now than I'd ever possessed in the past, when I'd supposedly had everything. Counting my blessings, as per requirements. Now, my muscles were trembling a little with hard use, which was also a good sign.

You could get a sort of aqua-leg that ended in a swim fin, and put a regular fin on your remaining leg. You'd be nearly superpowered then. I hadn't wanted to do that straight away, though. I'd needed to go out there under my own steam, unburdened by technology, and see what happened. And to let people see me outside of any kind of controlled environment, uncovered, scarred, and without my leg, and get the first time over with. If you couldn't look at things straight on, you couldn't see past them, and I needed to see past them. I had absolutely no intention of staying in this spot, because this spot sucked.

I wasn't wearing my specs, which was unfortunate, or maybe not, because I couldn't see people staring. If I were looking at things straight on, though, that included admitting that this was bloody awkward.

Don't fall over, and you're all good. This morning, I'd rolled out of bed after a dream in which I was running with my squad, my heart pounding, my lungs burning, and everything in me responding to the challenge. My body was weighed down with its usual thirty kilograms of kit, and I was holding my weapon like an extension of my hands, with the adrenaline flowing through me and making me feel invincible. Unbreakable. It had all been so vivid, and more real than anything in my life had felt for nearly half a year. It had been right there, under my feet, in my hands, all around me. Power. Hardship, and surmounting it. The possibility of death, and the awareness that you were alive.

I'd woken, realized it was daylight outside, I wasn't in the desert, and there was no life-and-death happening at all, had let the wave of disappointment wash over me, then thought, *Bathroom,* and headed for it. Upon which I'd fallen straight over, bang onto the floor, because I'd tried to set down a leg that wasn't there.

It was a good sign that I'd forgotten, I reckoned. It meant I felt like myself again, and not like a capital-A Amputee. It was one leg, and a few cosmetic alterations to my face and torso. *Half* of one leg, actually. It wasn't like I'd lost the wedding tackle.

I'd be remembering to forget some more right now, except that I was lacking the necessary equipment to do it. I couldn't see perfectly, but I could see that. My shirt was where I'd left it, four or five meters from the water's edge, but when I got there, my specs weren't on it as I'd left them. They were beside it instead, half buried in the sand. I shoved them onto my face, got my shirt on, and looked around.

Crowded beach by New Zealand standards, because it was January and the school holidays, it was Saturday, it was Mount Maunganui, and it was a warm afternoon by temperate New Zealand standards. On the beach in front of me, a dad was playing cricket with his kids above the high-tide mark. In the sea behind me, kids called to each other and dove under the waves in the familiar rhythm of home, fourteen thousand kilometers from the harsh, barren Afghan hills and even farther away in spirit. A few meters to my right, a mum came up from the sea, holding hands with a toddler in pink togs and water wings.

"All right?" she asked, catching my eye.

"All good," I said. "Cheers." Not quite true, but not the worst thing that had ever happened to me, either. There would be an answer. It would turn up any minute.

Ah. There you were. A group of teenaged boys well over to my left, aged maybe seventeen, running in a pack and cocky with it. One of them was trying out my crutches, and all of them were laughing.

First time, worst time. I was contemplating which would be worse—hopping, or walking on my knees over there, and deciding they were both fairly horrible—when I noticed the girl, and something happened in my gut, and in my lungs.

She was looking at me. Standing still. Her build was on the decidedly thin side, her black-and-gray camo bikini top and tiny black shorts were on the resolutely functional side, and her hair was on the absolutely short side, but that thing happened anyway.

Very long legs. Very nice waist. Very direct gaze. Very good . . . stance. The only problem was that two seconds after I'd registered all of that, she was flinging her bag onto the sand and heading over to the kids in a near-run like the goddess of vengeance, and you didn't need to be a mind reader to sort out why.

What. The. *Hell.* I didn't need a protector, and I needed a good-looking woman who felt sorry for me less than that. I started hopping, gritting my teeth at the effort of staying balanced on the sloping sand. Hopping had been surprisingly difficult at first. Good for the core strength, though, like swimming without part of your leg.

Focus on the strength, not the weakness.

I was still ten meters away when the girl started talking.

De-escalation was a skill. It was one I had. One she'd never heard of, apparently, because she led with, "Give those back, you little jerk," almost before she'd stopped moving. I could hear it, because she'd shouted it.

The kid, who was ginger-haired and swinging himself awkwardly along on my jet-black, custom-made titanium forearm crutches, glanced at his mates, then decided to say, "Piss off. They're not yours. Anyway, we're just borrowing them."

I breathed in and out, reminded myself, *De-escalation,* and hopped a few steps closer.

The girl—woman, because she was older than she'd looked at first—hadn't got the memo, because now, she grabbed a crutch, fast as a striking snake, and yanked the kid off-balance. He swung out with the other crutch, maybe reflexively, and in a blink-or-you'll-miss-it move, she shot a palm straight out in front of her—without pulling her elbow back and giving him warning, which said she was trained—caught him on the bridge of the nose, and sent him backward, then down to the sand. The other kids stood there looking gobsmacked, but she was over the ginger in an instant, wrenching the crutches off his forearms and standing up in a whirl of bikini straps and creamy skin, turning a circle, all but baring her teeth, and asking the rest of the kids, "Do you want some? Do you? Anybody?"

The answer was apparently "No," because they were backing off. Which was when I finally got there. I held out a hand and said, as calmly as I could possibly manage, "Thanks. I'll have those."

She blinked at me out of dark-lashed, whiskey-brown eyes, with the kind of returning-to-my-senses shift I recognized from my own less-controlled past, said, "Oh. Right," and handed them over.

The kid on the ground was moaning. He had a hand over his nose, the red blood dripping between his fingers, down his chin, and into the sand as he said, his voice muffled, "I think you broke it." The other three boys looked like they wanted to run, but also didn't want to, because it would be too embarrassing. Another emotion familiar from my past. That was why teenagers could be so annoying. They reminded you of all the dumb things you'd done yourself, and how you'd alternated between smug and hopelessly unsure, which you'd covered up by being even more of an arsehole. At least, that was the way I remembered it.

"Stand up," I told the kid with the nose, in the tone of voice that said, *No arguments.* "Let's have a look." I told the other kids, "Hang on."

"Yeah," my would-be rescuer said, bouncing on her toes a little more. "Try going anywhere, and I'll break *your* noses." That was an American accent, maybe.

"Thanks," I told her, "but I've got it now." She didn't appear to be what you'd call a good listener.

The ginger kid stood up, probably because he felt stupid lying on the ground, and I pried his bloody hand away and felt his nose between finger and thumb, which made him yelp. "Not broken," I told him, wiping my now-bloody hand on my togs. "It'll be sore, that's all. Put some ice on it when you get home."

"I was going to give them back," the kid muttered, not meeting my eyes. "Just having a laugh."

21

"Hmm," I said. "Not all that funny, was it, mate?" I had my forearms in the crutches now, and I felt about two hundred percent better, if that were mathematically possible. Nearly whole instead of nearly helpless, which gave me an idea. "Not that easy to use," I said, "are they?"

"You must be joking," one of the other kids said. "Dead easy." He was a tall, fit bloke with dark hair, king of the world. The ringleader.

The woman didn't say anything. She clearly still wanted to hit somebody, though. It was like she had a thought-bubble over her head, saying, *Let me punch him. One time. Come on. One little punch. Two, max.* The head was balanced on a very pretty neck, long and slim as the rest of her. You could see all of it, because her hair was so short, cut in a purely pixie sort of way, with a ragged fringe over her forehead. I'd never thought about the benefits of that. That neck would be so easy to kiss, and it needed kissing.

Whoa. Where had *that* come from? I hadn't had a sexual thought in quite a while. It had been alarming, in fact, in the rehab center, like I'd lost more than my leg and my career. One of the therapists had been very pretty indeed, she'd known who I was and had liked the idea, she may have used the words "hero" and even "warrior," and still . . . nothing. Maybe *because* she'd used the word "hero." It didn't take any heroism to get yourself blown up. It wasn't like I'd meant to do it. If you were an explosives expert, it was pretty much the opposite.

I was having one or two of those thoughts now, though. The girl had the kind of pretty, just-a-handful breasts that had you thinking about her not needing a bra, long muscle beneath the smooth skin, a line of three piercings in each earlobe and another line of four delicate little sparklers above and below her navel like flares along a landing strip, and fire all but coming out of her almond-shaped eyes.

She'd be a challenge, that was sure. A man would have to be on his toes, and he'd have to stay there. I wondered if she knew how to wrestle. Of course, you could always teach her. That was a happy little thought.

"Tell you what," I told the kids. "Meet me back here in— call it half an hour—and we'll have a friendly wee race. Running and swimming. Me against whoever's best at each of those. Losers shout the winner tea over at the Coffee Club. You'll notice I'm saying 'losers,' because that'll be you. Fair warning."

"We're not going to race a cripple," the good-looking kid said. "That's lame as." He laughed. "Good one, eh." He had a fairly enormous greenstone toki pendant hanging around his neck, like he was advertising the size of his axe. Full of bluster, and the least ashamed of the group.

The girl was about to do something. Possibly knee the kid in the groin. I turned my gaze on him and said, "Right, then. You're one of the racers. Thirty minutes." I paused a second, then added, "Unless you're a pussy. In that case, go home instead. Your choice."

That would probably work.

4

HENRY THE EIGHTH

KAREN

The sea god jerked his chin at me in a way that made my mouth open, and not from breathless wonder, then turned around and took off on the crutches without even checking for my reaction.

I'd thought I knew all about male arrogance, but that took the cake. He hadn't even thanked me. Now, I was mad at him *and* the kids. All I'd done was *help*.

If I followed him, it was just to give him a much-needed reality check. I hadn't even gone in the water yet, and that had been the whole point of coming here. For the time being, I went and grabbed my bag, but when I turned around, my heart pounding in a way that showed you the kind of shape I was in right now, he was standing off at a distance, clearly waiting for me, seeming oblivious to the stares he was garnering.

Well, I'd already figured out that he was tough in body and mind. That was why I was heading off to join him, somehow, despite the chin-jerking. That, and that I was the definition of "at loose ends," and maybe I was hoping that some of his toughness would rub off on me, since I was about a quart low.

When I caught up with him, I said, "You jerked your chin at me. Like you were *summoning* me. What was that about? Hello? Real world calling. Women don't go much for that. Also, don't say 'pussy.' That's a crappy insult, especially in front of me. You can do better." That was my compromise solution. Following him, but objecting.

He smiled. Unfortunately, he had a killer smile, slow, sweet, and crooked. It crinkled his eyes and his scar, and it was so unstudied. He said, with no lessening of calm in his voice, "You're probably right about the 'pussy.' Could be I've heard it too much and not thought about it enough. And I could've done that summoning thing, yeh. Could be you're being insensitive, too. I couldn't exactly crook my finger at you, could I? My hands were occupied."

I always think of men as having beer voices. I know that sounds weird, but I'm a food person. The beach kids were cheap pilsners. Too light and fizzy, without enough depth to them. My brother-in-law, Hemi Te Mana, was a stout, dark and deep, its sweetness all but buried. His grandfather, my Koro, was a porter, as comforting as a warm fire on a freezing winter day. Josh had been an IPA, fruit-forward and on trend. I'd forgotten until too late that I didn't actually like IPAs. This guy? He was a winter ale, layered, smooth, and deceptively potent, with an alcohol content that you should have checked first, because halfway through the first glass, you were already in trouble.

Too bad I liked trouble. And that matching wits was one of my favorite hobbies. "Good thing," I told him. "If you'd crooked your finger at me, I might have bitten it off. What are you, Henry the Eighth? I'm not even addressing the other part. You are not sensitive. And I was *helping.*"

"You wound me," he said. "In the emotional sense. And maybe I didn't need your help."

"Which would mean I didn't wound you at all." *I* was supposed to be wounded, in the emotional sense. Why did I want to laugh instead? Hysteria, probably. I asked him, "You aren't really going to do that, are you?"

"Do what?"

"Race. Why would you? And how could you think you'd win?" Up close, he had more scars than I'd realized, and they didn't look all that long-healed, which meant he must have lost his leg recently. The scars there were still pink. The facial ones, on the other hand, were dark blue, like somebody had drawn them with marker. One thin line down the center of his forehead and along the side of his nose, and another one, longer and messier, that sliced all the way down at the edge of his hairline, skimmed the outer corner of his eye in a way that made you wonder how he hadn't lost it, and only ended down near his earlobe. He could have grown his hair longer to hide some of it, but he hadn't, which was interesting. He had another one, pink again, just peeking out of the neckline of his T-shirt, or rather, a group of them, looking like the ends of a web woven by a very large, very drunk spider. I was guessing that one extended a ways.

Another man would have had a tattoo inked over that, tribal or not. Of course, he might just not have had time to have it done yet. He wasn't the god of the sea, he wasn't a merman, and he wasn't my hero.

"Why *not* race?" he said. "I don't have anything else on today, and win or lose, I'll make them think. I could also feel the need to regain my manhood, after having somebody else charge in and fight my battles for me. Somebody, I'll just say, that I wouldn't have chosen to do that. I need to go get my leg. Come along, if you like."

"Oh. You're kidding." I laughed. "That *is* what you meant. I hurt your ego, because you don't need help from a woman. Also, what does it matter whether they think or not? That's not your problem, surely."

He smiled. Slowly, like I'd drawn it out of him. Another good smile. It could be making me a little breathless, possibly. Now that I was up close, I realized that he had gray eyes behind the black-rimmed glasses. Not gray-blue. Actually *gray,* with a darker rim around the iris. He was quite a few wonderful inches taller than I was, too, which didn't happen often, and he'd put his shirt on like a man who didn't need to show off the breadth of his chest or the narrowness of his waist. Like a man with nothing to prove.

If the leg and the scars had happened in a motorcycle accident, I didn't want to know. I'd just make up a happy fantasy instead. Firefighter. Special Forces soldier. Man who dangled out of rescue helicopters and pulled people from cars balanced halfway down mountainsides, just before they teetered and fell. Hey, I saw it in a movie. It's a job.

Any of those would be good, and fantasizing generally made for a better outcome. Reality could be so disappointing.

If only I hadn't spent half my life feeling gigantic, I'd have walked away right then and kept things in fantasyland. Or maybe if he hadn't had that smile. But there you were. I'd been taller than my nine-years-older sister by the time I was twelve, which doesn't make you feel awkward much. At well over five-ten by the time I'd finally finished sprouting at eighteen, I was taller than every woman I'd ever known. I'd gone through most of my adolescence feeling like a hulking-but-skinny Jolly Green Giant, in the back row for every class picture. Then there was puking and being nearly bald, which were also extremely attractive. I wasn't feeling like that girl now, and it was heady stuff.

"Could be," he said. "That you hurt my ego, that is. I seem to have recovered, though. And, yeh, it matters that they think, or next time, they'll be picking on somebody weaker. If I can stop them doing that, I'm going to."

You see. A winter ale all the way. "I've never heard that one before," I said, possibly to cover my sudden lack of balance. "'Come with me to get my leg.' It's got novelty going for it, anyway."

"I could've asked you for a coffee instead," he agreed. "Or gone really mad and invited you for a drink. You could wonder why I didn't. Maybe I'm thinking I'll be more impressive this way."

"Well, if you win."

The lines around his eyes crinkled up some more. "Pardon me for saying it, but you seem a bit obsessed with winning. We'll have to see, I reckon." After that, he was swinging across the zebra crossing with a distracting amount of flex in his arm muscles, and no look at all behind him to see whether I was following.

I was. What else did I have to do? We were at the end of Marine Parade, where the enormous green mound of Mauao reared up from the flat land around it like a sentinel, forever looking out to sea. My favorite part of this beach, a reminder that you could only slap so much European veneer on the place. The ancient essence of it would still be lying there, just under the surface, pulsing like a heartbeat.

The guy must be staying at the holiday park, because the only other possibilities at the screaming end of the town were the two matching ultramodern buildings that looked like something out of a movie set in the future, and I had a pretty good idea of how much staying there would cost. No hard edges to them, just swooping lines of cream-colored multistoried goodness. Even the balconies were curved, and my merman didn't look like a high roller.

He stopped on the pavement outside the building closest to Mauao, though—the most exclusive of the exclusive— pulled a keycard from his board shorts, and swiped it, which forced me to look at the general torso area of his body in all its slim, muscular goodness. The shorts and the faded khaki T-shirt were the only things he was wearing, like he was too tough even to need protection on the soles of his feet. Foot.

"Huh," I said. "Well, this wasn't the accommodation I was expecting."

"Interesting," he said. "And possibly good to know."

"Some men," I told him in the lobby, after another few seconds went by with no more chat than that, "would do a whole lot more flirting than this. I'm just saying. If they were interested, of course, and not shy."

"Mm," he said. "So which do you think I am? Not interested, or shy? I'll give you a hint. I'm not shy. And there was the chin-jerking, after all."

Was he actually that self-assured? I couldn't tell. He was so . . . *wounded.* Shouldn't that make more difference? He pushed the button for the elevator, and I said, "I'm working it out. I'm really looking at two alternatives here. If you weren't actually crazy in challenging a whole group of teenagers to a race—a *foot* race—I'm going into an extremely strong man's apartment with him on zero acquaintance."

"What's the other alternative?" he asked. "I quite like the sound of that one. That I'm not crazy, and that I'm extremely strong." The lift doors opened with a smooth *whoosh* that said, "No expense spared," and he stepped inside and pushed the button for 2. The third floor, by U.S. measure.

I followed him again. "That you actually *are* crazy, *and* strong. Or that you're crazy to think you'll win, and also crazy as in 'nuts,' but not as strong as me. Or as well balanced, of course. Three alternatives, actually."

"I'm also homicidal, or a sex offender, is what you're saying in Alternative Two. Alternative Three as well, for that matter. In which case, you'd be madly self-destructive, wouldn't you? You should probably wait for me in the corridor."

"It could be that I'm too tired for good judgment," I said. "I just flew here from New York, over what feels like the past three days." I followed him off the elevator. "I'll bet you anything this place has security cameras, and I have mad self-defense skills, so I'm going along to get your leg. Maybe I want to watch the contest, also."

He said, "Mm," again, with some more of that almost-smile, then turned left from the elevator bank and went all the way to the end of the passage like he assumed I'd follow him.

You see? It was that bad-boy thing, pulling me in like a tractor beam. And I was *past* this.

He punched in a key code, held the door open, and stood there. "Are you coming in," he asked, "or waiting out here? The sand in my hourglass is draining away. Ten minutes gone already. It's an issue of strategy, the exact point at which you turn up for a challenge like that. Not early, definitely. Late is better, but not *too* late. Just late enough that they wonder if you're coming, and have a chance to realize they'd be relieved. If their heart sinks when you turn up, you're halfway home."

"I'm coming in," I said, and did.

"Right." He headed off, throwing back over his shoulder,

"Give me a few minutes. Find yourself something from the fridge, if you like."

The living space was fairly enormous, and it was also fairly special, New Zealand style. Which meant open-plan, absolutely spare, made of the best materials, and with acres of smooth surfaces, from the pale quartz counters to the oatmeal-colored kitchen drawers to the oversized floor tiles, which looked like quartz again. The couches were cream leather, and they were set in front of floor-to-ceiling, black-bordered accordion glass panels that opened up on two walls of the corner unit to form an L-shaped indoor/outdoor space.

One side looked out onto the green slopes of Mauao, almost like you could step onto it. That could have been forbidding, as close as the mountain was, as much of a contrast to the narrow, flat peninsula beyond it, but instead, it felt cozy. Watched over, because Mauao was a benign mountain. Maybe also because the other side was nothing but openness, looking out as it did over green grass and golden-sand beach to a wide swath of impossibly clear blue sky bisected by the sparkling, brilliant turquoise of the sea, dotted with green islands edged by wave-smoothed gray rock. A high-roller view all the way.

You didn't need decoration when that was your view. It was so beautiful, you couldn't look at anything else anyway, and it would change with every shift of cloud, every angle of sun.

I'd made it. I was here.

I found a glass in one of the roll-out drawers in the space-aged, cream-and-sand-colored kitchen, filled it with water from the bottle in the fridge, drank it down, and thought, *What are you going to do now?* And couldn't quite answer.

I always knew my direction. And when I knew it, I went that way. I *charged* that way, you could say. Right now, though, I was absolutely at a loss. I wasn't enjoying it, and yet . . . I almost was.

This was so confusing.

It would be better if I knew what tack I was supposed to

be on. I'd never had a breakdown before. I wasn't sure what the recovery technique was.

I'd figured that I just needed a break to figure out what to do next. That was what people did, right? They took a break. I'd been preparing to take it, a week or so ago. I'd been *deciding*. Unfortunately, my sister, Hope, had caught me doing my deciding while curled in a ball on the bathroom floor in the tiny Brooklyn apartment I'd moved into some weeks earlier. At that particular moment, I'd been taking a break from my deciding in order to think about how I was going to slide right across the floor and get myself wedged into the corner, because the bathroom floor sloped so much, and I didn't have the strength to resist. I'd be unable to get up again in my weakened state, and I'd end up as one of those stories in the *Post,* where the neighbors eventually started complaining about the smell, the super finally opened the door to check, the neighborhood was horrified and so saddened at the terrible isolation of modern life, and all of New York was left wondering how a twenty-nine-year-old woman with all the lucky breaks in the world could have ended up alone, friendless, and eaten by stray cats.

I'd had a whole narrative going, which said something for my imagination, anyway. It had been a weak moment, though, not a life choice. Unfortunately, my brother-in-law, the force of nature who was Hemi Te Mana, had stepped in and Made Things Happen. As usual. A woman couldn't even have a breakdown in peace with Hemi around.

He'd said, once Hope had helped me up off the floor, brought me a cup of tea, and fussed around me until I wished I *had* been eaten by cats, "You have two choices. Move in with us for a bit, or get back to work, if you're not actually as much of a mess as you look. Decide now. Make it good, though, or we're taking you home."

He'd been standing over me at the time, and Hope had been sitting beside me on the bed, rubbing my back and ignoring the fact that I hadn't showered for days and was disgusting, like I was one of her kids instead of a fully independent and capable woman with some very good degrees and all kinds of esoteric job skills. Who might

31

possibly not be as smart as she'd always thought she was, but everybody had downturns. From which you were supposed to emerge heart-whole, running through the winter streets for miles, then up several brutal flights of steps, before you turned to face the city, raised your arms over your head, and told the world that it hadn't beaten you after all.

And, yes, that would be *Rocky*. I was more of a boxing girl than a Cinderella girl. I'd thought that would happen, but it just . . . hadn't. Maybe I just wasn't quite at "conquering" stage yet, though. I'd been taking a *break*. That was why I said, "Forget moving in. I'm not sleeping on Maia's top bunk and having Hope check that my jacket is zipped before I go out. I am not your fourth child, and I'm not suicidal. I'm just . . . reflecting on my choices. I haven't had a personality transplant. I'm *upset*. Geez, can't a woman be upset for a day or two? And I know you were right about Josh. I'm *saying* you were right. 'You were right.' There you go. Done. I thought he was like you. Sue me. I thought he was the real deal, no artificial ingredients. I didn't realize he was cake mix. You did. Good job. Maybe someday, I'll be smart like that, too."

Hemi's mouth twitched, and he said, "Sounding more like yourself, anyway. And fair point. Maia's using her top bunk now, so there you are. Says she's five, and she can climb the ladder. Hope puts her on the bottom, and there she is an hour later, sneaked onto the top. Takes after her auntie, eh. Which means you'd be on the bottom bunk. Hitting your head."

"Ha," I said. "See? So—no." I was faking it, of course, but it was better than wondering which part of you the cats would eat first.

"New Zealand, then," Hemi said. "Change of scene would be good, I reckon. I'm considering an investment there, actually, a line of ecotourism properties. Glamour camping. Time to do some investing in Aotearoa, and I quite like the idea anyway. Diversification, eh. I can't buy it without checking it out, though, as well as meeting the staff, because that'll matter. You can only get so much from photos, and I've got too much on at the moment to leave."

You could say that, as Hemi had hit the billion-dollar mark

some years back and was still going strong. In the *fashion* industry, not the property industry. No pressure or anything, with him as your benchmark.

"My expertise is in food science," I reminded him, "not . . . sleeping bags, or whatever. So-called solar showers that are a trickle of lukewarm water out of a plastic bag. I went camping once. It was horrible. And I'm not even *talking* about the outhouse, because nobody needs to think about that. Hey, look, I'm giving you advice already, and I didn't even go! Besides, if you really don't have anybody else you trust to check it out, you have more problems than I do."

"Nobody I trust as much as you. Nobody better at forecasting shifts in consumer taste, either," he said, which knocked my breath out of my lungs one more time, and possibly made me struggle not to cry. I really *was* at the bottom. I. Did. Not. Cry. "I thought you were keen to learn survival skills. What happened with that?"

"I realized that discomfort's overrated?"

"Perfect for the job, then. You're the target customer. American, clueless, and spoilt. Besides, you're oddly disarming, I've noticed. I can put a seller's back up, for some reason."

"You're arrogant," I said. "That's the reason."

He almost smiled. "Mm. You could also spend some time with Koro and tell me how he's going."

How did I argue with that? Or with the way Hope was looking at me, like she was about to volunteer for some more Night Nurse duty, as if she hadn't worried about me enough in my life? And Koro? He wasn't my grandfather, but he was. I'd be going to Katikati to see him tomorrow morning, and it was the first thing I'd looked forward to in . . . however long this had been. The weeks had kind of run together there. New Zealand might heal my soul, if it hadn't already died a lonely, starved death, but being with Koro would heal my heart.

My sea god, though? He wasn't going to heal anything. Looking for a man to heal your ego was a bad bet all the way around, this guy looked as easy to handle as nitroglycerin, and I wasn't up for a juggling act. I was curious, that was all.

And, possibly, coming a tiny bit back to life.

5

No Mermaids, No Highlanders

JAX

I finished fastening my leg on, stood up, felt the bionics make contact with the nerves in my leg in a most reassuring way, and tried to get my breathing under control.

I'm not shy, I'd told her. It might be true, and it might not. I never had been, but I'd never looked like this before. At any rate, I now had ten minutes to make it across the road again to meet my new friends, and she was showing every sign of coming to watch me do it. Which meant I'd bloody well better be impressive.

Women were complicated. Men were simple. At least I was. I mostly just wanted to win.

I didn't check out my face in the bathroom mirror, or my shoulder, either. I knew what they looked like.

Did she have some *Beauty and the Beast* thing going on, looking to be treated badly by a hard, damaged man? That would be better than the women who wanted to take care of you, but not by much. I didn't think that was it, although there was vulnerability in her along with the toughness. She was bold as brass on the outside, but there was something else underneath, some siren song of the mermaids that called my name.

Stupid. How could she be a mermaid? I hadn't even seen her in the water. For all I knew, she couldn't even swim. She might be one of those women who wore a bikini she never got wet, because that would involve mussing her hair.

She wasn't that woman, though. I knew it. And I didn't want to treat her badly. I just wanted to thrill her. To leave her breathless. Wondering. Waiting. And then to make it all pay off. Very slowly.

Could I still take her on that kind of ride? I had no idea. I knew I wanted to try.

I'd order up some dinner, maybe, and we'd see how we went. And if that gave me nerves . . . well, all the best things did. But first, I needed to win.

When I got out there again, she was standing with her back to me and her hands wrapped around her upper arms, looking not out to sea, but at the Mount. Something wistful about that pose, surely. And then there was the thin strap of her bikini top, the tender nape of her neck, and the twin dimples at the base of her spine, their tops visible at the edge of her little black shorts, because they were that low. She turned at my footfall, took in my leg and both feet, the real one and the manufactured one, in their running shoes, and said, "Maybe you *can* run."

"We'll see," I said. "Ready?"

"Probably," she said, "though I should ask you first who you are. I don't want to, but I know I should." She studied me. No fear at all in her, despite what she'd said. She had more intelligence and definitely more personality behind those whiskey-colored eyes than any ten women had a right to. "You really care that much," she said. "That you . . . teach them a lesson, or whatever. More than you do about what's going on here, between us."

I had to smile at that, despite the way she unbalanced me. "Maybe you shouldn't put that to the test. But I committed back there, for whatever reason. I need to see it through. Not turning up isn't an option."

"Right," she said, picking up her bag again. "Then I'd better come help."

I gazed at her with as much severity as I could muster. She'd sounded as brisk as a headmistress. It was fortunate that my own headmistress hadn't messed me up like this, or I'd have got into even more trouble at school than I had done. "Thought I said I didn't need your help," I said. "I thought I'd made that point pretty clearly, in fact. Could be I'm not coming through with full authority."

"Oh, you've got lots of authority," she said, like she was reassuring me. "I just have authority, too. See, that's your problem. You're missing that."

Now, I was laughing. My laughter muscles weren't as well exercised as they'd ever been, but she was making me laugh now. "The name's Jax. Jackson MacGregor, at your service."

"Huh," she said. "I don't like J names much, but that sounds like some kind of sexy Highlander. Especially with the scars and all. Like you should have a sword."

She didn't like *J* names? Well, that was bizarre. "It may have been once," I said, heading out the door again. "Rob Roy was a MacGregor. Of course, they also lost their right to exist about five hundred years ago. Just using their name was a death sentence, which means no ancestral pile in Scotland, and no lands, either. There's a pit behind a castle, in fact, where their bodies were thrown by their enemies. Not what you'd call history's winners. Fortunately, history isn't destiny. They took the name back, anyway, eventually, and here I am."

"The question is," she said, getting ahead of me and pushing the button for the lift like a woman who'd never heard the phrase, "Let me take care of that" about anything, or if she had, hadn't listened to it, "whether you have a kilt. I'm more interested in that than your ancestral lands. I may have read a few novels in my past," she explained when I started to smile again. "While procrastinating, or taking a break, whichever way you want to look at it. My life can get a little intense at times. I have an issue with over-focus."

"Surprising me not at all," I said, because the lift had

opened, and she was already inside, punching buttons again. "I could have that issue myself, although in my case, it's considered a positive. Or it used to be. And, yeh, I have a kilt. I don't generally wear it out and about, but I've got it."

She sighed. "See. I *knew* it."

"How about you?" I asked. "Got an ancestral pile somewhere yourself, the reason for the confidence? Got a name?"

"Karen," she said. "Karen Sinclair. No ancestral pile, and no kilt. Not even any parents, for that matter, at least any who want to show themselves. Just a ticket to New Zealand and a job to do."

"What kind of job?" I asked. We were headed across the zebra crossing again, into which she'd charged like she'd never imagined the possibility that not every car might stop, or like she reckoned that if they didn't, she'd hold them off by force of her Wonder Woman magic bracelets. I caught up to her without effort, thanks to the New Zealand Defence Force's commitment to restoring my functionality and my own fairly rigorous rehab efforts, so all wasn't lost quite yet.

"I'm checking out an investment for my brother-in-law," she said. "Not really my skill set, but I'm adaptable. At least I want to be, which is half the battle, right? And look. Your friends showed. Cool." She was speeding up at sight of them, no matter what she'd had to say on the subject earlier. If she'd ever met a challenge she hadn't embraced, I missed my guess.

It wasn't that I didn't think women could be warriors. I'd known some girls who'd been as tough as any bloke around them. I just wasn't used to wanting to engage in close combat with them, so to speak. I said, "You *are* remembering that this is *my* challenge."

"Of course," she said. "That's the *point*. I can't help it if I'm excited about it."

I was still laughing when we joined the four boys, who were standing more or less where we'd left them. The ginger kid's nose was red and swollen, and he could have a black eye tomorrow as well. He looked absolutely miserable, but he hadn't left. The other two blokes were trying to fade into the background, but the ringleader still looked belligerent. As we approached, he spoke fast, like he was getting the words out before his courage failed him. "Thought you weren't coming. Also, you're wearing shoes. We're barefoot. Can't race like that. Not fair."

"He has one *leg*," my champion—Karen Sinclair—said, before I could say anything. Jumping straight in there again. "You have two. If it's not fair, that's not the way it isn't fair, and you know it. Chickenshit."

The kid's eyes narrowed, and I had my body between him and Karen before his leg muscles had finished tensing. Which she wasn't going to appreciate. Too bad. I said, keeping it calm, "I'll be swimming with one leg, of course. There's that."

"You also realize," Karen said, poking her head out from behind me like a woman who'd also never heard, "Let me handle this," "that this whole thing is the stupidest idea I've ever heard. Why are you racing at all, again? What are you trying to prove?"

"Who's a pussy now?" the kid said, then laughed, elbowed his mate, and said, "See what I did there? Because she's actually got one, eh."

I didn't lose my temper. Not ever. Not anymore. My job called for absolute cool, and I was very good at my job. Except that I didn't have my job anymore, and I apparently didn't have my cool, either. I said, "Ten seconds."

"What?" the kid asked.

"Ten seconds to accept the challenge, piss off, or find out what Option Three is," I said. "Make that four seconds now."

"I'm doing the swimming bit," the kid said, "and Dougie here's doing the running."

Karen was practically bouncing on her toes now. "Or better yet," she said, "both of us against both of you, so everybody has to run *and* swim. Since you care so much about fairness. What do you think? Think you can take a girl and a one-legged man? Think so? Huh?"

I'd have said, "Hang on," except that she was still talking. "We can run down to Tay Street, where that dead tree is, then back up to Moturiki Island. Swim around the island and back to shore. The other two of you can be the timekeepers. Simple. Let's hear you try to back out. I can't *wait.*"

"Hang on," I *did* say now. "That's a pretty long swim." And—wait. She'd said she just got here. How did she know the streets that well? How did she know the name of the island, and why did she pronounce it like a Maori? Who *was* this woman? She was as no-worries-rich-American as it was possible for a woman to be, perfect teeth and glorious skin and confidence and all, and yet she knew all that? And had laid out the rules of engagement like she was in charge of them?

"Not that long," she said. "One-point-two kilometers. Not even three quarters of a mile. They have a race, is how I know. I was looking at it on the flight over. A much longer race than this, I'll point out. And surely our friends here—" She snapped her fingers at the ringleader, who blinked and stared like she'd been summoning demons—"wouldn't have agreed to race at all unless they were as good at swimming as you and me. Right?"

"Run's all right," I said. "Five kilometers or so. We may want to shorten the swim, though. Get back here, say, then swim to the end of the beach and back." I pointed to where the strip of gold ended and the rocks began, at the base of the Mount. Six hundred meters total, maybe, and sheltered the entire way, which made much more sense.

"You scared, bro?" the leader-kid asked. "You sound scared."

"I'm concerned about your safety," I said. "How old are you?"

He said, "Never mind," then puffed up his chest and glanced at Karen, like he wanted to see if she'd noticed.

She noticed. Unfortunately for any hope of de-escalation, she laughed and said, "What, I'm impressed? I'm here with a guy whose *leg* is gone. Look at his face, too. I'm not going to be impressed by *you.*" Not a statement that was going to encourage any seventeen-year-old bloke to set sensible limits. Not one that was setting me on fire, either.

"Cheers," I told her. "Next time? Don't help."

She laughed.

The kid said, "I'm starting. Three—two—"

"Wait," I said. "Names."

"What d'you mean, names?" he asked.

"In case we're informing the police at some point," I said, "I think names are in order."

He scowled. "Artie Kamana, then. Me. And Dougie Daniels." He jerked his head at the kid next to him, a tall, skinny bloke with an oversized Adam's apple that had bobbed at the prospect of swimming around the island.

"Artie," I said, putting out my hand. "I'm Jax, and this is Karen." After a moment's hesitation, the leader-kid shook it. He would've tried to squeeze too hard, if I hadn't anticipated him and got my index finger onto his wrist, aligning my knuckles so he couldn't crush them. He needed to work on that predictability of his if he wanted to be a tough guy. "And Dougie." I shook his hand, too, and told him, "You don't have to do this. You and Karen can sit it out with the other fellas here. It's between Artie and me."

His brown eyes shifted, because he wanted nothing more. His Adam's apple bobbed again, and he said, "I'm doing it." His voice broke on the words, though.

Beside me, Karen was kicking off her jandals, then peeling off the black shorts, and all four of the boys got a bit distracted, even the one with the swollen nose. I may have done as well. When would the sight of a girl wriggling her pretty bum as she slid a tiny pair of shorts over it and down her endless legs, revealing an even tinier bikini, *not* be distracting? Never. I shot a hard glance at the boys that had them shifting their gaze, then put out a hand to her. She took it, which I was halfway surprised at, and used it to balance in the sand as she got the shorts off, though she probably didn't need it.

Her hand was warm, she smiled at me happily, like she was doing nothing but looking forward to this, and there was some more of that supercharging happening in the air. Her dark-brown hair was cut sleekly around her tidy ears, and her earlobes were the attached kind, shining with that row of winking studs. Then there were her high-cut bikini bottoms, which were only a few centimeters wide at the edges. Her togs were functional, I guessed, if you ignored her legs. And her endless length of flat belly, the sweet dip of her navel and the sparklers taking that downward path, the curve of her waist, her bum, which had some roundness to it that you might not have expected from somebody that thin, and the pretty bit of cleavage she was showing, pale against her tan, the just-visible inner swells of her breasts.

It was a lot to ignore. I'd have to take care to stay in front of her during the run, or I'd be forgetting what I was meant to be doing here.

"We ready?" she asked, and the two boys stripped off their shirts. I did, too, and everybody stared at the scars on my shoulder and chest. That was fun.

They could underestimate me. That was nothing but helpful. I was all good. Although it had dawned on me for the first time that racing hadn't been on the curriculum over the past three months.

Pushing past my comfort level had been, though. When it came to the willingness to do whatever it took to finish, even if you had to crawl? I'd be the winner there, every time.

Except that I didn't want to crawl. I felt fairly strongly on that point.

Too late for reservations now. Time to go.

6

⭐☆

WRONG TIME, WRONG TIDE

KAREN

I'd probably always known I was going to volunteer. Should I hold back, though, and not outrace Jax? Men could be so weird about things like that, like just because you were better at one physical thing, you were cutting off their junk and putting it in your purse. He only had one *leg*, which anybody—well, anybody female—would assume gave him a great excuse not to win a foot race.

He wouldn't think so, though. And—nah. If I had to damp myself down that much in order not to threaten a man, he wasn't a man worth having. Or, since I wasn't going to "have" him, or anybody, until I was normal again—he wasn't worth caring about. Surely, being with Josh had taught me that much.

Josh—Jax. See? No. Absolutely not. You didn't need to be struck by lightning to recognize a friggin' *sign*.

All of that took me about two seconds to work out. Or I may not have worked it out at all right then, or even thought about it until later. Maybe I just took off, once Jax got through the rules and regulations and *let* me. He was one of those guys who had to plan everything, when I would have just started running.

He said, "We circle the dead tree, then run back and touch the rock at Moturiki. An untimed stop for me to get my leg off, and then we're all off again, into the water. Race ends when you touch that same rock again. Stay close to the island. Shorter swim. Safer, too." He told the other two guys, Bloody-Nose-Boy and I'd-Rather-Be-Gone, "You lot can start the stopwatches on your phones on my 'Go,' bring everybody's gear along, and meet us at the island for the check-in. Take care you make a note of both times. You—" He gestured to the redhead. "You're timing Karen and me. Your mate's timing Artie and Dougie. Got it? At their nods, and the sight of their fingers hovering over their phones, he said, "Counting down from three. On go. Three, two, one . . . *Go!*"

The kids took off in a dead sprint, exactly like you'd have predicted. I got that surge of adrenaline, the way you do, nearly sick-making, and forced myself to hold back. Which meant Jax took off ahead of me, which—OK, I was surprised by. He didn't start out as fast as the kids, but he ran more easily than I'd have imagined, like he knew how, leg or not. The sand was firm at the edge of the water, as New Zealand sand tended to be on the wide beaches, but the ground still sloped a bit, especially at high tide, which was where we were, and that always made things harder.

I'd been on those planes for a long, *long* time. I forced myself to take it easy until I felt my muscles loosening, kept the breath coming slow and even, then lengthened my stride, caught up to Jax with some effort, and said, "You can run."

He glanced at me and said, "So can you. And I wouldn't have suggested it if I couldn't, would I." He didn't sound at all winded. I was getting that way, a tiny bit. Holding back or not, the pace he set was fast, and I may have done a little too much lying on the bathroom floor this past month or so. Suffering wasn't all that aerobic, apparently.

The kids kept looking back. Slowing them down, getting them in the wrong mindset, trying not to lose instead of trying to win. I got that racehorse-at-the-gate adrenaline surge again and said, "You'd better be here to win."

Jax smiled that almost-smile. "I usually am. Shut up, so we can do it."

I could have been outraged, but he was right. It was a decent run, and a fairly long swim. That would be the real test. I knew how well everybody ran now, and that was going to be no problem. I had no idea how well they swam, and Kiwi kids tended to be strong in the water. The boys hadn't increased their lead any, and when they'd rounded the tree, with its spindly brown branches, and were headed toward us again, I could see their chests heaving, their arms pumping. Dougie was in front, and Artie had fallen behind. He'd been supposed to be the swimmer, though. Figured. He was the bigger guy, while Dougie was the string bean.

Jax and I went past them, the two of us running together, in stride. His legs were longer, but I had two of them. Dougie went by with a sidelong look like a panicked racehorse and didn't say anything, but Artie looked over, veered up onto the softer sand, and wasted his breath saying, "You're dead slow, mate." On a gasp.

Jax didn't even answer him. He just kept going, letting out his stride a little more, heading up the beach, touching the tree, then running around it. I was starting to breathe a little harder myself, and asked, when we were on our way back, "Doesn't it . . . hurt? Your leg? The . . . pounding?"

"A bit," he said, "as it's new." And that was it. He sure wasn't slowing down, though, and the boys were only about ten meters ahead.

Or nine, now. Then eight. Seven. The land bridge to the island was still some way off, and the boys' gaits were getting choppy, their steps smaller, their heads down. They'd be laboring now, their legs leaden, their lungs on fire.

Jax said, "Pass them in the sea. I'll go around up high."

I said, "Harder. You go first. In the water. I'll follow."

"Can't," he said. "Leg isn't waterproof."

I just about stopped running. "You . . . idiot. That's got to be expensive . . . equipment. Not . . . worth it."

"Keep up," he said. "I'm going around." And did.

Maybe he should be letting *me* win. Wasn't that what a

gentleman would do? I found my fifth gear, finally, and went for it. The timekeeper kids were close now, standing on the sand facing us, their phones out as we slapped our hands onto the rock. And, yes, if you're wondering, Jax was a good three or four strides ahead of me doing it. He didn't stop, just slowed his pace, jogged it out, and circled slowly back, joining the timekeepers with me as Dougie came up, blowing like a locomotive. The kid hit the rock and doubled over right there, his hands on his knees.

Artie was about a football field behind, and hurting. When *he* finally got there, he threw up.

I laughed. It wasn't nice, but it sure was satisfying.

Jax waited until Artie was done, then told the kids, "Go get a drink at the fountain by the Cenotaph."

"We don't need a break," Artie said. Unfortunately, it came out more like, "We don't . . . need a . . . break," and he was hunkered down, his palms on the sand, his soaked hair dripping into his eyes, as he said it. Dougie looked at him and said, "Yeh. We're good," like that would convince us. Or himself.

Jax was sitting down himself now, sliding the mechanical part of his leg off as casually as if he were taking off a shoe. He peeled down the sleeve, or whatever you called it, that went over his knee, and took that off, too, and I saw some redness at the end of the remaining limb, no matter what he'd admit to. Skin didn't lie.

"Go get a drink of water," he said, "and then get another one. The sea will still be there in ten minutes." He glanced up at me and saw the direction of my gaze, and his face . . . hardened, I guess you'd say. He looked like a different man when he did that. That intense one again, like the calm face was his mask. All he said, though, was, "You too, Karen, if you need one."

"You don't, of course," I said, "because you're just that tough, and 5K is nothing." Actually, I could use a drink. Hey, flying was dehydrating.

He gave me a lopsided smile that was nothing but charming. Mask back in place, then. "You'll embarrass me."

That made me laugh. Maybe he *had* messed himself up doing the helicopter-rescue deal, and not in a drunken motorcycle crash. "You could've let me win," I told him. "It would probably have been gentlemanly, or something."

"Would you have let me?"

"Well," I said, "no."

He took off his other shoe and his male-model-pretending-to-be-a-nerd glasses, and I didn't watch, or not straight on, even though the sight of him was something to see. That was a *lot* of lean muscle, just enough black hair to say, 'I'm groomed, but I'm still a man,' and abs like you meant it, and the web of drunken-spider scars at the top of his chest just made him look tougher.

It was all pretty appealing. Fortunately, I was about ten years smarter than I'd been a couple months ago, so instead of throwing myself down on the sand at his feet like a woman asking to get used—or, possibly, a puppy—I told the boys, "Come on. Let's go get a drink and do some stretching. You too," I told the redhead, who wouldn't meet my eyes. Possibly because one of his was swelling. "What's your name?"

"Colin," he muttered.

"Well, Colin," I said, "let's go. All of you." If I didn't do it, they wouldn't, it *was* going to be a pretty long swim, and being a jerk wasn't a capital offense. Besides, I kind of liked Dougie. Dragged along out of loyalty, and doing his best. Dougie was all right.

JAX

Was I surprised that she'd kept up with me? Yes and no. No, because I wasn't anywhere close to my best. Yes, because even so, I was fast enough.

Was I *bothered* that she'd kept up with me? That one took more thought.

Nah. She'd pushed me, and that was good. So why was my

balance so off? The sympathetic look on her face when I'd taken off the leg, that was why. That was nothing I wanted to see. I'd rather have seen disgust.

She came back with the kids, eventually, and said, "Everybody ready to go? The tide's turning, but it's still high."

I said, "If anybody wants to quit now, or if both of you do, there's no shame in that. You did well. We can call it good."

Karen snorted, which I heard, then glanced at Dougie, who hadn't been too keen on any of this, and said, "Right. No shame."

Artie said, "Nah. We're all good." Dougie just nodded.

I shrugged. "Let's go, then. If you need a break along the way, take one. Let me get out into the water a bit, and you lot wade out as well, so we're starting even." I told the timekeepers, "On my go."

Karen asked, "Want my shoulder to get out there?"

"No." It came out too harsh. She'd asked it quietly, matter-of-factly. I was an arsehole. She stiffened, opened her mouth, and shut it again, and I said, keeping it quiet myself, "Came out wrong. Maybe that's not how I want to touch you."

She didn't flush, not exactly, but there was possibly a little more color in her cheeks. She said, "You wish."

"Yeh," I said. "I do."

"I'm sweaty," she said. "I'm *dirty.*"

I didn't say that dirty suited me. The kids were right there, they looked anxious, and I wanted to get this swim over with and take Karen's dirty, wet self back up to my apartment. After that? I had a few ideas. Maybe she did, too.

Meanwhile, here we were. I lowered myself down, got onto my knees, "walked" into the water, tried not to let that matter, and said, "Let's go."

The first half was all right. I was glad for the swim earlier, and knowing how to compensate for the foot. The outgoing current was giving me a boost, though I took care to stay clear of the tumbled rocks that lined the island. You could bash up against those if you weren't careful, and that wouldn't feel good. One-point-two kilometers was half an hour's easy swim, or twenty minutes' hard one, at my pace, and once again, Karen was doing a good job of keeping up, or at least staying close. It was fine.

She got ahead, then, because I turned around and treaded water to check on the kids. Artie was a splasher, and out in front, but Dougie was coming along all right, when I finally spotted him. All good, then. I swam across the top of the island, checked on the kids again, then headed back.

Ten minutes to go. Maybe twelve. The tide was definitely going out, and Karen was definitely ahead of me, but I wouldn't have a problem catching up.

A third of the way back to shore, and I was gaining on her very satisfactorily indeed. I didn't want to look back. I didn't want to take the time. Admirably or otherwise, I didn't care much for the idea of losing.

I looked back anyway. Too ingrained in me, by now, to check on the team.

It isn't always easy to spot a head in the water when there's any kind of swell. You have to bob up on the wave, hold yourself there, and scan until your quarry isn't hidden by a wave top. My vision also wasn't the best without my specs.

I squinted. Over there. That was a head, and an arm. Good.

I couldn't tell which of the kids it was, though, and I couldn't see the other one. I searched a while longer. No luck.

I headed back out. Fast.

You knew better. You should have insisted.

Not helpful.

I only found him, in the end, because of Dougie. I was still swimming, bobbing up every few meters to search, when I saw the kid hauling himself up on the boulders a quarter of the way down the island. Or more like—I saw a somewhat blurry, long, skinny shape against the rounded gray shapes. I swam over there as he waved at me. Frantically. I could see that, too.

"Over there!" he was yelling as he pointed. I saw the other kid, then. Farther out from the island than I'd expected, up toward the Mount. No arm waving going on, just the dark, round shape of a head, appearing and reappearing, almost languidly, as he drifted farther away from his goal. I knew what that meant. A swimmer who was losing his strength. Drowning isn't a noisy, splashing thing, the way people think. It's a quiet thing. Slipping under. Slipping away.

I covered the distance as fast as I ever had, pushing it, and then pushing it harder. It felt like ages before I found him, his head just slipping under the surface again. I grabbed the first thing I could reach, which was his hair, and yanked him up, kicking ferociously, damning the foot that wasn't there to help.

When I hauled him in and started to get my arm across his chest, he flailed. His fist caught me in the nose, and he nearly knocked me loose.

"Stop," I told him, putting all my command into it. "Hold still. I'm pulling you in. You'll be fine."

He wasn't listening. He was gasping, his arms windmilling in panic, and this time, he hit me harder, bang on the cheekbone. He got me around the neck, then, and pulled us both under the water.

No more mucking about. I got loose from his grasp by hitting him in the side of the head, yanked him to the surface, grabbed him tight under both arms, and shouted into his ear, "Shut the *fuck* up!" Words I was sure he'd heard before, that would get through. "I should let you drown, you ungrateful little shit."

"Wh-what?" At least he wasn't flailing anymore.

"Hold still. I'm getting you to shore. Pull me under again, though, and I'll leave you there." He could mess us both up well and truly if he started panicking. I needed him to trust me, and sounding like a Maori uncle was my best bet for that.

It wasn't fun, hauling along eighty Kg's of resistant Artie. But at least I wasn't getting hit anymore.

That was what I got for dragging two stupid seventeen-year-olds into a race I'd known was too much for them. But then, a man's wounded ego is a dangerous thing.

☆☆

49

KAREN

I was getting close to shore, and I hadn't even seen the flash of a long arm in the corner of my vision. I was that much faster than him? Huh. It was harder work swimming against the current, and I was getting the kind of endorphin rush I hadn't felt in too long. The kind that could lead a woman into foolish decisions.

I needed to know how far back he was. Would I rather beat him, or have him beat me? It wasn't a question that would even have occurred to me before. All I knew was—I wanted it to be a *contest.*

When I took a quick peek, I still didn't see him. I saw somebody wedged between two of the gray boulders that edged the steep slope of the island, though. Somebody in green board shorts. Dougie, who'd been nervous about the swim, stopping to take a rest.

Where were Artie and Jax, though? I hauled myself out of the water as far as I could, but I couldn't see them.

Five seconds. Ten. There. That was somebody, out there a ways. Or more than one somebody.

Something was wrong.

I headed back out, swimming hard, trying to focus, trying not to think too much. A few minutes, and I could see Dougie with every other breath when I turned my head that way. Still on his rock, his knees pulled up and his arms around himself. Getting cold, but he was OK.

Another stint of popping up like an otter, and this time, I saw them quickly. Not far away, and the water was churning. I was swimming on the sight, rising a couple times to find them again, and then I was turning onto my side so I could talk to Jax.

He had Artie on his back, holding him with an arm across his chest, under the arms, the way you did when you were rescuing somebody. Artie was struggling, though, saying, "I can . . . swim." Not sounding convincing at all, but at least sounding alive.

"Shut up," Jax said, "or you'll swallow more water. As

soon as we can climb out, I'll let go of you, no worries. Try pulling me under again, though, and I'll smack you."

"I can take over for a bit," I said.

Jax didn't look at me. "No," he said.

If I'd been his objective for a little while there, that was clearly over. But then, I wasn't loving myself right now, either. The kids had been dumb and overconfident, exactly like I'd been at their age. And I'd egged them on, pushed them into this, out of . . . what? My own bruised ego? Wanting to win at *something,* even if my opponents were kids?

Being honest with yourself isn't always fun.

I said, still swimming beside them while Jax motored along, perfectly calmly, like he'd done this a hundred times, "I'll go get Dougie."

"You do that," Jax said.

Dougie, needless to say, wasn't thrilled at the idea of my helping him. "I'm good," he said through chattering teeth. "Having a rest, eh."

I was doing the breaststroke below his rock to keep myself in place as I called out to him where he crouched, hugging himself. The sun had gone behind a cloud, and the wind had picked up, the way it did in the afternoon.

"Strong current," I said. "Surprised me, too. Wrong time, wrong tide, wrong decision. When I tell my Koro about this, he won't be happy with me."

Dougie's face shifted, a spasm of cold, or possibly of disgust. I was popular here, that was for sure.

"You're not Maori," he said. Ah. It *had* been disgust, then. He didn't say the rest. *You don't get to call him that. That's* our *name.*

I'd been so *sure* I was right, back there on the beach, when I'd punched that kid in the nose, and when I'd upped the challenge. Could life give me just a little more of a smackdown? Maybe I hadn't gotten the message yet. This whole thing, in fact, was a lovely referendum on my judgment. Exactly how much trouble had Artie been in out there, for Jax to need to haul him in? He'd been talking, fortunately, and I was about as sure as you could be that Jax would get him out safely. I was starting to suspect that he'd lost his leg in something much more dramatic than a motorcycle accident.

"Come on," I told Dougie. "We'll swim back together until we can climb out, and then we'll run back on the track. You'll still have run and swum the whole race, and it hasn't been easy. He toa taumata rau."

Courage has many resting places. I couldn't see those places, Koro had meant every time he'd said that to me, if I judged too fast. Which, of course, I always did. Which meant he always pointed it out. Which meant I had the proverb memorized.

"You're American, though," Dougie said. It wasn't just his teeth that were chattering. His whole body was shaking.

"Guilty," I said. "I'm also getting pretty cold hanging out like this, and the sooner you get yourself into the water, the sooner I'll be having a coffee. You're not going to finish this thing by wishing. He manako te koura e kore ai. The wish for fish will bring none. There, I did it again. I've got more, too. Pretty soon I'll be telling you not to die giving up like an octopus, and nobody wants to hear that they're a chickenshit. *Including* a girl. That's advice for your future, which you'll have a chance at if you swim back with me instead of freezing to death on the rocks."

"Maybe I believe you do have a grandfather," Dougie said. "And that he's Maori."

"You should," I said. "He's real. You had your rest. Get in. Swim hard, and you'll warm up. Kia kaha." Stay strong, that meant. I didn't say, *If you get in trouble again, I'll get you out.* He didn't want to hear it. Anyway, the fear was half the problem, and stinging his pride was half the answer.

I'd wait until I got him safely out of here to think about how close Artie had come to real trouble—or, face it, death—and that I'd put him there. Not to mention how much of a debt I owed to Jax, what he was going to say about it, and that I was going to have to take it, because he'd be right.

So much for the butterflies in my belly. So much for impressing a guy who knew how to do more than pretend to be tough. A guy who actually *was* that strong, and who'd watched me take off my shorts like he'd wanted me to keep going. I'd bet he didn't have a fountain pen. I'd bet he wrote with a cheap ballpoint, in whatever color ink the pen happened to have, and that his handwriting was that sexy, firm, angular kind. Too bad I was never going to find out now.

Way to do your first day, Karen.

7

PRETTY BLOODY WONDERFUL

KAREN

Dougie made it.

I stayed to the seaward side of him, swimming painfully slowly toward shore, counting off every ten meters aloud, and watching the slope of the island get less and less steep to our left, until finally, I said, "We can get out here, I think. I'll go first." I hauled myself out of the water and onto a sloping rock, got my body wedged into a crevice with only a moderate amount of shin-scraping and toe-stubbing, then turned and held out my hand for him.

"I can do it," he said, or more like—gasped.

I had to roll my eyes. "Pretend I'm another guy," I said, "and let's go." I hauled up his string-bean body, waited while he lay down and did some more gasping, then said, "One more push. Follow me," and didn't wait to hear about how he could do it himself. Honestly, boys were like four-year-olds on that one. I chose a path up the rocks, scraped my leg some more as I slipped, and grabbed his hand and hauled him up the hard parts, and he did OK. At least, he stayed with me all the way until we were up the tumbled rocks, over the scrubby grass, and onto the sandy track.

"All downhill from here," I told him.

A family was on the track, too, heading back to shore and looking about ninety-seven percent less disheveled than us. Mum, dad, a boy of five or six, and a toddler in dad's arms. The dad asked, "All right there?" Which, in Kiwispeak, meant, "You appear to possibly be dying. I'm here to help, but I'll be casual about it."

I asked him, "Do you have an extra water bottle, maybe?" The mum hauled one out of a beach bag and handed it over, and I gave it to Dougie and told the family, "Cheers." We stepped aside to let them go on ahead, then waited for another group coming up the track from shore, and the whole thing felt disconcertingly mild, like everybody else had just had a lovely day out, and nobody had realized there'd been a full-scale emergency. Except, of course, Jax.

When I saw him and Artie on shore, I got some trembling legs of my own, and one of those light-headed surges of adrenaline that's so much less useful after the fact. The redheaded kid, Colin, was with them, and the other kid was running back over the beach from the road holding a few more bottles. Artie was sitting on the sand, his head bowed and his hands laced over his legs, and Jax was putting his leg on.

Well, good, I told my stupid, overreactive body. Jax hadn't called for the ambulance, and I was guessing he knew how to evaluate the need for it.

I asked Dougie, who was still shivering, "Run or walk?"

He said, "Run," and started to do it. Jog, more like, and not the steadiest thing I'd ever seen, but he was moving.

"Well done," I told him again. We ran the last three hundred meters together, and Dougie finished slowly, but he finished.

Which was all good, except that when we got back, Jax wouldn't look at me.

Not an enormous surprise.

✩✩

JAX

I didn't breathe easy until I saw Karen hauling Dougie up the rocks. I'd been about thirty seconds away from going out again for him, once I'd known Artie was going to be all right. I hadn't done it, though, because Karen had stayed with him the whole way. When they started running, she kept on staying with him, too, instead of trying to prove that she was faster. He was going all right, but it was good that she wasn't pushing him.

When he staggered up the beach at last to join the rest of us, I handed him a bottle of Gatorade and said, "Well done, mate." After that, I handed my half-full one to Karen, and she took it without looking at me.

Ouch.

Dougie sank to his knees like he couldn't have run another meter, drank down half the bottle, and said, "I reckon you win." Which showed some mental fortitude.

"Nah," I said. "I put you both in danger to prove my point. That's not winning. We'll say we all did it, and good on us for getting out of there. And next time, we'll show a bit more respect for the sea."

He asked, "What happened to your leg?"

"Afghanistan," I said, and all the boys' heads came up. Karen's as well. I went on, "Which wasn't too different from this. You train for the situations you're likely to get into, you look out for your mates, you front up when you have to, and you try not to do anything too stupid. Rules worth remembering, eh."

They digested that a minute, and Karen got busy toweling off and pulling on a dress, a short thing with a flower print and a halter top that looked just bloody fine with all that arm and leg and neck. She still wasn't looking at me, and not in a sexy "I'm not looking at you, except when I glance over and look away again" sort of way. In a way that said, "Not much of a hero, are you, mate, letting that happen?" More or less what I'd been saying to myself for about half an hour now. Finally, she said, "I'm glad you're all right, Artie. You should

56

probably head on home, and Colin, you need to get some ice on your nose. My car isn't too close, but if you can wait fifteen minutes while I run to get it, I can give all four of you a lift."

"Already sorted," I said. "We were just waiting for you and Dougie. My own car's just across the road, in the apartment's garage. I've got room for four passengers, so we're all good. If you want to have a shower and warm up while I'm gone, Karen, I'll take you for that coffee once I'm back. We could let that run straight into dinner if you like."

"Oh," she said, "I think I'll quit while I'm behind, thanks." Which was easy enough to interpret. I'd probably issued the challenge in the first place to impress her, and it had worked about as well as that sort of thing generally did, all the way back to when I'd engaged in a rock-throwing competition at the age of six with Tom Harper during school recess. It'd had something to do with impressing a girl with blonde plaits, as I recalled, and had gone about as well as you'd expect. The girl had rolled her eyes, and Tom and I had been sent to the head's office.

On the other hand, I'd kissed that girl, seven or eight years later, standing in the shadows of a carpark after a school dance. Violet Carmichael. I still remembered the way my heart had pounded when I'd taken her hand for the first time, and how I'd thought I'd actually pass out when I'd finally been holding her, her body centimeters from mine. I'd wondered how this could be legal, getting to hold girls right there at school. I'd barely been able to breathe, and at the same time, I'd dreaded her getting any closer and finding out how hard I was. The shame and the thrill of it, and the shock, too, half an hour later, when my lips had met hers in that first-ever kiss. The sweet citrus of her scent, like girls just smelled better and *felt* better, too, so soft and pretty.

Maybe the rock-throwing hadn't been pointless after all, just a little slow on the payoff. Except that Violet had been six and fourteen during those events, I'd been better-looking and possessed of all my limbs, and Karen didn't seem like she'd be overwhelmed by the idea that I could throw rocks.

I wouldn't mind the dancing, though. Or the kissing. She

didn't look any worse wet and sandy than she had at any other time today, and her dress left her shoulders bare and swooped most of the way up her slim thighs at both sides. She wasn't as soft as Violet, but kissing her would be a contact sport all the way, and I could feel the electricity just from having her this close. Exactly like I was fourteen again, and pulling that girl into me for the very first time. Now, though, I knew what to do with her.

Oh, yeh, I wanted to take her out.

She was bleeding, though. A long scratch up her shin from which a trickle of red ran, and a bashed knee that looked painful. I finally got my leg on—not easy, when it was sticky with salt—stopped thinking about how I looked, and said, "You've hurt yourself. Come along to my place and clean that off. If you need bandaging, we'll get that sorted once I get home. We're headed over there now."

She shook her head, did some more not-looking at me, picked up her bag, shook hands with the boys, one after another, and told Artie and Dougie, "You did well. I pushed too hard. My fault." The words came out jerkily, like she'd forced them.

I said, "Stay."

She said, "I can't. I need to go."

The boys and I watched her head down the beach in the opposite direction from the apartment, and Dougie said, "She's pretty cool. Pity she doesn't like you better. Could be because you don't have a leg, I guess. Could put girls off, eh."

So, yes. Just a bloody wonderful afternoon all the way around.

8

LIKE AN ANCESTOR

KAREN

I'd been planning to visit Koro tomorrow morning, before my meeting. Once I'd had a chance to do those things you did—shower, and then eat something, preferably something full of salt and grease, the two essential food groups. Fish and chips from the Waihi Beach takeaway, for instance, not that I'd been thinking about that much. Eaten properly, through a hole ripped in the top of the paper wrapping so the heat stayed in, with vinegar and salt sprinkled over them and Wattie's tomato sauce for dipping. Mmm. Possibly—oh, let's face it, definitely—with a beer. After that, I planned to fall across the bed in the time-zone-change coma, and wake up about twelve hours later as a human being again. Which would also mean that the humiliating spectacle of Jax being kind to me, after I'd messed up as badly as a person could do, would be twelve hours in my past.

When I was headed northwest, though, past flax plants and fern trees, kiwifruit blocks and a whole lot of general sleepiness, the car just . . . *aimed* itself, and once I'd made it into town, no other destination was possible.

Colorful little kiwifruit-centric Katikati, with its murals

covering most of the downtown buildings. Perched at the edge of the sea, below the mountains, beside the river, and in nobody's tourist guidebook, because all it was—was perfect. The place where my sister and I had found a family.

Through the roundabout Hope had driven three times, squeaking all the way, before she'd had the nerve to take the turning. Down the street where we'd learned to parallel park, me by the bump-and-go method and her by inching cautiously forward and back about seventeen times before she finally got in. Past the Dave Hume Pools, where she'd become a slightly less timid swimmer and I'd learned how to go fast. And, of course, along the beach where I'd walked for hours, luxuriating in the delicious pain that was my undying love for Hemi's cousin Matiu, Sexiest Man Alive, glamorous single doctor, and our driving instructor.

I'd come up with so many scenarios in which Matiu would save my life in some extreme medical way, and then discover, as he held me in his arms and looked down into my beautiful, pale face, that he loved me deeply, passionately, and with every fiber of his manly being, and he couldn't live without me. They'd all tended to end the same way, with him casting aside the twelve-year age barrier between us as an artificial construct that couldn't hold back our timeless love. And kissing me in a way that made me understand that I'd never really been kissed before.

Too bad nobody I'd ever kissed in real life had done it as tenderly, as patiently, and then as absolutely possessively as a dream-man who'd never actually kissed me at all. Men kissed at the beginning, in my experience. It was a means to an end, the salad they had to eat before the main course came. After that, the kissing died down, because they didn't have to anymore, and most guys weren't all that crazy about salad.

Of course, there'd been the inconvenient fact that Matiu had been in love with Hope, even though she'd been pregnant—by his cousin—not to mention engaged to that cousin, with a three-carat rock on her finger and no eyes for any other man. I'd felt like—did *every* guy in the world secretly long for an ultra-feminine tiny blonde, so his manliness could blossom in full contrast? Because if so, I was doomed.

Oh, wait. I still felt that way.

Fortunately, I didn't have too long to stew in my misery, or maybe I just wasn't sixteen anymore, because I was coming up the hill, with the sea sparkling behind me and the mountains looming above me, to my favorite house in the world, and already feeling so much better. I pulled into the driveway behind a battered ute and a boat on a trailer, which meant somebody was still going out to fish for snapper and trevally for their tea, and probably gathering mussels and pipi from the rocks, and whitebait from the river in spring. Good times.

No second car anymore, because Koro had given that up five years ago, when he'd turned ninety. He'd said, "Handing over my keys before you lot take them from me, eh. A man doesn't need that humiliation." Or maybe he'd just been happy to stay at home with his garden, with the trees and the birds, the paddocks and orchards spreading out below him like a rumpled green quilt all the way to the sea. With the wind and the rain and the sun, and, of course, the whanau who loved him almost as much as he loved them. Well, most of them. The part of his whanau that didn't suck, anyway.

He was sitting under the avocado tree in the front yard, wearing a white T-shirt and baggy old-man pants, in the wooden Adirondack chair I'd painted for him ten years ago as a Christmas present. The moment my car pulled in, he was leaning on his stick and struggling to his feet, every line in his brown face creasing into a smile, until he looked like a man with a full-face moko. Like an ancestor. As for me—my chest was tight, my heart felt like it would burst straight out of it, and the tears were right there.

I couldn't even feel myself tumbling out of the car. I was across the yard, putting a careful hand on his shoulder, and feeling his ancient, gnarled hand come up to grip my own shoulder as he bent his head, touched his forehead and nose to mine, and we breathed together in a hongi.

I was breathing with my Koro again. I was here, in this place that had never been home and always would be, as long as he was here.

"I had a feeling you'd come today," he said after a minute. His own eyes were bright with old-man tears, and the hand that came up to touch my cheek was shaky. "I've been waiting, in case."

I was crying, and I couldn't care, a few tears that insisted on spilling over. "You should have told me you wanted me to," I said, brushing them back with the heel of my hand. "I almost didn't. I haven't even had a shower yet. I'm covered with sand."

"What do I care about that?" He lowered himself down into his chair again. Slowly, but I knew better than to try to help him. "You're here. That's good enough for me. Bring a chair and talk to me."

I dragged over another chair, made of weathered wood like he didn't have a billionaire grandson, or like he was more comfortable with familiar, homey things, and said, "Somebody's been keeping your peacock throne looking flash. Gave it a new coat of varnish." I'd painted it with bright blues, greens, and golds, and every slat was a peacock feather, with its iridescent eye.

He said, "Me, that's who."

"Koro. You know Hemi or I would do it. You know Nikau would do it. You know *anybody* would do it."

"Not dead yet, am I. I can still do a bit of sanding and varnishing, thank you very much. I'm old, though. Got no time to talk about this dull stuff. Tell me why you're bleeding."

"Oh, you know." I checked out the impressive scrape along my shin, which was stinging from the salt, and tried to laugh. "Doesn't everybody get off the plane after twenty-four hours, get into a stoush with a bunch of dumb teenagers absolutely immediately, because she gets all flustered by a sexy amputee, make two of the kids do a race that's way beyond them, which ends up with the sexy guy having to rescue one of them from drowning, and have to slink away in shame? What, how do *you* take a vacation?"

He smiled, or maybe he just looked amused, in Te Mana style, but his old eyes were wise. Also in Te Mana style.

It was no wonder I couldn't find a great man. My standards were too high, or they were too low, because I kept thinking that other men were like him and Hemi, and finding out too late that I was absolutely, positively, couldn't-be-wronger *wrong.* He said, "Sounds like you're getting over that fella, then, if you noticed the other one. That's good. Let him go. You worked hard, did your best. Got that company going, eh, and made sure all those people had work to do that'll keep their families fed and make them proud. You'll do it again, no worries. Why d'you reckon God gave you so much energy and made you so clever, if not to do that? And if you made a mistake today, you learned, that's all. That's what young people are here for, to learn. But you mean to tell me that this other fella, the one who rescued somebody, didn't want a strong, beautiful girl like you? No good, then. You can do better."

"I know," I said, and bit the inside of my cheek to keep from crying. "At least I keep trying to tell myself so. Why do I keep meeting guys like that, Koro? You've got to think it's me by now. You must have been wondering with Josh. Eight years, and I didn't even have a ring? I know I'm not Hope, but that's pretty lame."

"I wasn't wondering," Koro said. "I was glad. Meant you weren't being stupid, marrying him because he was pretty. You could get out fast, and you did. And of course you're not Hope. That's not who you were meant to be. Work on being Karen instead."

I sat back in my chair, stuck my legs out in front of me, and sighed. "You hated him, too. Why didn't you *say* so?"

"Thought you had enough with Hemi telling you, maybe. And you weren't listening to him, so why would you listen to me? You've got a hard head, same as Hemi. Have to learn everything the hard way, don't you. Never mind. You've learnt it now."

His hand was trembling on his stick. I said, "You're tired. You know what? So am I. Also, if I don't take a shower soon, I'm . . . I don't know. Something drastic will happen, anyway. Let me help you into the house, if that's where you're going.

I'll give Vanessa and the baby a kiss, and then I'll go to the beach house and collapse."

Vanessa was a local girl who'd married my almost-cousin Nikau a few years back. They'd come to live with Koro after he'd had flu, and stayed to care for him and be company for him, because Maori were like that. Nikau was exactly my age, and Vanessa was somewhere around that, too. Now, they had a baby, like everybody in the world except me.

A couple more trips down Memory Lane, and I'd be curled on the bathroom floor again. At least it wouldn't slope this time.

"That's good," Koro said, hauling himself slowly to his feet, leaning on his stick a whole lot more than the last time I'd seen him, which was had been six months ago. Too long ago. "I've seen you. Now I'm ready to take a nap. Vanessa went by the house earlier, ran the hoover, took you some milk and eggs and bread and avocadoes and that. The avos are doing well this year. Heaps of rain for them last winter. You go have your tea and a good sleep, then come back tomorrow. Back with the whanau now, aren't you. Home again, and that's good. Better for you, and better for us. Lucky for me, too, I think." He gave a sigh, or maybe he just breathed. "Lucky for me."

9

NOT IN THE BAMBOO

JAX

I crossed the street to the Coffee Club the next morning at one minute past ten. It was what I'd told Karen: You wanted to arrive just late enough for the other party to wonder whether you were turning up. Every soldier learned to wait, but I'd noticed that most other people didn't. Every soldier also knew what that wait could do to your head.

I might only be here for my sister's sake, but that didn't mean I wouldn't do my best.

I was thinking that, and then I wasn't, because she was there. Karen, that is, sitting at a table on the pavement despite the breeze ruffling the patio umbrellas. Choosing to be outside rather than inside every time it was remotely possible, exactly like a Kiwi.

She didn't look up at my approach. Maybe because she was frowning in absolute concentration, her laptop open in front of her as she wrote furiously in a spiral notebook.

It was like she had personality-rays all around her. I might not be spiritually evolved enough to tell what color her aura was, but it was definitely something bright. She also happened to be wearing a copper-colored T-shirt with a high neck. That would've been nothing out of the ordinary, except that the front had two sides that gathered at her collarbone, then opened up into a sort of narrow triangle whose bottom edge skimmed her cleavage. It didn't show much, but it showed enough, and it was knocking me flat. The middle-aged blokes at the next table seemed to agree, because they were checking her out like they were waiting for their moment, or waiting for their courage.

Too bad. I was here first. I was here *now*.

It could also have been the narrow blue skirt that didn't reach her knees, the length of thigh she was showing as she crossed her legs, and maybe even the blue canvas trainers she had on. Another woman would've done some kind of pretty sandals, maybe, with that outfit, but another woman wouldn't have looked like she'd leap to her feet at any moment and start chasing down villains, or possibly transform into a superhero. You needed to be wearing trainers for that.

And, yeh, I noticed all that. Noticing was my job. I also noticed that she was wearing a new earring in addition to the line of three sparklers in each lobe, a sort of gold cuff thing that crossed in an X on the edge of her upper ear. Whatever that part was called.

How could an earring look sexy? Unless, of course, you'd spent the last six years of your life around too many men who'd taken too few showers. After enough of that, almost anything a woman did started looking sexy, especially if she was the right woman. Taking off her coat? That worked. Wearing earrings? That, too. Showing a triangle of smooth skin, so close to everything you were dying to get your hands on, that had you wanting to trace along the edge of the fabric with your fingertips while you watched her eyes drift shut and, possibly, kissed her neck? That *absolutely* worked.

"Morning," I said, stopping at her table. Not that there had been any other choice. "You're looking intense. Diary entry? Ransom note? Hit list?"

She was frowning as she looked up, and then she wasn't, not quite. "Oh. You."

I had to laugh. "Don't throw yourself at me like that. It's embarrassing."

"Ha." Finally, she was smiling. "Guess we both recovered. Did the kids get home OK?"

"Yeh." I considered telling her that I'd wished she'd been waiting when *I* got home. That I'd had a long and frustrated night, broken up by a pretty special dream. Or rather, I didn't consider telling her. Telling a woman you'd had a dirty dream about her—a woman who'd run away from you the last time like she couldn't move fast enough—might not be the best way to her heart. Instead, I said, "I'm here to meet somebody, but if you give me your number, I could text you later, as we're both still here. We could go for a non-competitive swim. Have a drink. Indulge in a lively game of Chinese Checkers."

"Even though you're here to meet somebody," she said.

"Didn't say it was that kind of somebody."

My phone chose this inopportune moment to ring, and I pulled it out of my pocket, glanced at the screen, and told Karen, "Bugger. Hang on," before I put it to my ear and said, "Hi. Hang on a sec, would you?"

Karen had gone back to her writing, though, like I wasn't there. I was going to have to work on my X factor. I told my sister, "Nothing to report yet. Not a single over-stylish Maori billionaire in sight. You should've had him carry a red rose or something."

"I forgot to tell you," Poppy said. "He's not coming."

Karen was looking at me oddly. I thought back over what I'd said. I told Poppy, "Hang on," and told Karen, "No, I'm not into the gay dating scene. Haven't become an escort, either, lucrative as the amputee fetish market probably is. It was a joke."

She looked startled, or something like it, but Poppy was talking fast into my ear. Karen wasn't actually going anywhere, so I told Poppy, "Hang on. Let me look for him inside."

"I just *told* you." Poppy's voice was rising. "Bloody hell, Jax, *listen* a minute. Hemi's not the one coming. I forgot to tell you. It's somebody else."

"Right," I said in resignation. "Who?"

"I can't remember. Some relation of his. I wrote it

somewhere, on a sticky note." Poppy carried sticky notes the way other people carried tissues. Stuck into pockets, up sleeves, down her bra. Her pen was normally stuck safely through a topknot of hair, which was the only reason the sticky notes ever got written on. "I can't find it, though," she said, surprising me not at all. "I was being sick directly after, I think. Could've fallen into the loo, I suppose."

I did not roll my eyes. Before she'd first fallen pregnant, Poppy had been—well, not a model of rigorous efficiency, but brilliant all the same. Now, with two kids under the age of four and another on the way, the brilliance came in flashes, between bouts of sickness and other domestic emergencies. "You need a minder," I told her. "What am I meant to do, wander around every table and ask people if they're here to meet me?"

"Not you," she said, "me. No! Not in the bamboo! In the potty!"

I assumed that one wasn't meant for me, so I waited through some more urgent instruction, and eventually, she came back and said, "Olivia. She wants to be a kitty, and she says they go in the garden. I keep catching her trying with my plants. In the *house.* My bamboo's leaves are turning yellow. It'd be disgusting if it were somebody else's kid. It could still be disgusting, in fact. Potty training's hard enough when they don't want to be a cat. Why did I do this? Why?"

"Dunno," I said. "Research? To be fair, though, I suspect Max had something to do with it as well. Could be his fault. Maybe he has cat genes."

"You think you're funny. Wait until you have a kid who wants to be a dog. I'll be laughing then. Or a horse. A rhinoceros." Her voice got a faraway sound to it that I'd heard before. "That would be good, actually. Where's my pen?"

I recognized the signs. My sister wrote kids' books. I had about two seconds here. "Wait," I said loudly. "Stop. Why does this person expect to meet you and not me?"

"Oh. Because I think I forgot to ring him back and tell him it was going to be you instead. I *meant* to do it, but I have a feeling I forgot."

"Now I'm asking people if they have a date with my sister," I said. "I've gone from being an escort to being a pimp. Brilliant."

"Don't be silly," she said. "Oh, bugger. I'm going to be sick again. Oh, no. Why do bodily functions have to be so revolting? Hang on. No. Don't get up. Here. Talk to Uncle Jax."

After that, there was the sound of a toilet lid banging against the tank, some distant retching, and a piping little two-year-old voice saying, "Unkow Jax, I did a poo in the potty. Mummy says I can't go like a kitty, but I wanted to go like a kitty."

"Oh," I said. "Uh . . . well done."

"I need somebody to wipe me, and Mummy is being very sick. Can you come and wipe me?"

"No, sorry," I said. "Too far away. Wait for Mummy." The sound of the toilet flushing, fortunately, and I said, "Give Mummy back her phone," and escaped. Poppy could ring me back when she remembered the person's name. *If* she remembered.

On the other hand, the buyer's representative, whoever he was, would surely ring *her* and ask where she was, eventually, and she could tell him to look for the one-legged man. It was like a spy novel. One with kids in it, and spies of inadequate suavity, if suavity was a word. While I was waiting for the action to start, I could chat up Karen.

"Sorry," I told her, putting the phone back into my pocket. "My sister. She's pregnant, as well as various other issues. I'm meant to meet somebody here, but it turns out I don't know who, so I may as well get a coffee. Do you want something?"

"What?" she said. "No. It's me."

Women were not making sense today. I said, "Yours is cold, though, surely." Her bowl-sized mocha, in fact, still had the elaborate design of a fern drawn in milky foam across the cocoa-sprinkled top, like she hadn't taken a single sip. She hadn't even eaten the chocolate fish. Everybody ate the chocolate fish.

"Oh," she said. "I forgot about that. I do that sometimes. Forget. No. That's OK. I mean . . ." She drew her hand through her short hair, which was sticking up some today as if she were some kind of rocker chick, a look she'd intensified with black eyeliner. I liked it. "I mean," she said again, "I'm the person you're supposed to meet. I'm Hemi Te Mana's sister-in-law. You were supposed to be Poppy Cantwell, who was going to be showing me around various overpriced campgrounds for the next week or so. I'll warn you, they'd better come up to a pretty high standard if they're not aimed at Kiwis. Americans are not paying top dollar to go to the bathroom in a hole on the forest floor. Which they dug themselves."

She was negotiating already. That was interesting. "You sound like my niece," I said. "Or her opposite. We were just discussing that, in fact."

"Going to the bathroom on the forest floor?"

"Oddly enough, yes. She's two. So. Let's start again, shall we?" I stuck out a hand. "Hi. I'm Jackson MacGregor, here to represent Kiwi Luxe Eco Stays. Happy to meet you. Consider me your tour guide."

She looked away and muttered something. I thought it might be, "Fuck my life."

This never happened in the movies.

KAREN

Had I actually *said* the amputee fetish thing? Surely not. I'd been tired and stupid yesterday, but not *that* tired and stupid. Then why had *he* said it?

Also, why did it have to be him? Hadn't I made enough of a fool of myself already? And did he have to look that good? His hair was neat once more—not too hard, when it was that short—he'd shaved, and he was wearing a black T-shirt, in a radical departure from yesterday's khaki T-shirt, that wasn't one bit too loose, but also wasn't tight enough that it was saying, "Hey, girls." The T-shirt a man wore when he had a very good body, and he was used to having it.

He was also wearing shorts, like every other self-respecting Kiwi male. Somebody else might have worn jeans and hidden the leg. Jax, once again, was putting himself out there, and I thought that might not be easy. Before, people's first thought would probably have been, "Wow." At least if they were female people, it would be. Now, they'd see him and think, "Amputee." I'd hate that. He probably hated it more.

"So that was my sister," he said. "As we've established. She was planning this trip as a break from the kids. Besides that she needed to do it, of course. Turns out she's pregnant again and sick with it, so I said I'd do it, as I had the time. Hang on. I'm getting a coffee. I'll order you another as well."

He was gone before I could say more, and I sat there, went over my notes again, and tried to marshal my forces. I'd been exploring the company's website and making notes. Impressions, questions, things I wanted to check out. And, yes, you could say that it would've been better to do that, oh, say, any day before today. Hey, I'd been *depressed*. At least I was pretty sure that was what it had been. I'd never actually been depressed before. I was planning on avoiding it in future, because it sucked.

Jax came out of the café, putting his wallet into the back pocket of his shorts, which was a good look—biceps, et cetera—and stepping aside for a couple of young women, the kind with good hair and C cups—at least C, because I never got cup sizes right, except that they were "bigger than mine"—who wore cute clothes like they'd just thrown them on, and were never over five foot six. They looked at him, and then they stopped and looked again. After that, they said something, and he said something back. One of them shoved her long dark hair over her shoulder and did some posing, and I thought, *Hey. No.*

Jax looked over at me, smiled with his eyes, and said something else, at which the girls went inside at last. After that, he came over to the table and sat down, and I tried to remember what I'd been working on.

"I was feeling sorry for you," I told him, "before. I just decided to stop."

"And *I* was just thinking," he said, with, for once, no warmth in his eyes, "that I liked your honesty. I changed my mind."

"What?"

"You don't tell me that," he said. "Have you ever actually known a man?"

Talk about bumping back down to earth. "Yeah," I said. "It went about . . . uh . . . about . . . as well as you're thinking."

His face went still, and he said, "Aw, no," and put his hand over mine. It was a big hand. It had some scars, too. I knew that, because I was staring down at it. His voice was completely different when he said, "We'll rewind those last bits, eh."

I was choking up. It was like being with Koro the day before. The tears were rising, my throat was closing, and I couldn't do anything about it. I sat there, instead, staring down at his hand, concentrating on its warmth and trying not to panic. He wasn't Koro, and this was . . . it was way too . . .

"Karen," he said. "Breathe."

Oh. Good idea. I did it, and after a minute, he said, "All right?"

"Yeah. Sorry. I need a napkin." I'd managed to hold back the tears, but my nose hadn't gotten the message, and it was running. Some women cried beautifully. I melted down like a candle, and not one of those beautiful candles. The kind that puddled all over, so you had to scrape the wax off with a knife, and you wondered who the heck had decided that candles were romantic. Which was why I worked so hard on not crying.

I thought about that, because it was so much more appealing than thinking about what he'd said. I said, "Shoot. I do need a napkin. Hang on."

I was standing up, but he was faster. He said, "I've got it. Glass of water, too."

By the time he came back with them, I had myself under control, but my nose was also really running. I grabbed the napkins from him with more haste than delicacy, mopped up, took a drink of water, and asked, "So where were we? I was establishing dominance, business-wise. At least that's the way I'd like to remember it."

He gave me some more of his sweet smile, and I said, before I could stop myself, "Do all men really like long hair that much better? I'm not changing if they do, because screw that. I don't need that aggravation, and I work out a lot. I'm just asking."

He was still smiling. He wasn't holding my hand anymore, though, which was too bad. It was shocking how good that had felt.

I'd never wanted to be protected. I'd never *needed* to be protected. And yet it had felt exactly like that. Huh.

"Some men do," he said. "For other men? It probably depends."

"On what?"

"On how they feel about the woman."

Whoa. Talk about knocking your socks off. I was having some more trouble breathing. Fortunately, the coffee came at that moment. I said, "Thanks," he said, "No worries," and I took a sip. It was delicious, so I took another one. Nobody did coffee like New Zealand, the country responsible for my most expensive habit.

He said, "You're still not eating your chocolate fish."

"That's because it's disgusting. Fake marshmallow, artificial strawberry flavoring, cheap chocolate coating."

He had a hand over his heart. "You realize I took a bullet for Kiwiana."

"Really?" I asked. "You got shot, too? For chocolate fish?"

"Figuratively." He snatched the fish off my saucer and ate it in one bite. "Delicious." I rolled my eyes, and he laughed. "It's all in the comparison, eh."

We drank our coffees, and it was a whole lot better. "So," he said. "I seem to be taking you on a tour of some glamping properties. Four of them, is the plan, starting day after tomorrow. Two nights each, is what we have booked, so we'll have a chance for you to explore, get the full experience, talk to staff, or just poke around. With a break in between, since

73

the second two are in the South Island. By the way—thanks for not being Hemi Te Mana. I wasn't sure what the hell I was going to talk about with the bloke for a week. I don't know much about fashion anymore, and I'm not sure I see him in a kayak."

"He's surprisingly normal," I said. "In New Zealand, at least."

"Mm. Can I say that I'm glad you came instead?"

"Yeah," I said. I wasn't a shy person, but that was how I was feeling right now. Stupid breakdown. "You can."

"I can see *you* in a kayak, though," he said. "Ecotourism's all about adventure. Whatever you fancy."

"Good," I said. "Because I fancy everything." And got a look from him that sucked all the oxygen out of the air.

Whoa. The man could *smolder*.

I'd forgotten all about his fan club. Until the two girls came over to the table, that is, and the brunette said, "Pardon me. Jax? Can we get a selfie with you?"

"No worries," he said, then stood up, took a couple photos with an arm around a girl's shoulder, handed the phone firmly back, sat down again with me and ignored them, and said, "Now. Where were we? Oh, that's right. Planning our adventure."

10

⭐

LIFT AND SUPPORT

JAX

Karen could have left it there, possibly thinking, *Not really my business,* or *Could be awkward for him, so I'll wait and see if he volunteers the information.*

That didn't happen, of course. I did my best to move things along, saying, "Why do I think I'm about to hear that there's no 'I' in 'Team,' and that we'll be taking up your eminently logical arguments concerning the many ways I've already mucked up the plan for our working holiday? I've decided I need to be eating second breakfast while that happens. Won't have the emotional strength otherwise. And you'll want second breakfast as well, I'm thinking. Don't tell me. Cream donut. Almond croissant. Chocolate brioche."

Some women were experts at the cool, reserved face, keeping you off-balance and eager to please. Either nobody had ever taught Karen that game, or she refused to play it, or maybe she just wouldn't recognize "reserved" if it bit her on the backside.

That created a brief thought-diversion. Talk about your word pictures. I was still dragging my reluctant mind back to reality when she said, with the kind of fire in her eyes that I'd already come to recognize, "There is *so* much to unpack here. First—why would I go around eating cream donuts? Why wouldn't you assume I'm as disciplined as you are? Well, other than the gigantic mocha, but you just saw me running and swimming yesterday. I was about to win, too."

"Dunno," I said. "It's not that I think you're *not* disciplined, or not exactly. I suspect it's more like 'headed full tilt toward the objective,' though, and less like 'dutiful diligence.' I also think that anybody who lives as hard as you do burns calories doing it, and probably forgets to eat as well. And—no. I was going to win. But women tend to want sugar when they're hurting. Possibly chocolate as well. Or sugar *and* chocolate, of course. Cream donut with chocolate icing, maybe."

"I am not hurting. It was a few scrapes. How fragile do you think I *am*? Also—one word. Rematch."

I'd forgotten about the scrapes, possibly because she'd ignored them from the start. I said, "Yeh, nah. I wasn't thinking about your body. Not that way, anyway. I was thinking about your heart. That kind of healing can take longer. You don't want sugar? Avocado toast, then. An eggs benny. They do one with smoked salmon and spinach here that's quite good. I told you—whatever you fancy. Decide, though, because I know what I want. Smoked salmon benny with avocado on the side. And I want it now."

"How do you know about my heart?" she asked. "And— wait. Why are we talking about my heart?" As if she couldn't imagine a man caring that she'd looked like that, had fought the tears back that hard. That told you something. Mostly about the bastard who'd done it.

"Maybe I guessed," I said.

"Wait," she said again. "You're buying all this? Smoked salmon? Avocado toast? Who *are* you? You didn't lose that leg in Afghanistan. You're living too high to be any kind of soldier. I don't know much about soldiers, but I know that their families can be on food stamps. Which is wrong, by the way, but you're not buying smoked salmon or staying at that address if you're on food stamps. Of course, your sister owns all this pricey property we're visiting, so maybe you're on a per diem from her. Hot girls don't usually line up to get their pictures taken, though, with anonymous guys who are poor *and* have scars and—" she waved a casual arm—"so forth, not unless they also have something else. OK, one more. Women with crushed hearts probably don't pay off that well, investment-of-your-time-and-money-wise, so why bother with me? Or *do* they pay off? Huh. Interesting question. I never know those guy-type answers, and you'd know *and* actually tell. Is it a problem for you, being somebody's revenge sex? Or do you even care one way or the other? Does that even work? Does it make you—the other person, I mean, not you—feel better? Because I don't think so."

When you get hit by one of those sudden wind shifts out sailing, you find out pretty bloody quickly what it feels like to heel over. That was what Karen kept doing to me. There my rudder was, out of the water and no help at all. I said, "I'm both seriously insulted in a whole variety of ways, and reluctantly amused. Can't decide which is winning. Right, then. First, I did lose my leg in Afghanistan. Believe me or not. Second, I can afford to buy you an avocado toast, anyway. Third—is this third? They didn't recognize me because of my remarkable accomplishments, no worries. And, yes, I'd mind being your revenge sex, so never mind whether it works."

"I didn't say mine."

"Fine. Not yours, then. What do you want to eat?"

"If you're going to keep talking about smoked salmon, I have to have it. Also a cream donut. If they have one."

I was smiling all the way into the café, despite all the insulting, or because of it. You'd never wonder where you stood, anyway. How would a woman with that much vitality make love? It would be hard work for a man to keep the upper hand.

They did have a cream donut. With chocolate icing. Score.

☆☆

KAREN

When Jax came out again, I closed my laptop hastily and said, "You should have had me order that. You got the coffees."

"Nah," he said. "Call me old-fashioned." And then just shut up and sat there, ankles crossed in front of him like he had nothing to prove.

I said, "I looked you up. Just now."

"Oh?"

"What do you mean, 'Oh?' Aren't you going to . . ." I waved an arm. "Blow up at me about the Afghanistan thing? Wrong choice of words, I realize. And all right, I was wrong. Sorry."

He laughed. Which was aggravating. The man was the coolest person I'd ever met, with the exception of my brother-in-law. I'd thought Josh was cool, but what I'd told Hemi was true. Compared to Jax, Josh was cake mix.

"You're laughing," I informed him.

"I am." He was still smiling, in fact. "I don't think any bloke in the world has ever said 'Sorry' as reluctantly as you did just then. No worries."

"Except," I said, "that the reason the Afghanistan thing made the news at all is that you're a newsworthy guy. Rich-lister. Model. Bad boy. You could just have said."

"What, that I'm a rich-lister model? Not so much. Not a bad boy, either, whatever that is besides 'arsehole.' Or just a stupid kid who thought he was tough. I joined the Army for a lark and wished I hadn't about a week later, but too late. Eventually, I wasn't quite as much of a stupid kid anymore, and then I wasn't a kid at all. Also, I'm not rich. My family's rich."

"That's what rich people always say. Next you'll be telling me that you're not rich, you're comfortable."

"If you're Hemi Te Mana's sister-in-law, you probably know."

"Yes and no. Hemi's awesome, and he sent me to college and business school, because he loves my sister and she loves me, but he's not my dad. I'm not in the will, and that's fine.

But I grew up poor-almost-to-homelessness until the age of sixteen, and are-you-kidding-me-rich after that, and I know the difference. When 'new couch' means, 'Look what somebody threw away, right here on the sidewalk,' you're poor. And when 'Actually, quite a comfortable flight' means 'first class,' or even 'private jet,' you're rich. I'm doing all right, but I'm sure not rich. In fact . . ." I drew a breath and said it. "I'm unemployed. You could call it 'fired,' or you could call it 'severed.' That sounds appropriately bloody and abrupt."

"Ah," he said. "It wasn't just the bloke, then."

"No. It was both. You're a model, though. You modeled *underwear*. Famously. The face of Wallaby underwear, or maybe 'face' is the wrong word. Otherwise known as 'The Body.' That is such awesome news." Switching tracks like the coyote in the cartoon, exactly as fast as I could.

He gave me a hard look that made me want to laugh. "I modeled heaps of things."

"And yet," I said, feeling about a hundred times better, "it's the underwear ads that are sticking with me. Not just underwear. Special double-pocket *pouch* underwear, 'Because your boys deserve to breathe.' Except that so clearly isn't the point, because there was also, 'Show them what you're made of.' You saying, 'Show them what you're made of' with all that dangerous smolder has pretty much made my day. And—oh, the lifting and supporting. The *presentation*. The *enhancement*. Oh, what a crushing disappointment for a woman later on."

I was just about hanging over the chair, I was laughing so hard, and I thought he was having a hard time not laughing himself. "Stop it," he said. "I didn't write the slogans, and that wasn't my voiceover, either. Just wore the things, eh. It was a long time ago."

I was dying to ask him how they got the look that smooth in the commercials. Whether that was some sort of foam, or what, and how much of it they'd used. Maybe to tease him, and maybe more than that. I wasn't ready for revenge sex, but my battered ego could use some flirting. Also, I was curious, all right? Let's just say that the ad campaigns had been up-close and personal, and the combination of being the sexy-

and-single scion of a rich-list family in tiny, three-degrees-of-separation New Zealand, and the saxophone-lick-soundtracked, slow-mo videos of his seriously substantial assets in *very* clingy red boxer briefs had inspired some pretty furious sharing on both sides of the Ditch. The presentation, the lifting and supporting, had worked out just fine for him— if it *was* all him—and he also had about the best butt I'd ever seen. Just saying. I knew that part hadn't been padding, because I'd seen it during yesterday's run, since I'd never managed to pass him. I'd had to click through fast just now to make sure he wouldn't catch me looking, though. How creepy was it to want to look some more?

"And you're still famous," I said. "Modeling for the New Zealand Defence Force, too."

"I used to have a pretty face," he said. "The modeling was useful to both parties. They could put my name to it, and I was a feel-good Service to Country story, which made it more effective than filming some random good-looking bloke attempting to navigate an obstacle course whilst holding a nonfunctional weapon, generally looking bloody awkward and making you want to reach through the screen and slap him."

"So it was a public service."

"It's a good career, or a good start to one. Being in the services, that is, not modeling. Modeling wasn't that bad, either, once you separate out my own stupidity from the mix. Bought a house with it, and put a bit away. Not the apartment here. That belongs to the family."

"Able to buy me eggs benedict with smoked salmon, anyway," I said as the server brought out the plates. "And a cream donut. You are a tempting man."

"Good to know."

He didn't flirt like most guys, like he was either trying to score pick-up artist points or poised to backtrack and pretend it had all been a joke. What did you call serious flirting?

Hot, that was what.

We needed to plan the trip, and I needed to tell him what I wanted to see and do in order to report back to Hemi. That was why I was *here*. Too bad that the only thing I wanted to ask was how they'd got the look so smooth on the underwear. It would be such a bad idea. I was in no kind of emotional shape for a fling, he'd just said he wasn't interested in being my revenge sex, and Josh wouldn't have cared anyway. Besides, it wasn't what you had, it was what you could do with it. See "size not mattering," et cetera. I'd written what I had in that meeting to get back a tiny bit at Josh, that was all. Better than burning his entire stupid mostly-black wardrobe in our pellet stove. That had occurred to me, once I'd gone back to our so-called home and started flinging clothes into suitcases. That would have polluted the whole neighborhood, though, especially the polyester. And possibly started a fire, which would have been unfair to everybody else.

No reason to ask anyway, because it didn't matter. I was a mature, capable, professional woman, here to do a professional job. Every bit of this would become part of Hemi's negotiation, and whatever I'd said, I literally owed Hemi my life.

Fine. I wasn't asking. That was a No.

11

A New Normal

Jax

At nine o'clock two mornings later, after a bit of a rough night, I was crouched in the driveway of a modest house on a hillside above Katikati, sorting out gear, when Karen asked me, "When you're modeling underwear, Jax, how do they get the front to look that smooth?"

I shifted my weight to my right leg, did some careful balancing in order to stand up, and did not wince at the stab of pain from my stump. Beside Karen, a very old Maori man leaned on his cane, blinked tortoise eyes, and studied me with a calm certainty I recognized, the sort that came from seeing a lot of life. Beside *him,* a young woman named Vanessa said, "I always wanted to know that, too."

Her husband, who was holding their curly-haired baby, grinned at her. Yes, he was here as well, like we required an audience to pack the car, or possibly, as in my own family, that every activity was better if it were done together, and God forbid a person wouldn't want to share every single experience. The woman said, "You look all the time, Nikau. Why shouldn't I look, too? Heaps of gorgeous fish in the sea."

"Just remember that you've caught your limit," her

husband said. "You're done."

"Anyway," Karen said, "Jax hasn't answered my question. We probably should be taking my car, by the way, except that I wanted to leave it for Vanessa. I've seen bigger trunks on golf carts. Also, it's pretty, but it's a Lexus. That's disappointing, and not entirely surprising. My sister drives a Lexus."

"Got something against your sister?" I asked, beginning to arrange luggage in the impractical boot like pieces of a jigsaw puzzle, and ignoring the way Karen would start forward, then pull herself back, like a Border Collie waiting to get in amongst the sheep.

"She's cautious," she said. "Lexus is a cautious car. It's the *ultimate* cautious car. Their tagline should be, 'When you can afford the very best, and you think, "Lexus is the most reliable! Also extremely safe! I'll get that one!"' When you told me we'd take yours, because the rental company wouldn't like me driving on some of those roads, and sports cars are more fun anyway, I got all excited." She sighed. "And now you're packing. It's four days, and right now, we're driving a couple hours. We don't have to *pack*. Throw the stuff in the back seat and let's go. We'll be taking it out when we get there anyway."

"Oh, come on," Nikau said. "It's a sweet car." Karen had introduced him as "my cousin, more or less." Now, he put a hand on the swooping, black-stainless-colored bonnet of the Lexus LC500, which *was*, in fact, a pretty sweet car with some very sexy lines, possibly reminiscent of the way a tall, slim woman would look lying across your bed, and asked, "What kind of horsepower?"

"Four seventy-one," I said.

He whistled through his teeth. "Can't say I've ever seen one before. Your family's in the luxury auto business, eh. That'd be how you landed this, I reckon."

"Amongst a few other things, yeh, they are. This is a loaner." My family connections weren't something I much wanted to discuss at the moment, and they weren't doing me any favors with Karen, either. Neither was the modeling idea, for that matter, other than as a source of amusement. You could call that unusual. I'd swear she'd liked me better when I was some bloke who'd been in the Army. And if I liked that about her? I needed to balance that against the fragility I'd seen, which I was pretty sure was the source of the teasing, and the brittleness, too. She was nervous about all of this, but trying to pretend she was fine. I might know something about that.

Plus—business negotiation. Family. Et cetera.

"I bet it gets lousy gas mileage," Karen said, handing me a duffel, then shoving another one at me impatiently while I was still wedging the first into place, like the Border Collie was on the paddock at last and quivering to go about its business.

She didn't have a suitcase. She had two duffels, plus a bag of avocadoes and mandarins that she now decided needed to go into the back seat, which was why she was on a knee and a palm in there. She was wearing the black shorts again today, with a whisper-thin blue T-shirt that dipped into a low vee in front, letting you take in the multiple skinny black bra straps crisscrossing over her chest. Straps that weren't strictly necessary, because the bra had regular straps as well, although not as much coverage as you might have expected.

I'd seen sports bras. I'd taken off sports bras, for that matter. That was the only kind they issued in the New Zealand Defence Force. I'd never taken off one like that.

For a sporty woman, Karen had a surprisingly heart-pounding wardrobe. The shorts weren't any bigger than they had been the first time around, and I wasn't looking at those *or* the bra straps. Not in front of her grandfather. I may have been sweating a bit with the effort not to look. The woman had seriously good legs.

"You don't drive a car like this for the gas mileage." Nikau said. He wasn't any "more or less" cousin. He was a real one, or he felt like it. No other man could have looked at Karen from behind in that pose and talked about gas mileage.

Karen backed out of the car and said, "So explain about the smooth look on the undies, please, Jax. Vanessa says you were a big deal."

"Oh, bugger," Vanessa said. She was laughing, though. "Don't tell him what I said. And not that you aren't now, Jax. Just . . ."

Yeh. I didn't really need to hear how I'd changed, or to be Karen's amusement. When I'd washed my face this morning, my left non-foot still burning like it was on fire, I'd run a finger down the line beside my nose, which, like the thicker, messier one down the side of my face, had healed dark blue due to too many blood vessels in the area. I'd taken in the mess of pink scar tissue that was the left side of my chest and thought, *It's all good, mate. You didn't want to use your looks anymore anyway. This isn't the part that matters.* The phantom pain had answered with another lick of flame, the nerves refusing to get the message that there was no leg down there anymore, and I'd done my best not to think about my appointment with the Limb Centre next week, or the report they'd be sending in.

Technically, I was on leave. Being paid for nothing, and with nothing to do. At the rehab center, they'd showed all sorts of cheery videos and said all sorts of cheery things about "finding your new normal" and the advances in prostheses, but they hadn't answered the one question that burned above all others. "What do I do, now that I can't do my job?"

"Bread," I said.

"Pardon?" Vanessa asked. She had a tendency to turn red when she looked at me. A phantom sensation of her own, maybe, from the past. Her brain hadn't got the message yet that there was nothing to get excited about.

"They give you a slice of bread," I said, because I wasn't going to get away without an explanation, and it beat thinking about the future. "Bread's malleable. Lends itself to being mashed around and forming an . . . ah . . . screen of sorts. And you can do it yourself. There's a stylist fixing your hair and oiling you down and that, but nobody's actually putting her hand down the front of your kit, so it has to be something you can do yourself."

Karen was laughing, of course. "All those sexy videos, and you had *bread* down your shorts?"

"Whatever the job takes." I shoved one last bag into the boot, and we were done.

"I wonder what you were like before," she said. "Like—what was your rugby position, in school days? Don't tell me you didn't play, because I won't believe it."

"Surely you've already deduced it."

"A wing."

I bowed my head, keeping it cool. But bloody hell, how had she known that? I'd looked *her* up last night as well. I hadn't found much, but what little I had found didn't jibe a bit with the woman I saw. A biochemist who'd come up with a sort of mystery meat blend that actually tasted good, and a passionate believer in biodiversity, sustainability, animal welfare, and various other noble ideals. I knew that because she'd written the odd column and featured in the odd interview. Mostly, though, she'd stayed in the background, letting the CEO take the lead in the company's public life.

The CEO was named Josh something, which possibly explained the J-names objection, as well as the fragility under the toughness. She'd been engaged to him, and had lost her job *and* her engagement? I was guessing that was it, because he'd sold the company to a conglomerate in a buyout rumored to be very profitable, meaning tens of millions of U.S. dollars, and she'd left it on the same day, in a move that had surprised everybody, and missed out on the payout. That sounded messy, and like the kind of betrayal that could make a strong woman cry.

I could believe it, though, because Josh looked like a wanker. Dark and too good-looking, which, yes, was rich coming from me. It was the smolder, though. I'd done that smolder because it was my job. He did it because he was a wanker. Opinion of himself too high, actual life skills too low, because he'd think he could pay for anything he wanted. One of those rich blokes who came to New Zealand and couldn't figure out that you had to push the button to send power to the outlet, and that the button marked "Oven" was the one you pushed in order to turn on—yes, the oven.

Snap judgment on my part? Yeh, it was. Too bad. My

family was in the luxury-accommodation business. I knew all about those blokes. They might run companies, but put them outside their bubble, and they'd barely survive.

Josh-whoever was pictured all over the shop, as I'd have expected, but there were very few photos of Karen online, and she appeared to have no social media presence at all. You pictured somebody earnest and blonde, wearing clogs and cargo pants with the bottoms rolled up. Possibly with dreadlocks, especially when you saw the other hits that came up under her name, listing her as a member of a team competing in rowing races, an obscure hobby if there ever was one.

Nobody had said anything about a personality as big as the New Zealand sky, or a competitive fire that pushed her every minute of the day. Nothing at all about a brain that never stopped working, eyes shining with intelligence, a wide mouth that always seemed to be talking or laughing, or an intimidation factor that would have most men running far and fast.

"Let's hear how you know he's a wing, Karen," Nikau said. "Always entertaining to have around the place," he told me. "Get up every time you fall down, they say, and nobody falls down more or bobs up again quicker than Karen. Famous for it, you could say."

This time, Karen was the one who—not flushed, because she didn't. But whose chin went up, and whose eyes narrowed with the effort not to let that bother her.

"Why am I a wing?" I asked her, to turn the conversation.

"Fast," she said. "Flashy. And that's a winger car all the way."

"Except that it's a Lexus, and I'm just borrowing it," I said, and saw her grandfather smile.

"A *Kiwi* winger," she said. "Fast and powerful, yet polite and unassuming."

"Go on, then, you two," her grandfather said. "Take the winger off with you, Karen, but bring him back, eh. Bring him for the hangi."

☆☆

I finally got the chance to ask. "What hangi?"

We were in the car, headed down the hill. I downshifted, and the engine emitted a satisfactorily deep growl, which was juvenile but fun all the same.

She said, "For my birthday. Maybe we should have stuck around for another six hours or so while you packed the car with order and method, and everybody could have explained it to you. I thought we were never leaving."

"It was less than thirty minutes."

"It was an hour. Easy."

"I got there at nine o'clock. It is now nine thirty-one. We pulled out of the driveway at nine-twenty-nine."

She groaned and banged her head against the leather dashboard, then did it again. "Make the hurting stop."

I laughed, and she said, "Also, I'm going to need a coffee eventually. I'm telling you that in case you're one of those guys who thinks that once the car is in motion, it must remain in motion, and what do I mean, I don't know how to pee in a bottle?"

"Thought you were in a hurry."

"To *leave*. Five more minutes, and Nikau would've been reciting the Greatest Hits of my teenaged life. You were some kind of international sex god, and I was a science geek and the youngest person in my class, *with* the least developed chest, and a few other things, too. It's humbling, all right?"

"So it's a special birthday?" I asked, turning onto the highway.

"Thirtieth. Are you happy, now that I've admitted it?"

"Mm. You could've said it was twenty-nine, of course. Or not have answered at all."

"What, I'm going to lie? I'm not going to lie. I'd know the truth, so what would be the point? But, yes, I'm turning thirty. And since everybody thinks I'm going to be depressed, though they don't say so, they're doing a hangi and making a big thing of it. It's depressing *because* they think I'll be depressed, which means I'll have to slap a smile on my face all afternoon so they don't think so, which will *make* me depressed."

"I know what you mean," I said.

"Huh," she said. "I'll bet you actually do. You probably get that a lot."

"You could say so. People kept offering me tissues, at the beginning. Subtly."

She sat up straight in the car. "Yes! Exactly! With their calming voices. Asking if you have any questions, and if you'd like to 'talk to somebody.'"

Before I could ask how she knew, she said, "And now I have to invite you, because otherwise—nah, awkward. Saturday night, the day we get back. My birthday. On which I will be thirty, unemployed, and unengaged. My doors may all be closed, but a window will open any minute. Hooray."

I was smiling all the way through the roundabout, as we picked up speed, and as we headed north, out of town. I put on some music that had her tapping her feet like she was just bursting to get out and move, opened the sunroof, and let the smell of new leather and the feel of endless horsepower carry me along. I let myself think about nothing at all except this day, and it was good. Until, that is, we were driving through the outskirts of Paeroa, we passed a group of kids and bikes beside the road, and Karen said, "What *is* that? No way. Pull over."

12

☆☆

POWER DYNAMIC

KAREN

After a while, I forgot to think about wealthy men with sports cars (Josh had driven a Porsche), male models, or why on earth I was embarking on a trip with a wealthy male model in a sports car, when I was supposed to be having Girl Time with a lovely female entrepreneur who was also a children's book author and a mother. A woman who'd sounded, from her correspondence with Hemi, very much like my sister.

I knew how to deal with my sister. I knew how to *be* with my sister, and right now, I didn't quite know how to be with anybody else. I'd been planning to listen, watch, and explore for ten days or so, see Koro, and go back home and report to Hemi, hopefully with a vague feeling of life force returning and a clue in my head about what I was going to do next. That had been the plan.

Right now, though, the plan was to get out of this car. I was scrambling so fast, I got tangled in the shoulder belt, and had to spend valuable seconds swearing under my breath and unwrapping my arm, while Jax didn't say anything, in that way calm people had of not saying anything that told you all the things they weren't saying. Then I was finally free of the

Demon Car, and was running back along the pavement to where the kids were standing over the cardboard box.

Two of them, the bigger ones, ran away when I approached, and the three little ones didn't. They were barefoot, their bikes thrown down where they'd hopped off them. I came up fast, slowed down to a casual saunter in the last three strides, and said, "Hey, guys, what's going on?" at too late a stage not to alarm them.

One of them said, "Nothing." She was a girl, maybe ten or so, with her hair in a long brown braid and frizzing around her face, like she'd been in the water. A boy of about the same age said, "Nothing," for good measure. The littlest kid, somebody's brother, who might have been six, didn't say anything.

I looked into the box. I wasn't sure what I'd expected to find. A litter of too-young puppies. A kitten, crouching and terrified. Something I needed to make right, because I could at least do that. What I saw was . . . a duck.

A little white duck, in fact, with a short, rounded bill, a round head, a round body, and big, round eyes. It was the roundest little duck ever, and it was making a sort of tired little peeping noise, which wasn't the sound ducks were supposed to make, and shuffling around the box on its flat feet.

The outside of the box said FREE, in big black letters. What I'd seen when I'd made Jax stop. A cardboard box that said FREE, a flash of white, a bunch of kids, and too much excitement.

The girl said, "The big boys were teasing it. There were two ducks in the box before, when we went to the beach. Now there's only this one. It's hot, but if we put the box in the shade, nobody will take it, because they won't see. And the boys might come back. They're in Year Eight, and they're rough as. Plus, the duck should have water, I think."

"Yeh," the other boy said. "Ducks need to swim. We should take it to the sea, maybe."

"No, we shouldn't," the girl said. "That's salt water. Ducks need fresh water, like a pond or a river. I could take it home, except that the dogs will get it if I leave it outside, and I don't think Mum will let me have it in the house. We could take it to the river and let it go, maybe."

All three kids looked doubtfully at the duck, and so did I. If any animal had ever sent the message, *Free lunch!* to every predator in sight, it was this duck. This was, in fact, an absolutely defenseless duck.

That was the moment when Jax came up, still looking cool, and said, "Ah. A duck. I should've guessed a duck, clearly."

I said, "That makes no sense."

"In the context of my recent life? It makes as much sense as anything else." He looked the kids over. "Whose duck?"

"We don't know," the girl said. "It was just here. And it needs water. A water dish, like."

"You're right about that," Jax said, and told me, "I can't tell you how surprised and pleased I am not to be forced into a duel. I'll be back."

He took off toward the car, and the girl said, "We could ride to the dairy and buy something that comes in a punnet, maybe, and a bottled water, and pour the water from the bottle into the punnet once we eat what's in it."

"Ice cream," the little kid said.

"Not *ice* cream," the girl said. "Because you'd have to eat the whole thing at the dairy. It would melt by the time we brought it back here, and eating a whole carton of ice cream would take too long anyway. We need to give the duck water *now.*"

"But I like ice cream best," the little boy said. "So if we have to eat something up, I think we should get ice cream."

"We don't have any money," the older boy told the girl, ignoring the little kid. "We can't buy anything unless she gives us money, and people don't just give you money."

"I think Jax is getting water," I said. "My friend." I couldn't stand to watch the duck be hot. I lifted the box and carried it up onto the grass and into the shade, and when I put it down, I felt inside it. The bottom was uncomfortably warm, which was why the duck was hopping. I sat down on the grass, scooped the duck carefully out, and set it down between my legs, doing my best to make a barrier. I wasn't sure how flighty ducks were, and this was a very little duck, maybe six inches tall. It looked, in fact, a whole lot like Huey, Dewey, or Louie, except that it was missing the little shirt. It peeped some more and huddled there, looking feeble, and the three kids crouched down beside me to watch.

"Can I pat it?" the girl asked.

"I guess so," I said. "It doesn't seem very vicious." She gave it a careful stroke, and the duck gave another peep and edged closer to her, which made the other kids stick their hands in there, too. The duck, in response, nestled close to my leg like it wanted to snuggle in. Its feathers were soft against my skin, but it wasn't eating. Shouldn't it be eating the grass? I said, "OK, hands off, now. I think it's pretty stressed."

Jax came back, and, yes, Mr. Strong and Steady had a fair-sized water bottle with him, and not just that. He got down on his good knee, poured the water into a sort of expanding rubbery cup that was probably part of the survival kit he carried everywhere, and set it beside the duck, who instantly stuck its short bill in there and began to slurp, then raised its round head to swallow the water down. Jax squirted more water from the bottle over the duck's back, and it shook its tail feathers in a waggle that made the kids laugh, took a couple more drinks, and started to look less like a desperate case.

"All good," Jax said. "Job done."

The littlest kid had been staring at him without blinking the entire time. Now, he said, "You've got a metal leg."

"Shut up," his sister—she had to be his sister—said. "It's rude to say."

"Nah, no worries," Jax said. "I do have a metal leg."

"Does it come off?" the little boy wanted to know.

"Yeh. It does." Jax did some pressing down near his ankle, and the metal part of the leg slid out of the sleeve, leaving it dangling below what must be his real knee. "Easy as."

"Wicked," the older boy said on an admiring breath.

"Are you a superhero?" the little boy asked. "Because you

have a metal leg and lines on your face like a superhero."

"Nah," Jax said. "I'm a soldier, mate. I got blown up a bit, that's all." Which made all the eyes go wide. The duck, meanwhile, had finished drinking and was ripping up grass with its round beak, like a duck who'd been in that box for way too long. I petted its head with a finger, then ran my hand down its body. It waggled its tail some more, and I smiled.

I'd never had a pet. I'd never even thought much about it. I was always at work, or outdoors getting in a fast, efficient workout, which was fine. That was my life. But the duck was nice. Now, it decided to lie down, cuddling close to my thigh. I put my hand over its back, and I could swear it gave a little duck sigh, like it knew it was finally safe.

The older kid asked Jax, "How did you get blown up? Was it an IED?"

"Nah, mate," Jax said. "It was a truck bomb. A suicide bomber."

"What's sue-side?" the little boy asked.

"It's when you off yourself," the older boy said. "You kill yourself, like. With a bomb, so you're blown to bits. They might only find your head. The rest of you is just little pieces. But if you're a suicide bomber, you kill other people, too. You take them with you, that's the idea. Did heaps of people get killed?" he asked Jax.

"Two," Jax said. "And the bomber killed himself, of course, but that was the point, eh. He thought killing other people along with himself would take him to Paradise."

"Why did he want to kill people at all?" the little kid asked. "I wouldn't want to kill people."

"Good question," Jax said. "It's a war, and it's been going on for a long time. He may have grown up thinking it was his duty to fight that war. In Afghanistan, which is the other side of the world."

"How come they want to do a war?" the little kid pressed on.

"Also a good question," Jax said, not seeming the least bit fussed. "Wars happen when people fight over land, generally, or when one lot of people want to hurt other people and be the boss, and other people say it isn't fair."

"Like when the other kids were teasing the duck," the girl said, "and we didn't want to let them."

"Is that what happened, then?" Jax asked.

"Yeh," she said. "It wasn't fair, though. It's just a little duck. It wasn't doing anything to them."

"Lucky for it that you came along, then," Jax said. "Always better to be the protector, eh. Lets you sleep at night." He'd been putting his leg back on, which the kids were watching with a kind of morbid fascination. As for me, I was getting used to it. It was like the little boy had said. The blue scars on his face made him look a bit like a character from a fantasy novel, the kind I'd devoured in my teens. Not less than human. More than.

Now, my more-than-human got to his feet, and an expression flickered over his face that had to be pain. "Ready to go?" he asked me.

I didn't want an argument, especially if he was hurting. If he was more than human, I felt a bit less-than right now. I didn't want to be quirky, and I really, truly didn't want to be somebody's . . . pet. The way I had been for Josh. How much easier had that made it for him to dismiss me the way he had? I said, not being funny, and not being quirky, "I think we should take the duck."

I'd been afraid that Jax would sigh. If we'd taken my car, I wouldn't have worried about it, because I would have been in control. Power dynamics always messed me up when they got twisted together with sexual dynamics, but you couldn't help what you liked, could you?

He didn't sigh. He paused a minute and asked, "Why?"

"Because," I said, "I think it'll die otherwise. And I think it'll make my Koro smile. Call it a birthday present."

"You're the one with a birthday," he said.

"And what I need most for my birthday," I said, "is to make my Koro smile."

13

☆☆

MITRE 10

JAX

It took me a few minutes to rearrange the car in order to fit a box with a duck inside, and Karen, naturally, remarked on it.

"Good thing we don't have anything scheduled today," she said. She was leaning against the car again, ankles crossed, watching me work. Now, she emitted a sound like an air horn, and I jumped.

"Grass whistle," she said, showing me the strip of green between her thumbs. "I'm going to have run through all my talents pretty soon. Once I start in with my clogging routine, you'll know I'm out of ideas. I'm used to working. Plus, I don't actually know how to do clogging." She looked down at the blade of grass, fussed with its position for a minute, and said, "Thanks for not making a big deal of the duck. I didn't want it to die, that's all."

"Why would I make a big deal of it?" I got the duck's box wedged onto the floor with my wetsuit tucked around it, to make sure it wouldn't be sliding around back there. "Maybe I felt the same way. And what does it matter to me if you bring a duck along anyway? The owner's brother can get around the no-pets policy, and a duck isn't a cat that'll be killing the birds.

Besides, I'm just the tour guide."

"Oh." She looked disconcerted, and then blank. Almost shut down, if that were possible. "You're right. It's a few days, that's all."

Somehow, that had gone pear-shaped. I thought back over what I'd said. Still no clue. Was I supposed to pursue her harder? When I'd done it, she'd pretty much run. Correction—she *had* run. Getting any more insistent, when she was stuck with me in the car, and then in the wilds, would be creepy, surely.

We got going again at last, and made it almost a kilometer before she said, "Stop the car!"

"It's a roundabout," I said, navigating it, then pulling over once there was a verge again. "Not the best place to stop, generally. Also, shouting at me when I'm in it isn't your best choice. Where are you going?"

She was halfway out the window, waving to somebody standing at the side of the road. Somebody absolutely enormous. I was a tall fella, but the shaggy mess that came loping along like the larger species of elephant was half a head taller and a half-body broader. His red beard mingled with his curly hair, and I wasn't sure where you got shorts that big. His cardboard sign read *Wilson Bay,* a tiny settlement up the half-wild west coast of the Coromandel Peninsula, so I didn't have the excuse of not going his way.

"Cheers," the fella said when he got to the car. His grin was as big as the rest of him, and he was too hairy for me to guess his age. "It's bloody hard to get a lift from these bastards, isn't it. I've been waiting something shocking, and getting a wee bit worried that I wouldn't be there for the job tomorrow. Supposed to be hired onto a mussel boat. Thought I'd have to hire myself out down here instead, but never mind." All in a Highland accent so broad, I could barely make it out.

"Right," I said. It was an hour and a half's drive max. It would be all right. "We can take you as far as Thames. I'm Jax, and this is Karen."

He beamed some more, took my hand in a fist the size of

a reasonable ham, and shook with enthusiasm. "Jamie MacDougall here."

"Won't work with you in back," I said. "Not with that pack as well. Get in front. Karen, you can ride in back."

"*Excuse* me?" Karen said.

I said, "He won't fit." Which was true enough. This car had heaps of power and style, but what it didn't have was much of a back seat. The other reason, though, was that having somebody behind me that I didn't know made me itchy.

"Right," Karen said, perhaps remembering that she was the one who'd decided to give the bloke a lift. "I'll ride with Debbie." She squeezed herself into the back seat on the passenger side by putting a foot on either side of the box with the duck in it and lifting the bag of fruit into her lap. It was a squeeze. Karen wasn't exactly short herself.

"Who's Debbie, then?" Jamie asked, settling his bulk into the car and twisting between the seats to peer at Karen, which left roughly twenty centimeters for all of me. His hand on the glove box looked like something out of a monster picture, as if he'd rip it out of the dash at any minute.

"She's my duck," Karen said. "We just got her. She was free. Pretty sweet, huh?" She lifted up the duck to show him, and Debbie did some more peeping and a little raspy quacking.

"Oh, aye?" Jamie said, leaning forward a bit more and practically propelling me out of the side of the car, as if he had absolutely no idea how oversized he was. "That's a wee call duck, eh."

"I don't know," Karen said. "Is it?"

"Oh, aye," Jamie said again. "Taking it on a journey, are you? That's not quite usual, is it?"

"Maybe," I decided to interject here, "you could shift over to your side, mate, so I could see out the windscreen, and we *could* take a journey."

Jamie laughed some more, sat back, and hit me in the shoulder, which I didn't much appreciate. If not for Karen, I'd be turfing him out, genial as he was. Hitchhiking wasn't easy, though, and the bigger you were, the harder it got. He told me, "You could've just said, mate. Hang on. You've got a leg off. Driving all right with that, then? No clutch in this thing?"

"Yeh, nah," I said. "No clutch." I started the car, eased into traffic, headed north again, and wondered why people felt compelled to mention the leg. Little kids were one thing, but next time an adult did it, I was going to say, "I have? Bloody *hell,* you're right!" and politeness be damned.

Jamie was turned back around to talk to Karen again. Probably wise. "You taking the wee duck home, are you? Have a flock there?"

"No," she said. "She's a present for my grandfather, eventually. He likes to be outside. She can be company, I thought, and lay him eggs, too. Duck eggs are extremely nutritious. Bonus."

"Nah," Jamie said. "Probably not."

"Once she's grown some more, of course," Karen said. "She's still a little fuzzy and gawky, and not exactly duck-sized. I suspect she's a teenaged duck. I wonder when ducks start laying eggs? I only know about chickens."

"That one's never going to start," Jamie said. "That's a male. Reason he'd have been free, eh."

"Oh," Karen said. "Really, Debbie? You're a boy? How can you tell?"

"If it were a female, you'd have tossed her out the window by now," Jamie said. "She'd be that loud. The females do all the talking, and they're named 'call ducks' because they call to other ducks. Traitor ducks, more like, lead their mates straight into the trap."

"Well, shoot," Karen said. "I wanted her to be a girl. Oh, well. She'll—he'll—have to earn his keep by being adorable. Hear that, Debbie? That's your job." In response, Debbie-the-boy-duck peeped.

"Oh, aye," Jamie said. "Affectionate little buggers, call ducks. Easy pickings, though, small as they are. Best have a stout pen for him at home. That where you're headed?"

I shot a look at him. Second time he'd asked that. Karen

said, "I was worrying about that. Because—no. We're going to be camping out for quite a few days. We're—"

I said, "How do we keep him from running off during the day? You seem to know your ducks. Got a suggestion?"

"Dead easy," he said. "A bit of temporary fencing, and Bob's your uncle. Take him inside at night for now, maybe. Put some bedding in the box so he can settle down and you can change it when it's dirty, and you're golden."

"We don't have any fencing," Karen said.

"Aw, no?" Jamie said. "We could stop and get you some. Wouldn't want the little fella getting lost. Here. I'll find a place. Earn my keep, eh." He pulled out his phone and started tapping away.

That was how we ended up in Mitre 10 in Thames, once Jamie had directed me around the side where there was more shade, and had suggested we lower all the windows in the car to halfway in order to keep Debbie cool, which defeated the purpose of locking the doors, but what the hell. We wouldn't be long, and it was Thames, one of the sleepier towns on a sleepy peninsula. It was also how we ended up with Jamie climbing three tiers up the floor-to-ceiling shelving in a manner that had me putting my hand over his face, envisioning him bringing the whole thing down. Now, he tucked six two-meter lengths of plastic fencing under his arm like they weighed nothing, jumped down again with a force that threatened to knock the whole place flat, said, "Connectors," and grabbed a fistful of plastic packages.

"No," I said, and picked up a roll of flexible fencing instead. "That's not fitting in the car. We'll do this." I found rods that stuck into the earth, and some clips to fasten it all together. Calm and sure, that was the ticket. I wasn't fighting over duck fencing. I also wasn't entirely sure why he was putting my back up, but it was happening.

"Right," Jamie said. "Suit yourself. Shavings next, for bedding, so you aren't smelling duck all night. You'll want some feed as well. And maybe a couple dishes for food and water. Get a dishpan, like, and the duck can swim in it. Over here."

He set off, abandoning his fencing panels right there in the aisle, and Karen called, "Wait. We need to put them back, and Jax can't climb, not with his leg."

Tasks that involved heaps of knee-bending weren't the easiest, but that didn't make it any more wonderful to hear. Why were we climbing shelves anyway? Also—what the bloody hell was going on?

"Oh, right," Jamie said, turning back. "I've got it." Up he went again, and I handed up the panels silently, got a grin from him in return, and started to get a prickling sensation at the back of my neck.

I didn't feel anything violent from him, which made it odd. And yet—I trusted that prickle.

"If you'd chosen a more practical car," Karen told me, "we could have put the fencing in the trunk."

"Nah," Jamie said. "That car's a beauty. My dad's got that same one. It'll cost you a fair dollar, now. What's that go for, two hundred thousand?"

"Wait," Karen said. "Are you rich, too? Is *everybody* rich?"

"I'm not rich," Jamie said. "My family's rich."

Karen said, "Tell me your dad's the laird."

"He is that," he said.

"Is there a castle?" she asked.

"Oh, aye. A drafty one, mind."

Karen said, sounding absent-minded, "I had a thing about an English lord when I was sixteen. I was planning on marrying him."

"You were going to get married at sixteen?" I asked.

"I was precocious. Also, he was imaginary."

I looked at Jamie, then back at her, and told her, "Go wait in the car."

Her eyes did some shifting around of their own. "We do still need shavings," she said slowly. "And feed."

"I'll get them. Go wait in the car."

Jamie said, "What are you on about, mate? Stay here, Karen." He put out a hand and grabbed her upper arm.

She froze for a moment, then said, her voice tight, "No, I think I'll wait in the car."

Jamie didn't let go of her. I didn't look at him, just shot a fist straight into his solar plexus before he could notice me thinking about it. As soon as he doubled over, I took Karen's hand and said, "Let's go."

We went. Out the front doors of Mitre 10 and around to the side of the building. That was when I started to run. Both car doors were open, and so was the boot, exactly like I should have anticipated. Duffels lay on the pavement, spilling their contents, my wetsuit was flung down like a shapeless body, and Debbie's box had been tipped out and was lying on its side. A backpack that didn't belong to either of us sat on the ground, no doubt ready to receive anything worth taking, and Debbie was wandering around amongst the cars, peeping loudly and looking as nervous as it was possible for a duck to look.

As we approached, one fella turned from his interested perusal of the car boot, caught sight of us, grabbed the backpack, and took off. Karen kicked off her jandals and went after him barefoot. I shouted her name, and absolutely nothing happened in response.

The other fella had half his body in the back seat and hadn't seen us coming. He got the idea, though, when I grabbed him by the waistband and hauled him out.

He could've fought. He didn't. Instead, he wriggled out of my grasp and ran around the back like the hounds of hell were after him, which they were. It was the same direction the other bloke and Karen had gone, and he jumped a fence like he knew where he was going. I was after him, already leaping, grabbing at the top, cursing the leg, but even as I did it, Karen came pelting up on the other side, said, "Here," and handed me the backpack.

She was a mess again, I saw as I helped haul her over. Her forearm was covered with red scrapes, and both her palm and the knee she'd hurt rescuing Dougie had gravel embedded in them.

I asked, "All right? What did you do?"

"Caught up with him and tackled him, of course," she said, breathing hard and looking fierce. "Same thing you would've done. I may also have kicked him in the kidneys and the face, which you *wouldn't* have done. Ow. Never tackle on asphalt. Or kick somebody in the face barefoot. I think I broke my toe. They took my tablet and my camera. *Bastards.* That's why I kicked. Ow, my feet."

I had one eye on her and the other on the car, in case "Jamie" came back. He didn't, which wasn't a huge surprise. I was fairly sure he'd have run off as fast as his oversized legs would carry him, the moment the plan had turned to custard.

Karen didn't seem to be remembering him at all. She followed the direction of my gaze, said, "Oh, no. Debbie!" and started to run again. With a limp. I went with her, found the duck wandering between two other cars and peeping, and handed him over.

"Aw," Karen said, cuddling him. "Poor Debbie. That was pretty scary, huh? You've had a bad day, but it's all going to get better now. I'm going to be much smarter from now on, you'll see."

I started cleaning up the mess, putting gear back into duffels, and after a moment, Karen said, "Right, he was over the top. Especially naming himself 'Jamie.' The red hair, and the accent? The laird was too much. I was getting it, finally, though I just thought he was having some fun. How did you get it faster?"

"Explosives isn't just about the technology," I said, starting to load the car again. "It's about the eyes. There's a person wearing that suicide vest or driving that truck, and you need to know what he'll do. There's no clutch in a car with a semi-automatic transmission, which he'd know if he'd actually ever seen one, and he thought in New Zealand dollars. Also, the chief of Clan MacDougall isn't a man, it's a woman. We did a joint training exercise with the Highlanders regiment once. The chief of the clan does have at least one son, but he doesn't have that accent. Rich boys, even Highlanders, go to posh schools."

"Good memory," she said. "To remember his name."

"Possibly."

"But you knew before that," she said. "When he was

asking whether we were going home. The second time he said something about that? That was when you changed."

"Ah. You heard that, too. It was a niggle, that's all. And I started thinking about how well he knew Mitre 10, maybe, and why we had the car parked around the side. Pity that wasn't until we were inside."

"I heard it, too," she said slowly. "I didn't pick up on it fast enough, and I should have. Hemi worries about his wife and kids. He used to worry about me, but I'm not that much of a target. All I really do is be quiet online, and I'm not even sure that's necessary anymore. I have a different name than the rest of them, and anyway, the bad guys wouldn't be sure he'd pay." She put that out there like it didn't matter, but I thought it did. "He has a driver who taught me a few things, though."

"Like not to pick up hitchhikers," I said.

I could swear she winced. It could have been the scrapes, or it could have been something else. Thinking about impulsivity, maybe. Thinking about judgment. "Yeah," she said. "Nobody will be happy to hear about that. I'm not that happy myself. We have to call the cops, and hand over the backpack, but I sure wish we could just drive off and leave it behind. I thought it was OK. It's New Zealand, not Philadelphia, and I thought—I'll just go ahead for once. There can't be anything wrong with somebody that big, I thought. He's too recognizable. Like somebody with a facial tattoo."

She'd put Debbie back in his box and was folding clothes hastily and stuffing them back into her duffel, her movements quick and jerky. Toiletries as well, all of them scattered around like the blokes had emptied bags by the fistful, which they probably had. No silk or lace to be found, and nothing as stirring as that black bra she was wearing today, probably because this was meant to be an adventure outing. Red and purple and blue cotton undies and bras, that was all, showing nothing but a fondness for color, and a few tampons spilling out of a box. A comb, a lipstick, and a pink case that was probably something pretty intimate. All of it looking too personal, lying there. Like a violation, possibly.

She went on, her voice tight with the effort to keep it from trembling, "I hate that he went through my clothes. I hate that he touched my underwear. Why should that matter? And you don't have to say it. I was stupid. I'm from New York. I know 'wrong' when it's in front of me, or I should. Jamie texted a friend, because of your car. Because of *me*."

"Target of opportunity," I said. "Here. Maybe it'll be better if I pick up those things for you. What d'you reckon? Better than one of those blokes being the last to touch them?"

She sat back on her heels with a sigh and ran a hand through her hair. "Yeah. It shouldn't matter, but . . . it would help." She watched me tucking the tampons back into their box, and her throat moved as she swallowed.

There it was again, that glimpse of something wounded, something naked. In another second, she'd start talking and cover it up again. That was one of the worst things about crime. The way it left its victims feeling guilty and ashamed, like they were the ones who'd done something wrong. The way it made them second-guess and doubt themselves.

I could be going through a bit of that myself. I didn't want to tell her how I'd felt when Jaime's hand had closed over her upper arm, or when I'd been running after her, not knowing what would happen when she caught up to the bloke in the lead. Or when his mate joined them. The adrenaline was making me do some shaking myself, and I was used to it.

I didn't want to tell her? I needed to tell her. She needed to hear it. "I'm guessing I feel the same way you do," I said. "Questioning my judgment. Wondering why I didn't catch on quicker, and what I could've let you in for. The worst was when you ran off, and the other bloke ran as well."

"It wasn't your fault, though," she said. "It was mine."

"I let Jamie into the car," I said. "I don't much want to share this episode myself." I tucked the last bra into the duffel and zipped it shut. "Say we both made a mistake. Say there was no harm done. We're not the ones waiting for a knock on the door, hoping the cops don't show up. We're all good."

She was trying to roll up my wetsuit now, but her hands

were shaking, and she wasn't looking at me. "You're being kind."

"No," I said. "I'm being somebody who's made his own mistakes. The ones you make from a generous heart are the least of them."

She took a deep breath, finished with the wetsuit, and handed it to me. Nothing wrong with her courage, and nothing at all wrong with her heart. "You could say my judgment isn't great right now," she said. "But I think Jamie grabbed me, in there, because he didn't want me to come out here and possibly get hurt. And he really did know about ducks. I'd swear he liked Debbie. He didn't *feel* wrong."

"You're right," I said. "An opportunist, not a villain. Most people are a mixture, eh. He had more gray in him than he showed, that's all. I'm sure he *is* headed up to a job on a mussel boat. Not much else up in Wilson Bay. And he's got mates in Thames, because he's no Scot. And then there's the car. Lexus or not, it's tempting, if you've got those gray spots in you. Good thing the engine won't start without the fob, or we would've lost everything, I reckon." I stood up. "I've got a first-aid kit in the car. We'll find a toilet, get you cleaned up, and call the cops. Buy our fencing and feed, too. He was right about that, anyway. We need it."

"Why am I not surprised about the first-aid kit?" she asked. Getting her spirit back, then.

I slung the last two duffels into the boot and handed her the first-aid kit that of course I had in the car. We were going to be pretty remote. Who wouldn't take a first-aid kit? After that, I made sure the windows were up, like any other man locking the barn door after the horse had gone, and picked up Debbie's box. "We'll be smarter this time," I said, "and take our duck with us. With any luck, there's a phone in that backpack, or a utility bill. Something lovely and identifiable for the police. And we weren't such easy pickings after all. Good on us."

She'd started to smile, finally, and lose the shakes. "You weren't intimidated in there, were you? You were *waiting*. How did you know you could take him? The guy was enormous."

"Yeh," I said. "But I was trained. Training wins every time, just like it did for you. Somebody taught you to fight, eh. And what's even more important—they taught you to win."

14

An Accident of Genetics

Karen

Jax called the cops. While we waited for them, he insisted on cleaning and dressing my scrapes in the Mitre 10 restroom, which felt about as wonderful as you would imagine somebody picking out pieces of gravel from your palm and knee with tweezers would feel. Or maybe a little better than that.

When I told him I could do it myself, he looked up at me from where he was studying my various wounds and said, "Could be you'll be a baby and not go after them properly, though. Be a pity if I had to cut my holiday short to take you into Urgent Care," smiled at my huff of outrage, and kept on giving me directions in an absolutely calm, extremely assured sort of way that was surprisingly erotic.

What, you don't find it erotic to have a guy telling you to hold still while he tweezes gravel out of your knee, with a teenaged duck peeping and quacking from its cardboard box beside a hardware-store toilet? Maybe I had too much imagination, or maybe Jax was starting to fire it up, what with the scars and the decisiveness and the sweetness and all.

Josh had acted tough. Jax actually *was* tough, which seemed to make him want to be gentle with me. The combination was making me a little weak in the knees, and he was way, way too close not to notice.

Hope had babied me often enough—too many times, as far as I was concerned. At least until I'd put up a fight against being fussed over, and she'd had her own kids to divert her attention. When I had my bare foot on Jax's warm thigh and my hand on his shoulder, though, and was letting him take over the serious business of making sure I was protected from parking-lot bacteria, I discovered that there was something strangely seductive about having somebody want to keep you safe. And something seriously hot about it, too. It wasn't a dance, and it sure wasn't a sex act, but when I gripped the hard muscle of his shoulder and he held me a little tighter around the calf with a big hand, looked up at me, and said, "Keep it there, and don't move, or I could hurt you," I could've had to hold my breath. Fortunately, he misinterpreted that, saying, "Soon be over. Better if you breathe, though," and gave me some more of his sweet smile, like he had absolutely no idea what he was doing to me, or like he didn't care.

I didn't want to be anybody else's little sister, or his fun pal, even though that was what men always seemed to want from me, and exactly where I was comfortable right now. It wasn't like the thing with Josh had worked out that well, when I'd occasionally tried to be something else. But I couldn't help it. I wanted Jax to be thinking about how much he wanted to slide his hand up my thigh.

You know what they say, though. You can't always get what you want.

After my weak moment, we talked to a cop, which was about as satisfying as talking to cops generally was, as far as "We'll-get-them-no-worries" assurances. Not satisfying at all, in other words, because he looked dubious about the chances of finding anybody other than "Jamie." He was pretty distinctive, but he was out of Thames police jurisdiction and hadn't even been the one stealing from us, so there you were. I wanted more satisfaction than that, but then, I generally did.

The encounter *was* fairly satisfying as far as the "respect-for-our-brothers-in-khaki" went, though, because the cop sure did like Jax. He didn't even flinch much when I said, in describing the guy I'd tackled, "He could have a sore face, too. Some bleeding around the nasal area, possibly, from where he fell down." As far as I was concerned, when you stole people's stuff and risked the life of their duck, you might get accidentally kicked in the face during the struggle to get said stuff back. Thanks to Jax's influence factor, if the cop thought differently, he didn't say so.

When the two of us were eating lunch after all that, at a sidewalk table outside a bakery, I tucked into my chicken-and-mushroom pie, noticing, as always, that New Zealand pastry was heaven on earth, snuck a piece of it and some salad to Debbie, who shared my appreciation of Kiwi cuisine, and asked, "So what are we doing for the rest of today? I know we're going canyoning tomorrow, which I'm pretty excited about, and pretty interested to see how you manage, but are we hanging out in a tent this afternoon reading a book, or what? I'm not sure what's up there by the river, but doing activities is probably better. I need to know about them, so I can report back to Hemi."

"Doing activities, eh," Jax said. "As it happens, I did have a couple things in mind. Do you want me to tell you, or would you rather be surprised?"

Were there better words in the world for a woman to hear? They could cover everything from an erotic night to a marriage proposal. Or, of course, adventures in ecotourism, and never mind where I'd gone with it. "It might be better if I let you surprise me," I said. "For research purposes. The way I might be surprised if I had some vague ideas before my trip," I hurried to elaborate, "but I didn't exactly know the area, and when I got to my destination, some helpful Kiwi clued me in and showed me where the track started. Which is so often what does happen."

"Or," Jax said, "if you came to New Zealand on a holiday, being your fairly irresistible self, and met a bloke who wanted to show you a good time. Impress you, even. Whilst spending the night in his own tent, of course, because he's a slow mover. Takes his time, does it right, and so forth. Hypothetically."

Whoa. His eyes were doing that warm thing again, which gray eyes shouldn't be able to do. He hadn't shaved this morning, probably because he'd been about to set off on a five-day adventure with pit toilets and dubious hygiene, but I was forgetting about the reason and just liking it. That could be because the thick blue line on the side of his face ran into the scruff on his jaw in a way I just plain appreciated, and maybe also because it was such a contrast to the hot-geek black glasses.

A glamour boy he was not anymore, however short and neat his hair was, and however well his T-shirt fit him. However pleasingly his proportion of arm and leg length to torso had turned out, and however much your gaze wanted to rest on his face. The body and face, of course, were nothing more than a fortunate accident of genetics, having to do with things like inherited height, bilateral symmetry, ratios of eye spacing and nose length, and definition of jawline. His looks were nothing he'd done at all, just like I was genetically programmed to be tall and thin and energetic, and not to have much in the way of boobs. If it had taken years of hard work, though, for him to get that strong, hundreds of miles of long runs loaded down with gear, through the heat and cold, on days when he was hurting, when he was sick or tired or he'd had bad news from home? If it had taken obstacle courses and marching and whatever else soldiers did to achieve that level of functional fitness and that kind of stoicism? That part, he could take credit for.

The question I couldn't answer, though, and the one that was really messing me up, was this. How could he be even more attractive than he'd been in his modeling photos, before he'd gotten himself blown up? I found I couldn't think of him any other way. Why was that? And was my current level of judgment adequate to decide that?

That was an obvious "nope." Moving on.

"Hmm," I said, taking another bite of flaky pastry, melt-in-your-mouth chicken, creamy potato, and leek, all of it coated with gravy, and trying not to purr at the silky mix of flavors. "Right. First, I'm not that irresistible. I just got dumped after eight years, is how I know that. Personally *and* professionally, or rather—professionally, which meant 'personally' followed right along, since I found that being secretly cut out from everything I'd ever worked for sort of killed the 'love' idea. Second—this guy I'm meeting on my exotic holiday is a gentleman, is he? Or undersexed, in our hypothetical world?"

Jax just smiled. "Right, then. Challenge not quite accepted, because I still can't make out what the challenge is. Here's something for you to ponder, though. It could be that not every man is up to your weight. Could be you're intimidating. It could also just be that you haven't found the right man, one who *is* up to it. Fortunately, we don't have to worry about that right now. All we need to know is that I live for adventure, and so do you. So let's go have some."

☆☆

The campground didn't have pit toilets, and it started feeling good before we even got to our tents.

As we pulled our various bags and boxes along behind us from the carpark on a couple of helpful wagons, the forest track was dark and shaded. Overhead, the canopy was feathery with the tops of second-growth kauri, the one-time giants making their resurgence since the forest had been logged to the ground, the trees grown tall now and strung with vines as thick as my arm. There were a few other species I knew, too, because I knew New Zealand trees so much better than the ones back home. Credit Koro and Hemi for that, Hemi educating his kids, and me being along for the ride. You couldn't hang out with Maori and not learn the names of the other species inhabiting the world around you. Which was why I recognized the drooping branches of rimu and the exuberant crimson blossoms of rata, as well as the spiky shrubs of manuka in the open areas, in bloom now and offering up their nectar to the hovering bees. Ferns uncurled their fronds beside the track, and the bush beyond was full of birds in full summer-feeding voice. I told Debbie, who seemed to be enjoying the ride in his box, "Hear that? Those are your relatives. If they're OK here, you probably will be, too." I could hear a rustling that was the wind in the trees, or maybe the river below, the musical calls of tui and bellbird, the occasional cooing call and tree-rustling flight of a kereru, the New Zealand pigeon, and that was all. We were less than a half hour's drive from the outskirts of Thames, but separated from it by hills and the canyon and the river. I probably still had cell phone reception, but I didn't want to look.

This part, I liked fine. Of course, I preferred it followed by a hotel room.

Then we came around the corner, went down a short side track, and I saw my tent.

It was more like a yurt, a great big round thing made of white fabric, with a double fabric door that was pulled back to show a king-sized bed and rustic wooden night tables set with candle lanterns. You'd lie in there and look out at nothing but trees, which was actually pretty perfect. The patio outside had a table and a couple low chairs, and through the door of the little wooden building next door, I could see a wooden counter holding a stainless-steel sink and, above it, a log-framed mirror. I set Debbie's box down on the ground and told Jax, "It has a sink."

"Could be you'll survive, eh," he said, and I poked my head in and found a shower. And a toilet. Which was great, but it wasn't the best part. Around the corner from the bathroom cabin, tucked into a tiny clearing, was a bathtub. Yep, bathtub outside, in the middle of the forest. There was also a kitchen tent with a sink and a barbecue on the other side of the sleeping tent, but I was more interested in the bathtub.

"I'm next door," Jax said. "No worries, though, you'll be private. That's the whole idea. You're camping, and you're not."

"You going to have a bath tonight?" I asked him, starting to rip open the package holding Debbie's fencing.

"I could do," Jax said, getting on one knee again—the augmented one—and pulling some sort of survival tool from his pocket, with which he cut plastic. "Could feel good, eh. I have a bottle of wine in the car that may suit you. Worse things in the world than a warm candlelit bath in the trees, lying back and looking at the stars, and a glass of Marlborough Sauvignon Blanc. But we've got a few things to do first, as surprising you is part of our plan."

How could a man constructing a pen for a duck still have a voice that sent shivers down your back? I had a chance to ponder that as I helped him pound the ends of fencing poles into the ground with rocks and fasten netting to them with clips. He really was the most absurdly competent man, and he didn't seem to have any problem with me being competent, either. Between the two of us, we had a pen constructed in about ten minutes. I filled Debbie's food and water dishes, plus a plastic dish tub, put him in the pen and splashed my fingers in the water, and he flapped his way over the rim and was paddling around in seconds, quacking and peeping away and making me smile.

"Happy duck, happy . . . woman," Jax said, collecting plastic wrapping.

"That's your sexy talk?" I said. "Don't tell me what that was supposed to rhyme with. That's pitiful. You can do better."

He laughed, fortunately. "Come on, then. We'll get the rest of the gear, and I'll show you what I have in mind."

Which was how I came to be crossing a narrow swing bridge over the Kauaeranga River an hour later, then scrambling down to a rock outcrop, with the hypnotic burble of water over stones filling all the clamoring space in my head. The river was restless, and I wasn't. Already, my thoughts were ping-ponging around less than they had been for weeks, as if the folds of my brain were actually relaxing.

What was Jax doing? He was standing behind me, his strong hand over mine, showing me how to cast a line for rainbow trout.

"Whip it back there," he said, getting a little closer and putting his other arm around my waist, and not talking one little bit like he wanted to kiss my neck, even though his deep voice was giving me those shivers again, "and forward again. Keep it smooth. Aim for the deep pool under the rock, let the fly rest a minute, then pull it slowly back, skimming the surface. Be the bug, eh. A stupid bug, going where the trout are hiding."

"I'm not much for fishing," I said, trying to keep it cool. "Too boring, normally, but this is all right. At least I can move around and try different things, and I'm not sitting in a boat."

He was a warm man, and such a solid one. The late afternoon was still warm, but had lost some of the baking heat, and the light fell in slanting rays on the fast-flowing water, forming glinting prisms like so many crystal suncatchers hung in a kitchen window, making you slow down while you washed the dishes just to watch the light change.

Not that I washed dishes by hand. I normally flung them into the dishwasher fast and got back to work. I reeled my line in, and nothing bit at it along the way. Jax said, "You can move around, yeh. You'll still need a bit of patience, though. No side-arm. Here." He took my hand again. "Smooth motion overhead, and then an abrupt stop. Practice your aim, and you're good as gold."

"I hope you brought steaks," I said. "I suspect my fly is seriously unconvincing. I'd have to luck into a mentally deficient fish."

How could you feel a man smile just from the relaxed pressure of his shoulder on yours? "That would be giving up," he said. "We'll see how we go. Go on down and wade out there, if you like, try some other spots. The trout like the holes at the base of the rocks. Just don't hook me."

"This would be where you say I already did," I said.

"I would," he said, "but you'd tell me I could do better."

15

☆☆

A DIFFERENT MAN

JAX

I caught a couple good-sized rainbow trout. Karen caught three.

"And, yes, I realize I had to throw two of mine back for being too little," she'd said when we were gutting the fish at the cleaning station back at the campground, something she'd clearly done before, because she'd performed it neatly and with no fuss, "but still. Three to two." Why did she always make me smile? "I'm saving the heads and tails for Debbie," she'd added, wrapping them in a plastic carrier bag. "Ducks are omnivorous."

"Time to tell me why you've called your male duck Debbie," I said a lazy hour or two later. We were back at Karen's campsite, sitting on the wooden patio like we were sailing on an ocean of green, eating crispy golden-fried rainbow trout, grilled slices of kumara, and tender asparagus with lemon juice, along with slices of buttery, savory Turkish bread sprinkled with herbs, bits of which, along with every other item on the menu, Karen kept "accidentally" dropping for Debbie, who was going to be a very plump duck indeed in very short order. The shadows were long, the golden rays caught the edge of a fern tree and outlined its lacy pattern, the hum of insects merged with the sound of the river below, and Afghanistan felt as far away as the moon.

If only you could drift along like this forever. Or maybe that should be—if only you could be content to drift along like this forever. I couldn't, and I knew it. Skimming along the surface of life like a fly at the end of a fishing line, with all the world at your command, might look brilliant to somebody looking in, but it could also make you feel like a fraud who hadn't done much to earn all that he'd been given. At least, that was the way I remembered it.

But now? I'd take now. This moment, or the one when you were cleaning out the knee of a woman too brave for her own good, when she had her foot on your bare thigh and her hand clutching your shoulder, and you could see the skin of her own thigh pebbling into gooseflesh and catch the warm scent of her body, because she was just that close. Not perfume, not down here. That was all her, running and tackling and hurting and, just possibly, knowing I was holding her, because I'd swear I was smelling sex. The soles of her feet were dirty and bruised, and I'd cleaned those, too, wiping them off gently with paper towels, my hand around an ankle. I hadn't said anything, and fortunately, neither had she, because I wouldn't have trusted my response.

"Debbie Duck?" she asked now, finishing off her trout. She was sounding relaxed as well, even though she was probably hurting again, or still, just like I was. I should leave soon, let her get her bath and take one of my own. She'd pulled on a long-sleeved shirt and draped a blanket over her knees, but as soon as the sun set, it would get chilly fast. She went on, "I was thinking about Huey, Dewey, and Louie. Donald Duck's nephews, you know. And I realized—the only female animals in cartoons are the love interests, except Peppa Pig, maybe. Otherwise? You've got Daisy Duck. Minnie Mouse. Et cetera. All right, they're from a long time ago, but almost all cartoons are that way. Even SpongeBob is a boy sponge. So I thought—Debbie Duck. And I probably got stubborn after that, once I found out he was a boy, or maybe his name just makes me laugh, and I kind of miss laughing, you know? Or I *was* missing it, because you make me laugh, too. Huh. That's interesting."

"Brilliant," I said, although I was smiling. "Not quite what a man wants to hear."

"Hey," she said, "you asked."

"So how does a city girl from New York know what ducks eat?" I asked. "How did you come to like being outdoors so much? Even though you're a pretty reluctant camper."

"Why does anybody like being outdoors?" She said it lightly, but I thought there was some tension there. "Maybe because I couldn't always have adventures, and now, I want to do all the living I can. Why do you like it? Don't tell me you aren't a city boy. Your family lives in Dunedin. I looked you up."

"I'm a Kiwi, though. Fishing, camping, boating."

"Killing people in the desert."

An icy wind went through my body. "Or keeping other people from being killed."

She froze, exactly like I had. She started talking twice and cut herself off before she finally said, "Sometimes, the words come out before I have a chance to think them through. Maybe forget I said that."

I nodded, knowing it was stiff. So was my leg, for that matter. Too much time in the car, and last night's pain not wanting to leave.

"Jax." She reached across and put her hand on my forearm. I looked at it there and did my best to haul my emotions back under control. And for some reason, I couldn't. She said, "I've got it wrong, haven't I? Tell me how. I've never known anybody in the military. That's weird, but I haven't."

"Not so weird," I said, trying to get it together. "Not many millionaires' kids in the New Zealand Defence Force."

"Except you. Why did you join up? You did join up, right? There isn't a draft here, is there?"

"No. I volunteered." I stuck my legs out in front of me, crossed the good ankle over the prosthetic one, tried and failed to feel casual, and thought about what I wanted to say. *Whether* I wanted to say.

Karen said, "You don't have to say if you don't want to. You don't owe me anything."

I looked up. "That's what I was thinking just now. Whether I wanted to say. Odd. I had some requests for interviews, after I came home. Photos. Wounded warrior. All that."

Her face twisted. "Blech. I'd hate it."

I had to laugh once more. "Yeh. That was about the size of it. But I don't mind telling you, maybe."

"Hang on," she said. "We could need a little more wine for this." She poured it, and bent to light the candle lantern, too, her expressive face lit from beneath with its glow. After that, she sat back in her chair and took a sip of wine. I looked at my own glass and thought about readiness, and about how I didn't need to think about readiness anymore. It was twelve hours until we needed to drive back to Thames for our adventure, and I had nothing to do until then but sit here, take a bath, and wish I was kissing a girl's neck and, possibly, was sliding my hand up her thigh while I did it, the way I'd wanted to do in the Mitre 10 toilets.

Yeh, mate. Pick your moments. That hadn't been it.

"I wasn't drunk, or whatever you're thinking," I finally said. "Not when I enlisted. Before that? Maybe. I hadn't been feeling good about my life for a long time. Thought that was just growing up, maybe. Or maybe I didn't think much at all."

"How long ago?" she asked.

"Six years. Almost exactly. It was my birthday, in fact. Turning twenty-five, drinking much too much, out at a bar with some mates. In Sydney, that was. Too loud and too entitled. Went back to my hotel with somebody I didn't know, paid her fare home at four in the morning, walked into a flash bathroom on the fifty-second floor of a very flash hotel, in a suite that looked out onto Darling Harbour, looked in the mirror, and thought, 'What the hell are you doing, mate?' I didn't care about her and she didn't care about me, I'd been halfway bored even in the midst of having sex, and as soon as we were done, I'd wanted her to leave. Maybe that made one too many times like that, or a hundred times too many, if I'm honest. I didn't know if any of her own mates had even checked on her after she'd left with me. I'd turned twenty-five during those couple hours, and I wasn't looking at a man I wanted to see. I wasn't looking at the man I wanted to *be*. I thought—there must be something more than this, because I can't live this way anymore. It was all good, money and sex and autographs and all, except it wasn't, because it wasn't anything more than that."

"So you went out and joined the Army," Karen said. "Wow."

"Nah. Thought those things, that's all, and couldn't quite shake them loose once I had. The next time I flew home, there was a recruiting poster in the airport. Sounds stupid, maybe, but I looked at that photo and thought, 'Can't be worse.' That's the day I walked in and joined up."

"And you found out you loved it."

I laughed. "Are you joking? No. I thought, 'What the hell have you gone and done now, you wanker?' It was about as big a shock to the system as a man could get. I thought I was tough. No chance. There I was, spoilt rich boy who thought a hard day was a couple hours in the gym and ten more standing around in my undies, having a stylist mist me off when I got warm. Now, I had no privacy, bad food, not enough sleep, the kind of exercise that's more like torture, and a drill instructor and a barracks full of recruits who knew who I was and couldn't wait to take the piss. I'd joined up in winter, more fool me. I was cold, I was wet, parts of me hurt that I hadn't known *could* hurt, and I had to suck it up and do it anyway, because otherwise, everybody would be right that I couldn't take it. And then I went on for explosives training, and I wasn't just wet and sore and cold, I was terrified, too. Half of me was thinking I couldn't do it, and the other half was refusing to let that be true. That half won. I did it because I couldn't stand to quit, and that's the truth."

"But that's not how you feel now."

Dusk had fallen while we'd been talking, and in a few

minutes, the stars would start to appear. I'd thought I'd seen stars before I'd gone to Afghanistan. I'd never seen stars, though, like the ones in the mountains there, where the air was thin and the closest electric light was tens of kilometers away. Where the sky was lit with clouds made of thousands of pinpricks of soft light, and they looked like a blanket you could wrap around yourself, but in fact, you were still cold and still tense, and there was no blanket at all. Where life was so close to death, you could nearly taste both of them.

I hadn't told anybody all this before, or actually—*any* of this. Why was I telling somebody I'd met only days earlier? I'd touched her ankle, and almost nothing else, so why did it feel like more?

Intimacy, I guess you'd say, or not. The way you could be inside a woman and not feel like you were touching her at all. And the way you could touch another woman, and feel her touching you, when she was a meter away.

I said, "Two things. A couple weeks apart. The first one was driving down a street behind another armored vehicle, and having nobody look at us, the way they never do. Ghosting you, like you aren't there. I saw something that didn't fit, something odd thrown onto a rubbish heap beside the road. Backpack, I realized. A big one. Blue. I remember exactly what it looked like, the webbing straps and all. I thought, *Nobody would've thrown that away, not here,* and got on the radio. Before I even got the words out, that first vehicle went up like you'd chucked a firework, and we were in a firefight. My first one, and I didn't have a chance to be scared anymore. Or maybe it wasn't that at all. All I know is, my brain went cold, and everything got sharper. Vision. Hearing. Everything. Time slowed down. First time I saw somebody die, and the first time I made it happen, too. The first time I shot somebody and watched him fall. I helped drag the bodies of our own dead into our vehicle after a bit, blokes who'd been my mates and were just meat now, and I was still in that other space. That night, though . . . it all came home. When I closed my eyes, I saw my mates again."

"And they could've been you," Karen said. "Just luck."

"That part?" I said. "That part, I barely felt. Maybe because I already knew that. Maybe I'd already stopped thinking of myself as special. As separate. Whatever."

"You said two things," she said. "What was the second one?"

"Same, and not. The first time I saw that wrong thing and got to it first. The first time I neutralized an IED. It was a pressure cooker full of nails, with bits of rusty scrap metal and hunks of rotten meat, because that's what they do to make it worse. Get some rust, get some spoiled meat, drive those bacteria into somebody's body, and you've got infection that'll never clear. That time, though, nobody got hurt and nobody died, because I stopped it. First time I'd ever done it all by myself. I put myself in harm's way, and I knew why I was doing it. Things got sharp again, like the first time, and different, too."

I was right back there. The taste of dust on my tongue, the tire tracks in the fine brown silt on the road, how warm the sun had been, the sting of the sweat in my eyes, and the way I'd controlled my breathing and had taken it one step at a time, because I knew what to do. "There's this . . . shift," I said slowly, not sure why I was trying so hard to help her see it, "when you get to where you're ready every minute. Every move you make, you're making with intention. Every place you look, you're aware of what you're seeing, and you're evaluating it. Every second of the day, you're alive, because you know you may not be in the next second. And you've switched from thinking of yourself, of what you want, of protecting yourself, to thinking about keeping other people safe. When you're so sure that's what you have to do, it's not even a decision. That's the change. I wasn't nearly as worried that I'd blow myself up as that I'd get it wrong and blow up other people. That's what's better than being in that hotel bathroom, looking in that mirror, and having it all—easy sex, pricey drinks, flash car, all that flattery. Once you flip that switch, I'm not sure you ever really go back."

Karen didn't answer for a minute, but finally, she asked, her voice low in the gathering darkness, "Is it worth your leg?"

She'd said it softly, but the question lay there, sharp as a knife, and I had to think to answer it. "Dunno," I said. "When I was first recovering, when they'd just sewn me up, and I'd look down the bed and see nothing there but a bandaged stump, and get this hollow place in my stomach, this panic? A fella came in to talk to me. Fella with one hand. He didn't say much, just showed me everything he could do with his prosthesis. And I lay there, half-gone on pain meds, and asked him, 'What would you give to have it back?'"

I had to stop for a minute and look at the stars. They were beginning to wink into view now, looking like they always did, like they always would, and not, because the light I saw was coming to me from a century ago, or more. Because nothing stayed the same, and nothing lasted forever. Which made the good things you had now, the things that mattered, all the more precious.

Karen didn't say anything for a minute, but finally, she asked, "What did he say?"

I looked at her, and she reached her hand across the space between us and took mine. Lacing her fingers through mine. Holding on.

So I told her. "He said, 'I'd give anything to have the arm back, mate. Anything except my wife and kids. Anything except my mates. I'd give anything, except I wouldn't, I guess, because there are still a few things that matter more.' And I thought—if I'd stood there in the Auckland airport and looked at that recruiting poster, and known I'd lose my leg? I wouldn't have enlisted. I'd have found some other way to go on. Good way, bad way—I don't know. I'd have kept my leg, and I'd have kept my face. I'm not sure I miss my face. I know I miss my leg. I dream I have it, and it's a shock every time when I wake up and find out again that I don't."

"So you're sorry," Karen said. "It wasn't worth it after all." No judgment in her voice, just thoughtfulness. Almost . . . wonder, like she was trying with all her intensity and all her mental candlepower to get inside my head, to *know* what it was like to be me. I wasn't sure how well that would work. Since I'd lost the leg, *I* didn't even always know what it was like to be me.

"I don't know," I said. "I reckon it's what he said. The leg matters more than almost anything, and there's no perspective and no wisdom or whatever other bloody thing people talk about you getting in exchange that makes up for it. It's more than almost anything, but it's not more than everything. If I'd never signed up? If I'd never taken that first ride on the bus to Basic Training, never got my hair buzzed off and my ego battered? If I'd never sweated through all that heat and run through all that mud? If I didn't know what it's like to take a life, and I didn't know what it's like to hold a mate while he dies? I'd have my leg, and I wouldn't have to remember those things, but I'd have lost all those times when I did something that mattered. I don't know which is better. I just know that if I hadn't done it, I'd be a different man. And I'm not. I'm this man. I'm here now, and there's no going back."

16

TENTACLES

KAREN

I was having a hard time breathing. It was what Jax was saying, and it was his voice saying it, deep and rich as that winter ale. It was the stars, and the green darkness of the bush beyond us as the last light faded from the sky. He hadn't even touched the rest of his wine, which meant that explanation hadn't come from alcohol. It had come from needing to say it.

I said, "I admire you." I couldn't think of what else to say, since "I want to climb into your lap, kiss my way down that scar on the side of your face, and see if you can possibly want to hold me right now as much as I want to hold you" probably wasn't right. Besides, it was true. He was the sexiest man I'd ever met, but he was so much more than that.

He said, "Because I got myself blown up? Don't." He didn't sound smooth anymore, and now, he pulled his hand away, stood up, grabbed our plates, and said, "We should do the washing-up," which wasn't exactly leaning over and brushing his lips over mine, was it? He headed over to the kitchen tent with the dishes, and I'd swear he was limping.

"Wait," I said, scrambling to my feet. One of said feet had

gone to sleep, both soles were bruised, and I was limping myself. Or lurching, you could call it. I was dirty, too.

Oh, God. I probably smelled. I had a horrifying memory of him kneeling in front of me, cleaning me off after I'd been chasing that guy, and then standing behind me, helping me fly-fish. When women were trying to attract this kind of guy, they wore perfume. Dressed up. Took *showers*.

"Wait," I said again, focusing on the "friend" part, since the "girl" part was clearly out of the question. "Why was that wrong to say? Why shouldn't I admire you? And you're stiff. You were hurting this morning, and you're hurting more now. You need to take a bath, not do the dishes. Could you give yourself a break and let me take care of things? Also, what response *were* you going for? Because you're seriously confusing me."

What is your problem? I wanted to say, but I thought I knew what his problem was. That he'd put himself out there too much, and he was regretting it. I knew what *my* problem was, too. That I'd start thinking he was attracted to me, and then he'd pull away and act repelled.

I knew I wasn't girly, and I sure wasn't sweet. I was impulsive and outspoken and way too assertive for most men, and I hated being vulnerable, which meant I couldn't make them feel like heroes. I was pretty sure that what Jax needed was for a woman to burn for him, to want him for exactly the man he was now, but I was also pretty sure that I wasn't the woman he had in mind to do it. Whatever he'd said, he needed to be a hero.

He finished dumping fish bones into the rubbish, turned around at the sink as the water ran, and said, "Why should you admire me for missing a leg, or walking on an artificial one, or whatever it is you're thinking? What was my choice? Giving up and dying? You should be admiring the blokes who didn't come home instead. The one who was faster than I was, for instance, when that truck came up to the gate. Admire him. I didn't do anything this time except get myself blown up, and I'm not hurting that much. I'm good."

I moved around him and started scrubbing plates and

cutlery, splashing water onto my shirt in the inadequate lantern light, something he no doubt would never have done. He didn't want me to touch him, but he'd wanted to share his story, or why would he have said it? And now he was running away from it as fast as he could. I said, "You're making me kind of crazy. You just told me all kinds of things that tell me exactly why I *should* admire you, and they have nothing to do with your leg. I'm not supposed to tell you how I feel, though, because it would interfere with your internal narrative. All right, fine. I think you're being idiotic, how's that? You're trying not to show emotional weakness, which is unhelpful to personal growth and doesn't work that well anyway, because everybody can see you doing it, so what's the point? I might know about that, because I might be the same way. Also, you are the neatest cook I've ever seen. You cleaned everything up before we even ate. So now I think you're obsessive, too. Congratulations."

He might be smiling now. I couldn't quite see. We were back to Buddy Mode, then. If he was going to treat me that way, though, I could wish he wasn't leaning against the counter about eight inches from me while he did it, where I could practically feel his heat.

I hated being fussed over with a passion, and I hated being pitied more than that, so—yes, I got it. But there was also that other thing—that I was as aware of him as if he had tentacles coming out of his body and wrapping around mine. Or maybe coming from his mind and into mine, which was even scarier. Like he could see me, and he could touch me.

"And you're doing a sort of giant-spider deal now," I told him, because if you named something, you could be in control of it. "Maybe you could stop with the charisma and all, if you're going to be rejecting me because I heard your moment of self-reflection. The combination is confusing me."

He ran a hand over his perfectly neat hair and blew out a breath, then laughed softly, which wasn't attractive much. "Right," he said. "Arsehole thing to say, when you were being kind. Listening, and all that. And you could be a bit confusing yourself. I'm a giant spider *and* charismatic? You wouldn't think it was possible. Don't care much for spiders, myself. How am I one?"

I waved a soapy hand. "Like in a horror movie. You've got this thing going on where you're pulling me, like I want to step closer so you'll hold me. Except that if I do that, you'll probably tell me that I shouldn't be attracted to you, because you've got scars. Or I shouldn't be attracted to you, because handsomeness is superficial. I can't figure out which one is the problem." Distance. Distance was good. Also admitting the attraction, since I was sure he'd figured it out. I was stuck with him for another week, and if I didn't redefine this, it was going to be a mighty humiliating week. This thing right here—that I wasn't the kind of woman a man longed for, the kind he burned to have, and I never would be—was the way I wanted to be pitied absolutely least.

"I'm missing a leg, also," he said. "There's that."

"Thanks for pointing it out," I said. "I hadn't noticed. I've got scars, too, you know."

He stopped smiling. I couldn't quite see, but I could tell. He said, "You don't know what scars are."

Whoa. Before, we'd been . . . well, not flirting, because that was too superficial for what I was feeling. Dancing, you could call it, held close one minute, spinning away the next, but always reacting to each other. Now, I was just mad. I'd sure stopped dancing. "And you know this how?"

A long pause, and he picked up a tea towel and started drying dishes. "I apologize. Again. You lost your job and your boyfriend and so forth. It was scarring."

I could have said something. I could have explained. I didn't want to get into some sort of Dueling Banjos trauma-topping contest, though. He was off-balance, so was I, and suffering wasn't a contest anyway. If I'd wanted to hold him just now? If I still did? I'd already been through the five hundred reasons that was a bad idea, starting with "in no shape for this" and "volunteering for pain," ending with "possibly adversarial business relationship," and stopping off at all sorts of unfortunate stations along the way, like, "What if he pushes you away, his face twisting in revulsion?" Because if this was his courting technique, he sucked at it, and I'd bet he didn't. He was a seriously charming guy. He just wasn't serious about charming me.

I said, "I should take my bath, and so should you, except that I'm not supposed to say that, so I'll say that if you want to go chew on sticks or something to keep yourself from noticing that your leg hurts, now's the time. It feels late, I'm sore, and we have to be in Thames at eight-thirty in the morning."

Another pause, and he dropped his tea towel and said, "I'll put Debbie in his box for you and put him in your tent. I'll be back at six-thirty or so, and we can cook breakfast and have time to get a coffee before we start this thing. We won't sleep past six anyway. Birds, eh."

"Fine," I said. "Thanks. See you tomorrow."

JAX

When I called out, "Coming through," and headed around the corner into the campsite the next morning, with the pink of dawn already replaced by golden sunlight, and the clamor of avian voices that was the birds' dawn chorus having died down to chirps, trills, and calls from one treetop to another, Karen was already up. Debbie was in his pen, and Karen was dressed in flowered purple running shorts that were sadly longer than her black ones, a blue T-shirt over a red sports bra, and turquoise trainers, every bit of her looking like an advert for energy-enhancing vitamins. Living in color, you could call it. She'd also boiled water for tea, and was standing at the kitchen tent pouring it over the bag when I turned up.

"Morning," she said, handing me the mug.

"Morning," I said, and didn't kiss her, even though she smelled like everything I wanted, and the nape of her neck was right there. That scent was soap, maybe, but it was also something that was purely her. She said I pulled her? That couldn't be anything to how she pulled me, or she'd have been in my arms last night.

I didn't say anything about that, obviously. Instead, I went over to Debbie's pen and gave him a stroke. He peeped at me happily, resumed pecking at his feed dish, then waddled over and did an undignified scramble into his washtub. I told Karen, who was somewhere back there, if I could've managed to look at her, "I'd have come back last night and apologized, but I could hear your bath going."

I'd imagined her in it, too. Candlelight, glass of wine, long legs draped over the edge, sleepy eyes. A chance absolutely missed, or a woman who didn't want you, but if that was it, why didn't she ever feel that way to my body? Why did I keep getting the urge to pull her in close, to send my hand lightly down to the base of her spine so I could feel those two sweet dimples for myself, to kiss my way across her cheek to that spot under her ear, and to hear her sigh, if it wasn't coming from her, too? She'd said she felt it, so there you were.

She clearly had issues of her own, though, and the last thing I needed was to hurt somebody else. She wasn't a casual person. Whoever my first-time-this-way was going to be with, and whenever it was going to be, it wasn't going to be with her, and it wasn't going to be now. And maybe that was for the best, because if something horrible happened, if I worried about the leg, about what she was thinking, about how I was going to move into that next position, I could lose the ability to do anything at all.

Impotence. We'd move on from that horrible thought. If that happened, I didn't want it to be with her. I couldn't stand for it to matter that much.

I didn't say any of that, either. I said, "I'll say I was a wanker, and we'll move on, how's that?"

"That's good," she said. "I heard you in the bath, too. It's weird to be separated by just a few trees, and able to hear each other like that. It was kind of comforting."

Huh. Had she been lonely? Lain awake despite her fatigue the same way I had, one person taking up too little space in a king-sized bed? Or had I just made her feel bad? She said,

"Hopefully, the bath helped. And that's OK. I'm not always great at the vulnerability thing myself, and neither of us was at our best last night, let's face it." Her hair wasn't sticking up in spikes today, though it wasn't quite tamed, either, and there were some wisps around her forehead and ears that made her look like an elf. One of the strong kind, with a bow and arrow. She wasn't wearing makeup, which only made sense, and she was battered all to hell. Her shin had long red scratches all down it from her climb up the rocks to help Dougie, and the knee she'd fallen on yesterday looked swollen and red.

I stepped closer, took her hand, and checked out her forearm. Those scrapes were harsh and red, too, and I said, "Could be we should bandage this and your knee before you put on a wetsuit over them today, because this looks painful, and the knee looks worse."

"I would have," she said, "at least put a couple Band-Aids on, but I couldn't, uh . . . quite manage well enough on the arm. I'm left-handed."

"So am I," I said, for something to say. "Though I've trained myself to use both."

"Because you're perfect."

"No." I had to smile, just a bit. "Because that was my job. I can't do whatever it is you do. Food . . . science. Biochemistry. Agriculture. Consumer goods."

"You looked me up."

"I did." I was still holding her wrist, still feeling that pull from her body, like what she'd said. Tentacles, reaching out and wrapping around me. Or something less sinister than tentacles. Shining threads, twining around my body like a vine around a tree.

This time, she was the one who stepped back.

"Right," I said. "First aid. Breakfast."

She said, "I'll start the bacon." Not exactly, "Come on, boy," and we had an adventure to take. So I went and got the first-aid kit instead.

She had me completely confused. She turned my head around and got my body worked up, and then she acted like it was nothing. Maybe the problem was that we *were* both hurting, and we were trying to sort out how to be with somebody now. Or maybe it was something else. Revulsion at the idea of touching the barely healed stump of a man's leg, for example. I'd seen that look before from visitors to the trauma center. Looking, then looking away fast, like you would at a smash on the highway. It shouldn't sting, but it had. Sometimes, it still did. This would be one of those times.

Whatever the problem was, I wasn't going to find out this morning. I'd take her on an adventure instead. I hoped she was as fearless as she seemed. Otherwise, this could get difficult.

I wasn't worried about not being able to get her out of trouble. No matter what happened, I could do that. The question was whether she'd let me.

17

A REFINED WOMAN

KAREN

The canyoning adventure—my first—didn't start out the way I'd expected.

Being fitted for wetsuits back in Thames was nothing out of the ordinary, and neither was the Kiwi-casual way the lead guide, Nathan, assessed Jax's fitness.

"How d'you reckon you'll go with that leg, mate?" he asked. "OK to hike up three hundred pretty tough meters, and can the machinery get wet after that? Dunno how you'd get over the rocks to start rappelling without it, but you'll be in a fair bit of water all day."

"No worries," Jax said. "She'll be right." He'd brought his own wetsuit, which was cut off above the knee on the left side, because, he'd told me, his leg would rip a normal one to pieces. "I've got a waterproofing boot to put on it once we're at the top, and I can do the walk. I've done some rope work as well. Good as gold."

"You were in the Defence Force, weren't you, Jax? Special forces, or something heroic," a redhead named Megan said in an extremely perky sort of way. She was a Kiwi, and here with a friend, a blonde German backpacker. They both had long hair pulled back into cute high ponytails, and the German one had about three times my amount of breastage. I kind of hated both of them already. "I read about your leg," Megan went on. "It looks like you're fit again, though." She glanced at her friend, then down Jax's body in a way that wasn't nearly subtle enough. He was wearing a white T-shirt, which looked, if possible, even better than the black one, because it showed off his chest and shoulders so much more, and board shorts of the shorter, trimmer-fitting, Down Under type. Not *that* trim-fitting, though, so I didn't know what Megan and her pal Hilda, or whatever her name was, were staring at.

"Well known, are you, mate?" another guy, an Australian named Rog, asked Jax. "War hero, is that it? Good on ya." He was fortyish and here with his teenaged son, Andrew, who'd trailed up to the storefront behind his dad like he was doing Male Bonding Under Duress. Andrew had perked way, *way* up, though, when the Sexy Girls had walked in.

Jax looked like he wanted to be anywhere else, and also like he didn't much want to answer. Megan did it for him, saying, "I had his poster on the wall when I was seventeen. The jeans one," she told Jax. "I had an undies one as well, ripped out of a catalog, but my mum made me take it down. I cried. It was a dramatic time in my life, to be fair. Wrote you a letter as well, and imagined how you'd look reading it, realizing that I was your lifelong love. I told my mum that the undies ad was no different from my brother having the swimsuit calendar, and she said it was in his desk drawer, not on the wall, and if I wanted to keep you in my drawer as well, go ahead. So I did. And now I can tell her I've met you in the flesh. I'll get a selfie with you and text it to her. Revenge, eh."

Jax didn't look thrilled to know any of that, so I picked it up and told Rog, "He was an underwear model before the military, for a company called Wallaby. Named for the pouch. Australian company, but you obviously didn't pay keen attention to his commercials back in the day. It was five years ago, and it may not have been quite your thing. He's moved on."

"Wallaby? That's you?" Rog asked, clearly delighted. He

laughed and slapped Jax on the back. "I've got a couple pairs of those. The missus put them in my Christmas stocking last year. Not saying I look like you in them, mind. Always feel a bit of a prat, strutting around like that, but she seems to like them well enough. I'll have to get a photo as well, though it's likely to end up as the wallpaper on her computer. *And* she'll crop me out of it."

Jax's cool, for once, seemed entirely missing. Now, he *really* didn't know what to say. Andrew, for his part, looked mortified. *"Dad,"* he muttered in a despairing tone I understood completely.

"Righto," guide-Nathan said. He wasn't smiling, but I got the feeling it was taking an effort. The junior guide, a woman named Sheila, *was* smiling. "As we're all here, let's load up into the van. We've got a full day ahead."

When the van started up and pulled out of the driveway, we were in the far back. Which hadn't been easy for Jax to get into, but he'd gone there anyway, as if he were saying, "Save me." He muttered, low enough that the hot girls wouldn't hear it in the next row up, "I was not an underwear model. Not primarily. Cheers for that. I thought Nathan was about to tell us he wouldn't know, because he goes commando. What a topic. I'm sweating."

"You'd already been outed. And would you rather be a war hero?" I had to whisper it in his ear, because Megan and Hilda—I was going to have to ask her name again, even though I didn't want to—looked like their ears were actually pricked up to listen. Fortunately, I could get close enough to Jax to be discreet, as there were only two seats back here, and he was so close to me, our arms were brushing. He also smelled great, somehow, even though he wasn't wearing anything scented, except possibly deodorant, which *also* smelled good.

Responding to his scent wasn't True Love, it was histocompatibility. My body was telling me that his immune system code was suitably different from mine, the way female mammals' bodies had evolved to do in order to avoid interbreeding. If we'd been mice, I'd have picked him as my male mouse, assumed the lordosis posture, and let him know

I was ready to start makin' babies, but we weren't mice. If I wanted to bury my nose in his white T-shirt, it was my vomeronasal organs talking, and I didn't have to listen to them.

He wasn't exactly a colorful guy. So far, we'd had khaki, black, and white T-shirts. And yet his very presence still talked louder than Josh's had in his pumpkin sweater. All he had to do was stand there.

"Model's better than war hero," he murmured, his warm breath in my ear giving me goosebumps. "Just. The 'pouch' bit wasn't necessary, though."

"I was merely smoothing over an awkward moment. Besides, she also remembers the jeans. *Which* had the button undone. Very subtle message. Your chest was bare, so were your feet, and you were lounging back with a hand draped over your knee and smoldering again. That's practically the same thing as the underwear."

"It is not the same thing," he said. "And there were all sorts of others besides. Hiking in the mountains, fully clothed in merino. A luxury-car advert wearing a dinner jacket. I did a beer commercial as well, laughing with my mates and smiling at a girl. Earned heaps from that one, almost as much as the undies. Why aren't we talking about my suave glamour?"

"Because nobody cares about your dinner jacket. Why do you think they were checking out your package back there?"

"Anybody ever tell you that you're a refined woman?"

"No."

"Astonishing." I had to laugh, and so did he. "You look very nice as well," he decided to add.

"Ha." I had a white bandage fastened to my kneecap with adhesive tape and another one taped all the way around my forearm, and I felt about as alluring as Debbie the duck. The blonde girls were wearing bikini tops and tiny shorts with their running shoes. I had versions of those things myself, but they were back in my fancy tent, because I'd dressed for a full day of serious adrenaline sports, starting with a thousand-foot hike up a steep, rocky track. You didn't wear that kind of outfit to do that, unless you were interested in both acquiring a sunburn and allowing your male companions to pursue a careful evaluation of the lower curve of your butt cheeks. Besides, nobody'd ever accused me of being bootylicious, wedgies were uncomfortable, and I was here for the adventure.

The hike, when we got to the end of the road at the bottom of a steep, forested, impossibly deep canyon, was as tough as I'd expected, complete with rocks and roots that you had to pull yourself up by. I was sweating within ten minutes, and within an hour, Hilda—all right, her name was actually Margarete, which was as beautiful as she was, unfortunately— had some reddening happening on her shoulders and back despite her tan.

Jax told her, during a water stop, "You may want to put some more sunblock on. I think you're getting burned. D'you have some, or would you like mine?"

"Oh, no," she said in her sexily accented English. "Could I have some of yours, please?" A *gigantic* surprise. Jax pulled the tube out and handed it over, and she began to rub it into her chest and shoulders, pulling away the edges of her bikini top to do it, which had every guy in the place watching except Jax, who was engaged in offering me a water bottle.

"Thanks," I said, trying not to be grumpy. The scrapes on my forearm, for some reason, were burning like crazy. Probably sweat. I'd be all good once we got to the fun part. This was the effort that made the payoff even sweeter.

Jax took a long drink of water, and *I* watched *him*. So did Megan, the redhead, but that was probably because his scruff of beard was now a few days old and looking better than ever, the sweat was making the white T-shirt cling to him some, and he could definitely have modeled for a sports drink at this moment, scars and all. Scars even *better.* Which was probably why, when he'd finished, Margarete handed him the tube of sunblock and asked, "Could you put a little on my back, please?"

He didn't say anything. He just did it, and she pulled her ponytail aside and smiled at him over her shoulder like a woman on the screaming verge of coming out and asking for it, or possibly like a female mouse discovering his histocompatibility. When Jax had finished rubbing the white stuff in, though, he stuck the tube back into his pack and looked at Nathan, who said, "Right. Let's keep on, then," with another suppressed grin.

"Nathan's going to be talking about this one in the pub," I muttered to Jax as we took off up the track. I grabbed a root, swung up onto a rock outcrop, and ignored my elbow and knee, and also the view of Margarete's considerable butt cheek action up ahead of Jax.

He waited until I got up the trickiest section, then said, "Here, go ahead," and put his hand on my shoulder to help me pass him. "I could be slower on this part, and I know how much you enjoy winning." He grinned at me, and I got another flutter of the heart and thought, *Stand back, girls. The underwear model is mine.*

He wasn't, of course. But pretending was fun.

☆☆

JAX

Soon enough, I reminded myself as we kept going up the steep track, I'd be done with this. How many years could women remember the face of the fella on the undies packet? Surely not many more, even if he came with a missing leg for easy identification. All I had to do was stay out of the papers, and I was golden.

Ahead of me, Karen looked good. Slim and strong, and so much less obvious than either of the other girls. She wasn't here for me, or for her idea of me, she was here to have an adventure. We rounded a rare switchback, which made a change from climbing straight up, and I saw the Border Collie coming out in her again as she heard the sound of rushing water. She must have sensed that we were nearly at the top, because she picked up her pace.

Fifteen minutes more, and she wasn't looking at me at all.

She was standing with her arms out from her sides and a huge smile on her face, taking in the view. "Wow," she said happily. *"Wow."*

"Good, eh," I said, which was inadequate. The steep walls of the slot canyon dropped beneath us like you'd be stepping off into space—which you would—and the plume of spray from a series of waterfalls hovered like mist against a background of blue sky dotted with puffy white clouds, long, squared-off columns of gray rock, and foliage in every shade of green, the low, forested mountains stretching as far as you could see. The promise of adrenaline to come was all but hanging in the air, and I wondered who the first bloke had been who'd thought, "Let's try going over the edge of this thing!" Whoever he was, he'd probably been a Kiwi.

"Wetsuits, helmets, and harnesses on," Nathan said, and we started to suit up. I got the wetsuit on fast, then sat on the rocks and began to slide the waterproof boot over my left leg, pumping out the air when I was done to create a vacuum seal. Karen was going more slowly than I expected, wincing a little as she pulled the resistant, rubbery material over her knee, and I asked, "All right?"

"Sure," she said.

I handed over a tube of the stuff I used to lubricate the sleeve over my stump and said, "It'll chafe less with this," and for once, she didn't argue, just applied it.

"Scared?" I asked.

"No. It looks so cool. I can't wait." For all that, she winced a little more as she got the wetsuit over her elbow. I zipped up the back for her, got a strap on my specs and my helmet on, then stepped into my webbing harness, tightened it up, and helped her with hers, during which she put her hand on my shoulder again and I tried not to notice how close she was. We were first done, so I hauled out my water bottle, handed it to her, and said, "Keep it." She'd drunk all her own.

"Your glasses are going to do you no good at all while we're swimming," she told me once she'd taken a drink. "You're going to basically be blind. I guess I get why you don't wear contacts—I'm sure that's awkward out on a combat mission, when you're about to shoot somebody, but you get dust in your eye so you get shot instead—but I'm surprised you haven't had Lasik."

I said, "I haven't wanted to."

Did she drop it? Of course not. "Really?" she asked instead. "Why not? I had it. Both eyes, when I was still a teenager. It was totally cool. Your eyes are sore for maybe a day, and that's literally all. After that? You're not blind anymore. It was miraculous. You should do it. It's great for swimming, especially snorkeling."

Everybody was listening. This was wonderful. "I don't enjoy things touching my eyeball," I said. "And my eyesight's not that bad." Stiffly, I was sure.

Another perfect chance to tactfully drop it. Instead, she laughed. "Seriously? You're scared of something touching your *eyeball?* Jax. You're an *explosives* expert. You're a *beast.*"

"Really?" the kid, Andrew, said, a little shyly. He'd been too awed by Margarete, the German girl, to say much so far. Or too afraid to have anybody look at him, because I was sure he'd had an erection for so long by now, it was hurting, and that he couldn't wait to start rappelling so nobody would see. Something that made me extremely glad not to be fifteen anymore. "That's what you do?" he asked. "Is that how you lost your leg and all? That's so dope."

I grinned. He was so wrong, and he was so exactly what I'd been. "Yeh, mate," I said, "the job's pretty cool."

Karen said, "You won't get Lasik because you don't want your eye touched? You won't even get contacts? Jax. You have a phobia." She sounded delighted. "That's such a weird one, too, not like snakes or heights or public speaking, or something normal."

"I don't have a phobia," I said. "I have a preference. And I prefer not to have my eye held forcibly open whilst somebody cuts my eyeball."

"They put your head in a holder, too," she saw fit to inform me, "and the guy holds your head just in case. But it doesn't hurt."

I did *not* shudder. "Maybe they could put you under," she

suggested. "It takes about thirty seconds per eye, but maybe for you, being a hero and all, they'd do general anesthesia for three hours or whatever."

"Thank you," I said. "Are we finished?" I asked Nathan. He was smiling, finally. He'd reached his Impassive Limit, and I was the one who'd done it. "Yeh, mate," he said. "Gather round, everybody. We'll do a karanga first. A prayer, eh, to set us off right."

We stood in a circle, Nathan chanted a few Maori phrases, the vowel-intensive syllables lyrical to the ear, and powerful, too, even if you didn't know their meaning. It was the way they merged with the air, and the way you remembered that you were rooted to this ground. It was possible that I noticed that because of the way Karen looked out at the canyon below, heaved a deep breath, and let it out slowly.

She was such a contradiction, or she was a woman who'd stuffed down half of herself in order to get where she needed to go. I couldn't quite tell. Once we'd started on the rock scramble at the side of the waterfall that was the first part of the descent, I asked her, "How long since you started coming here? To En Zed?"

"Since I was sixteen," she said, putting a hand onto a rock and hopping down, so her knee couldn't be that sore. "When Hope and Hemi got engaged."

I wanted to ask her more, find out how deep her connection ran to the old man and to her not-cousins, but that was all we had time for. The scrambling got more serious, and then turned into wading across a rock-bottomed plunge pool at the base of that first part of the falls, during which my balance was tested and Karen's wasn't. After that, we were looking over a drop of thirty meters or so, and Nathan was saying, "Right. This is the short one, ease you into it. Remember—Kiwi rules. Be honest about how you're going and what you're up for, help your mate, and if you get into trouble, sing out so we can come help you. We'll send Sheila down first, and Jax, you go after her, as you've done it before. Watch how both of them use their legs," he told the others. "You're not letting yourself twist and bash into the rock.

You're kicking off, then swinging back and kicking off again as you get close, keeping your body facing the rock the whole way. Easy as." That didn't sound like he was pandering to my injury, and made me unreasonably, if quietly, satisfied.

There's nothing quite like the sound of the water in your head, the spray around you, the rainbows in the air as you descend an actual waterfall, or the soaring feeling of zipping down through all that space. There's nothing at all like finding you can still do it, when you've worried that the ability is gone forever. Exhilaration, that was the word. And when Karen got down and joined me, because she'd come next, the Border Collie needing to get in amongst it with every fiber of her being, she was laughing. Her whiskey eyes were bright, her smile enormous, as if she'd laughed the whole way down, and my heart flew a little bit higher.

"Oh, wow," she said, once she'd rid herself of the rope and swum across the deep plunge pool to me, and we were surrounded by rock and waterfall and bush, looking at a double rainbow that arched across the mist. "Wow. It's like being a bird. Or something better. A water bird, so you're soaring one minute, and swimming the next, part of all the worlds. Tell me we get to go hang-gliding next."

I had to laugh myself. "Can't believe nobody's taken you on an adventure like this before, keen as you are."

She was still smiling. "My sister's chicken. She won't even ski, and Hemi does what she likes. I haven't tagged along for a while anyway. And on my own? Adventure travel costs money. Anyway, I've worked pretty hard since I started college."

"Holidays?" I suggested.

"What are those? Never mind," she hastened to say, as if that had revealed too much. "I'm making up for it now."

Meaning a week or two in, what? Twelve years? Really? All I knew was, she went down the longest abseil of the day, the eighty-meter one that came next, first in line, because she so clearly couldn't wait, and plunged into the water afterwards with just as much jubilation. When we got to the next bit, a fifteen-meter slide on her back straight down a chute into another pool, she was nearly jumping up and down in her haste to get stuck into it, and she shouted all the way down like a kid on a roller coaster. And needless to say, when she was offered the choice of jumping fourteen meters into the water or doing another abseil instead, she didn't just jump. She did a flip in the air, went in with a splash, treaded water, and waved at me, while behind me, Margarete said, "I cannot do this one, I think. Perhaps I have a phobia as well."

Nathan said, "No worries. Whoever wants to jump can go on and jump, and we'll help anybody else abseil down."

The kid, Andrew, said, "I'll jump," and did, and Karen beckoned him to the other side of the pool, where he'd be out of the way. As for me, I hadn't decided. I wasn't sure how my prosthesis would do with that kind of impact, much as I hated having to consider it.

Margarete said quietly, as Andrew's dad jumped in with a whoop and an enormous splash, "It is very attractive to you, I think, this fearlessness."

"Yeh," I said, because why not say it? "It is."

She nodded once and looked away, and here I was, hurting somebody again. When I'd been that other bloke, the one I'd told Karen about, I'd barely tried *not* to hurt people, and yet I'd swear I'd done it less, or noticed it less, than I was doing now. Which was why I went on to say, "You're basically jumping off the roof of a four-story building, though. There's no shame in not wanting to do that. Probably more like good sense."

"Nah," Megan said with a laugh. "There's shame in it. Look around you. Everybody else is going. Kiwi rules, eh. You don't want to be that girl who won't try. And I'm off." She took the leap, and Margarete watched her go with a look on her face too much like hurt.

This wasn't anything to do with me. Despite the seriously curvy body and the seriously tiny shorts, Margarete had hiked up the track and done the rest of this so far without any dramas, and she certainly hadn't looked like she cared what I thought about it. All she'd actually done, when I thought back, was put sunblock on when she'd been getting burnt. It wasn't her fault that we'd all wanted to watch her doing it. I was also doubting that she'd meant anything by asking me to put some on her back. I'd overestimated my appeal, or maybe I'd forgotten that everybody you met was starring in their own movie. They weren't just extras in yours.

I said, "I've liked women who couldn't have done any of this, so I'm not sure how much any one . . . characteristic matters. It just has to be a match at the time, eh."

"A meeting of minds, you are thinking," Margarete said. "Or a meeting of hearts." She watched Megan swim across the plunge pool, but didn't say anything else.

Nathan cleared his throat, about to say, "Let's go, then, if you're not jumping." He could wait thirty seconds.

"Probably," I told Margarete. "A meeting of something, anyway." She'd come to New Zealand and lost her own heart, I was guessing, and was in that spot where you didn't know whether it would land in safe hands or be thrown to the ground like it was worthless. When you were so scared to find out, but you couldn't stand *not* to find out. I'd seen it before, but always in blokes. In a soldier who'd poured out his feelings in an email, when the thought of death had come too close, and had heard the wrong thing back, or, even worse, hadn't heard back at all. They never said much more than Margarete was saying now, mostly just went quiet. But when a fella handed you the photo he'd been carrying in his breast pocket for months and said, "You know how I said to let her know I loved her, if something happens to me? Fuck that," and climbed into the armored vehicle taking him into harm's way with nothing in his pocket anymore, you got to know the sound of hurt.

When I was younger, I'd probably tossed a fair few of those hearts to the ground myself. No "probably" about it, in fact. I'd told myself it wasn't my doing and wasn't my problem, but if you knew your feelings were that unequal and you went ahead anyway, it *was* your doing. Not a comfortable recollection.

Margarete nodded once, decisively, and said, "I am frightened, but I am jumping." Then she took a deep breath and leapt off the edge into space, not shrieking and not shouting with joy, because she was too scared for either. She hit the water, went down for long seconds, came up spluttering, and swam to join Megan.

I thought, *Good on ya. Hope it works,* and may have got a lump in my throat. After that? I jumped in myself. Bugger the prosthesis. I'd never find out if it could handle this if I didn't try.

I may have lost my leg. I may have lost my job. I didn't have to lose my courage.

18

⭐

ONE MORE DAY

KAREN

The guides started a barbecue once we were on the canyon floor again, and seven hours after we'd started out from Thames, we were sitting on boulders drinking specialty coffee and waiting for our hamburgers. Only in New Zealand would a freshly brewed cappuccino be part of your adventure outing in the woods, and I was glad of it. The clouds had moved in even as we'd moved down the canyon, and they were up there now, big and puffy, looking like "summer rain squalls tonight." We'd swum through more than ten plunge pools, and I cupped my hands around the warm drink in its metal cup, shivered some, and wished for sun. My scraped forearm was itching and my bruised knee was hurting, but I didn't really care. It had been worth it.

Beside me, Jax had stripped off his waterproofing boot and then his wetsuit and was inspecting his leg, and I forgot about my own knee. "Is it all right?" I asked him.

"Think so."

"It's pretty incredible that it's rated for fifty-foot jumps," I said.

"Ah," he said. "But is it?" I must have looked astonished,

146

because he grinned. "Say that I took a chance. Worth it, eh."

Once again, it was exactly what I'd been thinking. I wondered if he'd felt whole again, discovering how strong he still was, and suspected the answer was "yes," or at least "partly." I didn't say anything about it, though. I might not be the most tactful person on the planet, but even I'd noticed that it was a sensitive issue, and it wasn't the time or place. Instead, I said, "That was possibly the most awesome experience of my life. Thanks for taking me to do it. And taking the chance on your leg."

He said, "No worries. Could be that's the real Kiwi Rules, eh. When in doubt, jump."

He looked glad, I thought, although subdued. Tired, maybe, except that I didn't think he got tired easily, or that he succumbed to pain easily, either. I didn't myself, normally, but I was tired now. And cold. And when Megan came over and started chatting to Jax again in a cheerful, Kiwi kind of way, when Margarete shifted over to join her, and everybody else gravitated over to where Jax was and started taking selfies, I may have gotten even colder.

The hamburgers helped, but when we finally got back to our campsite, after a trip down the river valley in the van and back up it again in the car, I was more than ready to be done. I was still shivering, despite my sweatshirt and Jax turning on the heated seats in the car, and then the heat, without even asking, but when I saw Debbie, I had to pick him up and give him a cuddle. He was so happy to see us, he started peeping and giving his raspy quacks like crazy, and he did his best to hop over his fence to get to us faster. I stroked his fluffy white feathers and said, "Hey, boy. Did you miss us? Huh? Did you?" and he opened his round eyes at me and peeped in a way that said, "Yes, I did." I may have kissed his round little head, too. It may have happened.

While I was getting reacquainted with my duck, Jax dumped the water from the dishpan and bowl down my toilet and refilled them, then started scooping up the shavings from the pen with his expandable survival-bowl and putting them into a paper bag. I said, "You don't have to do that. I'll get it in a minute."

"Nah," he said. "I'm good. Sit down and have a rest."

I said, "I really want to. Rest, I mean. And here I was just thinking that I'm lousy at letting somebody be a hero." I sat down, though, grabbed the outdoor blanket that this absolutely perfect not-quite-campsite offered to make your experience even better, wrapped up in it, and watched him.

I liked his smile so much. He didn't do it often around other people, I'd noticed, but he sure did it for me. "Yeh," he said, still scooping smelly duck litter. "Noticed that, didn't I. Could be you were thinking about it because you saw that I like to do it. Not be a hero for losing a leg," he said, like I needed the explanation, "but for changing the shavings in your duck pen? I'll take that. Cheers for not going all damsel-in-distress on me today, though, when you wanted to be brave instead. Honesty's good. I'll take honesty as well."

He finished with the pen, then went and got Debbie's box and emptied and refilled it, too, and I said, "I could talk about that, but I think I need to warm up first, if I'm being honest. This was such a great day, but I may need one of those wearable blankets with sleeves right now, the ones they advertise in infomercials, that always look both seriously comfortable, and also like an embarrassment you'd never erase from your memory banks if anybody saw you in one."

He laughed, then came over and crouched down beside my chair. My heart picked up the pace, I lost my breath, and I thought, in the same moment, *Calm down. He's petting Debbie.*

He didn't. Instead, he put his arm around my shoulder and kissed my cheek, then moved his lips over it and kissed me again, near my ear. His lips were warm, the stubble on his jaw was rough against my skin, and his hand on my shoulder pulled me in, but gently. Like he was so strong, he didn't need to prove it.

I just about dropped the duck. My skin heated up like I'd lowered myself into the bathtub, my brain went numb, and I tried to come up with something to say and couldn't. He said, his voice low and warm, "You've got guts and no mistake. Time for a hot shower, though, I think. Or a bath, maybe." He stayed where he was, but he didn't kiss me again.

"And a beer," I said, doing my best to be normal and knowing I was absolutely failing. He made me lose my cool. He made me lose my words. "How . . . how about you?"

He stood up, and I was sorry, and I was glad, because I wasn't handling this well at all. "Definitely," he said. "I'll go take my own shower, but I'll be back. You can rug up, and we'll sit here one more time while the sun sets and have that beer. Could be we'll even go wild and have two. You never know."

☆☆

JAX

Something had happened when I'd taken that jump, or when Margarete had, and I hadn't been able to shift back since. Now that I'd kissed Karen, that shift was going to be impossible.

She'd frozen when I'd done it. I didn't know what that meant, and I needed to find out before I thought about touching her again.

As for me? I was already there.

Ever since the explosion, my life had been about getting through one more day. When I'd been medevac'd out and was lying flat on my back in the battering, mind-numbing clamor of a helicopter in flight with a medic bent over me checking the tourniquet on my leg, the drugs taking only the barest edge off the searing pain when he'd touched my skin, while I'd had my eyes squeezed shut, and my mouth, too, to try to keep from screaming, and I'd still seen my boot in the silty brown dirt and the torn body of Ali Madad, his arms and legs sprawled at impossible angles, his blood turning the sandy brown to liquid red—that had been nothing but a time to get through. I'd thought, *Hang on till we get there. Don't think. Hang on.* When I'd been flat on my back in a hospital bed, my face stitched shut, my chest covered by a dressing so enormous, I shied away from knowing what was under it, and I'd looked down at the outline of a single foot under the blanket, in the fuzz of a narcotic drip and the terror of knowing I was still alive, and I had to live this way from now on, forever, I'd thought, *Sit up. You can sit up, anyway, you bastard. Sit UP.*

Later, when my chest had healed enough for me to propel myself in a wheelchair, I'd got myself into it under the watchful eye of a nurse and told myself, *Get out there.* I'd wheeled myself through the door and into the corridor, had seen blokes missing both legs, missing an arm, a hand, and guessed they were thinking the same thing. *What am I, now that I'm not the man I was?* I'd felt like shit, and had known they all did, too, but I'd also known that they were hoping exactly what I was—that if they got stronger today, tomorrow would be better.

When I'd stood between the parallel bars for the first time and hopped and pulled my way down them, the sweat standing out on my forehead, my breath coming in gasps, the pain like fire, I'd thought, *Tomorrow, it'll be the second time. First time, worst time.* When I'd got my prosthesis and had taken the first steps on it, one arm still in a crutch, I'd thought, *Ten steps. Rest, then ten more.* When I'd walked down a city street for the first time and had seen every passerby's gaze go to my legs, then swivel hastily away, I'd thought, *Doesn't matter what they think. It matters what you can do.* And the day I'd met Karen, when I'd come out of the sea on my knees, then got to my foot, and she'd looked at my scars, I'd thought, *What do I do now? I try not to let it matter. Again.*

My life for the past months had been one long endurance test. A shameful one at that, for taking so long to adjust. I was still here, my mind intact. I was walking again, while all those flag-draped coffins had gone home in a cargo hold. I'd made it through all those first times, and moved on to the next one, because what I'd told Karen was true. What was the choice? Lying down and dying? I'd muscled my way onward, knowing that tomorrow, there'd be another step, and I'd have to take that one, too. Knowing that no matter how strong I got, no matter how hard I worked, my leg wasn't coming back.

For the first time in my life, there was a limit I'd never get past. Not with willpower, not with running until I vomited and swimming until every muscle was shaking, not with diet or strength training or protein powder or belief or faith. And still, there was no choice but to tell myself, *Push through it today, and tomorrow, you're that much stronger.*

Today, though? Today hadn't been another day of pushing through. I'd done things I hadn't been sure I could do anymore, which made it another first time, but it hadn't felt like that. Since I'd met Karen, none of the days had felt like that. Maybe it was me, but I thought it might be her, too. I'd made mistakes all over the shop, and it had still felt better, because I'd felt . . . alive again. Out there living my life, getting it wrong and having to make amends. So far, I'd engaged in a highly dubious race that had almost drowned a kid, picked up a morally deficient hitchhiker, had to explain myself to the police, collected the most useless duck known to man, and probably pushed both my own leg and my prosthesis past manufacturers' specifications. And maybe, somewhere in there, I'd remembered to listen to other people again, too.

Pain was a selfish beast. It wanted all your attention, and it took all your focus. Now, though, my focus had shifted at last. I'd started paying attention to something besides myself, and I wanted to keep doing it.

The other thing I wanted? I wanted to be in and out of that shower in two minutes. I wanted to be back there with a couple of beers when Karen stepped out of her own shower. I wanted to take her hand and lead her, wrapped in a towel or a dressing gown or whatever she'd be wearing over her nakedness, back through the drawn-back fabric of the tent door. I wanted to pull the ties on those flaps and shut out everything but the world of that enormous bed, and then I wanted to light the candle lanterns, take off my leg, and see what happened next.

And, no, I didn't really want that last bit. I wanted two legs. I wanted that with the aching, hopeless desire of knowing I could never have it again. I wanted not to have to worry about what she'd say or how she'd look at me when it came down to two bodies, one of them whole and beautiful and one of them . . . not, when there was no disguising what I felt and what I wanted, or what she did. I didn't want to have to think about anything except putting my hand in the top of that towel or at the neckline of that dressing gown, pulling the edges apart so I could see every bit of her, then coming down over her and kissing and touching and loving her slow and easy, all the way until the candles burned down.

Instead, I went over to my tent and took off my leg, and then my clothes. After that, I crutched over to my own bathroom block, indulged in five minutes of water as hot as I could stand it, headed back to my tent, still naked but for a towel, stood there and looked at my leg, and thought—*No.*

I didn't want to put it on. I didn't want to cover up my scars. I didn't want to hide what was missing. I wanted her to see who I was, and I wanted to know what she thought when she saw it.

It was the moment of truth. It was jumping off that cliff, accelerating through the air for those long, terrifying seconds, and not knowing what would happen when I hit. It might be pure exhilaration, and it might be the end. Whichever it was going to be, I needed to know.

19

✩✩

ALL THE MISSING PIECES

I came around the path into Jax's campsite fast. Fast because I'd heard the thunder as I'd stepped out of the shower, and it had now started to rain, and fast because I probably didn't want time to think twice. Part of me, what I thought of as the top of my head, the logical part, knew it was impulsive, and it wasn't like my impulsivity had yielded great dividends so far on this trip. But I was jumping off the cliff again anyway. I needed to take the fall, and I needed to hit the water hard and go down deep.

It was the way he'd kissed me. How gentle his lips had been, and how strong his hand had. When I'd taken my shower, the warm water had sluiced over me in that way warm water did, and I'd shuddered under it, but all I'd felt was that hand and that mouth. It was as if he were still there with me, wrapping his strong arms around me and holding me close, kissing my neck, being gentle, and being so firm, too, letting me know he was here to stay. I'd put on dry clothes to the *pat-pat-pat* of the first raindrops hitting my tent, and all I'd heard was his voice, warm and low, saying, "You've got guts and no mistake."

What, that isn't the way the man in your life does sexy talk? Maybe it depends on how desperately you want the man, because it had sent a shiver straight down my body. I'd been tingling ever since, and not just where you'd think. I had flutters in my belly. My inner *thighs* were tingling. It was like my whole self was being pulled along the track to him by those threads I'd stupidly told him about, the ones that wrapped around my body and my mind every time we were together and tried to drag me closer.

That wasn't the point, though, because however I felt, I wasn't coming over to drape myself across his bed, pull my shirt up sexily to reveal my belly piercings, and suggest that he could keep going until he reached my decidedly unimpressive breasts. I wasn't planning to lick my lips and breathe, "Take me now," and risk him saying, "Uh . . . maybe not the best idea." After which he'd come up with some excellent reason why that wasn't actually a rejection.

I was coming over for the first-aid kit. It just didn't feel that way, except in the top of my brain. The rest of me was having a problem with those stupid silver threads.

I would've knocked, but there was no door, and the rain was picking up. I called out, "Jax?" and stepped under the shelter of the tiny deck, and he was there. Standing by the bed on one leg in the low, flickering light of a single candle lantern, his hair wet, wearing only a white towel around his waist. The stump of his leg, the rough tangle of pink scars on his chest, and all the hard muscle and beautiful proportions of him. He got a hand on the bed and turned on his one foot to face me, and I couldn't read the look in his eyes at all.

"Sorry," I said, backing up a step. "Sorry. I . . . uh, I thought you might help me bandage my arm again. And, uh, it's raining, and I thought I'd do the work for once. Coming over, I mean. For the beer."

Yeah. Smooth. Not so much jumping off the cliff, then, as trying to get back onto it again, a cartoon character scrabbling in midair just before he plummeted toward the ground with a whistling *whoosh*. And an anvil landed on top of him.

"Come in," he said. "And we'll do that." He wasn't quite smiling, but his face had changed. I thought. I wasn't quite looking.

"I'll just . . ." I made some sort of vague gesture, kicked off my jandals, and stepped into the tent in my bare feet. "I'll turn around, if you want, so you can get dressed."

It was a bit late to realize that I could've dressed a little more seductively if I'd wanted him to get some other message than "Please bandage me." I was wearing wide-legged gray cotton pants with a drawstring and a red T-shirt. You didn't seduce a man in your comfy PJs, because, yes, that was what they were. My hair was wet, and I wasn't wearing any makeup, because I'd also forgotten that. I'd been in sort of a . . . hurry. To be bandaged.

"You can do that," he said. "Sit down on the other side of the bed, if you like."

I did. I faced the wall of the tent, heard the rustle of fabric behind me and the *thud* that was Jax hopping, and then he said, "All clear," and I turned around.

Blue rugby shorts. Another white T-shirt, with all that body under there. And no leg.

He said, "I'll grab us a couple beers, and we can do your arm. Bit of anesthetic, eh."

"I'll go," I said, hopping up. I needed a second. I needed a do-over. I was going to embarrass myself. I remembered too late how everybody had flirted with him today. If he realized how much I wanted to throw myself at him, and he let me down gently, I'd . . . well, I'd possibly die.

I was a mature woman who was turning thirty in about three days. I was highly intelligent. I was extremely capable. I was economically secure and emotionally stable. Just not right now.

"Nah," he said. "I've got it." He grabbed one crutch and headed out of the tent, and came back seconds later with two bottles, before I'd had nearly enough time to talk myself into the "stable" idea.

"It's good that you can still hold things," I said, still standing up. "With the crutches being on your forearms." Which was lame, yes.

His face hardened some. "Yeh." He got the tops off and set the bottles on the table at his side of the bed. "Come around here and sit next to the light, and I'll get your arm sorted."

"What, I'm not supposed to say that?" I asked as he grabbed his little first-aid kit and sat beside me.

"Let's say it begins to pale as a topic," he said. "Never mind." He'd picked up my wrist and was inspecting my forearm, and he was so close, I could feel his heat, and the prickle of the hair on his thighs next to mine. I could smell the rain-clean, full-man scent of him, like the smell of testosterone, and I could see the blue line on the side of his face. All I wanted was to kiss that line, wrap myself up in him, and climb inside. He looked up, his eyes caught mine, and he said, "This isn't looking too flash. Redness, eh. Got some swelling here, too."

See? Not sexy. Not even close. I swallowed and said, "I know. Could you put some more antibiotic ointment on it, maybe?"

"I could." He opened the little tube, and his hands were gentle as he dabbed the colorless ointment onto the considerable expanse of scraped, reddened flesh, draped gauze over the whole thing, and taped the top and bottom edges. "We'll let it breathe, eh."

How could you be turned on by the competent way a man tore *tape?* With his big, strong hands? I didn't know. All I knew was, those tingles had started up again, and they'd brought their friends. I was also getting flutters in my chest to match the ones in my belly, and even my throat felt tight. Jax started putting away his supplies and said, "You could hand me that beer, and drink your own. It's a dark ale. I'm telling you that, as you're a food person."

I handed his over. He was smiling, now, just a little. I checked out the bottle, just for something to do. "Emerson's Weizenbock. You brought out the big guns." I squinted at the label. "Whoa. More than eight percent alcohol."

"Good thing we don't have to drive anywhere. Born and brewed in Dunedin. Taste of home, eh." He tapped his bottle gently against mine. "Cheers. Well done today."

I took a sip, and then I took a few more, because it was absolutely, sinfully delicious, rich and malty and clove-scented and complex, like alcoholic gingerbread. Heady, too. I drank some more, realized I must be thirsty, wondered how half a beer could affect you this fast, and shivered some. The rain had picked up, the patter of drops becoming more of a drumming, and the beer was good, but it was chilling me more.

Jax asked, "Cold?"

"No. Yes. Sort of. It's funny—I think of men as having beer voices, and this is the kind you are. Winter ale, is what I thought that first day, on the beach. Like this. Darker. More complex. Stronger. Nothing like a grapefruit IPA." I was babbling. Yep, definitely babbling.

"Mm. I'll wait to be pleased about that until I find out whether you like it." He grabbed the throw from the bottom of the bed and put it around my shoulders. Is there a sweeter, more I've-got-you-baby gesture than a man wrapping you up to keep you warm?

"I like it," I said. "Actually, I love it." I was having trouble catching my breath, and now I'd said the *L*-word. I should suggest we go outside, where I wouldn't be sitting on his *bed*, except that it was raining, and he was looking at me, smiling over the bottle, then tipping his head back to drink. The leg that was beside mine was the left one, the one missing a foot, he was strong enough not to care about that, and I wanted him like you want dark-chocolate, high-butterfat ice cream when you're hurting. Straight out of the carton, because you don't have strength to resist anymore, and you just want to eat it all down. I reached my hand out, hesitated, touched his thigh lightly, hoped like hell that he wouldn't look at me like his little sister had just made a move on him—or worse, laugh—and said, "It was a good day. A little too focused on you, maybe, on the part of—oh, everybody else. I could've been a little . . ." I had to force myself to go on. *Come on, Karen. Say it.* "A little jealous. Because you looked so good and were so impressive, and everybody thought so. I was glad about that, but maybe I wasn't, too. Not exactly."

☆☆

157

JAX

She'd taken her hand away again, but she was so close, and this time, she hadn't frozen up. She was doing the opposite. I couldn't be wrong about that.

There were still a dozen reasons it was a bad idea. Somehow, I couldn't listen to any of them. Maybe it was that if she was wearing a bra under that thin little T-shirt, I couldn't see it, and I'd been watching her nipples harden for the past ten minutes, over and over again. When I'd sat down beside her. When I'd put the throw over her shoulders. When she'd touched me. And most of all—when I'd touched her. When I'd picked up her wrist and held it. She'd shivered, then, and I didn't think it was because she was cold.

I said, "You don't have to be jealous. A bit of leftover celebrity, that's all. Nobody was in love. Do you want to know who I was watching?"

"Yes," she said. "No. I don't know."

"I was watching you." I put a careful hand on the side of her face and brushed my thumb over her cheekbone, and she swallowed and didn't move away. Instead, she leaned in. I couldn't be wrong about that, either.

I was nearly as scared to do this as I had been that first time, when I'd been fourteen, and the surge of heat I got was, if possible, even more intense. I leaned in and brushed my lips over hers, felt her inhalation of breath, and got the kind of shock down my body that hit you like a two-by-four. And then she touched my thigh again with the other hand and drew it down my leg all the way to my knee, and I might be the one freezing up.

She moved her lips over and kissed me beside my ear. On my scar, I realized dimly, as she said, "Jax. I want to touch you so much. And I don't know what's OK."

I had to laugh, even though it came out choked. "Assume it's all OK." I leaned over her and set my beer on the table, and she put hers down, too. Which meant she stopped touching me, and I needed her to keep touching me, even if it scared me. Exactly like all of this was scaring her.

"Has anybody . . ." she said. "Right, I'm just going to ask." As if I'd have expected anything else. "Have you been, uh, trying stuff, since the leg and all? Having sex?"

I groaned. "You are the most direct woman I've ever met. No. I haven't."

"And it's a little rough," she said. "Maybe. Because you're not sure how it'll go."

"Yeh. It is." Saying it felt naked. Exposed. Much too vulnerable. This wasn't who I was in bed. I was careful, and I was attentive. I wasn't tentative. "Feels like the rules have changed. I hate that. I want my old rules back."

She traced her hand down my scar, her fingers gentle, and said, "I know. Me, too. Because I want to kiss you everywhere, and I don't know if that's all right. I need some rules myself, I think."

I was going to burst into flames. The blanket had fallen off from around her shoulders, and she didn't seem to have noticed. I said, "Could be the rules are just to be honest. Could be it's a first for you, too. First time, hardest time. I usually say, 'First time, worst time,' but this isn't that. This could just be us feeling our way, doing our best. Making sure it's a good time."

She swallowed again, and her eyes were bright, the tears rising too easily, the way they had earlier, at the café, after she'd told me she felt sorry for me. When she'd thought she'd gone too far, and she wasn't sure how to get herself back.

The rules hadn't changed that much, then. It was about taking care of her. Making her feel beautiful, and desired, and sure I could take her wherever she wanted to go, so she could relax and let me do it. Making her grab the sheets and call out loud, and know she could fall as hard as she needed to, because I'd be there to catch her. No change at all.

I took off my specs, leaning around her to put them on the table, and then I was doing just that. Touching her face, tracing the perfect lines of cheekbones and jaw, kissing her soft lips, and not trying to go anywhere else, not yet. I had my hand cradling her head and my other one around her waist, and there was nothing at all wrong with the way her slim body was yielding under mine. And when I pushed her gently down onto her back? She went.

Surely there's no feeling in the world like coming down over a woman, having her hold your shoulder to pull you in closer, hearing the hitch in her breath and watching her eyelids flutter shut. Feeling her start to believe that she can trust you, because you'll be here as long as it takes, and you won't take anything she doesn't want to give. When I got that message, I kissed a slow path across her mouth to her ear, touched each of those sparkling studs with my tongue, and told her, "I've been wanting to do this for so many days now. You've got the prettiest ears. The prettiest neck." I worked my way down to that, still going slowly, and when I set my mouth to her, she moaned and held me closer. That was a "yes," then.

"I need to . . . kiss you," she said, and her hands had gone under my T-shirt, were stroking up my sides, around to my back.

"You're not too convincing," I said, when I'd stopped being quite so busy sucking at the place on her neck that she liked best. "Because I'd say you want me to kiss you some more first."

"For a . . . while." She was tugging my shirt up my chest, and I thought for a second about the thick web of scar tissue, then forgot to think about it, because she'd levered herself off the bed and *was* kissing me, taking a nipple into her mouth and sucking on it, and if I wasn't careful, I wasn't going to be able to make this last long enough.

"Shit," I said, and she didn't answer, just kept going, and kept pulling my shirt up. "Karen. Stop. *Shit.*"

She sat back fast, and her eyes flew open. "What? Bad? Sorry. I don't . . ." She started rolling off the bed, and I put a hand on her shoulder.

"Wait," I said. "I don't want you to go. That's the last thing I want. No, that wasn't bad. That was bloody brilliant. I don't have a condom, that's all."

"Oh." She hovered halfway between sitting and lying down. Still feeling too vulnerable, I could tell. "Oh. Well, we could . . . uh . . . take a rain check, I guess. This is probably stupid anyway. I'm not really . . ."

The tenderness was right there. "Or," I said, "we could call it an exploratory session. See how good we could make each other feel. Or you could go. No worries."

Did I want to say that last bit? Not a hope. I wanted to hold her here. I wanted to lie over her, take her wrists in my hands, take her body over, push her all the way up the mountain and over the edge, and see how loud I could get her. But that wasn't how first times worked.

"I could be your . . . first time." Her voice was breathy, not like Karen at all. "So you wouldn't have that hanging over your head."

That wasn't what I wanted, either. I wasn't sure *what* I wanted, except that I was pretty sure one time wasn't going to be enough. The rain was pelting hard, and a gust of wind came into the tent and swirled. I sat up, pulled my shirt over my head, and said, "I'm closing the tent flap. Cozier, eh. Maybe you want to pull the duvet back and climb in."

And have time to think, I thought. Not for me. I knew what I thought. I wanted to be inside her. I needed to give her a chance to look at every one of my scars and missing pieces, though, and decide if they repelled her.

It took me a while, like it always did, and it wasn't anything like the picture I wanted to present. Hopping to the door on one crutch, and balancing on one foot as I unfastened the tapes holding the tent flaps back and zipped the opening closed. What daylight there still was went with it, and when I turned around again, it was to see Karen in the glow of a single candle. She *had* pulled back the bedclothes, and was sitting up against them and starting to pull up her shirt.

I could have told her to leave it on for me, but I didn't. I was enjoying the view just fine. I stood there on my one foot and watched as she showed me that, first, she still had that line of four sparklers down her belly, and second, that she'd come over here without a bra. She had the shirt over her head and was easing the sleeve over her bandaged arm when she said, "So you know. This is me."

Arms over her head, golden light flickering over honey-colored skin and small, taut pink nipples, the tender undersides of her breasts, the outline of triceps showing on the backs of her arms. "Yeh," I said. "I do see that. So far, I'm loving it. I'll keep letting you know, though, shall I?"

"I'm pretty athletic," she said.

I had to laugh. "Yes, you are. Wait a second, and I'll let you know what I think of that, too."

She took off the PJ pants, then. She was naked under there, and bloody *hell.* That was nice. She looked nervous. I didn't feel that way. I got my own shorts off in as much of a hurry as a man on one leg can do it, and left them where they fell.

I was still hopping when I headed back over there. I still had one leg when I came down over her again, when I stroked a slow hand all the way up her side and captured a breast, when I dipped my mouth down to taste, heard her draw in a sharp breath, and felt her hips rise under me.

I had one leg, and I didn't care.

I had one leg and too many scars, but I could still make a woman sing.

20

☆☆

NOTHING BUT WEAKNESS

KAREN

Have you ever wanted somebody so much it physically hurts? So much that when they come into the room, you freeze up, and you can't even talk? Jax had one hand on the tender flesh on the underside of my upper arm. He didn't just have his hand there. He was *stroking* me there with his thumb. I hadn't realized that was an erogenous zone. I was finding out now. His mouth was on my breast, too, and he had One. Patient. Talented. Mouth.

When I was nine, rubbing the insides of my forearms over the edge of the blankets in the bed I shared with my big sister, I'd thought, *That feels so good. Why?* And hadn't been able to put a name to it. Not tickling. Better than tickling. Stimulating and pleasurable, without that edge of panic you got when somebody tickled you. It had just felt *good,* and I'd wanted to keep doing it. When I was sixteen and a boy had run his hand up my side, then played with my breasts for the first time, touching and feeling his way around, I'd held my breath and thought, *Nothing can feel this good.* Like my forearms on the bed times a hundred.

Nothing I'd done in the team-sport arena *had* felt as good

as that, to be honest, for quite a while afterwards, because the men of my acquaintance had been more about the freeway than the scenic route, if you catch my drift. Straight shot to the objective, veering onto the onramp as fast as they possibly could, hurtling down the road with their foot smashing the accelerator. And somewhere along the way, I'd lost that—that breath-holding, knee-weakening, luxurious *wonder* that being touched could give you this kind of pure pleasure, so you wanted to drag your forearms across the edge of your school desk just to feel it some more. Like you wanted it never, ever to end.

It had been a while, but I still remembered. I was getting reminded now. I wanted to touch Jax, and I couldn't quite manage to do it enough, maybe because he was still holding my arm, and maybe because I was a little overwhelmed. That thing I'd thought, what? A few days ago, about how men didn't kiss for long enough, or touch you well enough? I wasn't thinking it anymore.

I said, "Jax," and he hummed and kept going.

I had one arm loose, so I grabbed his head. Then I forgot about things for a while, because he took that as an invitation to come back and kiss my neck some more, and I shuddered and did some more serious moaning. I did have to get my hands on him, though, and do some exploring of my own. His back was long and lean, and had the kind of shifting planes of muscle under his skin that let you know you were touching a man. If I'd been any doubt of that when he'd taken his clothes off. Let's just say that he hadn't needed the slice of bread to fill anything out, and that he was hard as iron all over.

I thought, *What are you doing? He's going to think you've got nothing to give, if you just lie here and whimper.* I said, "Jax. I need to . . . kiss you, too."

"Mm," he said, and sent a hand over my breast again as he sucked an earlobe into his mouth, then sent his tongue on an exploratory journey like what he wanted most of all tonight was to kiss the hell out of my ear. "Think I need to do this a little more first. You've got this line, you see." His hand drifted down my rib cage, over the four holes above and below my navel. "Been wanting to see where this goes since the first time I saw it. Time to find out. I'm going to eat you so slow. I'm going to hold you down so tight while I do it."

Oh. My. God. "Having a guy go down on you, uh . . . first," I tried to say as his mouth followed his hand, and I held onto his shoulders and tried to keep myself thinking straight, "doesn't happen."

"Shh," he said. "I'm concentrating." And he was. He kissed his slow way down between my breasts, then over my belly, swirled his tongue around each jewel-studded hole, then a couple tantalizing inches farther down, making my skin heat up some more, skipped the pertinent area altogether, slid his hands up my inner thighs, pressed them gently apart, and just . . . looked.

See, that's hardly awkward at all.

He did go slow. Boy, could the man go slow. The rain was beating on the canvas roof, like camping only so much better, the candle was flickering in its holder, and I was lying on a white bed with a man holding the backs of my thighs, letting him eat me up by excruciatingly slow degrees. When I started humming, he smiled against me, and I felt it. And when he had his fingers in there and was banging me good, and I started yelping some? He put a little more effort into it. I tightened up, and he said, "Oh, yeh." The first thing he'd said to me in what felt like an hour.

I said, "Jax." That was about the limit of my verbal abilities. "Oh, please. Please. Keep doing that. Please. Don't stop."

Not my most articulate moment ever, but he wasn't complaining. He didn't bother to answer at all, and he didn't stop.

I was making too much noise. He was going to think he was hurting me, and pretty soon, somebody was going to call the cops. I didn't care.

I didn't know how he was at preventing explosions, but the man sure knew how to cause one. I was going up in smoke. I was going up in flames. I was quite possibly going to die.

Holy *shit.*

☆☆

JAX

She didn't stop making noise for a good wee while.

She'd been loud, and then she'd been louder, and I'd loved it. There were a few feelings better than holding a woman open with your palms on the insides of her thighs and making her come so hard, her entire upper body rose from the mattress and her arms were flung out to either side, but there weren't many. They mostly involved being inside her while she was doing it, when she was squeezing you so tight that your eyes rolled back in your head, but never mind. Nothing wrong with having something to look forward to.

When her head made it back down onto the mattress, I played with her a little more, because those aftershocks could be delicious, and she shuddered and moaned and whimpered some more, so it was working. And when she was just shivering, her arms up over her head, her breath still coming hard, I climbed up the bed over her, dropping a kiss over her heart along the way, because I'd swear I could see it beating, and kissed her mouth, taking it deep, because I could. She'd be tasting herself, and I wanted her to. One more surrender.

"Jax," she said when I moved over to kiss her cheek again, because she loved having her face kissed, "you are really, really good at that."

I had to laugh. And, yeh, I was also dying for it. If I'd had a condom, I'd have been inside her five minutes ago, and it wouldn't have been gentle anymore, because I'd have lost some control. I knew that, and I also knew that I couldn't lose that control. "Good to know," I said. "Any time, eh."

Her wide mouth curved in a smile, even though her eyes were still closed, and her hands were drifting over my upper arms, over to my shoulders, down my back, like she wanted to touch me, too. The rain was so loud around us, you were practically wrapped in the storm, and things were exactly that way inside my body, too.

I thought I knew how she'd felt. I needed to come as badly as a man possibly could who hadn't had sex for too many long, lonely, painful months, and who suddenly had exactly the right beautiful, naked woman stretched out beneath him, but I didn't just need to do it. I needed it good, and I needed it to last. Quick and dirty wasn't enough for me, not tonight, and Karen wasn't a patient woman.

I thought about how to say it, then thought, *Nah, mate. You'll put her straight off, if you start giving instructions right off the bat. She doesn't have much confidence right now. She trusted you. Trust her to get you there, too. You can work on the "how" of it next time, give her all the lessons you want to.*

You'll notice the one thing I wasn't thinking about, at least not explicitly. My scars. My leg. How I felt about her touching all of that, about looking at it up close.

Which was when the candle went out.

Karen said, "Oh!" And then, "Well, that was unexpected." She got her hand on my face—actually, on my nose—laughed a little, a lovely soft sound, and said, "Maybe a sign. Want to roll over on your back and let me feel my way? I've got so much work to do, and I need to get started pretty desperately."

Yes, my heart may have thudded a few extra times at that. I said, "I need light. I want to watch." I did, but that wasn't all. I needed to *see*. The look on her face when she reached the broken parts of me. I needed to know. That was why I rolled off her, felt around for the box of matches and lit one, then followed it over to the lantern on the other side of the bed and lit that, since my candle was burnt down.

I was on my knees when the light flared up and I closed the lantern, and still on them when I turned around to look at Karen. She was sitting up, then scrambling to her own knees to face me, not thinking about covering herself, the skin of her chest and neck still rosy from the strength of that orgasm, her whiskey eyes warm and not quite sleepy. As I watched, she smiled at me with all the slow, sweet happiness in the world and said, "My turn. And you're so beautiful. I need to kiss you so much." She wrapped her arms around me, pressed closer, and did it. She wasn't shy, either. Her hand was on my arse, then stroking up to the base of my tailbone, and her other one was at the back of my neck.

Kissing her like that, looking at her in the lamplight, was like standing in front of a statue and seeing two lovers kissing in stone, their passion and their tenderness caught forever by the brilliance of the artist. Like when you looked at something like that in the midst of a bare room in the echoing space of some museum, and you thought, *I want that.* That was the way she was holding me now. Sinking down with me, her hands on either side of my face, then smoothing back my hair. She moved so she had a leg over me, propped herself on her elbows, kissed the center of my forehead, where my most visible scar began, and said, "If you don't want me to touch something, if it hurts, or if you just don't want it, tell me so."

I said, "All right." It was the only thing I could manage.

She smiled, and I felt it. She kissed her way gently down that scar, then over to the other one, as her other hand stroked over my shoulder, my arm, and she said, between butterfly touches of her lips, "The first time I saw you, I thought you were so beautiful, I was scared to look. I thought you'd see how I felt."

Something in my chest was twisting tight. I swallowed and closed my eyes, and I think she saw it, because she was kissing me there, first one eyelid, then the other. "And now I get to look all I want," she said, when her mouth had moved to my ear, was lingering there. "I get to touch you, and kiss you, and make you glad I'm here."

"I'm already . . ." I had to clear my throat. "Glad you're here."

"Mm." She'd regained all the confidence she'd lacked when she came in here, I thought fuzzily. Maybe I'd done that. Then I forgot to think, because she was tracing the web of scars on my chest with fingers and lips, and I was winding up tighter. Touching sensitive scar tissue didn't always feel good, but this did, because it was light, and it was . . . loving. Like she wanted to be there.

Oh, my God. Her lips had moved to my neck, then to my nipple, and she was biting it gently, then sucking hard, and I wasn't worried anymore that I'd lose my erection. I was worried that I was going to come before she even got there. Like right now. I had my hands in her hair already, and I wanted to shove her down my body fast, so at least she'd be there when it happened. Marginally less humiliating. I forced myself to hold still instead, tried to say the times tables backward like I was seventeen years old, and couldn't do it. She was rubbing her entire face over my rib cage, down to my belly, and it was making me shudder, but she wasn't going where I'd expected. Instead, her hands were on my thighs, the same way I'd done with her.

Wait. Not down my legs. Not . . . She'd reached my knees, and I was tensing.

It wasn't that nobody else had touched the stump. Every nurse had, and every therapist. I got a massage every day I could, and my left leg was what they worked on most, because it helped with the phantom pain that still plagued me most nights, and with the sensitivity of the scars down there. I massaged it myself, every night before bed.

Nobody had kissed it, though. Nobody had traced her fingers over it like she wanted to feel every stitch and said, "Jax. You're so gorgeous."

My eyes were still closed, and now, to my horror, my throat was closing up.

No. Stop. I couldn't cry.

I hadn't cried yet. Not when I'd known they'd taken my leg. Not when it had hurt the worst. Not when I'd seen the first person look away in revulsion. I *couldn't* do it now, at the worst possible time.

My body wasn't listening. The heat was rising in my chest, up my throat, and the pressure was building behind my eyes.

The sob ripped out of me like a wound opening, and more of them followed. I couldn't stand it. I couldn't do this. I had my hands over my eyes, and I couldn't hold back the tears. It was horrible, but it was happening anyway, and I couldn't *stop*.

Karen was up my body again, somehow, lying over me, her hands around my head, kissing my fingers, because she couldn't get to my face. "Shh," she said. "Jax. It's OK. It's OK."

I was scaring her. I was disgusting her. I needed to stop, and I couldn't. I cried for every time I hadn't, or that was how it felt. I sobbed, my chest heaving the emotion out of my body, until there were no tears left, and Karen got on her knees over me, stroked her hands over my shoulders and chest, kissed me some more there, and didn't say anything.

When I was done, I still didn't want to move my hands. How could I show her that? It was so much worse than my leg. My leg was a wound. This was weakness. No woman wanted to see weakness.

She got off me, I knew I'd been right, and my heart dropped until the pain and shame fell all the way into my belly.

I'd hear her leave, next. Wanting to leave me alone, she'd say. Wanting to get out, I'd know.

I didn't hear the raspy zip of the tent opening. I felt her coming over me again instead, and the press of rough fabric against my hands.

"Come on," she said. "Jax. Let me help you clean up. Let me see."

I took the towel from her, wiped myself up as best I could, and said, "Thanks," in a voice like a rusty hinge. I could manage that, anyway. After that, I needed to open my eyes.

It was one of the hardest things I'd ever done. I didn't want to see what I knew I would. I couldn't stand to see her pity.

I didn't see her expression at all, in fact, because she was too close for that. Kissing my mouth, her fingers threading through my short hair, her mouth gentle at first, then not so much, her tongue venturing out and exploring me.

I'd been right all along. I'd totally lost my erection. It didn't seem to work with crying. Surprise. Fortunately, she wasn't looking, and she didn't seem to care. Instead, she was kissing me like she didn't want to stop, and I had my hand around her own head, my other arm around her, and was kissing her back. I rolled her over, and an exultant wave of something washed through me. I couldn't have named it, except that I felt like the fella in that statue. Holding her so tight. Kissing her so deep. Wanting her so bad.

She said, when I came up for breath at last, "I want you inside me so much right now, I feel like I'll die if you don't do it." Because, yes, I was nearly ready to go again, just from that kiss.

"We can't," I said, and stroked a hand down her cheek. "I'd tell you I'm all good, but it's a bad idea for you to believe me. A bloke who hasn't had sex in this long isn't going to tell the truth, and I'm not even asking about birth control."

All of her heart was in her smile. "And you don't have any honor. Yeah, I'm believing that. Never mind. Lie down, then, and let me love you right. That's what you did for me, and I want to do it for you, too."

I did. And she did. And if I'd thought it would be over too soon, I'd been wrong, because she was over my body like it was everything she needed, and like all she wanted in the world was to make me know it.

"You're beautiful here, too," she was saying at last, stroking a hand over the length of me, then starting to kiss her way up. "Pictures don't lie after all. Come on. Hold my head. Move my hands. Show me what you want. Tell me what feels good. All I want right now is to give it to you."

Oh, God. I did, and bloody hell, but she did, too. And finally, after a long, long time, when I was staring up at the light flickering over the golden roof of the tent, starting to call out, beginning to groan in a way I couldn't help any more than I'd been able to help the tears, my chest may have tightened up again, and so did the rest of me.

I expected her to move away. Instead, she took me deeper. I held off as long as I could, and when I couldn't hold back a second longer, I emptied myself down her throat like it was the first time ever, and she swallowed me down like she loved it.

The whole thing had been the slowest, sweetest, most agonizing ride a man could take. And the finish? I wasn't sure I *could* take it. It was so good, it almost hurt.

Not the night I'd thought it would be. So much more than that. And bloody hell, what a woman.

21

☆☆

HORMONES, ETC.

KAREN

I didn't move for a minute or so afterwards. I wanted to stay down here, kissing that diagonal line of muscle down his abdomen, stroking his thighs, feeling him trying to catch his breath, the beating of his heart, like I was inside his body.

He felt like my resting spot, and what was even crazier— he felt like my forever. And I had to figure out how to be after this, so he wouldn't see.

Still no good at hooking up, then, whatever I'd told him about being his first time, and having him be mine. I *knew* that this was nothing but a brief pause for both of us, and as for our lives? Career interests, home countries, life choices, attractiveness to the opposite sex? Nope. Not even close. The only things we had in common were that we both worked hard, liked adventure sports, had wealthy relatives, and were on the rebound in the most profound possible way, everything we'd expected to be doing right now upended.

And all the same, when he'd cried, when I'd held him, and when he'd let me love him— something had happened despite all the reasons it shouldn't, and it felt major. It felt big. It felt like my heart had grown so much that my chest couldn't contain it, because it had to make room for him. And it terrified me.

This wasn't just being bad at hookups. I'd fallen straight over the edge.

Infatuation, my science brain tried to explain, as I moved up the bed at last and he wrapped his arms around me, rolled me over, and kissed me so deeply and so possessively, I was having trouble with my self-control. I could feel the stump of his leg against my calf, my thumb was brushing over the scar at the side of his face, and he wasn't trying to hide either one.

Norepinephrine levels. Dopamine levels. Testosterone levels. Hormones. That was why I couldn't look at him long enough, why I couldn't hold him close enough, why just hearing his voice made my knees go weak. But it didn't *feel* like hormones, or not only like hormones. It felt real, because it wasn't just his body I craved. It was him.

There was probably a reason for that, too. No doubt he embodied something I felt was missing in myself right now, certainty or fortitude or something like that. Or call it what it was. Mana, that most Kiwi of qualities. Honor. Dignity. Courage. The way you walked through the very worst things, and the way you put a hand out so the people around you could walk, too.

He waka eke noa, Koro would have said. A canoe we are all in with no exception, paddling or sinking together. That said everything about Jax: Why he'd been so unhappy being a star, and why his world had shifted into place when he'd realized his mission in it was to save people. It was also why he took my breath away, because that feeling wasn't just his gray eyes or the perfection of his features.

I couldn't look at that any more right now, which was why I kissed him back instead of indulging in further examination of my vulnerable heart. I tried to do it as sweetly as he was doing to me, to tell him everything I couldn't say. How strong he was, and how kind, too, from looking after the boys at the beach to taking care of a useless accidental-passenger duck. I couldn't say what I felt, but maybe I could show him, because I suspected he was feeling as raw as I was.

He definitely hadn't gotten the no-more-need-for-kissing memo, because by the time he was done, I was melting all over again, and he had both hands around my head and was looking down at me with so much intensity that I was way too close to crying myself.

And, yes, it was more than the noble stuff. It was that I wanted absolutely everything else, too. I wanted to give up control, and I wanted him to take it. I wanted to be sassy, and I wanted him to show me why I should stop. I wanted to let go. No limits.

Whoa. Danger. He didn't need to get to know me that well. I said, "I should go back before I fall asleep. Debbie, and so forth."

His eyes searched mine, which I could have done without. "Not hungry? You haven't even finished your beer, and you probably need your tea as well. It's still raining, but we could stay here and have a picnic, and another beer, too. Could be I'd get you drunk and have my way with you again. I could keep you up half the night, and I'd like to do it."

He smiled, because it had been a joke. If I *did* have another of those high-octane beers, though, after the day we'd had, who knew what I'd actually say or do? I'd tell him I loved him. I'd ask him to do something way too freaky. If he started holding my arms again? I wasn't all that fantastic at holding back. Plus, he'd said that thing before, about how he always wanted the woman to leave. Why would he have said that if it wasn't a hint?

I was panicking, and I knew it, but I couldn't help it. I also couldn't let him see it. I rolled out of bed, searched for my shirt and PJ pants, felt way too naked, and told him, "It's hard to sleep if I'm, uh, not alone. Plus, Debbie."

He sat up, seeming completely unconcerned about his own nakedness, but then, men with that kind of body didn't exactly have to worry about showing themselves. Except for the leg and the scars, but he knew I was all good with those. He was frowning, reaching for his glasses, handing me my T-shirt, which was on the bed, then studying my clearly panic-stricken self and frowning harder. "Something wrong?" he asked. "And—wait. You said you'd been engaged until recently. How would you not be able to sleep with somebody else? Did I do something you didn't like? Did I not do something you wanted? Don't bloody run away, and don't lie to me. Tell me."

Oh, God. He might be brave. I wasn't. Not brave enough for this, anyway. How did you say, *I just realized I'm flat-out in love with you, and I want to tell you all my secrets and hear all of yours and escape into a world that's just me and you, and because you're kind, I realize you will now say something gentle?* You didn't. I said instead, "My arm hurts, that's all." Which it did, but judging by the expression on his face, he wasn't buying it.

Wait. He thought it was him. What did I do now? I couldn't run away and leave him thinking that. I sat down beside him, leaned in and kissed his mouth, ran my fingers down his scar, and said, "It was great. I loved being with you. I loved everything we did. You're . . . you were amazing." Too many *L*-words. Too many words, period. Time to wrap it up. "I just need to go to bed."

I stood up again, found my pants under the bed, to my relief, and put them on, and then my shirt. He didn't pull me down by it the way I half-wished he would, right onto my back, or do any alpha-male-ing at all. Instead, he said, "Right. D'you have a torch to get back?" Which was a little alpha-male all by itself, actually, in the same sort of way Hemi did with his family. That competent thing. I was kind of a sucker for that, and I'd never had it, at least not a man doing it for just me. I'd been more competent than Josh, the one fixing the sink when it dripped, the one who knew how to change a tire, because Koro had taught me, and so had Hemi, since Kiwi men were the definition of "competent." It wasn't that I *didn't* want to be competent myself, it was just . . .

I was tying myself up in knots again. *This* was why you didn't have revenge sex, or breakup sex, or however you wanted to think of it. The person you'd broken up with wouldn't care, and you already had too many hormones and too many emotions happening. No need to heap on more.

Right. Flashlight. "No," I said. "I didn't think of it." That would be a great look, my getting lost in the rainy New Zealand bush, blundering around in the dark in circles until I came back soaked and weeping. If I wanted to look any more pathetic, that is. The alternative, though, was staying here, and I was getting short of breath at the thought.

He opened the drawer of the bedside table and handed me a head lamp on a neoprene band. I looked at it and said, "I'm not even going to comment about this."

He smiled. "Yeh. You keep on trying." After that, he stood up on one foot, kissed my mouth softly, touched my face, and said, "Sleep well. See you in the morning."

This was either the absolutely wrong thing to do, or the absolutely right one. All I knew was, I had to do it. So I left.

⭐☆

JAX

It was a hard night, and a hard awakening, too.

When I first heard the voice, I thought it was part of a dream. An anxious one, where I'd been running with my squad, dressed in full battle kit, the sweat on our faces gritty with dust. Dirt in my mouth, my nostrils, my eyes. Running hard, my weapon held in both hands, scanning the horizon and then the foreground for an enemy who could ambush us at any time, my body ready to react the instant it happened.

"Jax," the voice said. Alarm in it, urgency, and I bolted out of bed to answer.

The next second, I was toppling, and the second after that, I was hitting the bedside table a crack with my forearm and ribs, and then I was on the wooden floor, landing awkwardly.

"Jax! Oh, no. I'm sorry. Jax. Are you all right?"

This time, I knew who it was. Karen, and it was light out. The birds were so noisy outside, in fact, that I didn't know how they hadn't woken me, except that I'd only fallen asleep a few hours ago.

I shoved off with my palms, turned my head, confirmed

that it was indeed Karen, that she was dressed in shorts and a T-shirt, plus a bra this time, unfortunately, and that she was tugging on my arm and looking extremely concerned. I said, "I'm fine. No worries," got to my hands and knees, hauled myself up with a hand on the bed, sat down, and tried to look as casual as a man who'd just face-planted naked out of bed could manage.

Not how I'd wanted to start this day, not when she'd run out last night like her demons had been chasing her, and I hadn't been able to sort out why. Had I been too needy, with the crying and all, or on the flip side, too demanding? I hadn't been as demanding as I'd wanted to be. I hadn't wanted to scare her, and besides, I'd needed to be tender. It was her first time since whoever, and I'd needed to be careful. I *had* been careful.

Or was it nothing to do with me? Why had she seemed so . . . scared? I didn't have a clue. She was the last woman I'd have expected to play mind games, and I still couldn't believe she had. What was there to be scared of, though?

I'd spent some time trying to be narky about that, then told myself for another thirty minutes or so that it was fine, because we both had too much baggage and lived too far apart to get any more involved. After that, I'd made myself harden up, massaged my leg, and blown out the candle. After which I may or may not have lain on my back in the dark, listened to the rain, and revisited all the things we'd done, decided I was stopping to buy condoms in the morning no matter what, told myself that was stupid unless I was looking to complicate my life, and knew I'd do it anyway, because bloody *hell*, but I wanted to be inside that woman. My body didn't care that she wasn't ready for this. It just wanted her underneath me.

Yeh, I did some thinking about that. It was heaps more entertaining than worrying about questions to which I had no answers, and you could say it took my mind pretty smartly off the leg.

Right now, I pretended I hadn't imagined myself doing very dirty things to her, like a man who'd never heard the word "vulnerable," and said, "It's morning, eh. I overslept."

Her cheeks were flushed, I noticed, and so was her neck, which was odd. She sat down beside me and said, "I think I have a problem. But first—are you sure you're all right? Your ribs?"

"No worries," I said. "Assume I've fallen before. What sort of problem?"

She held up her arm to show me, because she'd taken off the bandage.

Oh. Yeh, that was a problem. The wound hadn't been looking too flash before, and now, it looked worse. The entire underside of her forearm was red and swollen, the scrapes looked angrier than ever, and most ominously of all, a red line like the tail of a tadpole had snaked its way from the worst scrape up and over her bicep, all the way to a few centimeters from her underarm and the lymph nodes there, where the infection could enter her bloodstream. That had happened fast, and it wasn't good. Bacteria in the water yesterday, maybe, taking advantage of all that open wound.

"Ah," I said. "Yes, you do." I touched the swollen area gently. It was hot, like you'd imagine, and when I put the back of my hand against her cheek, it was warm to the touch, too. "Hurts, eh. Feeling crook as well?"

"A little," she said, which I was guessing meant, "a lot." She went on, "This weakness thing's pretty awkward. Me being weak like this, I mean, given that I didn't do too great last night, either. We have to check out today, but maybe we could stop at a clinic on our way to the next place."

I thought about what to say. It wasn't easy. "First," I said, "you did brilliantly last night, other than the running-out bit. Best night I've had in a long time, at least the first part of it was. Also, I should probably remind you that you weren't the one who cried."

She looked away, and I picked up her hand and held it tight. It was warm, too, and surely it was trembling a little. "I got a little freaked out," she finally said, which was no news at all and told me exactly nothing. "Could we just . . . not talk about that right now?"

"Yeh," I said. "We could." I wanted to hold her tighter, but if I did, I had a feeling she'd run, so I settled for keeping hold of her hand.

"I packed my things already," she said. "I'd have loaded them into the car, but I'd probably have created a disturbance in the Force with that kind of unplanned behavior. Plus I didn't have the key. And by the way? Could you be a little more confident in your nudity, please? You're sitting here holding my hand like we're on a park bench."

I laughed. "Saucy to the end, eh. I reckon you're not dying quite yet. But—yeh. Let's get packed up and get you to a doctor before that gets any worse. I didn't come all the way from Dunedin to hang about in a hospital waiting room."

She wanted to be casual? I could be casual. I might be feeling the last thing from casual, but that didn't mean I had to fall in love.

I could still take care of her, though, and I was going to do it.

22

☆☆

AN ATTRACTIVE LIFE PARTNER

KAREN

A couple hours later, I'd had breakfast, which I'd mostly pushed around, given that I was shivering with fever and trying to hide it, and had drunk two coffees that hadn't helped as much as I'd hoped. After that, once the clinic had opened, a doctor had cleaned the wounds and rebandaged my arm, which had hurt. A lot. I'd listened to her talking about sepsis and warning signs and hospitals in more or less of a haze, and then had listened to her repeating it to Jax, because she'd noticed the haze and called him in.

Now, I was back in the car, and Jax was opening the door. He'd installed me here to wait for him while he got my medicines from the pharmacy next door, not listening one bit to my assurance that I was fine. I'd have been mad about that, but to tell the truth, sitting down felt better.

Debbie got all excited from the back seat at Jax's arrival, giving a raspy quack of welcome like a duck who was growing older by the day and getting his big-boy voice, and Jax handed me a box of antibiotic tablets, another one of Panadol, and a new water bottle, and said, "Take two now, then one with every meal. Do a couple Panadol now for the fever as well.

Get all that down you."

"Geez, you're bossy," I managed to tell him when he'd climbed in on his side, and then had reached across and opened the packets for me like I was helpless, just because I was fumbling a little.

"Yeh, I am. Get used to it." He sat with his hands on the steering wheel and frowned ahead of him at nothing, and I leaned back against the door, thought how beautiful he was, and considered going to sleep.

"The question is," he said, "where to take you."

"We're going to the next place," I said. "Camping near Rotorua." I'd looked forward to it. Rotorua was second only to Queenstown as an adrenaline-sports hub. Too bad that my adrenaline had vanished overnight, along with my dopamine and so forth.

"We're not camping," he said.

I sighed. "Glamping. I get the difference. Real beds, and no digging holes required. Also, you're being awfully authoritative for somebody who's had sex—*oral* sex—with me exactly one time."

He smiled. Still hot, unfortunately. Then he leaned across the car, kissed my mouth gently and so sweetly, looked into my eyes, and told me, "Like I said. Get used to it. We're not camping *or* glamping. Tell me whether you'd rather go home to your place, where I'm planning to stay with you, so you know, or go home to my place, where I can look after you better. More shops, eh. Closer hospital, too."

"I'll be better tomorrow," I said. "I want to go do what we came to do. Go . . . wherever that was. I can't remember. I'm a little fuzzy today, that's all. And tell me you haven't marched, or crawled under barbed wire in the mud, or fought bad guys or whatever heroic thing, when *you* had a little fever."

He was frowning again. The man looked so good frowning. He also had his hand on my face again, and I wanted to lean my cheek into it. "The doctor said, 'Watch for sepsis.' I heard her. We're not out in the bush with no electric. We're watching for sepsis, or rather, I'm watching *you* for sepsis."

I sighed. "And here I was hoping for sexy possessiveness. Dominance. Possibly a little bondage. Exerting your power by watching me for sepsis and making me drink orange juice isn't what I had in mind. This is my *vacation.*"

Whoops. Yes, I'd said it. Oh, well. Blame the fever. I really did not feel great. At least I hadn't told him I was in love with him.

His mouth opened, then closed, and he started the car and said, "Right. Option C."

"Which is what?"

"I take you to my place, where I can put you to bed and look after you and where the hospital's twenty minutes away, and if you do feel better tomorrow, we can go have an adventure. A very *mild* adventure. And indulge in some sexy possessiveness once I'm sure you're better. Dominance. Possibly a little bondage." He was about to pull out into the road when he stopped, turned to me, and said, "Wait. It's me doing this dominance-and-bondage bit, right?"

"Well, *yes,*" I said. *"Obviously.* Who was getting her legs held down last night? *I* wasn't the one doing that."

He'd looked fairly worried before, or as worried as a calm, competent guy could get. Now, he smiled, looking satisfied and not quite so sweet. "Good to know. I reckon I'd better take you home and get you well, then. If you need me to stop for a coffee or a snack, let me know. You didn't eat your breakfast."

"You have *major* control issues," I told him.

"Too late," he said, pulling out into traffic. "You already told me that's your weakness. Protest all you want, but we're doing this my way."

It only took an hour and a half to get to Katikati. I knew that, even though it seemed like six hours. One of those uncomfortable rides that got worse as you went along, despite Jax's butter-soft leather seats with their superior Lexus ergonomics. The kind of trip where you keep thinking, *This can be over any time now, OK?* Jax would look over at me occasionally and ask, "All right?" And I'd say, "Fine," because what was the alternative? This was a tiny bit of sickness. It wasn't any big deal, and never mind that all I wanted was to lie down. And possibly throw up.

When we pulled into Koro's drive, I said, "What if he doesn't want Debbie? I should've asked. I need to . . ." My teeth were chattering, and I was getting lightheaded from the sun, both of which were really annoying.

Jax leaned over, kissed my cheek, then put the back of his hand on it, frowned, and said, "No worries. I've got it." Which *sounded* good. Face it, it sounded perfect. Those were five pretty good words. It was lucky I wasn't a big believer.

Koro must have been sitting outside again, maybe ever since my text from Thames, because I'd barely closed my eyes again before I heard his voice saying, "Karen? What's happened?"

I was going to get out, but as soon as I started, the motion, and the nausea from the winding rural roads, kicked in all the way. I had the door half open and my seatbelt still half on, and I was leaning over and throwing up my coffee into Koro's driveway. See: How to Present as an Attractive Life Partner, Day 1. Fortunately, I hadn't eaten my breakfast, I wasn't auditioning as a life partner, and Jax was on the other side of the car.

Except that he wasn't. He was crouching down beside me halfway through the wreckage of my image, holding my head, and asking, "Karen? All right?"

I nodded, which was the wrong move, because it meant I was heaving again. Nothing to come up anymore, which at least meant I wasn't doing it on his shoes. "Fine," I managed to say, and he laughed. Gently, but still.

"Hey," I said, sitting up again and wiping the back of my mouth like the classy, mysterious seductress I most definitely was not, "that's what *you'd* say."

"Probably. Want me to take you into the house for a rest before we go any farther?" He was still right there, and beyond him, I could see Koro's legs in his baggy tan pants. Great.

"No." I just wanted to go *home*. And not have anybody fuss over me. I wanted that a whole lot. "What about Debbie?"

KIWI RULES

"I'm telling him about Debbie." He turned away at last, and I sat back and closed my eyes and heard him tell Koro, "I could bring your chair over if you like, sir, or we could talk over there."

My heart squeezed. Physically, I swear. I'd just been *thinking* that Koro should sit down. I wished Jax would stop being so perfect. I wished I'd stop being so weak. I was about to cry, and I didn't cry. Even when I'd been on that sloping bathroom floor, I hadn't cried.

They moved off, and after a minute, Jax came back and said, "I'm going to leave Debbie here with a bit of fencing, then do something more permanent for him once I've got you put to bed. And before you object to that—your grandfather told me to do it, too. You need a bed. And blankets."

"Who knew he was such a . . . traitor? I feel much better. Carsick, that's all. I'll go home instead, I've decided." I was still shivery and felt really, really crappy, but that would pass as soon as the antibiotics kicked in. "I *will* go in and rest a . . . few minutes, and then I'll be all good to drive myself. If you don't mind putting my . . . stuff in my car for me."

"No," he said. Absolutely calmly.

"I just threw up on you," I said, wishing he wasn't so tall, and that the sun wasn't right behind him. "You don't want that to . . . happen again. I'm fine. No big deal. I lie down, the antibiotics work, and I'm all good in the morning."

I didn't want to tell him the real thing. That I hated being sick more than anything in the world. More than being injured, by far. I knew that, because I'd broken a leg snowboarding once, and there was no contest. I didn't mind pain. I could handle pain. I hated throwing up and staggering around and feeling weak, though, especially in front of other people. Especially in front of a man. He didn't want to hear my life story, though, which was wonderful, because I didn't want to tell him. That wasn't what we were doing here.

He crouched down like he'd heard my wish/thought about standing up and the sun, took my hand, and said again, "No. *Because* you just threw up on me. What kind of new boyfriend would I be if I ran off on you now?"

185

"First," I said, closing my eyes, because it was easier, "a normal one. Second—is that what you are?"

His other hand was stroking over my hair. Not too much. Gently, the way Hope had always done. "Oh, yeh," he said. "And your boyfriend standards are seriously lacking for somebody who was engaged. Just saying."

"If you think men take care of . . . women that way," I told him, "you're living in . . . Dream World." Other than Hemi, but Hemi and Hope had a Great Love, because she was tiny and blonde and feminine and had big blue eyes and so forth, so forget that.

Was I grumpy? Yes, I was. As soon as he started driving down the hill and around the curves again, I was going to get nauseated again, too. I was already starting. He was also too close to my face, and I'd just thrown up. I concentrated on breathing shallowly and wished he'd stand up again, sun and all. "Save yourself," I told him. "Get out now."

"Makes me wonder," he said in a thoughtful sort of way, still holding my hand and not moving out of the danger zone, "what kind of wanker you chose. Could make me wonder what kind of wanker *I* am, too, but then—you didn't choose me so much as I chose you. I didn't give your bad taste a chance to operate, maybe. Snapped you up fast, didn't I."

"You did not . . . choose me."

"Can't hear you," he said, opening the back door. "Too noisy, with the duck and all. I'm leaving the fencing here, on second thought. Your cousin can get it sorted. He looked like a capable fella. Drink the rest of your water. All of it. I'll get you a plastic bag for the drive."

JAX

I'd joked because she'd needed me to, but bloody hell, she was burning up, and her chills were so bad, her teeth were chattering. She'd expected me to leave her like that? That bloke must have been a prince. But then, I already knew that from the night before. You could tell a lot about a woman by how surprised she was when you took care of her in bed.

She didn't say anything for the next twenty-five minutes, including about my speed, which was another sign of her state of mind, because Karen had been born to say, "You're going to get a ticket if you keep going that fast." A woman with no filter, except right now, because she'd shut right down on the sharing. No filter until she got ill, then, which was interesting. She did retch into her bag a couple times, though, and when I made a right turn instead of a left in Tauranga, she revived enough to say, "Wrong way."

Giving me directions. Surprise. Brain still operating, then.

"Yeh, thanks," I said, making another right, "but I know where I'm going."

I pulled up to the Emergency Department of the hospital, and she sat up and said, "No."

I didn't listen to that, either. I'd gone into binary mode, yes/no, next-thing. I jumped out of the car, came around fast, hauled her out of her side, and asked, "Can you walk?"

"I'm *fine,*" she said, wrenching out of my grasp. "Take me home." Her face twisted, and I thought she was going to cry, but instead, she said, her voice shaking and furious, "I don't need this. I need to go *home.* I'm fine." She groped for the car door, but the Lexus had done its thing, and the handles were recessed again. She did start to cry now. Angry tears, and I didn't care. Within two seconds, I'd picked her up and was heading for the entrance. "Jax," she said, doing her best to get free, like that was happening, "put me down. Your leg. You can't carry me. I'm saying a . . . safe word. Put me *down.*"

"Interesting," I said. "But not applicable. And I clearly *can* carry you. You're under my load limit, apparently." The doors opened with a *whoosh,* the air con settled over my skin like a chilled blanket, and Karen started shivering harder.

"Sepsis, I think," I told the woman behind the desk. "She's just started antibiotics, seen up at Thames this morning for a skin infection, and the doc up there warned us about this. Took the first tablets about two hours ago, but her fever's spiked pretty high, so has her pulse, she's got chills, she's vomiting, and she's irrational." I lowered Karen to the floor but kept my arm around her, lifted the sleeve of her T-shirt gently up, and showed the woman her arm. The swollen red flesh had extended past the bandage, and the pink line had broadened and snaked farther up. I couldn't see how far, but I was willing to bet it was all the way to the lymph node.

"I am not irrational," Karen said. After which she tried to bolt for the door. Fortunately, she wasn't moving very fast.

I grabbed her, wrapped both arms around her from behind, one around her chest and the other around her waist, and told the nurse, "She's irrational. Get her in there."

23

IF THE PIECES FIT

KAREN

So that was boring.

The ER, blah, blah, lots of people, IV, blood draw, throw up some more, then do it again, while Jax sat and watched and I wished he wasn't seeing this. By the time they were moving me into another bed, which felt really bad, and rolling down the corridor with me, I was even fuzzier. All I wanted was to be in a nice, big, comfortable bed with lots of fluffy pillows, and hospital beds aren't anything close. I was supposed to be at Jax's, looking out at the protective green slope of Mauao, maybe lying out on a chaise under a blanket in the warm sea breeze with the hiss and roar of the surf settling into my bones, not rolling down a freezing white hospital corridor getting seasick.

I watched Jax, because I needed to look at something good. He was coming along behind us, and when he caught my eye, he gave me a half-smile, like, "Yeah. Sucks. Soon be over." I could almost hear him saying it. That was nice. I'd just close my eyes, even though people were swinging me around and taking me through another door now, which was making me sick again. I had a line into the back of my hand

and a tube for oxygen in my nose, the pillowcase was way too scratchy, the pillow was thin and made of foam, and I didn't belong here. My arm hurt, that was all. I had an infection, and I had pills. I'd just . . . tell them so. In a . . . minute.

When I woke up, the room was dim, but the acoustic tiles overhead and the blinking IV tower beside me spelled "hospital" all the way. Worse than the broken leg. I hadn't had to stay overnight with the leg.

I didn't want to be here. Not at night. It was like I was going backwards, like everywhere I'd thought I'd got in the past fifteen years had been an illusion. I hadn't stayed overnight since . . .

I forced the panic down and turned my head, and Jax was there, sitting in an easy chair, his shoes off and his ankles crossed on my bed, reading a book. I had a roommate, it seemed. Sort of. I was the only one in here. No other bed. Why?

"Hey," he said, setting the book in his lap. "How ya goin'?"

"Oh, you know," I said, wishing my mind was working better and wondering what they'd given me, "hospitals. You must hate them too. Why are you here? Am I on . . . pain meds? I hate pain meds. Why is the room so big?" He was sort of advancing and retreating, and it was making my head spin, so I closed my eyes.

"A bit," he said. "On the meds. You're in the ICU. You're responding well, though, maybe because I got you here fast despite your serious lack of cooperation. You could be out tomorrow, possibly the next day. Only if you behave yourself, of course, and you so rarely *do* behave yourself, so . . ."

I tried to glare at him. I couldn't quite control my face, unfortunately. "I'm asking them for a . . . toothbrush. I threw up. A lot. So disgusting."

"Yeh," he said. "Never seen anything like it, have I. Sight of my leg the first time, looking like a chewed piece of meat on the bone?" He waved a hand. "Piece of cake compared to the sight of you spewing coffee. Practically had to use the basin myself."

"Not a . . . contest. I'm a woman. I'd kind of like to be . . . glamorous just once around you. Or . . . normal."

"Think I got that you're a woman," he said. "Can't remember how I discovered that, but it feels like something I know."

"Ha ha." A weak rejoinder, but it was what I had.

I did feel a little better when I'd brushed my teeth, even though it was hard and made my head swim. The nurse's aide who helped me do it was Kiwi-cheerful, which was great, since I hated fussing. Was I excited about exposing my half-naked back to Jax? No, but if it was a choice of "naked back" or "spit out toothpaste while he watched," I was going with "naked back."

"Wait," I said, once she'd left again. Jax had his feet on the floor now and wasn't reading his book. I couldn't tell what it was, but it was thick. What did he read? Spy stories? True crime? *Guns & Ammo?* "How come the whole whanau isn't here? Why don't I have many . . . annoying balloons?"

"Mm. Good question. Maybe I thought I'd let you wake up and decide who you wanted to tell, as they told me you weren't actually dying. You have an issue with weakness, I've noticed. Could be you don't like to worry people."

"That's oddly sensitive. And also cold-blooded. Huh." Talking was tiring, which was annoying again. I breathed in some more oxygen through my nose, closed my eyes, and took a little rest.

When I opened them again, I asked, "Where were we?"

"That I'm cold-blooded. You get what you get. Soldier, eh." He leaned over and kissed my cheek, and I was extremely glad I'd brushed my teeth. "But thanks for not dying."

"You carried me in. I remember that. Thanks, I guess. I hope your leg's OK."

This time, he laughed. "Don't get all sentimental on me. I could think I'm with the wrong woman."

I'd started getting that prickly feeling. I knew that feeling. My blood pressure was dropping. I was going to have to stop talking, or I'd throw up again. "You can leave. I'm fine. You're not comfortable. I need to sleep."

"It's a recliner. I've had base housing less comfortable than this chair. I'll go get some dinner in a bit, though, and get whatever you want as well, if the hospital's food isn't up to standard. What d'you fancy?"

It couldn't be time for dinner. I didn't care. I couldn't think about food. I closed my eyes again, heard him saying something, and sort of . . . waved it away.

Pain meds. I hated pain meds.

☆☆

JAX

I rubbed my hands over the legs of my shorts and thought about how she was going to feel when she found out the truth about who I'd told. Then I thought about how *I'd* felt when they'd been getting her hooked up to an IV, starting to pump antibiotics into her, and transferring her fast to the ICU. I'd followed behind the rolling bed with the bag of her belongings, and she'd lain there with her eyes closed, purple shadows like bruises under them, and her face nearly the color of the pillowcase, then opened them and looked at me, maybe focusing and maybe not, and I'd thought, *No. No.* After that, I'd watched the nurses come and go, checking on her, had seen her wake up halfway and then fall asleep again, and had tried not to think about how quickly she'd got worse, and how scared I'd been when I'd picked her up out in the carpark.

Not scared that I couldn't carry her. I'd known I'd carry her. Scared that I was too late.

Second-guessing was good for nothing, and "what-ifs" got you nowhere. And still, I wondered why I hadn't stopped and checked her temperature before I'd got to her grandfather's, and why I hadn't moved faster once I *had* checked it.

Eventually, I picked up my book again, since there was nothing else to do except listen to the thoughts in my head. I could've gone to get something to eat, but I couldn't tell how she really was, and I wasn't leaving like that.

It was only about forty-five minutes before she woke up again. It felt longer.

"Hey." This time, she'd turned her head, seen me, and smiled. That was good, or it was bad. She seemed different, but the nurse had told me during her last check that everything was going well.

My leg had been so much simpler. It had been right there, or rather—it hadn't. In any case, my wounds had been on the outside, or they'd felt like it. I hadn't worried that I was going to die. I'd been focusing on not wishing I was dead.

Also, I was discovering that it was worse when it was somebody else. Somebody who mattered.

I put the book down. "Hey."

"What are you reading?" Her voice was still a little slurred, but stronger.

I held it up. "Sci-Fi. Near-future. Pretty good."

"Seriously? That's what you read?"

"Sometimes. Imagination's a beautiful thing." She definitely sounded better. "How about you?"

She smiled some more. Drowsily, but I'd take it. "Not too much. Mostly . . . research now. Or up until now. I guess I don't need to read research now. That sucks, you know? I have so many things in my head. So much information, and so many ideas. I guess I should let them go."

I tried to think of something to say to that, but I couldn't. I knew how it felt to lose your purpose.

There was a tear at the corner of her eye, and as I watched, it rolled down her cheek. It wasn't followed up by any more. She said, "I used to read fantasy. Dragons, wise wizards, young people with powers they didn't know they had. That was my favorite, especially if the young person was a girl. Sci-fi, too, and romance. I like science. And imagination. And unrealistic scenarios, obviously. What time is it?"

"Six-thirty. Thereabouts."

"Six-*thirty?*" She tried to sit up, then didn't. "How? I fell asleep for a minute, that's all."

"No. You didn't. You've been pretty ill. And I should probably tell you that I asked my sister to text Te Mana and let him know."

Her mouth opened, then shut. "You said you didn't."

"No. Said I thought about not doing it, but I did it anyway. I didn't have anybody's number, and that was the only way I could think of to let your family know. I haven't heard back, though."

She closed her eyes and groaned. "Hope's probably already halfway here."

"They'd have rung me first, surely, for an update. Could be he didn't see it. Time difference and all, eh. It must be midnight or thereabouts in New York now. You can text him and give him the latest, if you like." I handed over her phone, which was on the table. "Also, I have your earrings, so you know, and the ones from down below as well. The belly ones. Have I mentioned how much I like those? Hot as hell."

She gave me some side-eye, so she was clearly feeling better, even though she was fumbling with her phone, then stabbing at it awkwardly. "OK, first—if you took those out and lusted over me in some weird way in the ER, I don't want to know. Second, I need you to type this. My thumbs don't work, or maybe my eyes don't. *Something* is definitely not working."

How could she still make me laugh? "Nah. I didn't take them out, and there was no lusting, not at the time. I let the nurse do it." I reached into the bag of her belongings and pulled out the packet to show her. "Six sparkly studs, and two little barbells. I have ninety-nine faults, but necrophilia isn't one of them. You were there. You don't remember? Give me the phone. OK, we've got a message to Hope. What d'you want me to say?"

"Necrophilia is when you're *dead.*"

"Yeh, well, say it was too close for my sexual tastes. Ready to type here."

"OK. Uh . . . 'Never mind text to Hemi. I'm fine. Got a little infection that is all. I'm only here for a day. Don't tell Koro. Do not come.' Put that last part in caps. The 'Do not come.' Oh, wait, one more thing. Say, 'Tell Hemi Jax is as bossy as him and he won't even leave me alone, so it's like

194

you're both here already. I was supposed to be having a rest. I'm having one.'"

"She won't wonder who composed it, anyway. That it?"

"Yeah. Oh—say 'LYL.' That's what we always say. Love you lots. Then she knows it's me."

"Done."

"Also, if it's six-thirty, you should leave and go get dinner."

"Maybe for a bit," I said. "As you're sounding better. Want something?"

"A smoothie, if you can find one? Fruit and vegetable something. No yoghurt, and no protein powder. They'll make me sick." She sighed. "I hate that I'm saying that again. I hate that I'm asking you. I hate that you think you have to be here. I hate being sick, OK? I'm going to whine for a second. I'm hating this." Her eyes were bright again, but she didn't cry, just blinked a few times, heaved in a breath, and closed them.

I leaned over, took her hand gently, and kissed her cheek, and saw the convulsive movement of her throat. "It's OK to cry," I told her. I tried to haul the tenderness back, and then thought, *What the hell, mate. You almost lost her today. Harden up and let her know.* "It's OK to tell me, too," I said. "You think I don't want to be here. You're wrong. It's the only place I want to be."

Her mouth twisted, and she opened her eyes, and then she tried to smile. Both of those things had taken guts. "Really?"

"Really. Seems you matter to me. Not sure how that happened, but it seems it has."

"But how can I . . . how can I feel that way? Already?"

It took me a second. She hadn't asked me how *I* could. She'd asked how *she* could, and something was happening to my heart. "Dunno," I said. "Maybe sometimes, the pieces just fit."

"We don't even know if our pieces fit. We haven't tried them out yet. Also, you could have a rescue complex. Or it could be a weird rebound thing. You know, coming back to life and all that." Her hand was shaking, and I was sitting on the side of the bed now, holding both of her hands. They were cold.

"Oh," I said, "I think we know our pieces are going to fit. Maybe you have a rescue complex as well, did you think of that? Could be we match, eh." I kissed her cheek again, and her hand came up to touch my face.

She said, "For the record? I think you're amazing."

"For the record," I said, "I think you are, too."

On the way out, I asked the woman at the desk to bring her another heated blanket. I gave them my phone number, too, in case they needed me, and I took Karen's phone, in case her sister or Te Mana rang back.

I had a feeling she was dearly loved, and I didn't have to wonder why. I also had a feeling she didn't quite believe it, and I wondered why not.

24

EVIL TE MANA

JAX

Something was buzzing. A fly. I batted it away and turned in the chair.

Bzzz. Bzzz. Bzzz.

My eyes opened fast, and I was grabbing for the phone on the table and leaping out of the chair, although "leaping" was perhaps not the exact word. "Staggering" out of the chair could be more like it, but at least I hadn't fallen over. I never slept in the leg, and I was stiff as hell. I looked at the phone in my hand. It was Karen's, its case covered with cheerful red polka dots, and the screen said, *Evil Te Mana.*

The buzzing stopped and the name went away, and I checked on Karen. She hadn't stirred, but her face looked peaceful, angelic in a way her mobile features never managed while she was awake. Too angelic for my comfort, except that her blood-oxygen levels and heart rate numbers were displayed right there on the screen, ticking up and down in reassuring fashion.

The phone started buzzing again. I swore a little internally and headed out into the corridor, limping hard. The rooms here were arranged in a square around a central nurse's station, and I nodded at the fella behind the desk, then got out of disturbance-range and into the main corridor. "Hello?"

"Who's this." It wasn't a question. It was more of a bark. Ah. Evil Te Mana.

"Jackson MacGregor. Here with Karen."

"She's in hospital? Why, exactly? Who are you, and where's Poppy Cantwell?"

"Poppy's my sister." I was starting to see a familiar Poppy-pattern emerging, as in—forgot to send the text for about six hours, or more like—composed it, then forgot to hit the button. "Let me guess," I said. "You've only just heard from her. First off—Karen's in hospital in Tauranga, in the ICU with sepsis, but we caught it pretty quickly, and she's responding well to treatment and is sleeping comfortably now. Being checked on regularly, and I've been in the room as well. If you check your wife's phone, you'll find that Karen sent her a text of her own."

"Hang on." This one was more of a growl. I'd heard of Te Mana, of course. It was hard for a Kiwi to avoid hearing of him, even in Afghanistan. It seemed the reputation was deserved.

I heard his voice from a distance, sounding different. Murmuring something soothing. Ten seconds later, and the command-voice was back. "Right. I'm looking at it. Seeing that she doesn't want Hope to worry, which tells me nothing. Explain."

I laid out Karen's injury and illness in a couple sentences, and got some brooding silence in return, until he finally said, "And you're there why? Where's Poppy?"

"Still in Dunedin. Pregnant, and feeling too crook to travel, so I was deputized."

"Jackson MacGregor," Te Mana said. "*Jax* MacGregor. The model. From the MacGregor family."

Ah. Rumor had it he never forgot anything, and rumor would appear to be correct. He also didn't seem to be a member of my fan club. I was trying not to get my back up, but it wasn't easy. I said, "She was anxious not to worry her sister. Please assure your wife that she's recovering well. I'd have her tell you herself, but she's asleep." I checked my watch. Midnight. What time was it there?

"Are you sleeping with her?"

What the *hell?* I said, "Not while she's in the ICU, anyway."

"Answering wasn't optional." You'd have expected a shout. Instead, he'd got quieter. More controlled. Definitely a scary fella, but then, I was an explosives-disposal expert.

"I'll let Karen share the details," I said. "Or not. I'm looking after her, no worries."

He must have realized that he couldn't actually reach through the phone and grab me by the throat—though I'd like to see him try—because all he said was, "We'll be there in about twenty-four hours. Karen won't want to ring Hope back. Tell her to do it anyway, once she wakes up. If she's moved, or if she's discharged, ring me back."

And . . . call ended.

The woman was nearly thirty years old, and Te Mana was her brother-in-law, not her dad. What was going on here?

☆☆

KAREN

When I woke up to light outside, I felt a whole lot more like a human being. They'd turned down my pain meds, maybe, and judging by the soaking-wet sheets the aide had changed in the middle of the night, my fever had broken, too. I checked my arm. Still red around the edges of the dressing, but not as swollen, and the pink tail was gone. Yay.

Of course, the second I stirred, Jax was sitting up in his recliner, grabbing for his glasses, and saying, "All right?" The same way he'd sat up every time somebody had come in to poke at me during the night. I might as well have Hope here after all.

"Yes," I said. *"*I can't believe you stayed this whole time. I'm fine."

He smiled so sweetly that I melted some. But then, I was

weak at the moment. He said, "I'm starting to think you're getting there. Your brother-in-law rang around midnight. Evil Te Mana?" He raised a dark eyebrow at me. "Scary fella."

I pushed the button on my bed to sit up, and it didn't even make me sick. I needed a shower really, really badly, though. I stank to *myself.* I said, "I may have been a little annoyed with him when I changed his name in my contacts. Wait. You slept in your leg. Ugh, did Hemi yell at you? You have to yell back. That's the secret."

He laughed. "You *are* better. The leg? That was in case I had to run to the nurse's station and pound on the desk for help."

He said it lightly, but I looked at him more closely. The dark stubble on his jaw was that much thicker, the lines on his beautiful face carved that much deeper. "Hey," I said, and reached for his hand. "Thanks. I've probably been pretty bitchy. I'm not good at the vulnerable thing. Kind of like you."

"No worries. Although I'd just as soon put that episode, the, ah, crying bit, behind us, if you don't mind. And sorry, but Hemi said they're coming. He and your sister."

I lay back and groaned. "You're kidding. Didn't you tell him I was OK? Didn't Hope read my *message?*"

"Yes and yes—or, rather, *Hemi* read your message. And said they were coming anyway. Why is he so protective?"

"Ask me an easy question," I said. "Why is the sky blue? Why does the tide go in and out? Why does a tiger attack? Hand me my toothbrush and my water, will you? And then you should go have breakfast. Also, if they let me out of here before Hope and Hemi come? Let's hide at your place and not tell."

JAX

I'd been gone for two hours, just time enough to shower and change at home, unload the car, and grab a few groceries for when I brought Karen back. I could be thinking about what all this meant and what I was doing, but I was pretty knackered. That was my excuse, anyway. The next thing was to go back to the hospital, so I did that.

When I found her new room, thankfully well away from the ICU, there were two bouquets of flowers on the wide ledge under the window, and one yellow happy-face balloon bumping up near the ceiling. There was also a bloke standing at the monitor, reading through her chart, who looked like a TV version of a doctor. Blue scrubs, neat hair, too-handsome Maori face with just enough lines in it to show his manly compassion and concern. Which would have been fine, except that as I watched, he smiled at Karen with his extra-white teeth, then picked up her hand and sat down. In my chair. What the hell?

Both of them looked up when I came in, but the bloke didn't drop Karen's hand. He said, "Who's this?"

"I could ask the same thing," I said. "Jax MacGregor." I handed Karen her smoothie. "Blueberry, spinach, and banana, with a bit of pea protein milk, which sounds disgusting, but the girl recommended it, so there you are. No protein powder, no yoghurt."

"Hey," Karen said, sounding perky and happy. "You're back. And thanks. This is Hemi's cousin, Matiu Te Mana. Dr. Te Mana. He works here. Flaw in my plan for secrecy, I guess."

The bloke rose and shook my hand, subjecting me to some fairly intense scrutiny. Looking at my scars, probably. I'd changed to track pants in case I ended up sleeping here again tonight, but I couldn't hide my face. Or maybe he was looking for more than that, because there was something else going on. I'd swear he'd been startled to see me. What was it with the Te Mana men? The grandfather had been all right, but here was another one who seemed to think Karen was his property.

"Look," Karen told me. "I got flowers, and it's not my birthday until tomorrow. The yellow roses are from Hemi, because of course they are. He always sends me yellow roses. He doesn't have much imagination. More like 'determinedly thoughtful' and 'tick all boxes.'" And again, I thought, *what the hell?* She went on, "But the other ones are a mystery."

"Ah," I said. "Those would be from me." The biggest and brightest bouquet the hospital's gift shop had held, tulips in shades of yellow, orange, and red.

"They are?" She looked as sunny as her flowers, like she radiated life. "Well, I love them. Thanks. You also sent me the happy-face balloon, I guess, because it was tied onto the vase."

"I did. Made me smile, and I thought it might make you laugh." I still had my eye on Matiu. "How's she doing?" I asked him. "I assume that's what you're here to find out."

"Yesterday was my day off," he said, "or I'd have known she was here and checked sooner. Hemi rang and told me this morning, though. And she's doing quite well. Infection's being controlled, and her vitals are looking much better. Everything responding as you'd hope."

"When do I get my IV out?" Karen asked. "I need a shower."

"Patience, grasshopper," Matiu said. "We're meant to heal you, you know. Give us a chance."

"I didn't want to come at all," Karen said. "Jax carried me in. Not because I couldn't walk, either. He looks easygoing, but it's an act. He was just supposed to be my tour guide."

"Lucky he did," Matiu said. "Your tour guide, eh. That explains it, then." He bent down, gave Karen a kiss on the cheek that lasted too long for my comfort, laid a hand on her face, said, "See you tomorrow at the hangi, as I'm guessing you'll be released this afternoon. Good that I'll be there to make sure you don't do any wild dancing, I reckon. Maybe just the slow stuff, with somebody strong holding you up. Will you need a lift?"

"No, thanks," she said. "Jax is bringing me."

"Ah." Matiu subjected me to some more penetrating assessment. "Back to work for me, but I'll be checking on your progress. See ya."

When he was gone, I didn't sit down. Instead, I leaned against the wall, folded my arms, and looked at Karen.

"What?" she said, but her gaze slid away. "Thanks for the

flowers. The balloon's awesome."

"Three options," I said. "One, you don't know what you're doing. Impossible. Two, you don't know that he fancies you, but you're hoping to make him. Three, you *do* know, and you're enjoying playing me off against him. I think it's three."

"It is not," she said. "I'm disgusting, in case you haven't noticed. Besides, I was in love with him for about five extremely embarrassing years, and Matiu's the definition of 'Playboy doctor bachelor.' The whole thing, *including* my undying love, is kind of a family joke now."

"Yeh," I said. "And you were with somebody else until just recently, and you're not a teenager anymore. Tell me he doesn't make a point of coming around when you're visiting, or that he never told you that fella wasn't good enough for you."

"That doesn't count," she said. *"Everybody* told me Josh wasn't good enough for me, even though he was almost as good-looking as you and Matiu, and he had a Porsche and was a CEO and was the closest thing to Hemi I could find. I thought I was doing it right. Go figure. Matiu was in love with my sister. Everybody's in love with my sister. When you meet her, you will be, too. Also, I'm vulnerable. You're supposed to be nicer."

I was baffled again. Matiu didn't sound like the one she was in love with. Sounded more like Hemi to me. I had to laugh, though, too. Very confusing emotional mix. "Twenty-four hours ago, I was so worried about you, I could barely see straight. Maybe *you're* supposed to be nicer to *me.*"

"Nah," she said, and smiled. "If you can't take it, run. Here's a tip: you probably will. I told you, I'm hard to love."

She said it lightly, and I said, "Actually, you're not. Drink your smoothie."

25

☆☆

EVILER TE MANA

KAREN

Boy, was I glad to get out of the hospital. I didn't much want to admit how tiring it was to get dressed again, or to get driven twenty minutes to Jax's apartment, *or* to stand up and do actual walking for the time it took to get from the basement parking garage to my room with a view. And I really didn't want to admit how nice it was, at around nine o'clock that night, to have Jax slide into bed beside me and turn out the light.

"This isn't quite the second date you had in mind," I said in the dark. I was wide awake now, probably because I'd slept most of the day.

I could practically hear his smile. "Is that what it is? Could be good enough, though." He rolled to his side and stroked a hand over my hair, even though I was wearing my PJs, not some slinky nightgown.

"It isn't good enough," I said. "And here tomorrow's my birthday and all."

He laughed, found my mouth in the dark, and kissed it, soft and sweet. "Never mind, baby. It'll be good enough anyway."

I thought that I'd never met a more confident man. I also thought that I shouldn't let him call me "baby." It was probably infantilizing. I'd never had to think about it before, because nobody had ever called me that in my life, except for Hope when I'd been sick, and our mom, maybe. She'd been gone so long, I couldn't always remember the look of her face. Just the sound of her voice, sometimes, when I was tired or too lonely, but that might be Hope's voice I remembered there, too.

I was too independent and too intimidating to be any man's baby. I'd found that out a long time ago, and it was fine.

Then I fell asleep again, because Jax was holding my hand.

I was still in my PJs, but out of bed, at least, when the doorbell rang the next morning. Jax wasn't there, so I checked out the camera, sighed, and buzzed them in, and three minutes later, I opened the apartment door.

"Wait," I said. "Where . . ." I was laughing, and hugging kids. "You guys hid from the camera. Awesome. What are you doing out of school?"

"It's your birthday!" the youngest, Maia, said. She had hold of me around the legs and was pressing her cheek against my thigh, which meant I had to put my good arm around her shoulders and snuggle her. "So we had to come. Did we surprise you? We wanted to surprise you, because surprising is more fun."

"We came because you're sick, and you're turning thirty," my nine-year-old nephew, Tama, said. "It's like when you turn ten. Birthdays that end in zero are the most important, even though you were already pretty old."

"Also, Mom's having another baby," eleven-year-old Aroha announced, and rolled her eyes. "Which is super embarrassing, when I'm in middle school already. Nobody has four kids. The most anybody has is *two*. But anyway, she's pregnant *again*, so you know she's all weird and everything. Dad said they should leave us in school, and she cried, so he caved. *As* usual."

Hope was hugging me now. Hemi was being his normal self, standing there looking impassive, like a Maori boulder. "You're kidding," I said. "You *guys*. They have measures you

205

can take for that now, you know." After that, I was hugging Hope back. She only came to my chin. "Congratulations. I can't wait. How far along?"

"Almost two months," she said, holding me tighter, then standing back, holding my face, and laughing, her blue-green eyes sparkling and her mouth trembling with emotion. Hemi was such toast. "I'm so glad you're OK, sweetie. I've been so worried. It was such a relief when Matiu called to let us know you were going to be all right. And I did not cry. I was a little conflicted, that's all, because I wanted to be with you so much, but I didn't want to leave the kids. I thought they could miss a day."

"She totally cried," Aroha said. "She got those big eyes and held onto Dad's arm and blinked a lot and then kind of hid her face in his chest, and it was Game Over. But I got straight A's on my last three report cards, so I can miss a *day,* and Maia's in baby school, so it doesn't matter. Tama's the only one who should've stayed home. He got three B's and one C last time, and he didn't even do his homework on the plane."

"I did so," Tama said. "You just didn't see. You aren't the boss of me."

"I'm not in baby school," Maia said. "I'm in *kindergarten.*"

"Inside," Hemi said. "Auntie Karen needs to lie down, and your mum needs to sit."

"Not lie down," I said. "Sit, maybe." I did, on the couch on the terrace, where I'd been hanging out, drinking the smoothie Jax had made me and reading his book, since I'd stolen it from him. It was extremely engrossing, or maybe I was just starved for entertainment. I'd forgotten how much fun reading could be. When I did it normally, it was during brief snatches of time before I fell asleep. I hadn't just lain around like this since . . . forever.

Maia climbed up beside me to snuggle, and Tama asked, "Can we see your wound? Is it, like, really gross?"

"Yeah," I said. "But the worst part is under a dressing." I showed him my forearm. "Look how red it still is around it, though. Pretty good, huh?"

"I thought they were going to have to, like, amputate it or something," he said.

"Sorry to disappoint you," I said. "Maybe next time."

Hemi was looking around. "So where's this fella? Gone off and left you alone? Doesn't sound too concerned. Never mind. Now that we're here, you can come stay at the house. If your things are packed, we'll take you straight to Koro's, and home from there after the hangi."

"I don't need taking care of," I said. "I'm fine. Also, tell me Hope isn't throwing up. Or don't, because I won't believe you anyway. She always throws up." My sister was, in fact, sitting in a basket chair with her legs tucked up under her, looking blonde and fragile and beautiful, and Hemi was standing as close to her as it was possible to be without actually carrying her around, which was probably what he wanted to do. He called her "baby" all the time, if you're wondering, and she was also the only person who could make him change his mind.

"Which means I'll be cooking," Hemi said. "Cooking for you as well. Six aren't any more trouble than five."

"And you can sleep with Aroha and me," Maia said. "We can be very quiet."

I hugged her a little closer. "I know you can." Which wasn't true. Staying in Hope and Hemi's child-intensive household was pretty much like living in a hurricane. "But look how great it is here. There's coffee right across the street, and the hot pools are a block away for when I heal up. I'm so comfortable, you wouldn't believe it."

That was when I heard the door open, and saw Hemi go to DEFCON-2. One step down from nuclear war. Oh, boy.

JAX

I knew they were there, of course. Two walls of this place were glass from floor to ceiling, which gave me a fortunate few seconds of warning.

I headed out to the terrace, handed Karen her mocha, and

said, "I ate your chocolate fish. Happy birthday anyway."

"Oh, goody," she said. "Exactly what I wanted. This is everybody. My small whanau. Hope, Hemi, Aroha, Tama, Maia. This is Jax. I can't believe they all showed up for my birthday. How good is that?"

"We didn't," Hemi said. "We came to look after you." His voice was more of the same growl I'd heard the other night, and he was looking me up and down in a way that had my muscles tensing. I relaxed them with an effort, took off my sunglasses, and left on my baseball cap. Could be I didn't feel like exposing all my scars, and could be I had a reason. I was also glad I wasn't wearing shorts. He was, but Hemi Te Mana in shorts and a T-shirt was still heaps of intimidation factor. For a civilian.

"Kia ora," I said. "And welcome." I put out my hand, and after a second, he took it. No attempt to crush mine, which told me he'd be subtler than that. I was a bit taller, but he was broader, built along Polynesian lines and with the heavy muscle and full-arm tattoo to go with it.

His wife, Karen's sister, Hope, had sat up in her chair at my entrance, and I took her hand next. She was very pretty indeed, with a head of tumbled blonde curls and some of the biggest, most innocent eyes I'd ever seen. She looked, in fact, as unlike Karen as a sister possibly could, like a Persian kitten next to a black panther.

"Thank you for taking care of Karen," she said. "Hemi and I both appreciate it so much. I still don't understand how she'd get that sick that fast. She does her best to be indestructible these days." Her voice was a little breathless, and she basically defined the word "sweet."

"Because she had a bacterial infection that got into her bloodstream," the older girl said. "From a wound. I *told* you."

"Aroha." Hemi's tone was perfectly controlled, but it made his daughter snap her mouth shut and mutter, "Sorry, Mom."

I asked, "Can I offer you something? I don't have coffee laid in yet, but I could run to a cup of tea. Water. Orange juice. Fruit. Karen's been working her way through an entire repertoire of smoothies, so we're well stocked with fruit. Got soup as well."

"No, thanks," Hemi said. "We aren't staying. We came to collect Karen."

"Except that you didn't," Karen said. "Would you guys sit down, please? You're making my neck hurt." She scooted over, and I sat beside her and put my arm around her for good measure. She leaned into me like she had a point to prove, which was interesting.

Hope had been looking at each of us in turn. Now, she stood up and said, "If you don't mind me helping myself, Jax, I'll have a look at that fruit."

"Please," I said. "Go ahead."

"Come on, kids," Hope said. "Let's check it out." Leaving me with her husband. Interesting again.

"I want to stay with Auntie Karen," the littlest girl said.

"You don't get to choose about that," Hope said. "Come on." All three kids hopped up. Hope was tougher than she looked, maybe.

Hemi watched them go, his expression brooding, then turned his gaze back on me. I met it. What was he going to do, try to throw me over my balcony? Good luck.

Finally, he spoke. "You realize," he told Karen, "that Jax MacGregor isn't any better a choice than Josh was. Worse. At least Josh made his own way."

"*Excuse* me?" She was sitting up straight, the color rising in her cheeks. "This is your business why?"

"Because I love you. That's why."

"I love you, too," she said. "That doesn't mean I go around telling you who to hang out with. How would that work out? Would you love it? I love it just exactly that much. You're also insulting Jax in his own *house*. I'm pretty sure that violates some kind of fundamental Maori hospitality rule."

I wanted to tell her to calm down. This couldn't be good for her. I didn't, because it would have had the opposite effect.

Te Mana said, "If I'm going to insult a man, I'll do it to his face." He directed his emotionless gaze at me. "Whose apartment is this?"

"Belongs to the family," I said.

"Thought so. There's a saying in the States. 'Born on third base, and thinks he hit a triple.' Could apply here."

"He has a house of his own," Karen said. "Just not here. And—"

I put a hand on her arm, and she looked at me, then shut up. That was encouraging. "Got any other objections?" I asked Te Mana. "Other than my occupation and my unfortunate family connections?"

"Other than that you've had too many women and have never got serious with any of them, and you've got no skills other than looking pretty in your undies, and Karen's judgment is a bit compromised just now? Those would be the main ones, yeh."

Karen said, "All right. I'm going to say just *one* thing. *One.*" She wasn't, I could tell. "I don't think you're exactly in a spot to lecture anybody about their romantic behavior, Hemi. I was there, remember? Like when Hope cried in the bathtub after your first *date?* Oh, wait. I was there on your second date, too. That didn't go a whole lot better. And, oh, let's see. Maybe when she ran nine thousand miles to get away from you, when she was *pregnant,* because you were such a jerk, and you kept lying to her?"

"Thought you were on my side back then," he said. "This is a blow." I thought I could see a smile trying to get out, though.

"I was," she said. "I thought you were the most wonderful man in the world. I couldn't believe Hope kept screwing it up. I was fifteen. It took me a while to get the whole dynamic. Meanwhile, I have a caffeine addiction from all the times you sent me off while you guys had a fight, and if I'd invested all those twenties you handed me to do it, I'd be a whole lot richer. And, yes, I get that you paid for my surgery and may have saved my life, and, yes, when I got older, I also realized that you didn't have to do that, because—guess what? Hope had broken up with you again! And, yes, you moved me into your apartment and paid my private-school tuition and supported me and paid for me to go to college *and* get my

MBA, and you treated me every single time like I was your sister, not just Hope's. More than that. You treated me like you wanted me, and like you loved me. I'm grateful to you for everything. For showing me what a man is supposed to be. For loving me even when I was the one being a jerk. For how much you've loved my sister, because she deserves it."

Her voice was trembling, and I'd swear she was shaking. There were spots of color on her cheeks, and I didn't think this was good for her, but maybe it was necessary. Opposite her, Hemi was sitting absolutely still, his eyes fixed on her. Letting her have her say. Not quite the man I'd thought him, then. A better one, maybe.

In the end, I just held Karen a little tighter as she went on to tell him, "But none of that gives you the right to come here and insult Jax, or to tell me I can't judge what I see. I'm here to do a job for you, and I've been doing it. I've been taking notes and pictures, and you'll get a full report. I've also already told him that I'm not in the will, so his big plan to marry an heiress is busted, and you notice? He's still here. *And* he's never made me run away *or* cry. So far, I'd say I'm doing great. Also, he's not a model anymore, and he hasn't been a model for about six years. Your research skills are slipping. I'm just saying."

Spirit returning, but then, I'd already noticed that Karen rallied every time. She'd have made one hell of a soldier. Mental strength like steel.

"Working in the family business now, are you?" Hemi asked me. "Clearly, if you're doing this. Not so much business as recreation, I'd say." After that, he asked Karen, "Why d'you think I told you I wouldn't hire you at the company, and you'd need to find something else and make your own way instead? Because that's not a good path, not until you've proved yourself. You'd never have known what you could do on your own, or that you'd earned your spot, if you'd taken the easy road. He hasn't had to find that out, and that's a problem."

"I asked you that, what, when I was eighteen?" Karen said. "You notice how I haven't asked again in twelve years? I've *made* my own way, and I'm not interested in you hiring me. I don't think you're in the food business. And you just assumed again, by the way, about Jax, and were wrong again. You're not doing well at all here."

I told Te Mana, "I'm not working at the moment. Recovering from an occupational injury, and I'm not sure what I'll do next. You're right that I'm not in my most stable place, but I'm still a bit unclear as to why that's your concern. Surely Karen can decide for herself about the company she keeps." *And,* I didn't say, *she's getting too tired.* I was going to say it in about thirty seconds, though.

"Not doing too well at deciding, is she," Te Mana said. "An occupational injury? She told Hope she was jumping off waterfalls with you. Doesn't sound like it's getting in your way much."

I took off my baseball cap, and his face went still. Then I lifted the leg of my jeans. "Staff sergeant, First New Zealand Special Air Services. Currently on medical leave. Future career prospects uncertain."

Karen said, "Annndddd . . . busted. It feels like I've waited all my life for this moment. Hemi Te Mana, absolutely wrong."

26

☆☆

WHAT GOES AROUND

KAREN

Hemi had gone still, and I was coming down out of the red-mist zone and starting to realize what I'd just done. I had no idea what he'd say. What he'd do.

Or, rather—I knew it wouldn't be horrible, or that it wouldn't be that way forever. Hope wouldn't let it be horrible. When Hemi told her about this, and he would, she'd say the right thing. She'd explain, and because he loved her more than life, he'd listen.

I couldn't do any explaining, not anymore. I'd started to shake like I'd done with the chills, and things were going a little black around the edges. I put my hand out for my coffee, and knocked it over. My beautiful birthday mocha spilled out over the table, onto the stone terrace, and I let out a cry like a seagull deprived of a donut.

Jax said, "That's enough, I reckon. Let's have you lie down."

"I really wanted that mocha." I was having trouble with my eyes now, too. "It's my . . . birthday, and I'm thirty, and . . ."

I didn't say the other thing. *And I've lost control with Hemi.*

I've talked to him like I'm Hope, and I don't know what's going to happen with that. They're my family. They're all I've got. But they're each other's family first, and I might have just blown it, because I can never shut up.

"I'll get you another mocha," Jax said. "I'm putting you to bed first, though."

"I'm not a child," I said. "That was the whole point of my . . . speech."

"Got that, didn't I. I'm guessing Hemi did, too. It was an awesome speech, but it didn't do much to balance your electrolytes." He was standing with me, practically holding me up, because things were going even darker, like a black curtain coming down over my vision. I was familiar with that curtain, and I didn't want to be. I couldn't stand that this was happening.

Hope was coming out as we were coming in. I could only see the shape of her, practically running across the room, because I'd stopped being able to concentrate. She asked, "What's wrong?"

"A little crook, that's all," Jax said. "Too much excitement, I reckon." And then I tipped over, because he'd picked me up again. I didn't try to fight it this time. I just let the whole thing wash over me. Jax setting me down on the bed, pulling the throw over me. Hope saying, "I'll go get her a glass of water." Maia asking, "What's wrong with Auntie Karen?" And Jax saying, "She needs a rest, that's all. She was pretty ill."

I wanted to tell the kids I was OK. I *needed* to tell Hope so. I'd do that. In a minute.

JAX

She fell asleep fast. At first, I hovered between wanting to take her back to hospital, and knowing that was an overreaction. I may have checked her for fever, and I may have checked her pulse. I'd have done it more if her sister hadn't been there, because, yes, Hope stayed.

"You look tired yourself," she said. "It sounds like it's been a pretty crazy few days. I have to wonder how much you've even eaten, and I definitely wonder how much you've slept. Also, I need a sandwich fast—like right now—and if I stay here, you can go get us both one, and I can stay with Karen. I'll ride with you to Koro's—a bit later, Hemi, because I don't think Karen should stay too long—and Hemi won't even have to come back to get me. Easy."

"I'll get the sandwich," Hemi said. "The kids need to eat anyway. Want a chicken and veggie panini, sweetheart? Herb tea?" At her nod, his gaze swung to me. It was absolutely neutral. "Jax?"

"Ham," I said. "And a large flat white. Cheers. You could get Karen a new mocha as well, and maybe a sandwich, in case she wants it. All she's had are the smoothies. Not much protein in those." I considered reimbursing him, but abandoned the idea pretty smartly. I didn't need another dick-measuring contest, especially when it came to who paid for his sister-in-law's sandwich. He needed to do something for her right now, maybe, after what she'd said to him. Not easy to apologize. Easier to buy the lunch.

"Ten minutes," he said, gazed at Hope some more, and asked me, "Got a biscuit? A packet of cheese?"

"Uh . . . yeh," I said. "Come with me."

Hope curled up in the chair in the corner of the bedroom, told the kids, "Go into the living room and wait for Daddy, please," pulled her phone from her purse like this was all perfectly normal, smiled at me, and said, "Here's my chance to sit in peace and answer my work emails. Secret agenda."

In the kitchen, Te Mana found a plate, arranged cheese-topped biscuits on it, poured a glass of orange juice, said, "One second," and took it back into the bedroom. When he came back, he told me, "Pregnant," and looked absolutely satisfied to be saying it.

"Ah," I said. "Congratulations."

He nodded. "Seems I may have been wrong about you as

well." He hesitated, and I thought I knew where Karen got her reluctance to say "sorry." Except that Te Mana wasn't actually her dad, or her brother. An influence, though? Clearly.

"No worries," I said, rescuing him from having to utter the dreaded word. "Reckon you had your reasons."

"Too right I did,"

"What was that fella's name again?" I asked. "Karen's? In case I ever meet him."

"Not if I meet him first," he said, like he knew exactly why I was asking. "Josh Ranfeld. Wanker."

"Daddy, that's a bad word." His youngest was leaning against his thigh, her arm wrapped around his leg. "You're not s'posed to say bad words."

He picked her up and settled her on his hip. "You're right. Let's go get Mummy a sandwich, eh."

"And muffins," the little girl said.

"No," Hemi said. "And *lunch*. Don't want to spoil your appetite before we go to Koro's. Not before the hangi."

"Plus Koro always has lollies," she said. "In his pockets."

Hemi smiled. I hadn't realized he could do it. "That's a secret for the mokopuna. Don't tell Jax. He may want to share."

She looked at me doubtfully, and I laughed and said, "Nah. You can have all the lollies."

"Daddy," she said, staring at me wide-eyed, "that man has blue lines on his face."

The other two kids, who'd been sitting at the kitchen island, spinning idly around on the stools, stopped spinning, and Hemi said, "Not polite. We don't talk about how people look. Tell him you're sorry."

"No worries," I said. "They're scars, that's all."

She studied me some more. She was cute, with a ponytail of curly brown hair, golden skin, big hazel eyes, and a rosebud of a mouth. Going to be a heartbreaker, it was clear. "Oh," she said. "I'm sorry I said about the lines. Did you draw them on with a marker?"

"No," I said. "I got some cuts, and when my skin closed up, the scar was blue."

"Like magic?"

"No," the older girl said. "Like healing. Really?" she asked me. "They just ended up blue like that?"

"Yeh," I said. "It happens."

She got a faraway look, like she was considering researching the phenomenon. Karen all over again. In another minute, we were going to get into the bomb, and then the leg discussion. It wasn't that I minded, exactly, not with kids. It got a bit boring, though. Hemi hadn't said the "hero" word, at least. I'd hear it sometime today, though. That, I minded.

"Come on," Hemi told his kids. "Lunch." He told me, "Ten minutes."

☆☆

After a bit, I was alone with Hope. I checked on Karen again, and her sister looked me over and said, "Why don't you take a couple hours' break? I'm guessing you need it."

She didn't say, *You look like hell,* but she may as well have. I hadn't massaged my leg or got any exercise for days. The burning phantom-limb pain had woken me every hour or so during the night, and my stump was swollen enough that it had been hard to fasten the leg on this morning. I said, "I could do with a swim. Even more than lunch. I'll take my phone, though, so you can ring me if you need me."

She handed over her phone without a word, and I punched my info in and handed it back, then rang up the Mount hot pools, booked a deep-tissue massage, and packed a bag. I told Hope, "Ninety-five minutes. If she's worse, if you're concerned, I can be back in five. I'll be across the road."

Half an hour's fast swim helped, ignoring the curious looks my leg earned me on another busy Saturday. The first five minutes were rough, but once I settled into it and started working out the tight places in my shoulders, things got better. When I'd showered and headed into a massage room, though, the remedial work began in earnest.

"Ouch," Joni, a brunette who'd seen me a few times, said, when she came into the room and checked out the leg. "You haven't been looking after that."

"Life's been complicated," I said, and then I didn't talk, because my face was stuck down in a hole, and the rest of me was getting tortured. She started out easy at first, but when she was working my back, I started to sweat, and when I'd rolled over and she got to the leg, I had to blow out the breaths.

"I'm going easy," she said, checking my face. "Let me know if it's too much." It was definitely too much, but it was also definitely necessary, so I didn't let her know. She added, "Coming every day would be better. And working it for a good wee while twice a day yourself, if you can't do that."

"Gotcha." I looked at the ceiling and told myself, *Breathe in. Breathe out.* And then told myself again.

Afterwards, I was glad I'd taken off the leg before I'd come, because I wouldn't have got it back on. I took the crutches over to the shower, and then to the hot pool, lay in there, thought hazily that ice might be better than heat, and then that I didn't care, because I needed this. In fact, not to put too fine a point on it, I fell asleep.

I woke up with a start, accidentally slipped under the water, and got myself upright again. A beefy fella asked, "You doing OK there, buddy?" American, like Karen.

Oh, God. Karen.

I pulled myself out of the pool, and the fella averted his gaze. His wife looked for a horrified second, then did the same. I barely noticed. I was back in the changing room, grabbing my things, checking my phone—nothing—and crutching across the street and home.

When I came in the door of the flat, Hope came out. "Sorry," I said, breathing hard from my near-run. "How is she?"

Hope's eyes widened. She hadn't seen me take the leg off before I'd left, because I'd done it in the guest bath. Clearly, Hemi hadn't told her, and neither had Karen. She got her face under control and said, "Still sleeping. She's not feverish, though."

"Geez," I said, grabbing the towel from around my neck and giving my hair a scrub while I balanced on one foot. "It's been nearly two and a half hours. Sorry."

She laughed. "I don't mind. Mount Maunganui is one of my favorite places, and nobody's saying 'Mommy.' You have no idea how refreshing that is. Hemi's the one doing all the hard work. He's at Koro's already, shoveling dirt onto the pit for the hangi and no doubt building a new porch or something equally Kiwi and industrious. I've just been sitting on the terrace, looking at the sea and pretending to work. Possibly taking a nap. Go on and get changed. We're fine."

I checked on Karen—turned onto her side with her hand under her cheek and looking peaceful, if pale—took my third shower of the day, and didn't put my leg on. I'd prop the stump up instead for a bit, I decided, and give the swelling a chance to go down. I heated my cold panini in the microwave and headed outside, then went back for a glass of water. I could manage carrying things in one hand by using one crutch, but it meant more trips. Just one of the many things I'd had to get used to.

When I was sitting down, grateful for the shade of the terrace and the cooling green of the Mount—I'd probably burned up a bit, after an unexpected half-hour in the spa bath and the sun—Hope put down her phone, on which she'd been typing, and said, "I didn't realize you'd lost a leg. I *wondered,* when you called about the massage. You didn't seem like the massage type. Were you in the military? Hemi said you were a model."

"Still am," I said. "In the military, that is, not a model anymore. On medical leave." She'd seen the scars on my chest as well. They weren't a secret, and Karen would have shared all of it eventually. Nobody would ever call her anything but "outspoken," and the sisters might be opposites, but they felt close to me. Hope had planted herself in the room with Karen like it was the only place she wanted to be.

I ate some of my sandwich, belatedly realizing how famished I was, and Hope looked out at the Mount and said, after a while, "I'm guessing it's helpful to Karen that you've been injured. Not that I'm saying it's good that you were injured, but it's hard, when you've been through something so physically traumatic, to explain to somebody else what it's like, or how it changes you. She seems so strong to other people. Physically and mentally. She *is* strong. Maybe she can let her guard down with you, though, because you get it." She glanced over at me. "Forgive me if I'm assuming. She let you carry her. That normally involves a whole lot more protesting."

"You seem happier about that idea than your husband was," I said.

She laughed. A very pretty woman indeed, with a face like a flower and an air of serenity that was, again, the opposite of Karen. "Hemi's protective. You could call it his defining characteristic. And he's especially protective of—well, I was going to say Karen, but Karen and the kids, of course."

"And you."

"Oh, yeah." She smiled again. "I still have to call him on it sometimes. Other times, to be honest, I just enjoy it."

"It's seemed to me," I said, feeling my way, "a bit . . . odd, though. That he'd have to be so protective of her." *Or that you would,* I didn't say. I was close to my sisters, but I wouldn't have flown halfway around the world because one of them was ill. "She was fifteen, sixteen, she said, when he was first in her life, and she went off to Uni shortly after that, surely. She mentioned surgery before, and that her parents are dead. There are some things I don't understand here. Or possibly everything."

Hope was silent for a long time, but finally said, "I'm not sure what to say. I'm not sure how much is my story to tell. I have a feeling I may have underestimated how much she needs to feel . . . free."

"Ah," I said. "You heard that, then."

"Some of it. She's accomplished so much, it didn't occur to me that we still treated her like—well, a child."

"You're older," I said.

"Nine years. And our mom died when Karen was nine herself, so you see . . ."

"Your dad, though."

"No dad. Mine took off a long time earlier, and Karen's took off a year or so before Mom died. He's probably still alive. He just isn't around. So you see, we both may have had some trust issues, especially some trust in . . . life, I guess you'd call it. I found somebody to work through them with me, eventually. Karen hasn't. And she deserves to."

"She said the same thing about you, you know," I said. "That you deserved to be happy. I couldn't quite suss out what her problem was with Hemi, though. Why he loomed so large."

"Well, he *does* loom a little large," Hope said with a smile.

"True. If he paid for her to go to school, and to Uni, and took her in as well—I reckon I get it. Eternal gratitude may not be easy to sit with."

From behind us, a voice said, "Hey. You guys talking about me? Can't leave you alone for a minute."

Her hair was sticking up some. Her eyes were sleepy. And I was pretty bloody happy to see her. "Hey," I said. "How ya goin'? Come sit down. Need a tea?"

"Oh, you know," she said. "Probably. How long did I sleep? I feel like the princess in the tower, like there should be brambles all around us. How come you aren't wearing your leg? Why is your skin looking like that? Oh. Wait. You haven't been taking care of it. *Jax.*"

I'd propped both legs on the chair beside me, as planned, and Hope hadn't seemed too fussed, even though she was sitting opposite me, with too good a view of the damage. She hadn't stared at it, but she also hadn't looked like she was trying *not* to stare at it. Karen, on the other hand, shoved at both legs, said, "Lift up," sat down, laid them across her lap, and asked, "Does it help if I rub it?"

I cleared my throat. Something was happening to my chest, like a band tightening around it. It was bloody uncomfortable. "Yeh," I said. "I had a swim and a massage while you were asleep, but I've been neglecting it, I guess."

"Mm," she said. "I'd say you have, since all you've done for the past few days is take care of me."

I could let her do it for a few minutes, surely, if she wanted to. She'd asked. Her hands were strong, she wasn't one bit shy about touching my stump, and when it got sore like this, there was no such thing as too much massage.

Hope stood up and said, "Hemi got you a mocha, sweetie. Also a sandwich. Want me to heat them up for you?"

"Yes, please," Karen said. "You could bring me out some lotion from the bathroom, too. That'd feel better for Jax while I do this." She put out a hand and gripped her sister's. "Thanks for coming, you know? I'm really glad to see you. And hey—you can take care of me a little, and I'll take care of Jax a little, and when you get home tonight, Hemi will take care of you. You know how they always say, 'What goes around comes around?' It never seemed true to me. I mean, I'd love to think karma bites people in the butt, but it almost never seems to happen, does it? Maybe that's what it really means, though. Maybe it's more of a 'paying it forward' thing. Huh. It's an approach, anyway. It's a concept. I kind of like it. I think I'll start believing that instead."

"That way," Hope said, "somebody else could hurt Josh."

Karen laughed. "Yeah. Exactly. Hey, I didn't say I was going to be a Buddhist."

27

⭐

TOSSING THE BOMB

JAX

I wore shorts to the hangi. I also wore my leg.

My reception wasn't too bad. Hemi had told people about the leg already, maybe, because nobody but the kids mentioned it or my face, and the "hero" word wasn't uttered. I did have to take off the leg to show the kids—my one party trick—but that was it.

At the moment, I was standing in the back garden with a few dozen others, looking out over the gentle green folds and hillocks leading to the sea below in the golden glow of late afternoon, watching Debbie-the-boy-duck waddle around the party in search of attention and pats like a golden retriever, and having a post-dinner beer with Hemi, Matiu, and Matiu's older brother, a cheerful bloke named Tane who lived up the road.

Karen was right. Hemi seemed a bit more natural here, fully immersed in the rhythms of Aotearoa and his whanau, though nobody would ever mistake him for a relaxed fella. He hadn't built a porch earlier in the day. He'd put up trellises instead.

Just as I was thinking that it felt good to be normal, Matiu said, "Something I was wondering, if you don't mind a bit of shop talk."

Here we went. I tried not to tense up for a discussion of whatever an emergency doc would find fascinating. What my initial treatment had been, probably. Pity I didn't remember much other than a tourniquet, the coppery smell of blood, helpless anger for the dead, and too much pain.

I said, "No worries," and didn't mean it.

Matiu asked, "How do you actually disarm a bomb? You see the bomb squad taking it away, but what happens after that, and how do you determine whether you can move it? And what about a suicide vest? Do you clear the area and let them do their thing, or . . ."

I said, "'Or,' if you can, which you usually can't. A handler sews them into the vests, usually, so they can't have second thoughts. Mostly half out of their heads anyway, drugged to the eyeballs on tramadol. And in any case, the chance of somebody being around at the proper time who can stop it happening are pretty slim. You've got a better shot if the suspicious package isn't on a person. As to how we do it—we use bomb-disposal robots as much as possible, that's how. And hope we don't get our legs blown off."

Matiu asked a few more questions, Hemi jumped in as well, and Tane looked amused, his eyes going from one to the other of us like he'd have opinions later on. While he was in bed with his wife, possibly, talking over the party, laughing over how hard some people made things for themselves, in the way that kind of bloke did, the kind to whom life came easy and laughing came easiest of all.

We were all good—other than the amused judgment from Tane and the not-amused judgment from Hemi, of course—until Matiu said, "I'm wondering how that skill translates to civilian fields. There's the cool head, of course. Otherwise, what? Something in electronics, maybe, or law enforcement, depending which part's more important—the puzzle of it, or being on the sharp end."

"That's cheerful," Tane said with a laugh. "Don't go into psychiatry, bro. You'd be a dead loss. Have patients killing themselves left and right, wouldn't you."

"What?" Matiu asked.

"The bloke could be wondering what comes next for him, now that he's lost the leg and all," Tane said. "Since you need me to draw you a map, you've just told him he's got nothing to take with him. Good work. Of course, this could be about Karen. Subtle, boy. Very subtle." He shook his head. "Should've made your move earlier, I reckon. Hard luck. You were never much chop at choosing between two good things." He told me, "If you had two types of cake? Matiu'd ask for a bit of each. Maybe if you hadn't kept on asking for a bit of each for the past twenty years or so, bro . . ."

Matiu said, "Oh, I think I still have time." Lightly, but I froze.

"Pardon?" I asked.

He didn't answer me, just told his brother, "It's not like he lost an arm or the use of his brain. I went to a conference a while back in Aussie, and there was a fella speaking with two blades on his legs. He was doing ice climbing, mountain triathlons, everything I'm not doing now with two good legs. They've got the next generation coming, he was telling us. Mind-controlled, with myoelectric sensors implanted in the remaining tissue. Means your mind's talking to your leg in real time, relaying the message instantaneously." He asked me, "What can that thing do? How far along are you in the process? That matters as well, probably." Switching to doctor-mode just like that. I could still have been in jealous-partner mode. It was possible.

"Going on five months from amputation," I said, which was, yes, discussing my least-favorite subject, but as long as we kept it at the technical level, and nobody was asking me whether I wept at night—or what other skills I had, which were basically "none"—it wasn't too bad. "Dynamic-response design, so you're pushing off more like a regular foot. Running's pretty good so far, but you're right that I'm still new in it, and the stump's still changing. The leg's not mind-controlled, that's for sure." I paused, because I didn't want to ask. Or rather—I wanted to ask. I just didn't want to

ROSALIND JAMES

ask *him.* "Maybe you could send me a link to that talk," I finally said. "If there is one."

"No worries," Matiu said, and took another pull on his beer.

"And if you're looking for me to get myself blown up again and clear the field," I said, "you should think again. I don't plan to get out of the way."

A voice at my elbow said, "I hope somebody's fighting over me. I feel entitled, as it's my birthday."

Karen, coming up behind me. I put my arm around her and asked, "Good party, baby? Feeling all right?"

"Yes." Bright eyes, saucy smile. "And I should probably object to that, the 'baby' thing. We'll talk about it later."

"Mm," I said. "I could have that discussion."

Matiu said, "We could've been doing some fighting. Sounds like I lose, though." He shot me a look and drank some more beer. "When you said she needed distraction, cuz," he told Hemi, "I didn't realize what you were planning. *I* could've distracted her."

Karen said, "What?"

Hemi said, "Nothing. Should you be sitting?"

"No," she said. "I should be asking. What do you mean, I needed distraction? And—wait. What were you planning, and why did everybody else know?" She stepped out from under my arm. Not a good sign.

Hemi said, "I told you. I was planning to check out those properties, and I didn't have time."

Her mouth opened, her eyes narrowed, and then she snapped her mouth shut. "Wait. *Wait.* You *never* would have had time. I can't believe I didn't see that right away. It's like I've been in a . . . a coma. A half coma. Whatever. If you'd been doing it yourself, you'd have come down here, flown around in a helicopter for a couple days with maximum efficiency, and shot your questions at Jax's sister, preferably across a conference table for increased intimidation factor. You'd have looked at balance sheets in absolute silence, and gone home again without offering a clue about your decision. You were going to be camping with her for a week, so you

226

could casually lose all your scary advantage, insisting on carrying everything that needed carrying and generally showing her your soft side? Yeah, right. Never mind that Hope's pregnant, because you'd never have traveled around like that alone with another woman anyway. You'd have worried that Hope wouldn't like it. In fact, you made the whole thing up. You *did.* You made it all up, and I'm here for nothing."

"No," Hemi said, his face inscrutable. "I didn't. I'm capable of doing business with a woman on a purely professional basis, and I was considering the investment." He glanced at me. "I still am. We'll discuss this later."

Did Karen listen to him? She did not. "Wait," she said. "Wait. Jax. The other half doesn't make sense, either. Why would the buyer and seller look at the places together at all? For a *week?* Was your sister ever really going? Didn't it occur to you that this isn't how real-estate deals work? She didn't need you. She was giving you something to do so you'd feel useful, because she was worried about how depressed you were, with no leg and no job and all. She was pretending you could be helpful so you wouldn't feel so useless."

Matiu was looking down at his beer, Tane was looking wise, and I was feeling stupid, exposed, and at a total loss. I'd never been in business. I'd bought one house in my life, and my agent had done all the career negotiations that needed doing. I'd never even bought a car, and I was standing here with two entrepreneurs, both of them wondering why I hadn't known better, not to mention the too-handsome, too-charming doctor who'd just told me he wanted my woman and was here looking at and listening to all the reasons she could've made a better choice. And then there was the other part. That my sister—my *family*—had thought I needed rescuing, when I'd thought they'd seen that I was getting my strength back, and I'd made it completely clear that I didn't need their help.

I tried to think of something to say, and couldn't. "Another beer," I finally managed. And walked away with as little limp as I could possibly manage.

The leg still felt like shit. The leg was the least of it.

28

☆☆

THE FIRST THIRTY

KAREN

I expected Jax to come back. Instead, he walked around the corner of the house, pulling his phone out of his pocket as he went.

Fine. He was either getting upset and walking out, or, since Jax never got upset, he was walking out because *I* was upset, in which case, I didn't need him, right?

Of *course* I was upset. I wasn't going to apologize for it. I told Hemi, "That was a crappy thing to do."

Tane said, "Music," and melted away. Matiu looked between Hemi and me and said, "This should be interesting. Much as I'd love to hang about for the next chapter, though, I think I won't."

"Been pushing it, mate, haven't you," Hemi said.

"No," Matiu said. "I don't think I have. I think I'm throwing in my hand and walking away. If it doesn't work out, though, Karen, you know where I live."

"Because that would be a great idea," I said, but my heart wasn't in it. Was I supposed to go after Jax, or was I not? I never knew these relationship rules. What had just happened? I asked Hemi, "Did I say something wrong, or is he being too

228

sensitive? Or is he just . . . taking a break, or something?"

"And I'm off," Matiu said. "My limit on nobility is fast approaching." And he was gone.

I'd have killed—well, not *killed,* but I'd have done something stupid, at twenty, to have Matiu look at me like that, and to have him say something like that. Now, I barely registered him leaving. Partly because Koro was headed over, with Debbie following him like a duck who'd found her destiny. When he reached us, he said, "Something's happened, eh. Everybody running off like they've been scalded, and Karen the birthday girl and all."

"Just that Hemi didn't need me here at all, on this trip," I said, "and he pretended he did. And that Jax's family did the same thing to him. Like we're both *needy.*"

"You could think that everybody's needy sometimes," Hemi said. "There's an idea for you. Could think that when you are, your whanau wants to help."

"You could also think," I said, "that people who are feeling worthless don't need to find out they actually *are* worthless."

"Nobody said you were worthless," Hemi said.

"You didn't have to say it. I got it anyway. I should go find Jax." Why *had* he left? He'd been so sweet, earlier today. And yesterday. And all the days before that. Could you really wreck all of that by saying one tactless thing? If you could, did you want to have to walk on eggshells like that with a man?

No. You didn't. I had to fight the wave of desolation from that one. Was my judgment *still* that bad? It hadn't felt like it. It had felt like I was getting it right. It had felt perfect.

Koro said, "You could give him a minute. If he walked away, it could be he needs some calm before he talks to you."

"Or to get hold of his temper," Hemi said.

"I don't want him to be calm or to hold his temper," I said. "At least, *I* don't want to do it." Koro smiled, and I said, "All right. He needs to be calm. Obviously he does, because he always is. I'll just stay here and yell at Hemi." Or put off finding out the truth. One or the other.

"You do that," Koro said, and then *he* headed off. So did

Debbie. I was a man-magnet, all right. One whose polarity had been reversed. Even with *ducks.*

Once we were alone, I asked Hemi, "So tell me what I did wrong just now. I can tell you're dying to." I was hanging onto things, but not by much.

"And here I thought," he said, "that I'd set such a low bar for being in a relationship, anybody could clear it. You called him out in front of everybody and told him he was stupid. Think you also explained to everybody that he was depressed and not functioning well, but it's hard to remember, as I had a metaphorical palm over my face at the time. You didn't just do it in front of anybody, either. You did it in front of Matiu and me. Brilliant for his pride. At least you didn't bring up his impotence problem, so there's that."

"Oh." That didn't answer the question about the walking-on-eggshells thing. "All right, first off—how was I supposed to know Matiu had any interest in me? Not like he ever has before."

"Not when you were sixteen, maybe. Since then? You could be wrong. Never mind. You're not a match."

"How do you know? You're crushing my girlhood dreams here, you realize." Which I cared about not at all. That was extremely weird. Matiu had made my heart flutter for half my life.

Hemi said, "He needs somebody he doesn't hesitate about. Somebody who makes him have to jump in, no matter how bad an idea it is. Somebody he'd lay down his life for. He needs to be worried he won't get a chance with her, because she lets him know that the way he's always done things isn't good enough. How do I know that? Possibly from personal experience, as you've already pointed out."

"Gee, thanks," I said. "That makes me feel tons better." In fact, it felt so terrible, it was almost funny. *I* wasn't tactful? What would you call Hemi, then, a wrecking ball? "All right. Moving on. Jax *won,* if there's actually winning happening, so the idea that he'd care about Matiu—or about you, because he won with you, too—is just stupid. You know what I just realized? The reason Matiu and I aren't a match, besides that

I'm not dying-for-you material? I want somebody who doesn't keep me guessing. I used to think that was so sexy, so mysterious and all—I mean, obviously I thought that, or I wouldn't have gone for Josh in the first place. I've changed my mind, though. I don't want to play some game, at least I don't want to play that one. So if Jax *is* that furious with me, why'd he walk off instead of telling me so?"

"Could be he didn't want to embarrass you. A good man supports a woman in public. If he humiliates you in public, it's a sure bet he'll be worse in private."

"Oh. Well, that's probably a positive, then."

He laughed. "Yeh, I'd say so."

"In another minute," I said, "you're also going to have to say that you were absolutely scary-R-word *wrong* about him." I saw his amusement vanish, right on cue, and added, "Maybe I said the wrong thing. Maybe so. But you *did* the wrong thing. You're not supposed to make somebody you love feel stupid? Do you have any idea how stupid I feel right now?"

He paused a moment, possibly looking a teeny bit less than comfortable, then said, "Could be I don't always get it right. Could be I was a bit desperate, too."

"You? You're never desperate."

He said, "Let's sit down."

Much as I'd have liked to say I didn't need to, I actually did. I still wanted to go talk to Jax, or maybe I wanted to see if he'd come back to talk to me. I didn't know which was better, so I perched beside Hemi on the low concrete wall edging the patio instead, away from the center of the action.

People were finishing up their seconds and thirds of pork and chicken, of potatoes and carrots and kumara, the succulent hangi that had been roasting in the ground for hours today. Normally, I'd have been doing the same thing, but I still didn't have much appetite. I'd seen my ribs even better in the mirror this morning, and my collarbone didn't look all that great, either. Some women were voluptuous. Others were ribby.

Hemi said, "Hang on," then came back with a bottled water and handed it over, sat down beside me, and said, "I've seen you hurting so much you couldn't even open your eyes. I've seen you when Hope went off to New Zealand without you and left you alone with me, and when the first of the many arseholes you've fancied dumped you when you thought you'd found romance. Then there's the time when you thought you were going to fail that International Economics class, and they'd turf you out of the MBA program, because for the first time ever, you weren't always the smartest person in the room, which meant you must actually be the dimmest. I've seen you cry a time or two, and I've seen you rage heaps more. I've never seen you give up. When we found you this time, you'd given up."

"It was a *break.*" Hemi *also* didn't get bonus points for recounting all the lowest moments of my earlier years, like some kind of This Is Your Life for the clinically depressed. It was a good thing he hadn't been around when my dad took off because he didn't want my mother and he didn't want me, or when my mom died. I was surprised he hadn't thrown them in there anyway just to round out the whole pathetic picture.

On the other hand, *I'd* just thrown them in there. All aboard the Trauma Train. It was leaving the station now and picking up speed, trying to carry me with it. I opened my water and thought, *Stop it. It's antibiotics, making you depressed. You're fine.*

Hemi said, "Let's recap. Hope and I found you curled on the floor of the bathroom with tomato sauce on your shirt and some kind of crusty brown stuff on your chin, smelling like you hadn't had a bath in a week. Nobody'd cleaned that floor in a while, either."

I took a drink of water. "You aren't supposed to say you noticed the smell. Or that I had something on my face. Which was probably peanut butter chocolate ice cream with hot fudge sauce, because I ate a pint of it at some point there. Out of the carton, standing up at the kitchen counter. You're also not supposed to say that I'm a bad house cleaner and my bathroom was disgusting. That's just a wonderful list of additional failures to put into the memory banks. Thank you.

You're extremely bad at this comforting thing. Tell Hope I said so. She should probably do it next time."

"If it's the smell and the look of somebody I love giving up," he said, "I'm noticing, and I'm acting on it. What was I meant to do, then?"

"I don't know, maybe leave me alone to wallow? I'd have been done soon. I'd have made a plan. I'd have taken a shower and cleaned my bathroom eventually. And if I'd needed help, I'd have asked you."

"Would you?" Hemi's gaze could look as remote as the icy peaks of the Southern Alps. Right now, it was nothing like that, because he was absolutely, one hundred percent focused on me. Which did not feel wonderful. "Or would you think, 'Nobody's ever been as dumb as me, which means I can't tell anybody, or they'll know?' Would you think, 'Hemi would never have done this, invested this much of himself with the wrong person, gone this far down the wrong road, and lost everything just because he was too stupid to defend himself?' You forget that I did nearly all those things. I actually *married* that wrong person, in fact."

"That doesn't help," I said. "It makes it worse. At least she wanted to marry you. I would've married Josh if he'd asked me for real. If he'd asked me to set a date. If he'd given me a . . ." I had to stop and breathe. "A ring." There I went, slicing myself open, hauling out one more painful stone from the bottom of my gut and setting it on the table. "Every time I came home, Hope looked at my finger and didn't ask, and I could feel her not asking. I could *hear* her talking to you, afterwards, being all concerned for me again. And every time I thought about it, I got this panicky feeling, like nobody was ever going to love me, not the way you said, like he'd . . ." I'd never had my voice wobble as much in my *life* as it had these past few weeks. I was not a fan. I went on confessing anyway. "I didn't know what to do about it. I told myself Josh was as smart as me, and he wasn't threatened by my intelligence, and we were physically compatible and great business partners, and where would I ever find another man like that? Then there was the company. What would happen if we broke up?

How would I work with him? If I didn't—what would happen to everybody's job? They had mortgages. They had *babies.* I couldn't even think about that, so I thought that Josh and I could discuss everything in the world, and I was work-driven anyway, and that was fine, because I wasn't the kind of woman that men have a Great Love with. Not the kind they give huge diamonds to and can't live without and would lay down their life for. You know it's true. You just said it about Matiu and me, that I'm . . . wrong. That I'm not . . ."

I knew this was another low point. It was just that it was a *really* low point. I'd hauled out the stone, so why was all of that still lying so heavy inside me? I thought that when you faced it, you started getting over it. Another lie.

I kept talking, because as horrible as it felt, I was on the train now, and it was running away with me while Hemi watched. "And never mind, because I already knew that. You wouldn't have done any of those dumb things I did. You wouldn't have let yourself lie like that about somebody for that many years. You'd have gotten out so much sooner. I know what I was doing wrong. I always have, because I *didn't* actually fail economics. It's the Sunk Cost fallacy, where you double down on your investment even when you have no hope of getting it back, because you've put so much in already. It's called a fallacy because it's stupid, and I knew it and did it anyway. You didn't do that, and you also didn't work seven years for almost nothing. That was my *chance.* It was going to be my . . . my Hemi-thing. My brilliant start. It isn't just that I failed. It's that I failed *twice.* The business thing, and the romance thing, and the life thing. I don't have part of a company. I don't have equity in a house. I don't have a . . . a . . ." *A baby,* I wanted to say, but I couldn't get the word out. "That's three times. I pretty much . . ." I took a breath and said it. "I failed at everything. And I didn't have any . . . resilience left. I always get up again, but I couldn't. I *couldn't.*"

Boy, did that make the panic rise. I wanted to get up and walk around. Well, actually, I wanted to get up and run away.

"I wouldn't have done that?" Hemi said. "I came close enough to doing worse than that. Also, you just described my first marriage. Failing just means you find out what doesn't work for you. And of course you're going to have a Great Love. You found out what it doesn't look like, and maybe that means you'll recognize it when it turns up. Here's a tip. It's not the diamond part that matters, it's the laying-down-your-life part. Find that bloke. He's out there. You're awesome as you are, and he's going to know it."

He put his arm around me, and I leaned my head against his shoulder, just for a minute. Hemi had the broadest, most comforting shoulders in the world. I'd never had much of a dad, and I'd never had a brother at all. I knew how it felt to have both, though.

I said, "I so want to believe you right now."

Some more of that low laughter, and he hugged me a little closer. "You should. Getting your kick up the arse, that's all, realizing you may not be quite as clever as you always thought. You got it faster than I did. Comfort yourself with that."

"Have I ever said that I kind of appreciate you?" I asked.

"Think you said so today. There was a 'but' attached, though, as I recall."

"All right, I'm going to say it now. Pay attention. I appreciate you. And . . ." I had to swallow to get the words out. "I love you."

He kissed my cheek. "Goes both ways, eh. Happy birthday. The first thirty years are the hardest. Maybe you should go find that Jax fella, tell him what you're thinking, and let him tell you what he's thinking, too."

"He's probably gone. In fact, I'm sure he's gone. All my stuff is at his place, too. I'm going to have to go back there and apologize. Probably over the intercom, standing on the sidewalk and yelling out my weaknesses for the entire clientele of the Coffee Club to hear. There's a horrifying thought."

"If that's what happens," he said, "you've got the wrong bloke again. This time, you'll get out before you've sunk so much of your cost. Only one way to find out."

"Does that mean that if he's left, you'll give me a ride back there?"

"I will," he said. "And I'll hang around, too, in case you need a ride home again."

29

☆☆

FIND YOUR REASON

JAX

I got my beer, but I didn't drink it. I couldn't anyway, not if I was going to drive home, so why had I picked it up? I stuck it back in the tub, walked around to the front of the house, and thumbed a number.

"Hey," Poppy said. "I was just about to call you. Where *are* you? Leave the doggie alone. Leave it *alone.*"

"Poppy," I said. "Focus."

"Leave it *alone,*" she said, and then, "If I focus on you, either Hamish will get bitten and we'll probably have to go for rabies shots, he'll get mange, because that's definitely happening, or he'll drop the poor thing and I'll have to tick the 'yes' box when they ask me whether your kid has a history of harming animals. Hang on."

Some only slightly muffled talking, some high-pitched, pint-sized arguing, and she was back. "Right. This isn't working. Why didn't you answer my last two calls? How's a loving sister meant to get you your flowers if you aren't even there? Thought you said you were back at the Mount for the weekend."

"I'm at a hangi in Katikati," I said, "and I don't need

flowers. I'd also tell you that I was furthering your negotiations by establishing good relations with Hemi Te Mana, his grandfather, and about forty members of his whanau, but turns out I'm wondering instead whether I actually have anything to do with this venture or not. I'm guessing 'not.'"

"What? I have to go. Where exactly in Katikati? I'll get the flowers delivered there, then."

"Just leave them." I not only didn't need flowers, I *absolutely* didn't need flowers. I never had, which was why nobody had ever sent them to me. I especially didn't need them from my sister.

"Address," Poppy said. "There's meant to be singing."

Brilliant. Karen's birthday party was about to be crashed by a stripper. Or something bizarre, like a *male* stripper. In a gorilla suit. That was exactly the sort of thing Poppy would think was hilarious.

I needed a stripper, male or female, only slightly less than I needed flowers, or another burst of shrapnel through the chest. If Poppy thought I'd be excited by the prospect of a woman taking off her clothes for money, she knew nothing about life in the military. Feeling sorry for a girl with nothing but blankness behind her eyes, because she'd told herself, "Don't think, just do it and get it over" too many hundreds of times, didn't much make me want to climb into bed with her.

"Tell me it's not a stripper," I said.

"It could be," she said. "What's the address?"

"No stripper. I mean it. Absolutely not."

"Address," she said.

I gave it to her, because I needed to get off the phone, and because she wouldn't really do a stripper. She'd have feminist objections. I hoped. The male one in the gorilla suit was still a possibility, but those probably weren't too easy to come by in Tauranga. A thought to cling to.

I stuck the phone back in my pocket and contemplated whether to just drive off and leave all this behind, and then, once I was home and could explode in peace, to do the thing

I needed to do most, which was ring my dad. The whole ridiculous setup had his fingerprints all over it. Sending me all over New Zealand like I was on some high-end Outward Bound expedition for troubled teens, as if all I needed, as I adjusted to life on one leg and a brand-new career in the luxury-auto and more-luxury-real-estate business, was to learn self-reliance and teamwork via some camping and rock climbing. If one of these stops featured a campfire sharing circle and a vision quest, twenty-four hours on your own in the bush eating what you could gather and a heavy dose of journaling, I was out. I'd spent six years in the military. Same thing, except no journaling. And people tried to kill you.

Somebody came around the house. Unfortunately, it was the old man, so turning my back and driving off wasn't on. He headed for the brightly-painted chair that sat like a throne under the avocado tree, lowered his skinny backside into it, and said, when I came over, "Taking a break, eh. Probably wise. I'll take one with you."

"Nice chair," I said, for something to say. It was elaborate, with the entire back painted like a peacock's feather, and the peacock's body painted on the seat. Hand-painted, definitely.

"Karen made it for me. She's a special one, eh."

"Yeh," I said. "She is." Right now, "special" could mean "specially tactless," as well as "specially damaging to my ego," but I didn't tell him that.

"Sit down," he said, and when I sank into the chair beside him, he looked at me more keenly than I appreciated. I'd been evaluated by enough Te Mana men today to last a lifetime. He said, "Thought you might've got your knickers in a twist and driven off, from what I heard. People don't surprise me much anymore, but you could've done it. Still here, aren't you."

I stuck my legs out in front of me, crossed my ankles, and looked down at them. No matter what miracles medical technology came up with, I'd still have to take my leg off at night. I'd still face-plant out of bed when I forgot. People would still define me by what I'd lost, and they'd still pity me for it. And I still wouldn't be able to stand the thought of it.

That was weak. It was the last thing from the man I wanted

to be. It was who I was anyway, and I wasn't sure how to explain it. Actually, I *was* sure. I didn't want to explain it at all. I also couldn't drive off without Karen. If I'd started to, I'd have turned the car around. I wasn't sure which prospect scared me more—that I'd be enough of an arsehole to leave her here alone, or that I'd have had to come back. I was so far out of my depth here.

He said, "Never mind. Karen told me about what happened, about Hemi arranging for her to come down here, pretending she was helping, and that it may have happened to you as well. Right now, I expect she's telling Hemi. Worse things in the world than your whanau trying to help out, though, I reckon."

"Yeh," I said. "I'm sure she feels stupid." I should go talk to her. I needed another couple minutes first, though. After that, maybe I'd find something to say to make us both think we had something left to offer. That this was a pause, and then we were moving on.

Which looked like what? The realization hit me like a shot of cold water to the face. This was not how romance worked. Romance had rules. I hadn't followed them, maybe, but I knew what they were. What we were having didn't look much like that. More like ships passing in the night.

The old man said, "Not easy to think the people you want to take care of are trying to take care of you instead. I'll tell you a secret. Getting old doesn't make it any easier."

"I never thought of that," I said, because I had to say something, "but I reckon you're right."

"No man wants to be helpless," he said. "Can't feel like a hard man when somebody's propping you up, especially if you've made your life about being that hard man. And if they don't tell you they're doing it, it could be worse."

That one was so true that I had no answer at all, so I didn't try. Anyway, I was still stuck back at the "moving on" bit.

"On the other hand," he said, "it could be that a woman wants the same thing. Some women, anyway."

"Like Karen."

"Never seen a girl want to be taken care of less. Maybe

because she didn't want to count on it. Hope says she's letting you do it, though."

I had to smile despite the uncomfortable battle of emotions in my gut. I guessed those were emotions, because otherwise, I had food poisoning. "Under duress," I said. "There could've been some picking up and carrying involved, and a fair amount of protest."

He laughed, a wheezy, near-soundless chuckle, and looked up at the deep-green, shiny leaves of the avocado. "Same as you, then. Scared of being weak. Scared of what it would mean."

Well, that was about a mile too close for comfort. If I wasn't going to leave, though, and it seemed I wasn't, it was time to get some answers. I said, "She's done nothing but succeed, from what I've read. That had to take heaps of work. Why would she be afraid of being weak?"

He was quiet a minute. Sound drifted around from the back—laughter, the shriek of kids chasing each other through the orchard, a Kiwi-centric version of reggae playing on backyard speakers, somebody singing a snatch of a verse, and more voices joining in. Maori, singing their way through life, in celebration or in mourning. Giving voice to whatever it was, and sharing it. The old man said, "Of course, when I met her, she was mostly over it. Had barely any hair, still, but with the life bursting out of her."

"Because . . ." I said.

"She was ill. Hard on her. Hard on Hope. Hard on Hemi, because all he wanted to do was help, and Hope nearly wouldn't let him. There you are. Could be you're not the first man in the world to be frustrated by that, eh. But I don't think life was a treat before that for either one of those girls. Karen was alone too much, I'm guessing, as a wee girl, with Hope away at work. Proud of being so good on her own, telling you she'd rather have it that way, and maybe scared, too. Not much point in being scared, though, if there's nobody to help you through it. You harden up instead, don't you. And once Hemi was in the frame . . . could be she wasn't always sure where she stood."

"Because it was just her and her sister before," I said, the pieces falling into place in the one and only way they fit, "and then her sister had somebody else, and Karen was tagging along. Hope *did* let him help, though, obviously, and it's clear Karen loves him almost like a dad, so . . ."

I got a smile from him. Missing a few teeth, and not bothered by it. What would you be bothered by, if you were ninety-five? "And you wonder why. Hemi doesn't always put his most lovable foot forward, especially when he's worried. Straight to defensive mode, eh."

I had to smile, too, even though I didn't really feel like it. "Or offensive mode, maybe."

The old man laughed, then turned the carved wooden stick in arthritic hands, digging out a spot in the grass. A raspy quacking broke through the rest of the party noise, and there came Debbie, waddling around from the back of the house like a duck in a hurry, quacking all the way. When he made it to us, he ignored me and headed straight to the old man, parked himself on his foot, and settled down with a waggle of tail feathers.

"I hope you wanted a duck," I said.

"Got one, anyway, didn't I." He wiggled his foot, which made the duck fluff up and nibble at his toes, and smiled. "Sometimes you go with what comes along, eh. Just because you didn't expect it to happen, that doesn't mean it's no good."

That was a little too close to too many things that I couldn't sort out just now, so I leaned over and gave Debbie a stroke, and he leaned his body into me the same way Karen had that morning on my terrace. Like she was making a point to her brother-in-law, or maybe like she wanted to be closer to me. Like an upfront woman showing what she felt, and what she wanted.

"She's got a strong will," I said, still patting the duck. "Karen. A fair bit like Hemi, I'm thinking."

"A fair bit like her sister as well," the old man said. "Can't always tell by looking, eh. Sometimes, you're strong because you were born that way. Other times, you're strong because you have to be, and letting down your guard's something you can't afford. Karen's strong both ways, same as Hemi. The reason they understand each other, and the reason they butt heads, too. Too much alike, and both of them having a hard time believing things could change for them. Could be different from the way you grew up, I'm thinking."

"Yeh," I said. "Two parents, and too much money." I didn't say anything about the modeling. I didn't feel much like adding that onto the pile. If nobody mentioned underwear again today, I'd be just as glad. Which was worse? Underwear, or the "hero" thing? It was a close call.

"Gifts," he said. "That's what you'd call what you've got, I reckon. Still got them, by how interested the girls are." And, yes, we were on to the undies. Fortunately, we didn't stay there, because he said, "That would be the other kind of strength, then. The kind you don't know you have until you need it. The kind you build. Rough to think you're losing it, maybe, when you worked so long to get it."

Bloody hell, was the man *trying* to make me squirm? I thought people this old were supposed to get senile. I also couldn't pat the duck anymore without looking like I was avoiding something. "Maybe," I said, and sat up.

He didn't say, "No 'maybe' about it, mate," which he very well might have. Instead, he said, with another look up into the tree like he was checking on avocado ripeness, "A woman needs to feel cherished, unless she doesn't think she'll ever get it. Then, maybe she tries not to need it instead."

"In other words," I said, "it's not about me."

"Reckon it's always about us, but it isn't only about us. Not about what we get, anyway, because it could be that what we get is the least important thing, in the end. That could scare a young girl, thinking about the end, being brave anyway for her sister. Reckon both Hope and Karen could tell you about that, because it's harder to be the one left behind. Could scare a fella, too, whether he's sitting under his avocado tree with his mokopuna around him, or off in the desert somewhere, wondering if he's about to die too far from home. Wondering if he ought to, because it was his turn, and somebody else took it."

I couldn't answer, and he sighed and didn't look at me. He looked at the mountain instead. His voice was deep and scratchy, the sound of the ancient limbs of a totara rubbing together in the wind, when he said, "I may know a bit about that myself. I had a granddaughter once, one you haven't met. Tane and June's youngest. Kahukura."

I did not have a good feeling about this. "Rainbow."

"Yeh. She had the right name, because she came out just like that. From the time she learnt to laugh, seemed like she never stopped. Never stopped moving, either. Cheeky monkey, always into something. Full of life, full of opinions from the moment she learnt to talk. Miss Sauce, same as Karen. Always thinking she ought to be going somewhere, ought to be doing whatever the big boys were. Boys are meant to be the ones getting into everything, but nobody told Kahukura that." He sighed, leaned on his stick, and looked up at the mountain again before he went on, every word slow. Measured, or maybe painful. "We were having a hangi like this one. Matiu's fifteenth birthday, it was, and we did it at Tane and June's place. Not at the house where they are now. It was another one, down toward Tauranga. They moved, afterwards. Couldn't bear to stay there, I reckon, though they said it was to be closer to me."

This was going to be something I absolutely didn't want to hear. I could tell by the way my scalp was prickling.

I was right. "She was meant to be having a nap," he said. "June went into the house after an hour or so, though, and found her gone from her crib and nowhere in the house. Some of us were looking at first, and then we all were. Thinking we'd find her any minute, that any second, she'd come running, laughing again, thinking how funny she was to have slipped out. She'd be hiding somewhere, maybe, or off to visit the chickens. Must've got out of the front door while we were all around the back. Somebody'd left it unlatched, maybe, with all the coming and going. Anyway, we looked for half an hour or so, checking with the neighbors, more worried with every minute that went by. Imagining the worst, and trying to tell ourselves a different story instead."

Another sigh. I didn't want him to go on, but he did anyway, because you couldn't stop life from happening. "Tane'd already called the cops to help when Matiu found her. Down at the neighbor's pond, wasn't she, gone to look at the ducks. She loved those ducks. She was wearing a pink shirt. That's what he saw. That pink, in the reeds, and the ducks swimming around."

Debbie gave a quack like he'd heard his name, waggled his tail feathers, and took a nibble at the grass. The leaves rustled overhead in the late-afternoon breeze, the music and the laughter floated around the house, and the old man said, "You've never seen a man move as fast as Tane when Matiu came over the hill with her. You've never seen a face like his when he took her from Matiu, or a man work as hard as he did trying to bring her back. And you've never heard a sound like the one that came out of June when they got her to hospital at last and the doctor told us she was gone. Didn't even sound human."

My throat hurt, and so did my stomach, with that kind of tight, balled-up pain that comes from something too hard to swallow. So much for my idea that Tane had laughed his way through life. I'd been bowled out today every time I'd been on the pitch, emotional-intelligence-wise.

"That was a sad day, if you like," the old man said. "Maybe the saddest day. Maybe so. June was crying, and Tane wasn't. Holding her, wasn't he, putting the rest of it aside for now so he could do it. Still with that look on his face. That he should've stopped it. That he should've checked the door. That he should've noticed sooner. That he'd failed at the one thing a man needs to do more than anything else. He hadn't protected his family. And me? I was thinking the same thing. I was thinking that other thing you always think, too."

"That it wasn't fair."

He shook his head slowly. "Nah, mate. I'd given up on expecting 'fair' a long time before that. I was thinking it was my turn to go, not that wee girl's, and that I'd have traded places in a heartbeat, if somebody had just asked me. I'd have said I'd given up on that idea as well, but you can't help thinking it, can you, at a time like that. You don't get to trade, though, because nobody did ask. And if you waste your life regretting that you're still here instead, what's the point? You could say it disrespects the dead when you feel that way." He bent painfully down and gave Debbie a stroke. "Reckon you could say that."

He sat up again and was still, and so was I. I said, "I'm sorry." The two most inadequate words in the English language.

"Mm. You could have a think about this, maybe. That even if you live to be as old as me, you still won't have a leg when you pass. Karen still won't have a mum and dad, and Tane and June still won't have their rainbow girl. Everybody loses too much. That's life, eh. It's not what you've lost that matters in the end, though. It's what you leave behind after you go. Maybe that's your mokopuna. Maybe it's just being that space in somebody's heart, someplace you filled that nobody else ever could. Got to be a reason you were left here, whatever you lost doing it. You could think about that, eh. Maybe it's time to find out what that is. Maybe it's time to find your reason."

30

☆☆

TRUE LOVE

KAREN

I went around the corner of the house to find Jax. What else
was I going to do?

I knew he wasn't my True Love, or if I didn't, I was trying
to know it. I'd met him about a week ago, I hadn't covered
myself with glory since, I didn't live in New Zealand, I didn't
even know where his house was, and he'd never offered to
show it to me. I could at least talk to him, though. If he hadn't
left, that is.

He hadn't. He was sitting beside Koro, his elbows on his
knees, everything about him looking like listening. He still had
the almost-beard, but he'd shaved neatly around it this
morning. The side of his face I could see was the one with the
scar, and all he looked to me was beautiful.

Koro looked up, and so did Jax. I couldn't tell what he was
thinking. He stood up, and I said, "Hey."

He smiled, slow and sweet, and his gray eyes were so
warm. "Hey," he said. "Hi." My pulse kicked up, my knees
shook, and I thought, *Wait. Wait.* In total confusion. I tried
to tell myself the not-your-true-love thing, but it wasn't
working.

That was where we were when a white SUV came up the road and stopped at the driveway. It didn't pull in, because there was no room, with cars filling the verge on both sides of the drive. The driver's door opened, a pretty redhead leaned out of it and threw up onto the pavement, the same way I'd done a few days earlier, and Jax muttered something under his breath and headed over there fast.

Koro was still in his chair, and Debbie appeared to have gone to sleep on his foot, like a duck who'd partied too hard. I asked, "Who's that?"

"Dunno," Koro said. "Not somebody I know. Could be Jax does."

Jax was crouched beside the woman, his hand on her back. I told Koro, "He's got a . . . pattern going here." He had more than that. How had this woman known he was here? He must have called her. He must have been *talking* to her, when I'd thought he was with me. He had his arm around her now and was kissing her cheek in the exact same way he'd done with me when I'd done the exact same thing. After a minute, though, he stood up, opened the back door of the car, and leaned inside. A boy of four or five, his hair red and wildly curly, climbed out, and the fuzziest little dog in the world jumped out with him. Its black fur was matted, and it had a white muzzle, white paws, and a hairy, white-tipped tail that was going like mad. It was a very messy dog indeed, and as I watched, it lifted its leg against the car's rear tire and took a long, luxurious pee.

When Jax turned around at last, he had a toddler in his arms. She was dressed in short pink flowered overalls and had her strawberry-blonde hair fixed in two pigtails high on her head, and Jax adjusted her on his hip with too much familiarity and said something to the dog, who wagged his tail some more and panted happily. The girl had her own arms around his neck, and something cold was happening in my stomach, because what I was seeing was a family.

The car was still running, but Jax headed up the walk to us, with the rest of them, dog and all, around him. When he got there, he told Koro, who'd risen to his feet, dislodging

Debbie, "Seems my family decided to turn up and crash your party."

"Your . . . family," I said.

"Yeh," he said, not fazed a bit. "Poppy, Hamish, and Olivia. And dog. The dog is a surprise, but then, the whole thing's a surprise, eh. This is Wiremu Te Mana, Hemi's grandfather. And Karen, who's been checking out those sites with me, of course."

"Kia ora," Koro said. "Haere mai. Welcome."

The dog had discovered Debbie. He uttered a joyous *Woof,* bowed down with his head on his paws and his butt in the air, wagged his tail furiously, and then leaped straight into the air and lunged at the duck. I grabbed Debbie fast, and Jax said, "He looks OK to me." He was crouched down, giving the dog a scratch around the neck area like a man who hadn't just tipped my world sideways. "You're friendly, huh, boy? Want to play? You could use a bath, though. Didn't know you'd got a dog," he said to the redhead.

"We haven't," she said. "I thought you could take him to Animal Control on Monday. Somebody's lost him, probably. Besides, Max is allergic. But I couldn't just leave him there. He was running up and down the pavement outside the apartment. He seemed so thirsty, and I think his foot pads are sore. He's lost, or abandoned, because he doesn't have a collar. We gave him water, but he needs feeding, and brushing, too."

"Which you reckoned I'd do," Jax said. "Of course, the apartment has a no-pets policy, so there's that." He looked amused, not at all like a man whose wife and girlfriend were standing three feet apart.

"You could hide him," the boy said. "You could put him in a basket with a very long rope and hold the rope, and he could go lower and lower, and then he could jump out at the bottom and do his wees, and then jump back in the basket so you could pull him up again, and nobody would see, except if they looked out their window. But if it was a very big basket, the dog could hide inside. He's just a little dog."

"Mm," Jax said. "I could do, if I didn't think he'd jump

out." He gave the little girl a bounce, because he hadn't set her down, and asked, "What do you think?"

"You could has a garden," she said, "and the doggie could go in the garden." She took a breath. "Like a kitty. Maybe he could turn into a kitty."

Jax looked at me. Finally. "All right?" he asked.

"Oh," I said, and waved a careless arm, wondering who'd sucked all the air out of my body, "I'm just great, thanks."

He frowned. "What?"

What? What did he mean, "what"? The boy said, "We came to sing to you! Because it's your birthday! Mummy said you'd be sad if we didn't, because you're used to being with your mates, but you don't have any mates here, because it's not the Army. And we brought you some flowers and a piece of cake, except the dog sat on the flowers in the car and spilt all the water, so they're a bit squashed. And he ate the cake, too. He even ate some of the bag it was in. So we don't have the cake anymore."

Jax said, "I appreciate the thought, anyway. It's Karen's birthday, too, so you can sing to both of us, how's that?"

"You have a duck," the boy said to me.

"Yes," I said. "I do have a duck. You didn't mention that it was your birthday, Jax. And here you had so many opportunities to do it." I was so mad, I could barely see. That must be mad, anyway. It had *better* be mad. I wasn't going to cry, not here. Instead, I kissed Debbie's head and didn't look up, then set him down and headed off.

Jax could protect Debbie from the dog. He was supposed to be good at protecting. At least for people he cared about. I couldn't do this, though. I couldn't be here. Not possible.

Jax said, "Hang on. Karen." He set the little girl down and came to put his arm around *me,* now, which meant I couldn't escape. "What's wrong?"

"Oh," I said wildly, "nothing much. I need to go." I needed to find Hemi. I needed somewhere I could actually cry, and there wasn't anywhere. I couldn't do it around Hope, or around my nieces and nephew, either. I needed to go home and lie on the bathroom floor again. Someplace I could be *alone.* I needed to crawl under a porch like a sick dog and wait to feel better. Sometime, I'd feel better. Why couldn't I ever be *alone?*

Jax was peering down into my face, and now, Hope was coming around the house with Maia running ahead of her. When she saw me, Maia shouted, "Auntie Karen! It's time for cake! And you get to blow out all the candles, and there are lots of candles, because thirty is so old. And Koro has to come and help."

Hope said, "Wait, sweetie. We have new company. Hi. I'm Hope, Karen's sister, and this is Maia. Welcome."

"My sister, Poppy," Jax said. "And her kids. They've come to surprise me. Karen. What?"

"What kind of cake is it?" Hamish asked. "I hope it's chocolate. That's my favorite."

"Hamish," his mother said. "We don't say that. We say, 'Thank you.'"

Jax said, *"Karen.* Sit down." He had both arms around me now, and to my horror, was sitting down with me in his lap, and I had a hand over my face and had started to cry. Not just cry. Sob. Shoulders shaking, nose running, ragged, ugly noise-making. The works.

I didn't cry. I. Did. Not. *Cry.* I couldn't help it, though. Both hands were over my face now, and I was losing it big-time. Jax was rocking me back and forth, stroking a hand over my hair, saying, "Baby. No. What's wrong? Tell me."

"Your sister," I managed to say. I shook my head and didn't move my hands. "She's your . . . *sister."*

"What? I told you she was my sister."

"No."

I heard Koro's voice, then, saying, "Come on. We'll go put off the cake for a few minutes, eh, give these two time to get themselves sorted. Could be you're hungry for lunch anyway, big kids like you. Got heaps of food back there. We'll get that down you. Could be the dog needs a bite to eat as well. He looks like a hungry little fella."

"Mummy always wants to eat," Hamish said. "But then she spews, so I don't know why she wants to eat. When I'm sick, I only have apple juice and things. She's having a baby, and ladies who are having a baby get very sick."

"My mummy gets very sick too," Maia piped up. "Because she's having a baby too. Ladies always have babies."

Which could have made me cry some more.

☆☆

JAX

I couldn't figure out what was wrong. Why would Karen be crying now? Had Hemi said something to her? She'd looked fine, though, when she'd first come up to me. She'd looked like she wanted to be there.

Everybody else left, finally, which was better. She was embarrassed, I could tell. She hadn't liked being ill. She was going to like that she'd cried even less. I rocked her and kissed her hair, and after a couple minutes, the sobs eased. She said, "I'm . . . heavy."

This tenderness. It hurt my heart. "No," I said. "You're just exactly not. What's wrong?"

"I'm also disgusting," she said. "Oh, yuck. Kleenex."

This time, I laughed, and she kept her hand over the lower part of her face and tried to glare at me out of reddened eyes. "Let's go inside," I suggested. "You can clean up, and then you can tell me. You may also want to remember that I cried, too, much as I'd like to forget it. You could think that we're even."

"The car. It's still . . ." She sniffed. "Running." Practical and logical even in extremis.

"Right," I said. "Go inside and clean up, then, and I'll come join you in a second, once I've moved it."

The little house was empty, fortunately, when I got inside. Nothing at all flash about this place, which I was guessing was because Hemi's grandfather hadn't allowed him to fix it up, because Hemi seemed like the type to offer. I sat on the couch, thought that my leg was still pretty sore, tried to make sense of all this, and failed.

When Karen came out, she was still wiping her face with a wad of toilet paper, and her nose was red. She said, "If I were one of those women who always had an extra makeup kit in her purse, I'd look better right now. I'm not, and I don't even have a purse, because I was supposed to be camping, so too bad."

"Sounding more like yourself, anyway," I said. "What happened out there? That can't be because I got a bit narky earlier, unless you're actually barking mad, and I don't think so. Not quite."

She sighed, sat down beside me, and stuck her bare feet up on the edge of the coffee table like she'd done it a hundred times. "I thought you were married."

"What?" I laughed. "Me? No. To who?"

"To *Poppy*. Obviously." She was glaring again. "What do you expect me to think, when you kiss her and hold the little girl and act like they're all your family? You *said* they were your family."

"But . . ." I tried to think it out. "Poppy's my sister. You know she is. She's who you were meant to meet in the Coffee Club, remember? What, my wife and my sister are both named Poppy? That'd be unusual. Off-putting, too."

"See," she said, "and now I feel stupid, because I realize you did say her name. I just . . . you looked . . ." Her arm was going again. "Like you loved her. And I was kind of . . . off balance anyway."

"Geez, I'd be casual. That'd be cool, introducing you like that." I'd started to laugh. I couldn't help it. She smiled, reluctantly, and then she started to laugh, too.

The hilarity rose in me like a bubble. The duck. The dog. The old man. All the times I'd held women's heads these past few days while they vomited. The hospital. The absolutely ridiculous amounts of emotion. I had my arms around Karen, she had hers around me, and as the laughter died down, I pressed my forehead to hers, smiled into her eyes, and said, "So. Wanna fuck?" And we were off again, laughing like fools.

It was the oddest romantic interlude you could possibly

come up with. The whole thing. And it had also been the best, and the worst, I'd felt in about . . .

Well, in forever.

31

STAR SIBLINGS

KAREN

I couldn't stop smiling. The daylight was fading, the air smelled like roast pork and citrus, a very relaxed Maori version of a Bob Marley song was playing over the speakers, half of the whanau had gone home, and I was dancing with Jax. Swaying to the sweet rhythm, the voices around us picking up the chorus, the stone of the patio warm under my bare feet, my lips against Jax's neck and his big hand splayed over my lower back.

He said, "OK?" His voice was very nearly a hum. A lovely *low* hum, vibrating through his chest and into mine.

I sighed, said, "Oh, yeah," and could practically hear his smile. Beside us, Tane and June were dancing, too, and Hemi and Hope were behind me somewhere. All that love, and I had some, too. At least that was how it felt.

"I used to be better at this," Jax said. "Had some moves. I'll have to ask my physio for help, I reckon. I wonder if that counts as operational fitness. Depends what you're trying to get operational in, maybe."

"Mm," I said. "Or you could figure that I'm liking it fine." I pulled back a little and smiled up at him. "Happy birthday."

He bent his head and kissed me like he didn't care who was watching. "Happy birthday, baby. You're beautiful."

When the song ended, we sat on the curved concrete wall again, my hand in his, and I realized how wonderful it was for a man to want—really *want*—to hold your hand, because he needed that connection as much as you did. His thumb was brushing over my knuckles, and I was listening to his sister, who was sitting on his other side. Her daughter, Olivia, was sleeping on Koro's bed along with Maia and a couple other little ones, arranged beside each other like bundled loaves of bread, or a demonstration of fertility, and for once, that didn't even hurt my heart.

Poppy said, "Sternengeschwister. That's what you two could be. Star siblings, destined for each other. That's romantic, eh. Wheeling round the heavens together like Ranginui and Papatuanuku."

"Mixing up your myths," Jax said. "The Sky Father and the Earth Mother." He sounded amused, though, and relaxed, too, not like he was running screaming at the mention of destiny with a woman he'd only just met. Somehow, I wasn't running, either.

"Holding each other tight in the dark," Poppy said. "But maybe with some space between them, so they don't have to worry about being separated." Something sad in her voice, but then, the Maori creation myth *was* sad. The Sky Father and the Earth Mother, together through all the pitch-dark ages at the beginning of the world, until they were separated forever by their children. The Sky Father's tears falling onto the earth for all the years and all the centuries that followed, blessing his wife again, longing to touch her one more time. And her longing just as much, only able to reach him via the morning mist, the vapor left behind by her sighs as she ached for her husband through the long nights.

It was sad, kind of like life. I was a realist, or I tried to be, but I liked the Star Siblings idea much better. Well, maybe not so much the "siblings" idea.

Hamish was playing with pocket-sized trucks on the patio at his mother's feet with Tama, who was enjoying being the big kid as they built a ramp out of blocks. Now, he sighed and said, "Mum. Boys don't like *romantic.*"

"Hush," she said. "It's not for a story. It's for Uncle Jax."

"Uncle Jax doesn't like romantic either," he said. "He's a soldier."

"Actually," Jax said, "Uncle Jax likes romantic fine." He lifted my hand to his lips, kissed my knuckles, smiled into my eyes, and said, "So tell us, Poppy," as I tried not to fall even harder and absolutely failed.

"It's German," she said. "I read it in a book. A *romantic* book. Research, you could say. Imagination work. In the story, they were both Gemini, which is even more romantic. Star twins."

"Jax is a year older, though," I said. "Also—incest." I'd got a shiver down my back all the same, though. *Star twins.*

"Doesn't matter which year," she said. "It's the same, astrologically. Want to know?"

"I'm an Aquarius," I said. "Which I don't believe in. It makes zero logical sense that eight-point-three percent of everybody on earth would share the same characteristics. Also, Jax and I don't have the same personality."

"You're exactly on the cusp with Capricorn, though," Poppy said. "Which means you have both. He's got more Capricorn, even though he's left-handed, and you're more Aquarius, at least I think so, although the 'eight-point-three-percent' thing sounds like Jax. Science, eh. Or math. Whatever."

"Karen *is* a scientist, as it happens," Jax said. "So maybe not so Aquarian. She's left-handed as well, which is interesting, maybe. Also excellent in the water, though. First day I met her, she reminded me of a mermaid."

I had one of those moments where your world tilts, and you aren't sure if you're looking at things upside down, or whether you just now realized how you ought to have been looking at them all along. I said, "The first time I saw you, coming out of the sea? I thought you were a merman. The way you swam, and how lean and strong you were. And how beautiful. You were walking on your knees, and that seemed so *right*. I thought I just had jet lag."

Hope, who was sitting on the ground with Hemi, raised her head like she was hearing extra-low-frequency noise, in that way she did. Hope didn't have extra-sensory perception, she had *ultra*-sensory perception, and right now, so did I. I felt a prickle along my arms, and looked down to see goosebumps.

Beside me, Jax had gone still. Or "more still," because Jax was good at stillness. Boy, I was hanging out here. Talking about how beautiful he was in front of everybody, letting him know how I felt. Now, the goosebumps weren't just about the connection. They might be about the fear, too.

He didn't let go of my hand, though, as Poppy went on, "There you are, then. Aquarius is all about the inner world, your waking dreams, where what's going on inside your head, what you're reading or thinking, is more real than what's actually happening. Born to create, eh, like being left-handed, but the Capricorn side means all that's based in logic and reason. You want security and balance, but you want freedom, too. Your need for grounding will always be fighting with your need to fly. I looked it *up,*" she said at a probably-sardonic look from Jax. "A long time ago, when I was looking up birthdays. I didn't say I believed it. I said it was interesting."

"That's you, Karen," Hope said. She was sitting against Hemi's chest, his arms around her, and just for tonight, I didn't have to be one bit jealous of that.

"What do you do for work?" Poppy asked me.

Oh, boy. Not my favorite subject. "I'm separated from work right now," I said.

She laughed. "Sounds like a divorce."

"Exactly like that," I said, and Jax squeezed my hand. I was tired, worn out by the day despite my long nap, and probably ready to leave, but I went on and said this anyway. I was tired of running away from the doubt and the disappointment. Tired of running from the fear most of all. That I wasn't enough.

I'd shown myself, front and center, all through the past eight years. At work. With Josh. With everything. I'd given all of myself, and everything I was had been rejected. And the fear was—maybe I always would be.

I was tired of the fear, though, too. I had a feeling I'd come too close to dying a few days ago. I'd looked up sepsis today, when I'd been resting after Hope and Hemi had left, and had realized how close I'd come. I'd almost died fifteen years ago, too. How many do-overs could a woman expect to get? I was taking this one. I was moving on.

"Before," I said, "I was an . . . an entrepreneur. In food technology, developing new products. My degrees are in biochemistry and business." That was another of those stones, the ones that had been weighing me down. Loss, or call it what it was. Grief. That was the only word, surely, to describe what it felt like to lose what had defined you for your entire adult life, to lose your purpose and your home and your community.

Well, I'd lost it. It was over. It was done, and it was time to put those stones down and walk on without them. Or at least to take the first few steps, if I wanted to leave them behind.

"So interesting," Poppy said. "Jax is the same, but different. Got the drive and the curiosity, anyway."

"And the calm and logic. And by the way—being left-handed doesn't actually make you more creative. That idea's based on one misinterpreted study, sadly. Means you're more likely to have certain mental illnesses, though. Which he clearly doesn't." I leaned my head against his shoulder, he put his arm around me, and that was even better. "I kind of like you," I told him, "you know?"

He kissed my temple. "I kind of like you, too. Want to go home?"

"Yeah." I asked Koro, who was sitting in his chair, which Hemi had brought around back, "You sure you're OK with the dog for now, if we come back tomorrow? I'd take him, but we probably shouldn't. I don't want to get Jax kicked out of his apartment." We'd given the little thing a bath after cake time. Its fur wasn't matted anymore, but it was now *extremely* fuzzy. It was adorable, just like Debbie, with big, round

brown eyes that looked at you worshipfully and brown
eyebrows on its black-and-white face, but it desperately
needed grooming. Also dog food, and a few other things. If
it was a breed, I couldn't imagine what. "I'm not worried
about Debbie, at least," I said. That was because Debbie was
already the boss of the dog. In fact, right now, they were both
asleep at the edge of the terrace, Debbie's bill resting on the
dog's back like he was making sure the dog would wake up
still knowing what was what. Debbie didn't mess around.

Koro waved a hand. "No worries. Nikau will get it sorted
tomorrow. The dog's good with the babies, and that's enough
for me."

"I feel bad," Poppy said. "Dumping a dog on you. I meant
to dump it on Jax."

Jax laughed, got up, gave his sister a kiss, and said,
"Breakfast tomorrow, then. We'll meet you at eight-thirty,
along with Hemi and Hope. Family time, eh. If you're too
sick, ring me, and Karen and I will come get the kids and feed
them."

They were staying over, Poppy had told me brightly,
because her husband, Max, was "traveling. *Again.*" I thought
she might have come up to see Jax as much because she didn't
want to be alone as because she'd wanted to be with him, but
there was no better antidote to loneliness than being with
Hemi's whanau. Or, it seemed, than being with Jax.

JAX

I thought Karen was asleep. The long summer daylight was
fading at last, streaks of pink and orange lighting up the
electric-blue twilight as we headed south, the muscular growl
of the car a bass note to the soft music playing over the
speakers, the wheels hugging the curves in the winding road.
It occurred to me how different this drive was from the last
time I'd done it, with Karen hot and listless beside me and the

anxiety winding up tight in my body.

As I was thinking it, she said, "I didn't hear you yell at your sister. Did you do it?"

"Nah." I downshifted as I slowed for the Tauranga limits. "Hard to do, when she's being sick."

"Mm. I've noticed you have a weakness when it comes to sick women. Could be alarming. A pretty terrible tendency toward gentleness with women in general. What happened to my tough guy? You've barely yelled at me since I got sick. What's up with that?"

Geez, she made me smile, even when she was heating me up. "I don't think I ever yelled much. And I like well women even better, if this is about you. Ones who jump off waterfalls with me and make love like they've thrown their heart over that fence already and are sending their body after it. No limits. I could have had a few moments, though, when I wanted to show you what I was thinking. You're a bit . . . frustrating. I'm keeping score, no worries. As for Poppy? I'm guessing it wasn't her idea. My dad's, more likely."

"So are you going to let him know how you feel?" She put a hand on my thigh below my shorts. It was my left one, but her hand didn't feel like it was assessing an amputated limb. It felt like a woman who wanted to touch you, and was doing it. "By the way—I thought that 'no limits' thing, after the first time. I thought I shouldn't say it, though. I thought it would put you off. Why are you always saying exactly what I'm thinking?"

I cleared my throat. "I'm going to have a discussion with my dad, yeh. And in what possible world would I be put off by you saying, 'No limits'? Also, that's a bit distracting, what you're doing there."

"Yeah?" She ran her hand under the edge of the shorts and stroked it up my inner thigh. "How about now?"

We were headed across the bridge into Mount Maunganui. Unfortunately, that meant we still had five minutes to go. I asked, "How are you feeling?"

I tried to ask it neutrally. I probably wasn't entirely successful, because she laughed, leaned across the center console, kissed my neck, sending a shock wave through me and seriously endangering both of us, and said, "I'm feeling like I want to touch you. I'm feeling like I want you to touch me a whole lot more than that. I'm feeling like I'm ready to be done being sick. You have a beautiful body. Have I mentioned that?"

"Yeh," I managed to say. "I think you have."

It felt like a very long time before I was pulling into the underground garage. When I'd eased the car into its space at last, Karen didn't wait for me to kiss her, like I'd expected her to. Instead, she jumped out. I climbed out myself, but I caught her hand as she headed off toward the lifts, pulled her back, got a hand behind her head and an arm around her waist, and kissed her. Harder than I had before, because if I'd ever had an invitation to do it, this was it. And she made a noise under my mouth and let herself be kissed just like that.

I'd have done it against the car. I was in that deep that fast, my hands tightening on her, the need pounding in my body. Footsteps on concrete, echoing from around a corner, brought me back to myself, and I pulled back a fraction and said, "Upstairs."

She pulled my head back down, kissed me again, got a hand under my T-shirt and sent it up my side, moved her mouth over until she was kissing my neck, and said, "I don't want to wait. I *can't* wait. Jax. Come on. I'm better."

I was a self-disciplined man. It wasn't easy to remember that. I got my hands on her shoulders, set her away from me, and then, because I possibly wasn't as self-disciplined as all that just now, I gave her a slap on the bum, did my best to smolder, and said, "Upstairs."

This was going to be hard. Hard to remember that whatever she said, she was still fragile in all sorts of ways. Hard to be everything she needed right now. Hard not to get carried away.

Fortunately, I was good at hard.

32

☆☆

DIRTY SECRETS

KAREN

How had he jumped so fast to exactly what I needed? How did he always *know?* Right now, he was pushing the floor button, then shifting his gaze to me. I thought I'd hear something sexy, but instead, he picked up my arm by the wrist and inspected it. The scrapes were still bandaged—he'd changed the dressing for me, in fact, before we'd gone to the hangi—but the visible skin was only a little pink and mottled now. I said, "It doesn't hurt."

He said, "It does, though. I've noticed you lie." In a remote sort of way that was weirdly sexy, or maybe that was the excitement rippling through my body. I shuddered, he smiled, the elevator doors opened, and he took my hand and said, "Come on."

I didn't know what I was going to get, but I had a feeling it was going to be good. When he was opening the door to his apartment, I kicked off my jandals and said, "I hope you bought condoms."

He shut the door behind us, got his own shoes off, put his arm around me, kissed my mouth, ran his hand down my neck until he was holding my shoulder, and said, "You've had a pretty rough few days. Maybe it'd be a good idea to let me take over now. All right?"

He kissed me again, and it was like his lips carried electricity. Not like a shock. More like a buzz of silver energy. I said, "All . . . right."

I should say something about how this was only in bed, and probably something about limits. I didn't, because I didn't want to.

He said, "Go on into the bedroom, then. When you're ready, you can lie down on the bed for me." He ran a hand up my thigh. I'd worn the halter dress that was my swim cover-up today, because it was the prettiest thing I had with me, and right now, I was glad I had. He kissed my neck, sent his hand a little higher, then brushed his fingers lightly between my legs, making me quiver. He smiled some more and said, "Leave all this on." Like he couldn't wait. Or like *I* couldn't, and he was going to make me do it anyway.

Oh, yeah.

I brushed my teeth, washed off my feet and a few other necessary areas, feeling jumpy and off-balance, wondering if he'd come in and watch me do it. When he didn't, I wondered what he was doing. I couldn't hear him, but surely he was out there. And finally, when he *didn't* come in, I went to sit on the edge of the bed. And burned.

He came in, finally, with a couple bottles of beer, sat down beside me, handed me a beer, and said, "You liked it the first time, eh."

Well, *this* wasn't exactly sexy. Then he said, "Thought I said to lie down, though," which was.

I took another sip of beer, shrugged, and said, "If I lie down, I can't drink my beer. Your plan has flaws."

He ran a hand over my hair, traced the hair at the nape of my neck, then leaned down and kissed me there. Gently. He whispered in my ear, "Suppose we make a new rule for tonight. No talking."

He was kissing my nape again, not touching me anywhere else, and I was having a hard time focusing. "A little hard to communicate what we want, maybe," I said.

"Oh, I can talk," he said. "This rule only applies to you."

I froze. He said, "If it hurts your arm, if I do something you don't want—tell me. Otherwise?" He kissed my lips again, smiled into my eyes, and said, "Shut up and do what I tell you."

The jolt of heat went right down my body. It was like he saw straight into me. I took another sip of beer. My hand was shaking, though, and it was hard to hold the bottle. Jax took it from me, set it down on the bedside table, sighed, and said, "You can start by taking off my leg."

I saw something in his eyes, then. Something that said, *I need to know you will. I need to feel like it doesn't matter.* And, maybe, that he needed to feel like a man. That worked for me, because I needed him to feel like one, too. So I did it. I got off the bed, knelt in front of him, found the button to take the leg off, and pushed it. He put his hand on my head, and when I looked up, there was an expression on his face I couldn't read. I leaned over, kissed his thigh above the white sleeve, and started rolling it down. I took his leg apart like foreplay, and when I had all the pieces off, I rubbed my hands over the stump, up his thigh, tried my very best to let him know with my touch that he was the most beautiful man I'd ever seen, and waited.

His voice was strained when he said, "Matches in the kitchen. Candles, too. Drawer by the fridge. Bring them in, light the candles, and turn out the light."

How could it be so hot, I wondered when I was touching the match to the second one, then going to the door and flipping the switch, simply not to be able to talk? How could I already be soaking wet, longing for one more touch of his finger? I knew why he'd chosen to do it this way. Because he was afraid of hurting me, but he wanted to excite me. I wanted to say, *Hey, buddy. It's working. Could we get the show on the road?* But I couldn't, so I just came back and stood in front of him. He put his hands on my waist, looked up at me, his expression hard in the flickering light, and said, "Take off your dress."

I did it. Slowly. I still wasn't voluptuous, and I was still ribby. I was wearing a thong, but I was also wearing a sports bra. It was the black one with the extra straps between my breasts, because it was the cutest—but still. It was a sports bra. And when I pulled the flimsy cotton fabric of the dress over my head and dropped it on the floor, Jax's hands went to those ribs of mine, traced over them, one by one, like they were beautiful, pushed the thrum in my body up another notch, then pulled me forward and kissed me just under my breastbone before he moved over and did some more kissing. Gently. And I thought fuzzily, *How can it feel this hot to have a man kiss your midriff?*

His hand touched each of the four shiny jewels in my belly, one at a time, and then his fingers drifted, light as smoke, on down to the edge of the thong. He said, "Take off the bra," and I did, being careful over my bandaged arm and wincing anyway.

He said, "Hurts, eh," and I nodded.

"Feeling all right?" he asked. "Need to lie down?" When I shook my head, he smiled and said, "Take off my shirt, then."

I did, even more slowly than I'd removed my dress, my hands brushing over the ridges of his abs, up his chest, over his shoulders and back. And when he said, "Take off the rest," I did that, too. Slowly, and with plenty of attention.

Was he beautiful? Yes, he was, and I wanted to touch everything, but I wanted him to touch me more than that. My hands went to my thong, and his hands closed around my wrists.

"Oh, no," he said. "You've got to earn that. We're not getting there for a long, long time."

The arousal was a steady pulse now, making me shudder. He said, "Seems to me you've been standing up long enough. Maybe you should get on your knees instead, start doing some of that earning. Nice and slow. Make it last."

I looked in his eyes. I dropped to my knees. And I did it.

He didn't touch me. He didn't push. He gave me directions, and that was all. And I was practically coming already. I wanted to touch myself. I *needed* it. And I didn't do it. I focused on him instead, and there were some whimpers in the back of my throat while I did it.

He'd begun breathing harder as soon as I started, but was *he* whimpering? No, he wasn't. The man had some serious self-control. I could feel the rigidity in his thighs, though, the tension in his body, and when he finally said, "Stop," it was a gasp.

I did, sat back, and looked up at him. He had both hands on the bed and his head bowed, his chest rising and falling. He looked at me, tried to smile, and said, "You're killing me. Come get up on the bed. We're going to play with you now."

He was still careful. When he said, "Put your arms up over your head, baby, and keep them there," his voice was gentle, and when he took my nipple into his mouth, that was gentle, too. But the second he did, my hips started to move. I started to say, "Please," and he lifted his head and said, "Don't talk. In fact, we'll make another rule. Don't open your mouth. I don't want to hear any noise."

Oh. My. God. The spasm went straight through my body, just like that. Over and over again, slamming into me like when the wave hit you wrong and you lost your breath and your strength, overtaken by the wall of water. I had my mouth closed, muffling the sounds, my hands stretched over my head. My back arched, my legs stiffened, and Jax was swearing, yanking down my thong, and shoving a finger up inside me. And I did it all again.

JAX

I'd been selfish. I'd been demanding. And all she wanted to do was obey me some more.

I wanted to make her come again. I wanted to keep on doing it. I needed to be inside her. All of that at once. I was rolling over, grabbing a condom from the drawer, getting it on with fingers that insisted on trembling, and she had her mouth and eyes screwed shut, her legs shaking, her thong not even off, and some noises coming out of the back of her throat. Absolutely unself-conscious. Absolutely gone.

I got the thong off. It was an effort. Her legs were long. After that, I took her inner thighs in my hands and spread them slowly apart, and she didn't open her eyes. Her pink-tipped breasts were right there, so I sucked on them a little more, and she bit her lip to keep from calling out. Did she turn me on? Oh, yeh, she did. And when I slid inside her at last, I was the one who moaned.

Doing it slow and easy took even more effort of will than not coming in her mouth had. If I'd made her ache, she was doing it to me and then some. When I got on my palms and was driving deep, looking down at her spread out underneath me, her eyes closed, her head flung back, her hands trying to grab the sheet overhead, her long, slim thighs tightening again? I wanted to get there right the hell now, but I needed to get her there again first. And I needed to make her wait just a little more to do it.

I wanted to flip her over, too. I wanted it more than I'd ever wanted anything. I said, still moving inside her, my eyes trying to roll back in my head at the pleasure of it, "Can you do . . . hands and knees? Without . . . hurting?"

She didn't open her eyes. She just nodded.

I pulled out of her with the effort of a lifetime and said, "Then do it." And she did.

If there's a better sight in the world than the woman you want most, naked on her hands and knees, head down, waiting for you, I don't know what it could possibly be. I ran a hand slowly down her spine, and she shuddered. I caressed her pretty bum, and she shook. I spanked it two or three times, and she started to moan, then stopped. Being quiet for me. I got on my knees behind her, spread her wide, and said, "You don't listen. You don't do what I say. You push it every time. Right now? I'm pushing you." And then I did. I fucked her until she was shaking, until she was panting, until she was so swollen around me, I could feel her grabbing hold there. And finally, I got my fingers around that little nub, started to press them together in time with my thrusts, and said, "No noise. I don't want to hear a thing."

I didn't. But I felt her spasms all the way through my body. And when the sweet sin of it spread over me and inside me the same way I was over her, inside her, and I was wound up so tight, it nearly hurt? When I finally let go? I called out loud. I went down deep, and she shook with it, but she took it.

I lit her up. I burned her down. I made her mine.

KAREN

Jax's hands were gentle on me, afterwards, when he helped me turn over, taking care of my arm. His lips were gentler than that when he kissed my closed eyes, one after the other, my cheeks, and, finally, my mouth. He stroked a hand down the side of my face, over my neck, my shoulder, and asked, "All right? Not hurting?"

I nodded, then shook my head, still with my eyes closed, and when he said, "You can talk now," his voice was amused. I opened my eyes, and he grinned, looking entirely too self-satisfied, and said, "Worked, eh."

I tried my best to glare. I had a reputation to uphold. I asked him, "How could that be so hot? I should be so mad at you right now, except that's part of the thrill of it. How are you so good at that?"

"Dunno." He kissed me again. "Maybe because you turn me on like you were made for me."

I wound a lazy arm around his shoulders and did some kissing of my own. "Mm. Way to be dominant without hurting."

"It was a challenge," he said. "Fortunately, I'm good at challenges. I think you came about three times there."

"I can't even count. And you sound ridiculously smug. Want a glass of water?"

"Yeh." He hoisted himself up against the pillows. "I'm going to let you get it, too, so I can watch you do it.

Tomorrow, I'll do some babying again. Tonight, you're still mine, and you're staying naked as long as I want you to." He watched me, and when he saw the shiver, he smiled, slow and satisfied, and said, "Pity I know so many of your dirty secrets. And the ones I don't know? I'm going to make you show them to me."

33

☆☆

THE LONELY MOUNTAIN

JAX

I didn't actually push her any more, of course. If she'd been well, I'd have done it, no worries. I'd have kept her up, and I'd have shown her plenty. She *wasn't* well, though, and she'd had a long day, so I didn't.

I didn't let her put on her PJs, though. There was a limit.

She was lying on her side, her bandaged arm propped on a pillow, and I was wrapped around her spoon fashion, my arm across her chest, when her voice came out of the dark, after I'd thought she was asleep. Sounding soft, and not like Karen at all. "Jax?"

"Mm?" I kissed the back of her head.

"Can you just . . . not promise anything? Not tell me you love me, or anything like that? You might think you're supposed to. You're not. I don't need to hear that."

Something was twisting in my chest. I held her a little tighter, kissed her again, and asked, "Why not?"

A long hesitation, and then she said, "Normally, I'm strong. I'm kind of . . . off balance right now, though. Anyway, I don't live here, and neither do you. I don't have a plan for my life anymore, and I'm not sure what yours is. So could this just be a . . . a good time?"

The same thing I'd told myself. My body and my mind were going in two different directions, or rather, they were going in no clear direction at all. I waited a minute, but nothing magically got any clearer, so I said, "I don't know. It should be that, but it doesn't feel like it to me. Maybe we don't get to have a plan right now. Maybe we just have to roll with it. Jump off that waterfall. Could feel a little scary, but I'm not sure we've got a choice."

"I always have a plan, though. A plan helps you get through the hard things."

She sounded so sad, and my chest hurt. Physically hurt. I asked, "What happened to you? When you were fifteen, sixteen, whenever it was?"

"I had a brain tumor." The words were quiet. She took my hand and moved it to the top of her head, but she was still facing away from me. "You can feel the plate here, under my skin. It's metal, and it's screwed in. You must have felt all of that, as much as you've touched me there. That's why it feels so good to me when you do, because that was where I hurt. See? That's another thing you somehow know. That's what's making this so hard."

"Oh." I felt stupid once again. "I thought you just had a lumpy head."

A soft exhalation that was possibly laughter. "No. I was really sick for a long time. It took almost a year to get it diagnosed, and I got sicker and sicker. It hurt a lot. Pretty . . . pretty scary, actually. I wanted to be normal so bad. Sometimes, I still do."

She paused, and I didn't say anything, because I didn't know what to say. I just waited, instead, until she went on. "I was a freshman in high school. It was a very fancy school. Private. I was on a scholarship. I mean, *totally* on a scholarship. That meant I had to do well, or I'd lose it, and my head hurt so much, and I was so sick, it was hard to focus. I was poor, too, and almost nobody else was, let me tell you. I not only had glasses and no chest and no money for lattes or cute after-school clothes, I was *also* the only one puking all the time. And I couldn't stand that Hope worried. I couldn't let anybody worry, or it would be true."

"It was Hope," I said carefully, feeling my way, "because your mum was gone."

"Yeah. Since I was nine. Hope was eighteen when she died, and she became my guardian. I didn't think about that then, but how scared must she have been? She worked so hard. We were so broke. I didn't realize how poor we actually were until I started going to that school. We never had a car, but that's New York. I never had a bike, though. I learned how to ride one here. I never went to a restaurant, a real one, until I was sixteen. I never learned how to swim until we lived with Hemi. Hope and I shared a bed until we moved in with him. Before my mom died, we slept on a fold-out couch in the living room. After she died, that couch was still there, and it stayed there until Hope and Hemi got married and Hope officially moved out. Which was, by the way, twenty-five years from when our mom probably got it, because as far as I know, Hope always slept on it. I didn't realize that people bought new furniture. I thought you bought one thing, and you used it forever. I slept with Hope my whole life. She rescued me. She always has. And then Hemi rescued both of us."

"He paid for your surgery."

"He paid for everything. He had ginger soup delivered when that was all I could eat. He got me diagnosed. He got me into the specialist. We didn't even have insurance. I think he probably saved my life. I kept my scholarship, somehow or other, until we moved in with him, and after that, he paid for school. Even when they were fighting and Hope left, he kept me with him and let me know he'd always help me. I know he's too protective, and he's way too bossy. He's not always good at boundaries. But you know—he's almost like my dad. And he didn't have to be."

I couldn't stand this. I couldn't. The tears were there behind my eyes. "And that makes you not able to trust this, to trust me, how?"

It took a long time for her to answer. "I think maybe I've reached my limit," she finally said. "I know how to work. I know how to figure things out. I have good ideas, or I used to. I don't think I know how to . . . how to make somebody love me. I'm not asking you to feel sorry for me." She said that fast, like being vulnerable was something to run away from. I might understand that, too. "I've been lucky. I had Hope, and then I had Hemi. I've got a good brain. I'm strong physically, other than right now. Strong enough to get over anything. I'm lucky."

"Or maybe," I said, "you could think that you're absolutely bloody fantastic at making somebody love you. Maybe you could think that that's why you *did* have Hope, and you had Hemi. Could be that Hope's good at loving. I'm sure that's true. But she got good at it by loving you."

Her shoulders shook, and I felt it. She said, "I don't . . . cry." The words came out tight. Choked.

"Maybe you should," I said, "if you've got somebody to hold you while you do it. It could make you feel better. That's what happened to me. Somebody held me and told me I was strong. I think she even said I was beautiful. Maybe it'd help if I told you that."

"But . . ." She was still fighting the tears, and I wanted to tell her not to. I wanted to tell her I was here, and I wasn't sure how to say it. It was pretty bloody frustrating, if you want to know the truth. "It's . . . dangerous," she said. "Believing. Like the legend of Mauao."

"Uh . . . you've stumped me here. What legend of Mauao? The mountain, you mean?"

"Yeah. Hope loves it here. I mean, right here. Mount Maunganui. It's where Hemi proposed to her, on the beach. It's where all her good things happened. I love it around here, too. It's home, or almost, because I know it isn't really. Maybe I've always felt a little like Mauao."

"Which is what?"

"If I tell you . . . you realize I'm doing the thing you're not supposed to do. Expressing negativity about myself to a potential mate. Off-putting and unromantic. Confidence is sexy."

"Or," I said, "allowing him to see all of you." I kissed the back of her head again, below the spot where the metal plate would be. "In case you haven't noticed, I enjoy looking at all of you, and you've got heaps of sexy confidence. Let's hear this legend, then."

"Mauao wasn't always here," she said. "That's the story. He was in the Hautere forest, in the ancient days, and there were three mountains overlooking Makahei Marae. Koro's marae, and Hemi's."

But not hers, because she wasn't Maori, and this wasn't quite her whanau, or she thought it wasn't. "Go on," I said.

"He stood in the forest then," she said, "beside Otanewainuku, the tallest mountain, the strongest one. A male mountain. He stood with Puwhenua, too, the most beautiful mountain. The two of them were in love. Mauao didn't even have a name then. He just stood there, year after year, being the little one, the fifth wheel, in love with Puwhenua and knowing he could never have her heart. It's a Maori legend, so you'd think he'd fight, somehow, but instead, he decided to take himself away instead, because he couldn't stand it anymore, loving and losing and having to know it every day. He decided to drown himself in the sea."

"So far," I said, "this is a pretty depressing legend."

She laughed. "I know, right? So he called to the patupaiarehe, the people of the night, and asked them to plait a magical rope and haul him down towards the ocean, and they agreed. They came in the early hours of the night with their magic rope, fastened it around him, and chanted the hauling song, pulling him towards the sea little by little, like you pull a waka. They pulled so hard, they carved out the valley where the Waimapu River flows. That's what the name means. 'Weeping waters,' for the nameless mountain's tears as he was pulled farther and farther away from his home and his lady mountain. Also what formed the channel between the Mount and Tauranga, so you know."

"Right," I said. "So he's drowned now. Very romantic. Not."

"No, obviously, because he's still right here, outside your window. They were almost to the sea when it got too close to dawn. The patupaiarehe had to flee back to the forest where they live, and when the sun rose, the mountain was fixed to that place forever. The patupaiarehe gave him his name before they left, though. Mauao. Means 'Caught by the morning light.' Now, he's not nameless, and he has a job to do, being a home for the birds and the trees, watching over the people. He does his job, but he never got any of his wishes."

"And you think that's you," I said.

Her shoulder lifted in a shrug. "No. Not really. He wanted to die, and I've never wanted to die."

"Good," I said, "because that's rubbish. Why are Maori stories always so bloody sad?"

"Because life can be sad?"

"It can be happy, though, too. That mountain sounds like a quitter to me. The very last thing you are, and I'll bet the very last thing you've ever been."

She rolled over, finally, and I said, "Take care of your arm."

"I *am.*" I could see her face, just, in the moonlight from the window. A moon that shone on the mountain watching over us, over the sea and the trees and the birds. And the woman in the bed beside me. "You're right," she said. "That's a stupid comparison."

"You could think," I said, "that he found his job, and he did it. Maybe that's what he was meant to do all along."

"Ah," she said. "But that's the other thing."

"What's that? If it's the ex—I've already decided the ex is a wanker. If Hemi hasn't already told you so, too, I miss my guess. Besides, I'm better than him."

She laughed again, and I got a little closer and kissed her mouth. She said, "Yep. Hemi used the same exact word. And, yes, you are."

"And how did we both know? Because we could see he wasn't good enough."

"You've never even *met* him."

"Don't have to."

"Anyway," she said, "that isn't the worst thing, no. I don't miss him. That's what's weird. I miss work. I miss it like crazy, but I don't miss him. I don't think I ever really had him, so maybe I didn't lose him. Plus, I hated him for what he did. A lot. I probably still do. I'm not too good at the love/hate thing. It's one or the other."

"Same with me," I said. "Frustrated, yes. Hate, no. Not along with love. Could be we're passionate, eh. Could be we see things in black and white."

"The worst thing," she said, like she hadn't heard me, "is that I keep thinking I'll know what to do next. That I'll get an idea, like I did when I started Prairie Plus. And I just . . . haven't. I've got nothing. I used to wake up every *day* with ideas. I had a notebook by the bed to write them down, because otherwise, I'd be blundering around in the middle of the night, trying to find a piece of paper so I wouldn't forget. They were usually something bizarre, like 'Banana garbanzo muffins,' because I was eating them in a dream. That one doesn't work, by the way. I tried making them, just in case I'd been subconsciously brilliant. The texture's disgusting. But ever since that last day? I've got nothing. It's like I took the money, and they took my *brain*. I signed a noncompete agreement anyway, so I don't think I can even see if there actually is some way to make baked goods with legume flour. Brownies, maybe. Never mind. Anyway, when I try to think of an idea for something completely different, something I *could* do with the agreement, I'm just . . . blank. And I think— what if I've already blown my only lucky shot? What if I never *do* think of something else? I'll have to join somebody else's company, I know I will, and I won't get to say what we do, but what am I even going to bring to the table if I don't have any more ideas?"

I laughed, and she said, "Hey. It isn't funny. I'm *confessing* here. You wanted vulnerable? There you go. Vulnerable."

"Nah," I said. "It *is* funny, a bit. Let me guess. You were lying in hospital, half dead, thinking about how you should be having brilliant ideas for a brand-new kind of product that'll take the States by storm, and that you'd clearly lost all your mojo because it wasn't coming to you somehow, between the

IV and the infection and the pain and all. Have you ever heard of resting time?"

"What, like sleep? Of course. I'm hearing of it right now. Hey, *I'm* not the one who asked all these questions and kept me awake."

Now, I was the one laughing. "Who was the one who said, 'What are those?' when I asked her about holidays, though? Farmers don't plant the same thing in a field every year, do they? They switch it out, right?"

"Yes," she said. "They plant a cover crop that they plow under. That was part of the idea of Prairie Plus. You have to use a whole lot less fertilizer and so forth if you rotate the right crops. Better weed control, less nutrient leaching, increased water infiltration, et cetera. If you plant the right cover crop, you can use it for things like, oh, for example, mixing with grass-fed meat to create a better burger, *while* you improve the land. And this is a worse metaphor than my mountain one. It's making me really depressed."

"No." I kissed her again. "It's a brilliant one. Wait and see. You know the right term, and all the benefits, whilst I exhausted my agricultural knowledge with the general idea. If your brainwaves didn't get killed by having a tumor in there, I think it'll take more than losing a job and a wanker boyfriend to do it. Maybe your brain just needs a cover crop, did you think of that? Maybe it needs to take a walk on the beach and feel the waves coming in. Have a swim, be a mermaid for a while. Take a walk up Mauao and hear those birds. Jump off some waterfalls. See some dolphins. Make some space for the ideas to come. Pretty hard to get that space when you're in the depths of despair, or when you're back in hospital, with all those feelings from before crowding back in the way they must have done."

She sighed. "How did you get so smart? It's like you're in my *head.*"

"Dunno. I just am, I guess." I sighed myself. "It's my gift, eh."

She laughed and hit me in the arm, and I grinned back in the darkness and said, "You're pretty good at that yourself, being in *my* head. Could be that our pieces fit after all."

"Even though I said the absolute wrong thing today, which you haven't given me a hard time about yet, because you're being careful. OK, I'm putting it on the table, because I'm *not* careful. I was tactless. About the real-estate thing," she clarified, when I didn't answer. "And how you should have known. Which I said in front of everybody. And don't say you didn't care, because I know you cared. You walked off. Besides, Hemi told me I shouldn't have said it."

"Oh. Yeh, I did care. On the other hand—that's you, eh. If it's a choice between waiting for the right moment and choosing the right words, and blurting it out the second it occurs to you? Reckon you'll blurt it out every time. Also, I *was* pretty stupid, obviously. But then, if we hadn't both been stupid about that, we wouldn't be here, and yet here we are. Maybe we should take advantage of it and go make some more room for ideas in that brain of yours."

"What will we be doing for you, though?" she asked. "I'm not the only one at loose ends here."

"And there you go, blurting it out again. Well, on Monday, I'm going to Dunedin, to the Limb Centre, for my next appointment. That's not too exciting. I could show you my house, though, maybe. We could also have some more sex. There's an idea. That could help pass the time while we wait for inspiration to strike."

34

UNDERCURRENT CITY

KAREN

When I opened my eyes, it was to the comforting sight of my lonely guardian of a mountain, because the blinds were open. The doors to the terrace were open, too. I knew that because I could feel the touch of the breeze and hear the faint roar of the sea. Possibly my favorite sound in the world, so I closed my eyes and dozed a little more, drifting on the ebb and flow of that roar, the call and answer of the seabirds.

The next time I woke up, I was a little more with it. I rolled over, looked at the digital clock on the bedside table, sat up straight, tried to blink the sleep away, and remembered about four things at once.

One: That Jax had seriously rocked my world last night. I was still a little swollen and sore from an excess of usage, in fact, and all it took was remembering the look on his face when he'd told me, "Shut up and do what I tell you," to set up some major throbbing. Two: He hadn't woken me up to do it again, so maybe all of that hadn't been as hot to him as it had been to me. He'd said he hadn't had sex since before he'd gotten injured, and before that, he'd been in the Special *Forces*. In Afghanistan, where I couldn't believe there'd been tons of opportunity. He wasn't any more eager for me than that? Three: That I'd somehow spilled absolutely everything to him in the aftermath, like he really *was* my star twin, or possibly like I'd been drunk—on half a beer—and that I couldn't remember quite what he'd said in response to all that oversharing of my seriously not-hot weaknesses. I'd told him about my *head.* And my early poverty, probably in a woe-is-me way, which I *never* did. Nobody wanted to hear that. And then there was my business failure. I wasn't sure which of those was worse, and the memory made my skin flush. Not in a sexy way.

Oh, and four. *Wait.* Four was that it was . . . eight-eleven, and we were meeting Hemi and Hope, and Jax's sister, whose name I somehow couldn't remember right now, plus five kids, in nineteen *minutes.* I stumbled out of bed fast, caught my foot in the duvet, and nearly crashed to the ground. Which was when Jax came through the door. He was across the room, somehow, before I'd hit the floor, his hands under my arms, setting me on my feet.

I said, "Thanks." My head was still fuzzy, and I was a little dizzy, too. "How did I sleep that long? That had to be ten hours at least. Why didn't you wake me *up?* Wait. I'm naked. Shoot. Where are my clothes?"

I was searching in my duffel, which was sitting on the dresser. I'd never unpacked it, since I'd spent almost all my time in this apartment in bed. Jax said, "Those may be rhetorical questions, but in order: Because you were tired, because you were tired, and your clothes are right there under your hands, except for the things you've been wearing, because I did your washing along with mine this morning and hung it on the rack. Sorry, baby, but your pretty dress is all wet. Almost as wet as you were last night."

I'd found a pair of bikinis and a seriously not-hot sports bra, and now, I pulled on the underwear and tried to get the bra the right way around. "And, see," I told Jax, "it's hardly awkward at all having you say that, and having you look at me naked and messy in the, uh, genital area, after only the second time we've had sex, or the first, depending how you count, while you're all cool and dressed and ready to go. Also, I have a bad feeling that I overshared."

He sat on the edge of the bed, his expression amused, and said, "And here I thought I'd established that I get to look at you naked while I'm all cool and dressed, and that I get to mess you up in the genital area, too. Thought I'd made that point pretty clearly, in fact. Can't remember what the other thing was. You're distracting me. Have I mentioned that I plan to fuck the hell out of your pretty body?"

I stopped in the midst of pulling the bra on. Which, yes, was another slightly awkward position, what with my hands being over my head and all. He stood up, got his fingers on my nipple, and did a little pinching, and I swear, my legs shook. I was also kind of speechless. Finally, I said, "You've always been so . . . gentlemanly, though." Breathlessly.

"Yeh?" He was backing me up against the dresser. That was before he sent his other hand down, straight under the edge of my bikinis, and did some exploring, which may have had me leaning back and moaning. "Think you'll find that's about to change." After that, he spun me around, gave me a hard slap on the butt, said, "Get dressed, or we'll be late," and walked out.

Oh, boy.

He wasn't one bit like that ten minutes later, which was hardly disconcerting at all. Instead, he asked me, when I came out of the bathroom, hastily dressed in the first shorts and top I'd pulled out of the bag, and with two minutes' worth of makeup on, "Did you take your medicine and drink some water?" The same way he'd reminded me last night, when I'd been about sixty seconds from falling asleep. He'd gone into the bathroom to get the pill for me, in fact, despite the fact that he hadn't been wearing his leg, and had stood over me, and said, "Drink all your water. You need to stay hydrated," in a way that could have felt like fussing but had felt more like bossing, in a way I could handle. If a man could be said to bring you your antibiotic in a hot way, Jax had done it.

I said, "Yes," and he said, "Good. Ready to go, then?"

"Wait." I put my hand against the door so he couldn't

open it. "I need to ask . . . which guy is you? All right, you asked how I was doing, but aren't you going to talk about all those embarrassing details I shared last night? Say something reassuring? I'm seriously confused."

He was smiling, and then he was laughing. Leaning against the door, too, and saying, "You make it so bloody difficult to dominate you."

"Oh." I considered that. "Well, that's disappointing, if it's a paint-by-numbers thing." I was laughing too, even though I was trying not to.

He was still smiling when he pulled me in, kissed me softly on the mouth, and said, "It's not a paint-by-numbers thing. It seems to be a contradictory thing. It's that I want to take care of you, and I want to take *care* of you. You could say that means, 'Take care that I've got you where I want you,' and that I don't need any help at all to be that fella. You could call that first one new territory for me, though. Also, there's the leg."

"The *leg?*" I looked down at it. "What, it's hurting?"

"No. Yeh. Never mind. Say that it's not as easy to be that fella you want when you're massaging my leg."

"You don't like fussing," I guessed.

"No. I don't." No laughing, now.

I kissed him back and said, "Well, good, because neither do I. Except that I like it a tiny bit when you do it. Maybe because of that contradiction you mentioned. Maybe because I know you're just waiting to be that other guy. Maybe you could think, when I'm massaging your leg . . . that I want to do it for you." Was I going to say this? It seemed I was. "That I want to . . . serve you."

He went still, and he also went hard. He was close enough that I knew that for sure. I rubbed my cheek against his scruff-roughened one, felt like the kitten I absolutely wasn't, and sighed. "So . . . want to buy me a cream donut before you dominate me?"

☆☆

JAX

I was rocked off my pins already. Or off my pin, more like. And then there was breakfast.

Five kids, three of them needing their food cut up. One pair of very shrewd and speculative eyes, which would be Hemi's, noticing the faint love bite I'd somehow left on the side of Karen's neck, because she loved having her neck sucked so much, and she'd tightened up so gorgeously around me when I'd been doing it, while I'd been fucking her hard from behind, that I'd got a little carried away. He was noticing the way I held her hand under the table, too. I was doing that because I had the feeling that she felt a bit less-than with her sister and Hemi and the kids, despite all her achievements.

I'd never thought much about kids. Or, rather, I'd thought pretty hard about taking care I didn't make any. Somehow, though, when I'd been lying beside Karen last night, my arm and good leg over hers like I could hold her there with me and never let her go, I'd found myself wondering about the whole subject. About how both of us were in the middle of some fairly serious transition, I hadn't had sex without a condom in ten years, and I wanted to have it that way with her anyway. I'd wondered if she'd trust me enough to let me do that. I'd also wondered if I'd trust *her* enough to make sure she was safe from pregnancy, and had realized I didn't care. More than that. I'd realized I'd rather she wasn't safe.

Whoa. I tried to tell myself, "Brakes on, mate," once again, and couldn't do it. Sexy possessiveness might be a game I enjoyed playing, but that was all it had been. When she'd told me everything she had the night before, though, it had been what I'd said. I'd wanted to wrap her up and hold her safe. I'd wanted to tell her she didn't have to feel alone anymore, and she didn't have to feel scared.

I'd never in my life believed the thing you heard from time to time, that some fella had looked across a room at a girl and thought, *That one. That's mine,* and had it work out for a lifetime. Sexual attraction, I'd thought, and that was all. Karen would have said that you only heard about the stories that ended up being true love and soulmates, which were probably about one percent of the total, and not the ninety-nine percent that burnt up and fizzled out, or that never got started in the first place. Or, of course, the ones that were just some rando stalking a woman he thought was his destiny. Karen was as logical as I was, or more so. Maddeningly so.

And yet—it *felt* true.

I knew I was off-balance now, for the obvious reason that I was . . . well, literally off-balance. One of the things they'd told me at the rehab center was not to make any major life decisions for at least six months after the loss, and I still had more than a month to go.

"The grieving process is a complex one," the therapist had said. "Give yourself time to process the emotions, and remember that every choice you make during this time will be influenced by the loss of your limb, and may not resemble the choices you'll make once you've worked through it."

Which all sounded reasonable enough. There'd be a reason behind what I was feeling now, too. That the recognition of my own mortality had made me want to leave biological descendants behind, to get that seed planted fast in the most fertile soil I could find, and to watch it grow there, preferably under my eye and hand, the most primitive impulse that had ever held a man in its grip. That on a perhaps more elevated level, I needed to know I'd have somebody's photo in the pocket over my heart next time I was bleeding into the dirt, and that I wanted to think I'd know for sure, in that moment, that I was living, and maybe dying, for something beyond my mates and my country and my duty. Possibly to know there was somebody who needed me more than life, so I'd bloody well better live. Even though I was probably never going to be in that position again, so the desire made no sense.

All of that was true, and yet there was this as well. That I'd woken about three times during the night and had to touch Karen to make sure she was still all right before I'd been able to fall asleep again. That I'd pinned her washing onto the rack this morning with mine, thought about her easy-breezy confidence, and had thought, too, about her being fifteen, trying to study through sickness and pain so she wouldn't lose her scholarship. I'd realized how tough she'd been, and that she still didn't know how rare that kind of toughness was. I'd clipped her pretty little dress to the line and heard Hope saying, "Maybe she can let her guard down with you, because you get it." Right now, I was watching her sister's eyes going to her again and again, like a mother cat stretching out a paw to pat her kitten, making sure it was there and getting everything it needed, and was feeling a bit humbled, if I were honest. I'd always thought I was a pretty good brother. I hadn't known anything about it.

Poppy asked, "What are you two doing next? Still going to the South Island? I shouldn't say it, as here we all are together, but I do want to sell this business, and having you show the places to Karen *would* be helpful. It wasn't all Dad's idea. I should tell you to take care you're impressing her, in case she has influence over Hemi."

"If Hemi weren't such a good businessman," I said, "he'd be doing a face-palm right now. I'm no kind of negotiator, and even I know that you just gave away your position."

"Nah," Poppy said. "I didn't say I wasn't going to ask a good price for it. He knows I want to sell it, and that I don't want to sell it to just anybody. That's been established. I want it to be a Kiwi, and somebody who cares about the land."

"Tangata whenua," Karen said.

Somebody Maori, she meant. A person of the land. Poppy said, "Or somebody who feels that same way about it, anyway. Somebody who gets why I bought each parcel, how special it is, and why I set it up the sites up the way I did. I want the buyer to feel the heart beating there the same way I do."

Hope said, "That's beautiful." Hemi, of course, said nothing. He was probably rubbing his hands together in glee inside, though.

"I don't want to have to keep track of all of it," Poppy said, "not with the new baby coming and my books doing well, but I can if I have to. If I don't find the right person, if I'm not convinced. I've done it so far, after all."

She'd had a partner, in the beginning, when she'd bought the first couple slices of paradise on some of the money she'd received in trust from our grandfather at the ripe old age of twenty-one. A few years later, she'd bought another two properties, bought out the partner, hired some people to help run things, and been off to the races. "Three kids feels like heaps," she said to Hope. "Is it?"

Hope said, "It feels like more, definitely. You're outnumbered, with three. That's surprisingly important."

"I'm outnumbered with two," Poppy said, and I wondered a couple things for the first time. First—why wasn't Max taking care of this sale? He was in the import/export trade, and from what he said, he was doing bloody well at it. Surely he could handle a real-estate negotiation for his wife while she was this sick. Poppy had had to make a dash for the toilets twice already this morning, and she wasn't doing any better at eating her breakfast than Hope was. Hope had Hemi sitting beside her, though, cutting his youngest daughter's pancakes and issuing the odd quiet command, whereas Poppy was doing it herself and looking green. Second—why were they having another kid, when Poppy already seemed so stretched? She'd always made me laugh. She made everybody laugh. Maybe she wasn't always laughing inside, though.

"You should come visit at our house, Uncle Jax," my nephew, Hamish, said. "You could bring the dog to live with us when you come. You could bring him on the airplane, if you packed him in a suitcase. Livvy and me want to have a dog. In Mummy's stories, kids always have dogs. Or they have cats, sometimes, but I think dogs are better. You can throw a ball for a dog. You can't throw a ball for a cat. Or we could have a snake."

"You can throw it," Poppy said. "The cat just won't care. And Daddy's allergic, remember? We've talked about this. Also—no snakes. Absolutely not. I draw the line at snakes."

"Daddy doesn't live at our house all the time, though," Hamish said. "So the dog could live at our house when Daddy isn't home, and Uncle Jax could live there too and be our company and throw the ball for the dog with me. And then the dog could go live with Uncle Jax when Daddy comes home."

"He travels," Poppy told Hope. "Excuse me. Jax, could you—" She didn't finish the sentence. She was off to the toilets again. Hope's eyes followed her, and she exchanged a look with Hemi.

Poppy was never what you'd call meaty, but now, she looked positively fragile. From what I'd seen of Hemi, that was a better weapon than any brilliant negotiating. Maybe Poppy hadn't put herself at such a disadvantage after all.

In another minute, I was sure of it, because Olivia announced, "More juice," Hemi asked, "What's the magic word?" and when Olivia answered by saying "More juice" again with a determined look on her face that made me want to laugh, he waited with his Inscrutable Negotiation Face until she gave an exasperated toddler sigh and said, "More juice *pease,*" upon which he smiled and poured a bit into her glass. Soft spot uncovered, if I hadn't already seen it.

When Poppy came back, I said, "To answer your question—yeh, Karen and I will go check out one or two of those places, as long as she's still keen. We're going to my house first, though."

"Dad knows you're coming, of course," Poppy said. "He's tracking your movements. Possibly on his wall board. He texted me this morning and said he hasn't heard from you. He says you've got an appointment tomorrow at the Limb Centre, and you should come for dinner afterwards. I'm supposed to remind you to answer him."

There were so many undercurrents at this table, the place was practically underwater. I said, "Thanks, but I've got it," then asked Karen, "Did you want to go see your grandfather before we go? I need to see to the dog anyway." Whatever the old man had said, I wasn't dumping Poppy's impulsive good deed on him. He'd been given an unexpected duck already. He didn't need two new pets in one week.

"Yes, please," Karen said. "I need to return the rental car to the airport, so if you want to take me, that'd be good. You probably wouldn't want me to drive your fancy Lexus anyway."

"I don't care if you drive it," I said. "First, because I suspect you're a good driver, though you probably speed, and second, because it's not mine. A bit like the apartment."

Hemi murmured something like, "Too right, mate," and Karen ignored him. "So what kind of car do *you* have, then?" she asked. Saucily, of course. "I'm torn between the battered ute and the top-of-the-line Jaguar. Oh, wait. It'll be something much more reliable, with excellent resale value. BMW, maybe. Which you bought used, because you have no need for ego, being so tough and all. I can't decide on your house, either. Sophisticated urban bachelor? Full-on Kiwi bloke, complete with shed, and your gumboots by the back door? Don't tell me," she said to Poppy. "It's more fun to guess. Whichever it is, it'll be *extremely* well maintained. I feel confident in that assertion."

Poppy said, "Sounds like she's got your number, Jax." She was laughing, which made the first time today. "You've even distracted me from being sick," she told Karen. "Cheers for that."

"I'm thinking," Karen decided to share, "that he might not care anymore whether he impresses the girls or not. He could be that confident now. It's possible. Something to do with all that military toughness, maybe." She took a final sip of her mocha. Feeling good, apparently, because she'd eaten every bit of her eggs benny. *With* smoked salmon.

Feeling good was very good news for me, because I knew exactly what she was doing. Teasing me where I couldn't respond well enough, in front of both of our sisters, too many kids, and Hemi Te Mana. Seeing if she could get a reaction. I smiled and said, "Could be you'll have to wait and see on all of that."

"Oh? Not going to tell me?" Karen tilted her head at me and managed to look saucy and asking-for-it as hell, despite being dressed in a pair of shorts sadly longer than the black ones, her blue T-shirt, and the plain purple cotton sports bra we both knew she had on under there. "I'll just be excited to find out, then."

35

☆☆

A Quick Errand

Karen

I'd kissed Hope and the kids goodbye, Jax and I were walking across the street again, and my body started to hum, right on cue. Or rather—the hum that had been happening all morning increased in frequency. Something about how calmly Jax had looked at me, especially at the end there.

Well, to be honest, probably more the way he'd looked at me earlier. When I'd been naked, and he'd backed me against the dresser like he was two seconds away from putting me up there, pulling my hips to the edge, and doing it right there and then. You know. That.

He held the door for me into the lobby, and I said, "I like your sister."

"So do I," he said. "And that isn't what you want to talk about." We were in the elevator, but he was pushing the button for the garage.

"Wait," I said. "Are we going to visit Koro now?"

He was doing that remote look again. "Why? What did you want to do?"

I waved an arm. "Oh, nothing. It's not like you promised or anything."

He smiled, we stepped out of the elevator, and he put an arm around me, dropped a kiss on my mouth, and said, "I did promise. And I keep my promises. You'll see."

"So I'm just supposed to wait for it?"

The smile grew some. "That's the idea." Then he opened the car door for me. Back to being a gentleman.

I told him, when we were driving over the bridge into Tauranga, "I'm not a patient person."

This time, he laughed out loud. "I think I've grasped that."

He turned off the highway, though, barely fifteen minutes from home, and I asked, "Why are we stopping?"

"We're going to have to do something about this tendency you have to take control," he said, as he took a left on Wharf Street, the fronds of the palms by the shore rustling in the breeze, the winding footpath beside the water already busy with runners and bicyclists. He found a parking space up a side street, and slid the car neatly into it. "I have an errand to run first. Do you want me to be in charge here or not?"

"I'm talking about in *bed,*" I said, not getting out of the car, because I needed to establish this. "Or sexually, anyway. Different rules."

"Ah," he said. "Consider this foreplay, then. Get out of the car."

I did. He had me curious, that was why. If he thought he just got to boss me around in general, I'd . . . Well, I was on vacation. I'd let him boss me a little. Just because it was hot.

We walked a block up the road, which wasn't busy yet, at ten-fifteen on a Sunday morning, other than the half of Tauranga that was inhabiting the ubiquitous sidewalk cafes, because one thing Kiwis knew how to do was relax and enjoy themselves. Jax passed two of them and stopped in front of a jeweler's, whose black velvet display stands were mostly empty, and said, "This is it."

"Uh . . . Jax," I said, reading the sign on the door. "They don't open until eleven." My heart was beating like a kettledrum all the same. *Boom. Boom. Boom.* Which was stupid, because the store was closed. The pieces that *were* in the window, though, were gorgeous, modern and swooping, the rose and yellow gold settings, in lush, thick curls, enclosing jade, opals, and pearls of both the blue paua-shell and the creamy-pink oyster-shell variety. It might all be semiprecious, but it sure was beautiful.

Jax had his phone out and was texting, and as I peered into the shadowy interior, a guy came out of a door in back, then turned a key and opened the door.

"Morning, Bevin," Jax said. "Cheers for this."

"No worries," the man—Bevin—said. He was short, neat, sandy-haired, and middle-aged. He didn't actually have a loupe screwed into his eye socket, but he looked like it was in the back room. "Here you are." He went behind a counter and handed over a bag. "Always happy to help the family. Be sure to give your dad my best."

"I'll do that," Jax said, pulling out his wallet.

Oh. We were picking something up for his father, because Jax was seeing him tomorrow. The place at the Mount was a family apartment, he'd said. Their holiday spot, obviously. Even the fancy car wasn't his. I remembered the other thing he'd said. "I'm not rich. My family's rich."

The glass covering the counter was heavy and thick, and the case beneath it held rings, and not the kind you see at the mall. It was the kind of jewelry Hemi bought Hope, and not. The settings he chose for her were always delicate, the motifs tending toward the floral. This was bolder, more modern.

I looked at the case on the wall, because the man had slipped an invoice onto the counter—in the way purveyors to the rich and famous had of doing it, like money was a slightly dirty afterthought—and Jax was busy paying. Or, possibly, because there were some things in there I had to see. A pendant like a twist of ribbon, diamonds on gold. A shining circle of paua pearl in all its deep-blue luminescence, surrounded by diamonds in a rim of white gold, on a white-gold chain as thick as cable. Oh, that was gorgeous. A thick, wavelike chunk of yellow gold with a diamond sunk into its middle, with more diamonds set roughly into the roughly beveled edge along one side, so it looked like it had been mined that way. It was on a heavy yellow-gold chain that looked exactly like that—like a chain—and it was nothing Hope would ever have worn. I loved it.

Jax came over and said, "So. Which one's nicest?"

"Is this where your dad buys your mom her special things?" I asked.

"Yeh. They do mostly bespoke pieces here. Why, d'you like them?"

"Well, *yes,*" I said. "Only extremely." He laughed, and I said, "Your mom has good taste. By which I mean what people usually mean by 'good taste.' That it's the same as mine."

"Which is your favorite?" he asked.

"I wouldn't know how to choose. One of the pendants. This one, maybe." I pointed to the chunky wavelike one. "It looks like it was mined by magic dwarves. I love how the basic shape is all organically smooth and curved and pleasing, but it has that roughness where the diamonds are set, like it's stone. Like the diamonds were inside, and they've cut the edge out to show them. That's really clever. It would be amazing in other colors of gold, too."

He studied it. "Yeh. Nice. Ready to go?"

"Awkward," I said, "looking at jewelry like you expect it. I don't expect it, so you know. Just to put it out there."

"Ah," he said. "Yes. Always good to have it out there." We headed out again, and the jeweler locked the door after us.

"Fun to look, though," I said.

Jax had picked up my hand and threaded his fingers through mine. Now, he said, "I think we should have another coffee before we go. You could need hydration."

"Caffeine is dehydrating," I pointed out.

He laughed. "All right. You can have decaf. Here." He stopped in front of a building that *didn't* have a café on the ground floor. "Upstairs. My secret place."

We climbed the stairs, and I sat down at a table on the balcony looking at, what else, Mauao, at the end of the channel he'd carved out being hauled by the magic rope, while Jax went and ordered. When he came back, he looked at me for a minute, and I asked, "What?"

"I don't want to ask," he said slowly. "But I'm going to ask anyway."

"Oh, boy. What?"

"That bloke. Josh. He was the CEO of your firm, right? Got the big payout?"

"Yes." I wished my coffee were here. I'd like to have something to look down at. I didn't, so I looked at Jax instead.

"But he didn't buy you jewelry?" he asked. "Or did you just not bring it along with you on the trip? Other than the earrings and belly rings, because those are all I've seen."

"The earrings were a graduation present from Hope and Hemi," I said. "They're diamonds, and I love them. I don't usually wear anything else in those holes, because they kind of do the job, you know?" I touched the ones on the left, the way I sometimes did. My talismans, and my reminders. They were small, which I liked, but they shone like Hope's eyes had that day, when I'd achieved the dream for both of us. The college degree she'd never had a chance to get, because she'd been taking care of me, the one she'd been determined I would. "The others are fake," I told Jax. "You know, they're belly rings. You're not going to go whole hog there. And, no. Josh bought me kitchen stuff, the high-end type. I have all kinds of amazing Williams-Sonoma bakeware, for example, and a really pretty KitchenAid mixer. Cherry red. I'm a good baker. That's what I do when I'm tense. I don't eat it, because I don't like sweets as much. I love to bake it, though, and give it away. If you're trying to motivate a staff and create a cheerful creative atmosphere, there's nothing like delicious baked goods, and it's good thinking time. Call that a business secret."

I hurried on, because it wasn't too much fun to remember being in the Old City condo with its high ceilings and industrial black-framed windows, pulling a coffee cake out of the oven at eleven o'clock at night with the spicy smell of cinnamon perfuming the air and some brand-new idea tickling at the back of my brain, and said, "All that's in boxes now. In my new place. I don't really have anybody to bake for now that I've moved back to New York, except Hope and Hemi and the kids, and Hemi has a housekeeper the likes of which you've never seen. They're all taken care of, cooking-wise."

Wait. Why *had* I moved to Brooklyn, anyway? Especially into an apartment with an electric stove and an oven with a wonky thermostat? Because it had been what I could find in a hurry, and I'd been planning that move anyway, with Prairie Plus. Because I'd told all my rowing friends I was leaving, and I couldn't stand to tell them I'd been left behind. Because the condo had belonged to Josh, and all I'd wanted was to get out of it. To get away.

I wasn't going to be working at Prairie Plus, though, so . . . why? Because I needed another job, and they were easier to find in New York, that was why. On the other hand, I could afford an apartment with level flooring in Philadelphia. Maybe even one on the river. Maybe even one I *liked*.

Oh. Jax. He was frowning in concentration, looking out the window. If he'd been the kind of guy to tap his fingers, he would have tapped. He was a still guy, though, so he didn't. I asked, "What?"

"I'm trying to figure out," he said, "what kind of a bloke gives a woman kitchen gear as a present."

"I love kitchen gear," I said. "Hey, it's not a vacuum cleaner." I didn't tell him how much I'd longed to see a little box, just once or twice. Cute earrings. Or, you know. A ring. I didn't need to actually expose more of my wounds here.

A young man in a black apron came out with our coffees. He set down Jax's, and then he set down mine. It was a flower. A chrysanthemum, or something like that, etched in foam on the top. It was so pretty, I almost cried. I was still recovering, though. That was my excuse.

"Wow," I said. "Thank you."

"No worries," he said. "Enjoy."

I asked Jax, after the guy had left, "Did you ask for this?"

"Asked for something special, yeh. Family time's good and all, but sometimes, you need to be alone. We haven't had much chance at that lately." He reached onto the chair next to him and set the jeweler's bag on the table. "Happy birthday."

There went my heart again. *Boom. Boom. Boom.* I was actually having trouble catching my breath. I said, not opening the bag, "Uh . . . Jax."

"You know how I said you needed to trust me?" he said. "Open it up."

"You didn't say . . . trust you." I still wasn't opening the bag. I couldn't. I was getting those shakes again.

He had his hand over mine, just like that first day, and I was staring down at it, at the scars on the backs of his fingers, wondering if they'd come on that last day, or from some earlier accident. "I'm saying it now," he said, absolutely gently.

"But . . ." I couldn't think what else to say, but I looked at him, finally.

"When you were in hospital," he said, his gray eyes steady on mine, "in the ICU. When the nurses kept coming in and checking those numbers, and not telling me enough. Your face was white as paper, and you had these shadows under your eyes. They were almost purple. I'd never seen somebody's face change as fast as that. I had this plastic bag with your earrings and belly rings inside, and I felt those little diamonds through the plastic and thought—I finally found out what it feels like to fall in love, and I'm watching her slip away. And it terrified me."

"It . . . did?" I was going to cry again. The heat was rising in my head. I wasn't going to be able to help it.

There was a look on his face that almost hurt me to see. Tenderness, I thought that was. The way Hemi looked at Hope, but this was for me. "Yeh," he said. "It did. Open your present, baby. I'm so glad you turned thirty."

All right. That was it. I cried. Jax had to go get me napkins again. I said, when I was mopping up, gulping air and then gulping water, "This probably wasn't how you expected this to . . . go."

"Well, no," he said, but he was smiling. "But then, I didn't have much to compare with. I've never told a woman I loved her before. At least not when I meant it."

"Oh," I said, wiping my eyes again and glad that I hadn't worn more makeup, "that's just great. That's, like, such a character reference."

This time, he laughed. "I told you, I was an arsehole. I haven't done it since I stopped being an arsehole."

I said, "OK, I'm opening my bag. Here I go."

It was like a Chinese puzzle. Inside the little paper bag was a nest of gold tissue. Inside that was a square white box with a lid. Inside *that* was a blue velvet case. Not a tiny one. And inside *that* . . .

"I used the ones you had," Jax said. "Took a photo and sent it over, and asked Bevin to do something like that, but different."

They were barbells. Rose gold. One of them had a faceted, round-cut red stone on either end, set in more rose gold. The other one was the same, except that it had something else below the bottom stone. A tiny bow made of rose-gold mesh, hanging from a teeny-weeny chain. I took that barbell out of the box and held it up, and Jax said, "The bow's my favorite," and touched it. It swung on its chain, and he sighed and said, "I know I'm meant to be romantic here, but that's going to be sexy as hell hanging down your pretty belly. I can't wait."

"Are they garnets?" I asked. "That's our birthstone. January. And I didn't get you anything."

"Oh, I think you did," he said. "You didn't die. Worked for me. And no, baby. They're rubies."

The bow swayed, because my hand was shaking. "Oh," I said. Not my most brilliant rejoinder ever.

He laughed. "Think I finally found a way to shut you up. Well, another way." He stood up, leaned over, kissed my mouth, smiled into my eyes, and said, "Happy birthday, sweetheart. Thirty looks good on you."

36

☆☆

THE LIGHT IN HER EYES

JAX

We still had to go visit the old man, even though I didn't want to. I wanted to go home, lay Karen down, take out those sparklers stuck into her belly, and put mine in instead.

It was an ownership thing, probably. A dominant thing. That primitive instinct again, like tattooing my name on her bum. The thought of that gave me a rush I could barely conceal.

She asked, "What are you thinking?" She was driving this time, and enjoying the hell out of it. Using the paddle shifters, testing the car's limits.

"Thinking about tattooing my name on your bum," I said, like a man who'd never heard the words, "Too much information." Exactly like that, because I went on to say, "Diagonally, across that sweet curve at the bottom, so if you're wearing a bikini and it rides up a bit, everybody can see it. Written in my handwriting. And if you're wearing a thong and I turn you around and pull up your dress, in a lift, say—*I* can see it. But mostly, I'm thinking about doing the tattooing." She shot an outraged glance at me, or a shocked one, and I said, "Well, you asked."

She downshifted, took the car around a tight turn that had us both leaning, and said, "Do you even know how to tattoo?"

I laughed out loud. "Not the question I thought you'd ask. No. I didn't say I'd do it. I said it was fun to imagine."

"Geez," she said. "One weak moment, and I unleash the beast. I'm scared to fall asleep now."

She was smiling, though, and so was I. "Why is that so hot?" she asked.

"Dunno. That's what I was wondering. It's a new fantasy for me. Hasn't cropped up before. Speed limit's a hundred most places in New Zealand, by the way."

"I'm going a hundred."

"Around the corners, maybe."

"Too bad, buddy. This is my time. You had your chance to drive. This is a great car, too. I forgive you for it being a Lexus." She was slowing as we got near the turnoff to her grandfather's place. "You do realize that expensive presents early in a relationship are red flags. Like moving too fast is in general."

"I can see that," I said.

Up the hill, now, and another of those quick glances at me. "You can?"

"Of course. A fella who gets obsessed, too possessive. Too much too fast, like he doesn't want you to have a life outside him. Stalking, and so forth. Entitlement. I've known a few like that in the military, and I've seen to it that they left it, when I had something to say about it. They join up for the violence, and they tend to wash out, too. Anger management issues tend to come out, and the Defence Force isn't too keen about giving blokes like that automatic weapons."

"And, see," she burst out, "I'd be *worried*, if I saw that. Wouldn't I? I mean, obviously, I've been rejected, so it's going to appeal to me to be desperately wanted, but wouldn't I know if it was something pathological?"

"Well, I'd hope so," I said, "and so would I, hopefully. It's not like I haven't been seeing a therapist who's been poking and prodding into my brain. She'd be pretty quick to point it out, I imagine."

"Oh." Karen considered that, and I thought once again that I'd never in my life known a more upfront woman. "That's true. Also, if you were that kind of guy, you'd have a history, and you've got pretty much the opposite one, from what I've seen. And if I had that kind of issue, *I'd* have a history, and seeing as the guy I was with didn't exactly break down in heartrending sobs at my departure, much less come running after me, I don't. I've got ninety-nine problems, but a stalker isn't one of them. Maybe sometimes, rubies just mean—" She waved a hand. "Whatever. Rich boyfriend."

"Passion, power, courage, and life force," I said, "supposedly. In other words—you. That's why I chose them, not just because I thought they'd look good against your skin, which I did. I had heaps of time to look it up, sitting in the room with you. It could be they were a . . ." I stopped.

"A what?" She'd slowed down again, like she didn't want to get there quite yet.

"A talisman," I said. Reluctantly. I wasn't the bare-your-soul type. The lose-your-self-control type. I'd never broken down in heartrending sobs at *anybody's* departure, other than a dog when I was eight. He was a golden retriever, though, and we'd had him ever since I could remember, so there you were. I'd also never gone running after anybody, not even the golden retriever. I'd sure as hell never stalked anyone.

She pulled over at the entrance to somebody's drive, and I asked, "What?"

"I have to concentrate." She held out an arm. It was covered in gooseflesh.

"Not sure what I'm seeing here," I said, but my heart was sinking. I was remembering the thing I should have noticed before. That I'd told her I'd fallen in love, and she hadn't said it back.

"That's what I've always thought about my earrings," she said. "I've never told anybody. How could you say the same word?"

This sounded better. "Tell me."

"My talismans." She touched the ones in her left ear, one at a time. With her left hand, her heart hand. "Hope said, when she gave them to me on the day I graduated from college, that they were to remind me of everything I'd done, and how I'd kept going even when it was hardest. That they were in my head to remind me of how strong my brain was, even under pressure, and how I was bright enough for anything. And that they were in my ears so I'd always hear her telling me how much she loved me."

I said, "I'm suddenly feeling much less satisfied with my own speech."

"And I thought," she went on, as if she hadn't heard me, "exactly what you said. *Talisman.* I don't believe in magic, and I don't believe in destiny, but I believed in that anyway. I still do."

"Just because you can't see the love," I said, "that doesn't mean it isn't there. Holding you up. Holding you close. Maybe that's what you felt. And maybe she thought you needed the reminder."

"See?" she cried out. *"See?* It's the same thing. You just gave me goosebumps again. So tell me why my rubies are a talisman."

I now felt incredibly stupid. I was the one who'd used the word, and I was going to have to say this. "Maybe just that if I ordered them, you'd be there to wear them. Call it an investment in the future." I'd already said that, basically. I was all good.

She waited a minute, and so did I, and finally, she said, "I decided how I feel about the expensive-present, going-too-fast thing."

"And what's that?" I asked.

"I decided I don't care what the rules are. The law of averages is a fallacy. *Famously* a fallacy."

"Uh . . . pardon?" I liked the not-caring about the rules part. I wasn't sure about the rest.

"Just because something's statistically likely," she said, "that doesn't mean it's inevitable. Statistics aren't individuals, and just because the roulette wheel's landed on red the last three times, it isn't any more likely to land on black the fourth time. The odds are still exactly the same. Fifty-fifty. In other words—who cares what moving too fast means in somebody else's life? In *most* people's life? We're not most people. We get to make our own destiny, and we get to make our own rules. But I'm still not letting you tattoo my butt. Not if you don't even know *how*."

☆☆

KAREN

Jax had smiled, after I'd said that, and hadn't said anything else, and I'd pulled out again, driven the mile or so up to Koro's, and parked in the drive.

He was in his chair. Debbie was over in the flower border, presumably searching for snails or something appropriately ducklike, and the dog was following him around.

Koro didn't get up, which was unusual. I came over and hongi'd him, and when we breathed in together, my heart eased the way it always did. I stood up, and he said, "Come on, mate," and gestured to Jax. Something about seeing Jax lean down, lay his palm lightly on Koro's shoulder, and Koro's own old hand on Jax's shoulder, made my throat tighten, and when they touched foreheads and noses, I may actually have teared up.

Respect. It was a thing.

I gave the dog a pat, since he'd come wagging over, bouncing some, with his tongue out and his brown eyes bright, and then I patted Debbie, who wasn't one bit happy about being second in line and basically elbowed the dog out of the way. Debbie was not a polite duck. After that, I sat down beside Koro, and he told Jax, "Go grab a chair from the kitchen, mate. There's a plate of sandwich buns in the fridge that Vanessa made from the leftover roast, when we knew you'd be coming. She's in the back with the baby. We won't bother her. You could bring them out, maybe. Make a cup of tea as well, if you like, and one for Karen."

"I'll do that," Jax said. "Can I get you one as well?"

301

"Yeh," Koro said. "That'd be good." And Jax headed off, seeming not one bit put out at finding his own way.

"You like him," I said to Koro as we watched Jax disappear through the front door.

"Not much not to like," he said. "Takes care of you. Good to his sister, too. Hemi says he's all right as well, and he's a hard judge. Did you have a good brekkie?"

"Yes," I said. "That was a *lot* of kids, though. Did they stop by, Hemi and Hope and the kids? They've flown out by now, I guess. It was a long way to come for a hangi."

"Stopped by on their way down to meet you," he said. "And never mind. I reckon Hope needed to come, and Hemi needed to come with her. She'll be feeling better now, able to rest easy, knowing you're in good hands."

"You're sorry to see them go, though," I said. "And you're tired today, huh. Too long a day yesterday?"

"Nah. A good day, and I don't spend much time anymore being sorry. Better to spend my time being happy for what I've got."

"I wish I could be like that." I stuck my legs out in front of me, kicked off my jandals, wiggled my toes in the green grass, then rubbed the dog's belly with my foot, since he'd decided to flop down at my feet. He really was cute.

"Could be you have to be ninety-five to do it," Koro said, and gave a wheezing laugh. "Could be a downside, eh. Nah. You're passionate. That's nothing but a good thing. Got that passion to give to your work, and maybe to that fella as well. You put it where it's needed."

I'd bent down to scratch the dog around the neck, and he was wagging his fluffy tail so hard, his whole back end wiggled. "It's so soon, though." I'd said I didn't care, but maybe I still did, a little. "And Jax said the 'passion' thing, too, this morning. He gave me rubies for my birthday. I tried to be bothered by that, that it's too much too soon, but I just feel . . ." I sighed. "Just . . . *delighted,* you know? Like— cherished. Is that dangerous?"

"Yeh," Koro said. "It is." And my heart sank. That hadn't been one bit the answer I was going for. He went on, though,

"Living all the way's always dangerous. Heaps of things are dangerous. Doesn't mean you shouldn't do them."

I leaned my head lightly against his shoulder, and his rough hand with its paper-thin skin came up and smoothed my cheek. I asked, "When did you know it was right, with your wife? When did you decide? Did you know her a long time, or not? What sort of . . . tipped you over the edge?"

I'd never met his wife—she'd died when Hemi was a teenager—and I'd never asked Koro about her. I'd never asked him so many things I needed to know. Why hadn't I taken every minute I had to do it? It wasn't like I didn't know that you could lose people you loved.

He said, "We went to school together. I didn't see her again, though, for a few years after that."

Jax came out of the house with three cups of tea, set them down on the little table between the chairs, said, "Back in a second," and took off again.

"So," I said. "You saw her again. What was her name?"

"Airini. A pretty name, and she had the prettiest hair of any of the girls. Had some red in it, and it curled. First time I saw her with her hair down, when I came back, which was that first day . . ." He sighed. "I thought—that's what I want. She had a smile, too, and a light in her eye. I needed that light, then. I needed that smile."

Jax again, with a chair and the plate of sandwiches. He looked between us and said, "Want a minute?"

"Nah, mate," Koro said. "Sit down. I'm just telling Karen about how I knew my wife was the one for me. Old men's stories. All you really have in the end are your memories, eh. You can have all the precious things, take them out of their box, think about what they cost, maybe, but if they don't have memories attached, they're not good for much. Taking a memory out of that box, now . . . that's different. That lasts."

Jax handed me the plate of sandwiches, and I took one and said, "So tell us. It had been a few years, and then you saw her again."

"Yeh." Koro lifted his mug to his lips with a trembling hand. "Just back from the war, I was. Seen too many things, maybe, and I needed to see something good. That's what she was. Something good."

"Which war?" I asked.

"World War Two," Koro said. "With the 28th Battalion."

Jax's head had come up, his gray eyes sharpening. "The Maori Battalion. That's a proud history, sir. A tough one, too. Fifty percent casualty rate."

"It was," Koro said. "Reckon you know that it can be hard to sit with afterwards. Not that we weren't on the right side of it, or that it didn't have to be done. Too many good mates left behind, though. Too many bad dreams."

"Yeh," Jax said. Quietly.

"When we came home," Koro said, "they gave us a parade, here in Katikati. She was there. Airini. They did a dance, the girls, and some songs. In their flax skirts, and her hair was down. She could sing, now." He sighed. "She could sing. Seemed like I hadn't heard anything as good as that song since I'd left home, and I hadn't seen anything as good as that saucy smile of hers, or that light in her eyes. I asked if she wanted to go for a picnic, and she said yes."

"And how did you know?" I asked. "That she was the one? Or did you just want to get married?" Jax looked at me, a half-smile on his face, and I said, "Whoops. Not tactful."

"Could be I did," Koro said, "but that wasn't how it felt. Woke up one Friday morning, that was how, after a month or so. I had a job by then, down in Tauranga, doing mechanic's work. I woke up with her on my mind, thinking that I was going to see her that night, because we were going to a dance, and how happy I was about that. I thought that next day, maybe we'd go fishing off the rocks." He took another slow sip of tea. "And I realized that I couldn't think of a day when I wouldn't want to see her face, and I couldn't think of a future that didn't have her in it."

JAX

We didn't take the dog.

I offered, and the old man said, "Nah, mate. Vanessa will look on the computer, see if he belongs to somebody. She had him into the vet already this morning, though, to get his jabs. He's a bit skinny, the vet says, under the hair. Probably been missing from someplace for a while, or dumped, maybe. Anyway, seems like he fits around the place. Could be we needed a dog. Sometimes, the thing you need comes along."

"I wonder what kind he is," Karen said. "He's pretty funny-looking." She threw a stick, and the dog tore after it, with Debbie hustling along behind with no hope of catching up.

The old man said, "Border collie and miniature poodle in there, the vet says." The Nameless Dog trotted up with the stick in his mouth, dropped it at Karen's feet, and stood staring fixedly at it as if he could make her throw it via thought-rays. "Maybe a few other things as well. That's why he's got so much hair on him. Take him to the groomer's, she said, and get it cut off him, and he'll be more comfortable. Vanessa will see to that, too."

I said, "Let me help with that, anyway," and pulled out my wallet.

The old man waved a knobby hand. "Nah, mate. Hemi gives me more than I can spend, and he keeps it coming. May as well spend it on grooming a dog. It's not doing me any good in the bank. Besides . . ." He smiled, showing off those spaces where teeth had once been, "you could need to buy Karen something else, eh. Save your money for that."

"I told him about my birthday present," Karen said. There was a little color in her cheeks. "How you went overboard in the generosity department. It's not like I'm broke, you know. I got something when they cut me loose."

"Nah," the old man said. "Reckon he needed to do it."

"Reckon I did," I said.

"Right, then," Karen said. "I'll go on and take my car back to the airport." She leaned over the old man and hongi'd him one more time, and when she stood up, there were tears in her eyes. "I love you. I'll come see you again before I leave New Zealand. I'm not sure when that'll be."

"Doesn't matter," the old man said. "I'll be here."

37

BEYOND REASON

KAREN

I cried all the way to the airport.

I never cried, and somehow, I kept doing it anyway. I wanted my old self back, please. At least they weren't heaving sobs this time, just a steady stream of tears that wouldn't stop, like a river overflowing its banks because the water had no place else to go. Like the emotion had to get out somehow.

Jax was behind me in the Power Car, and I glanced in the rearview mirror every thirty seconds or so, just to see him. I couldn't even have told you what I was thinking. Koro, and how much I loved him. Jax, and how much he felt like a resting place. Like *my* resting place. And maybe, with both of them, the thing I wasn't allowing myself to look at. How I'd feel when they were gone.

By the time I pulled into the lot, I was a mess. I found a spot in the right aisle, pulled in, opened my door, and Jax was there. He looked startled, as well he might. "All right?" he asked.

I waved an arm. "Oh, you know." I wiped my face on the inside of my T-shirt again. It was fairly soaked, and fairly disgusting, too. I sure knew how to show a guy my best side.

"Go on and get in my car," Jax said, and popped the lock for me. "Give me the key. I'll take it in."

"You have to get the . . . odometer reading." I was *still* crying. Well, this was awkward.

He smiled. "Could be I knew that. Maybe you should just get in the car and assume I can handle it."

"Bossing again," I said.

This time, he laughed. "You can tell me how you feel about that. Later."

When he came back, I'd finished crying, at least. I asked him, as he pulled out onto the street, "Are your grandparents still alive?"

"On my dad's side, no. On my mum's side, yes."

"In Dunedin?"

"Yeh. They live not too far from my parents, in fact. My sisters and I used to go there after school, because my mum and dad were both working in the business. That was a good place. A warm place. And right now, I'm feeling like an inadequate grandson, so you know. Feeling like I need to sit with them more, ask them to tell their stories."

"It's weird, of course," I said, "because Koro isn't even really my grandfather."

"Maybe he is, though," Jax said, "in all the ways that count. Pretty sure that if you asked him, he'd say he was. Maybe it's time to stop thinking of yourself as that lonely mountain, and start thinking of what you really are instead. Loved beyond reason."

"Oh, thanks," I said, escaping into the collar of my T-shirt. "You made me start up again. Well, this is . . ." I sniffed. "Extremely attractive."

He smiled. "Maybe we should take a shower together when we get home. Wash all that away."

"You probably need a massage. Also exercise. Why do I feel like I want to go to sleep again?"

"Because you got out of hospital forty hours ago?" He pulled into the entrance to the parking garage, and then into his spot. He turned the car off, unclipped his seatbelt, leaned across the car, took my face in his hand, and kissed me. My nose was probably red, and my cheeks were probably blotchy, and he didn't seem to care. He stroked a thumb down my cheek and said, "I was thinking something else about us, too."

"Oh, yeah?" I did my best to haul myself back under control. "I'm still not letting you tattoo me."

He laughed and kissed me again. Still taking his time. "No. About birth control."

I tried to give him some side-eye. It wasn't easy, not when he was kissing me like he had all day, and the warm tendrils were curling down inside me, tingling every place they touched, like he was in my very veins. His thumb was on the side of my neck now, because he was holding me there, his fingers brushing the hair at my nape. "If you want to insert my IUD," I said, when he let my mouth go enough that I could talk, "that's also not happening. It's already in, and I'm not letting you practice medicine on me, either."

I could feel the curve of his lips against my neck, because that's where he was kissing me now. I had my hand in his hair, and he had *his* hand up my shirt, stroking a lazy path northward. The warm tendrils had some silver streaks in them now, and they were going right there. *Zing. Zing. Zing.* I might be having some trouble with my breathing, and I also might be doing some moaning.

He said, "I don't want to put in your IUD. I could want to take it out of you, but we'll talk about that later. Right now . . . I want to be inside you without a condom."

Oh, boy. Talk about moving too fast. I said, "Even though I've been crying? You've got weird . . . taste. And I'm, uh, good. I got . . . tested." It came out on a gasp, because he had his hand under my stretchy cotton sports bra, he was teasing my nipple, and I didn't care that we were in a parking garage. I wanted to do it *now.* "In case Josh wasn't just a . . . wanker."

He kissed my neck some more, and then he sucked on it, and my hips were already trying to move. "Do you trust me?" he asked. Low and soft, against my neck.

"Oh, yeah," I said. "I want you to . . . do it." You could say that. "Would you . . . stop talking and take me upstairs?"

This time, he laughed. "You're meant to have this

conversation beforehand. So there's no pressure."

"Other than that you're already . . ." I couldn't say anything, because his mouth and his hand had both found exactly the right spots. In another minute, he was going to be taking off my clothes right here in the car. In another minute, I wasn't going to care.

In the elevator, then, fortunately not with anybody else, because the second the doors had closed, he'd grabbed me again. Getting down the hallway, somehow, with his hands around my head and his mouth on mine, and in the door. The second we were inside, he had his hands on my T-shirt, pulling it over my head, taking care over my arm, and when he got to my shorts, he popped the button right off and basically ripped them down my legs along with my bikinis. I could swear I heard fabric tear. I'd dropped my jeweler's bag, and I had my back against the wall again and was getting his shirt off, too.

He said, "Shower."

I may have moaned. "No," I said. "I want to do it now." I was working on his shorts, and he was helping me. "I changed my mind," I told him, when I had my hand on him. "Size matters. I want it."

"Come on," he said. "Shower. Grab my crutches for me." He put his forehead against mine, held my face in his hands, and said, "I need to slow this down. I need to feel it."

"Oh. Right," I said. "Your leg. You have to take it off. I kept forgetting."

He looked at me sharply, and I said, "What?"

He said, "Nothing." When we were in the bathroom, though, I was the one who took off the leg. I turned on the water first, so the room would fill with steam. The shower was Kiwi style, separated from the rest of the room only by a partial glass wall, it had seven shower heads, and the air was already misty when I was kneeling on the floor, peeling the sleeve down Jax's leg, kissing his thigh where he sat on the closed toilet lid, running my hands all the way up and down it, then, finally, kissing the stump. And if you think that isn't sexy, that it isn't romantic . . . all I can say is—it was. It was absolutely sexual, touching him there, and it was service. His hands were in my hair, and he wasn't saying anything at all, but he felt it, too.

It was like we were in that waterfall again, but this time, it was just the two of us, swimming around each other in the plunge pool, kissing and touching, with all the time in the world. His hands were on my injured arm, peeling away the dressing, disposing of it, checking out the wounds. He lifted my hand, kissed the inside of my wrist, his touch so gentle, and when I got up from the floor, he came with me. Hopping on one leg, his hand on the wall, and into the shower. The warm water hit us from overhead, and from all the way down the wall. Jax had a hand out, propping himself up, and I covered my own hands with body wash, soaped him down, and kissed his mouth, his neck, his chest.

He didn't ask me, for once, if the water stung my arm. It did, a little, and I didn't care. He pulled me in with one hand, kissed me like he wanted to take my soul into his body, ran his hand down my back and up my side, and I was barely keeping myself upright.

I wasn't the one who turned off the water. That was him. He let me dry him off, and he let me bring him his crutches, but when we got into the bedroom, he said, "Go get the bag with your present." No smile at all.

Oh, boy. I did it, and when I came back into the bedroom with it, he took it from me and said, "Lie down."

It wasn't tattooing, no, but it felt like that when he unfastened first one belly ring, and then the next, and pulled them out. When he brushed a hand over my skin, touching each of the four little holes in turn, exploring them like he wanted to be there. And when he was threading the rubies into me, through me, fastening them closed? It felt like . . . something. I couldn't even have said what.

Yes, I could. It felt like absolute domination.

He got the second one in, got himself over me, lowered himself down in a move like a ballet, and kissed each stone in turn. When he got to the little bow, he sucked it into his mouth, tugging at my piercings. His hands were on either side of my waist, his lips were warm against my skin, and still, he didn't say anything at all.

☆☆

JAX

It wasn't tattooing her, no. I still wanted to do that. You could say so, because just the thought of it was winding me up tighter. Putting my rings in her, though, was hot as hell. And when I was done, I made my meandering way south and teased her a while longer, because I needed to make her beg. When she did, because she couldn't help it anymore? I gave her what she was asking for. I set my mouth to her in earnest, and she rose up into it and called out. She grabbed my hair, and she made some noise. Mostly, she said my name, and it felt like I *had* tattooed her. Exactly like that. Like triumph.

I made her come, and then I made her do it twice more, each time wilder than the last, and when she was lying on her back, her arms and legs flung wide, when she was spent and gasping and weak with it, and I said, "Turn over"—

She struggled up and did it. Hands and knees again, as if she wanted to do exactly what I said. She might not want me to control her outside of bed, but she sure as hell wanted me to control her in it.

I traced my name on her bum with my hand, exactly where I could see that ink, and she trembled. I spanked her a few times, and then a few more, a little harder, and she gasped. I opened her up and touched her everywhere, and she shook. And when I slid inside her, she moaned.

Too hot. Too tight. I had to hold still a minute. She didn't. She said, "Jax."

I didn't answer. I kissed her nape instead, and then I put my hand there, circling her neck, keeping it gentle, but letting her know. And she tightened around me like I'd just told her to.

"This is mine," I said.

She whimpered.

Oh, yeh.

I ran my hand slowly down her spine, stopping at those two little dimples at the base. "That first day," I said, rubbing her there just beneath her tailbone, feeling her tightening some more, in a rhythm now, "you had your back to me, showing me this, and I wanted it. And now I've got it. Now it's mine."

She said, "Jax. Fuck me. Please."

So I did. Hard and fast. She was hot and tight around me, the sensation plunging all the way through my body the same way I was driving into hers, sharp as a knife. She came again, with plenty of shuddering and gasping, and by the time I was spilling into her? I had her saying some things she might be embarrassed to remember. Some things I'd remind her of next time.

I was going to have to keep her exactly like this. It was going to be necessary.

⭐

When we were lying together, after she'd cleaned herself up, and cleaned me as well, like she wanted to do it, I kissed the back of her neck one more time, and she said, her voice slow and sleepy, "I'll be walking around today being a mess. Leaking. Why is that so sexy? It's wet. It's sticky."

I ran my hand over her thigh, then between her legs, and felt for myself. Oh, yeh. That was nice. "Reckon I know why it's sexy to me."

"Right," she said, when I didn't say anything else. "Why?"

I smiled. That could be because I felt good. "If you have to ask, I can't explain. Say it's a bit like the tattooing idea. Or like everything I just did to you."

She sighed. "Or the way you put my rubies in. That was seriously hot. I feel kind of . . . tattooed. So you know."

I kissed her again, between the shoulder blades this time, because I was moving down the bed. "I know. That was why I did it."

She rolled over, her whiskey-brown eyes sleepy, her wide mouth for once not smiling. I'd been right. The rubies looked exactly right against her honey-colored skin, and so did that pink gold. She said, "I should probably say something to remind you again. Make some rules."

"Mm." I cupped a breast, because it was right there, then leaned down and kissed the pink nipple. "You could. We could have a talk about limits. Tell you what. You can think about that, and we'll talk about it over dinner. Very quietly, because I'm taking you out. Right now, I'm going to go for my swim and to have that massage, because I have a feeling that I'm going to have to fuck you again after that conversation, and I need to get in shape to give you all my attention. I'll dress your arm first, though. Want to come with me?"

She stared at me for a minute, then inspected her arm like she wasn't sure what else to do, and I said, "Before you ask—you're not good to swim yet. And, no, that's not me failing to appreciate the difference between in bed and out of it. That's me listening to your discharge instructions, and you still being pretty wonky at the time. You could come with me and lie by the pool, though, if you like. Hang on one sec first."

I got my crutches, headed into the bathroom, and found the stuff for her dressings, and when I came back, she said, "I'm going to say no. I'm going to lie on a chaise on your terrace instead, read the rest of your book, listen to the surf, and maybe fall asleep. And that's all I want to do today." She put her arm out for me to take hold of, sighed when I did it, and said, "You're pretty great, by the way. In case I didn't say so. Even though you keep switching back and forth between personas and throwing me off."

"Well, no," I said, getting down to the business of dressing her arm, "you didn't say so."

Her expression changed. I wasn't exactly looking, but I wasn't exactly not. "Oh," she said. "Did I forget to say the words?"

Somehow, I was laughing again. I should be tense, maybe. I should be thinking about what we were doing here, how impermanent our current setup was, and why that seemed to matter so much. I couldn't manage it. "Well, yeh," I said. "You did."

"Oh. All right. This feels a little momentous, so you know."

I finished smearing on the antibiotic ointment, laid the gauze gently over her healing flesh, and tore off a strip of adhesive tape. "I know."

"The first time I thought I was in love with you," she said, "was that first night in the tent, after the waterfalls. And ever since then, I can't stop thinking it. It's the way you're so sweet, and then the way you're not. You just . . . burn me down. You make my knees shake. You make me weak. And every time you do it, I want it more."

That seemed to be all I was going to get. I guessed I'd take it. I finished bandaging her, pressed my mouth to the tender inside of her wrist, and said, "Well, good. You keep on thinking about that. Think about how bad you'll want it by tonight, maybe, and how much advantage I may take of that. I'm going swimming."

38

☆☆

DINNER CONVERSATION

KAREN

I had two guys here, I thought at eleven o'clock the next morning, as we lifted off for a three-hour flight after dropping the Actually Sexy Lexus off at a very high-end car dealership whose manager was more deferential to Jax, even if he expressed that with typical Kiwi understatement, than Jax was comfortable with. There was the Jax who was holding my hand now and saying, "You don't have to do this with me today unless you want to. The Limb Centre, or even dinner with my parents, for that matter. You could visit Poppy and report on the dog, or go to the Settlers' Museum, maybe. That's not bad, and it's only about ten minutes' walk from the hospital. Or go shopping, of course."

I said, "You're sounding pretty eager to get rid of me. Do you actually not want me at your appointment, do you not want to introduce me to your parents, or do you think I don't want to come? I'm good either way. Any way. Just tell me, because I can't guess." Which, of course, I wasn't, but if he really *didn't* want to introduce me to his parents, I needed to know.

He looked a little less remote. "You have to know I want

you. I keep forgetting that I can actually come out and tell the truth."

"I could point out that you've met my family, complete with me exposing all of my weaknesses and insecurities around them. If I were the arguing type, that is."

Now, he actually laughed. "If anybody in the known universe is now or ever has been the arguing type, it's you."

"Not what you said last night." I didn't grab him while I said it, or do anything similarly unrefined. I may have looked at him from under my lashes, though. It was the sort of thing that was normally beyond my level of subtlety, or my level of flirting ability, but it could be I was learning.

Because, yes, that was the *other* guy. The one who'd camouflaged himself at first by holding my hand while we'd walked the few blocks down Maunganui Road to a little restaurant called Post Bank as the evening shadows grew longer, then sat beside me on a red velvet banquette in an intimate room lined, for some reason, with shelves of books reaching all the way to the ceiling, so you were eating haute cuisine in a library, hence combining two of my favorite things in the world. The one who'd enjoyed some truly delectable examples of high-end New Zealand cuisine with me, had drunk almost certainly too much Otago Pinot Noir with me, and had proceeded to ask me, two feet from the diners beside us, low-voiced questions about my sexual limits that had had me alternately trying and failing not to gasp, which he loved, and trying and failing not to squirm, which he loved more.

If you've never been asked exactly how much bondage you're into while you're tipping a green-lipped mussel into your mouth, I'll clue you in. It's seriously distracting. Are scarves as far as you want to push things, or do ropes sound better, and how do you feel about having both your wrists and ankles tied down, so you can't move? Also, how comfortable are you with having him move you into different positions and take you different ways? Once your arm's healed, of course, because until then, he's going to be so careful, baby. Or how about being asked what your safe word is, when you've just taken your first bite of roast lamb with balsamic and rosemary? And when you've just swallowed that first, incredible mouthful of dark, rich chocolate torte with raspberry sauce and are absolutely dying from the taste of it sliding down your throat, and he asks how hard you want him to spank you? And is his hand enough? Because if it's up to him—he wants to feel it.

Well, yeah.

I finally whispered, with half of my torte left, as well as a third of whatever-glass-of-wine this was, "I'm still *injured.*"

"Yeh. I know." He picked up my hand and kissed my knuckles, smiled at me, and said, "That's why I want to make sure I take special care with you."

"Oh, yeah?" I did my best to scowl at him. It wasn't easy, since I couldn't feel my face, or much of anything other than the insistent throb that had started up with the first question, and the kind of shocks you'd normally expect from scuffing your feet across the carpeting and then touching the lamp. "I'd say you're just exactly *not* trying to do that. I'd say you're trying to make me suffer."

"Well," he said, "maybe a bit. Here's something else you could do for me, if you want to suffer a wee bit more."

"Uh . . ." I said, half of me wondering pretty hard whether he was thinking about doing any of this tonight, or if it was just dinner conversation. I'd had at least four orgasms already today, and, yes, I wanted another one. Or three. But whatever guys said—all right, I was talking about Josh here—they didn't really want it as much as I did. Also, it wasn't like a man carried around his bondage supplies in his luggage, just in case he got lucky. And found a woman who liked it a little kinky. He'd jumped straight to ropes? Seriously? And we hadn't even *discussed* sex toys.

"Because if you do," he said, leaning in a little closer and running his thumb slowly over the inside of my wrist, then my palm, like he wanted to let me know how patient he was willing to be, "you'll get up right now, go on back there, and take off your undies for me, so I know you're ready. If you say you'll do it, I'm going to check your purse for them, so you know. And if you haven't done it . . ." He sighed and took a sip of wine. "I could do a bit of . . . punishing. I could do it anyway, in fact. Maybe I could think of some way you've disappointed me."

Did I do it? Of course I did. And when he *did* take my purse from me, when I came back, unzip it, check inside, then lift his eyes to me with all that slow smolder? I may have shuddered.

It was four blocks home. I counted. Jax held my hand again, he didn't hurry, and he didn't say anything at all. He just went into the apartment with me, and then into the bedroom, and said, "Get on the bed and lie down. And tell me how you're feeling. Arm still OK? Too tired?"

And there was that other guy again, confusing me. "No," I said. "I'm not too tired, and I can't even feel my arm." Well, *that* was true, so I decided to tell him so. "The only things I can feel right now are the parts of my body that contain erectile tissue, but I'm feeling all of those to the point of serious discomfort, because that's what happens when you have too much blood flow to those areas for about two friggin' *hours*. You get engorgement. After that long, it's almost painful, and the only way to relieve it is with an orgasm. Or several of them. Which can happen any time now. Since you asked."

He was laughing, and then he was sitting on the bed, leaning over, kissing my mouth, and brushing his thumb over my cheek. Still smiling. "Got a scientific explanation for everything, eh. You do know your biology. Here's another question for you."

I eyed him with some suspicion, because he was looking smug. "What?"

"Where'd you get this dress?" It was my sundress, the one I'd been wearing the first day, and every time since that I'd had to dress up at all. His hand was tracing the neckline, and not where you'd expect, between my breasts. Around the outer edges of the halter top instead, in that tender place between your shoulder and the start of your breast that no man touches enough. Except that he was doing it. His hand drifted up to the side of my throat, and then circled it gently, barely touching, but I remembered how he'd held the back of my neck earlier today, and swallowed.

"I don't want to be choked," I said. "Something you neglected to ask about. That's not hot, it's just scary. Also dangerous. And I'm a big, big believer in lube. Just putting that out there."

He looked, fortunately, horrified, and took his hand away. "I'm not going to choke you. I'm not going to hurt you."

"Oh. Well, good." I was right at that edge, where you're so excited, you're trembling, and you know you could tip over to being scared too easily.

"I do want to know, though," he said, "where you got the dress. And you're not answering me." I thought he'd kiss me, but he didn't do that, either. Instead, he moved down the bed and unfastened the little ankle straps of my sandals, because I somehow hadn't remembered to take them off at the door. He slipped them off, dropped them beside the bed, put his hands around my ankles, and moved them a couple inches apart. And—whoa. Just that was making me ache harder. Maybe it was remembering that I wasn't even wearing a thong, and that I'd been as aware of that as a woman could possibly be during that walk. And now. Maybe it was wondering what was coming next. Maybe it was all of it.

"Uh . . ." I said. "Athleta. It's a . . . catalog. Are you buying your sister a present? You know, there's sexy two-steps-forward-one-step-back, and then there's just plain getting a woman out of the mood."

He smiled, but he didn't let go of my ankles. "Could be that I want to know for another reason."

"All . . . right?" I was still pretty confused. "I guess."

He stood up and said, "Stay there," then went into the bathroom and came back with a plastic bag. And pulled out a thick coil of rope. It was red.

"I don't even want to know," I said.

Blue scars. Black nerd glasses. Hard body. And smolder. "And yet I'd swear you do. It's silk rope. So I can tie you down as tight as I want to, but it won't hurt. Could be I did some shopping as well as some swimming today, because I wanted to make sure I had everything you needed."

"Oh, yeah," I said. "I'm sure that's the reason."

I was trying, but I wasn't too convincing. He said, "Because pleasing you is going to make me so bloody happy. Or maybe it's torturing you that's going to do that. Can't decide." He leaned over me, brushed my hair back from my forehead, kissed me again, nice and slowly, and said, "Put your hands over your head. Right now."

When he wrapped the thick silken strands around my wrists, over and over again, then ran the rope between them, tightening the bonds, before he tied me tight to the head of the bed, I started breathing harder. Silk rope, it turned out, felt amazing, strong but soft. When he left the room, I tugged at it, testing the bonds, and honestly wondered how long I was going to hold out. And how long he was going to make me.

That was before he came back with a pair of scissors.

I said, "Jax."

He said, "Shh." After that, he pushed my dress up as far as it would go, put the blade of the scissors against my skin, and started to cut. I heard the rasp as the wispy cotton fabric parted, felt the cold metal on my midriff, and shuddered.

JAX

I wasn't sure how I'd made it through that dinner. Seeing the flush rise in her cheeks, hearing her trying her hardest to be saucy, to be cool, guessing how wet she was and wanting to feel it for myself. It was a bit like that fantasy I'd had about the tattooing. I'd wanted to put my hand right there and tell her to sit still, order her not to make a sound, while I made her come in front of the entire room.

Well, I didn't literally want to. I definitely wanted to think about it, though, so I did. By the time I opened her purse and saw the black thong in there, I wasn't sure I'd make it back to the apartment. And right now, while I stood over her, looked at her arms pulled overhead, the red rope wrapped around her wrists, and the knot fastening it to the headboard, and watched her dress fall away? It was one of those moments when you don't have to think about anything else, because the fantasy's right here.

Her eyes were closing as the scissors reached the spot between her breasts, and I said, "Karen. Look at me."

She shivered. And she did it. Dark lashes fluttering open, absolutely no artifice in them. Whiskey-brown eyes staring into mine, and her breasts rising and falling fast and hard. Fear, excitement, or a bit of both.

I was holding onto the fabric with one hand now, careful, as I cut the last bit of fabric, not to nick her skin. The two halves of the dress fell away, and I set the scissors down, put my hand against her face, took her mouth in a kiss, and told her, "I'm not going to hurt you, baby. I'm going to tease you, though, until you don't think you can stand it, and I'm going to make you come too hard. If I scare you, if you don't like it—use your safe word."

"You're not . . . scaring me," she said. "Or only a little."

I smiled. If she was aching? So was I. The only thing she was still wearing was the strappy black bra, because she'd already taken off her thong for me. She'd sat beside me on that banquette without it while I'd delayed over the last glass of wine, and had finally walked home with me with the wetness all but running out of her.

She was going to be feeling that way tomorrow, too, because I wasn't going to be using a condom. When I was done with her, she was going to know I'd been there.

That bra was another thing I'd wanted to take off every time I'd seen it on her. I cut it off instead, one tiny strap at a time, and she trembled more with every one. Afterwards, I brushed my hand over one breast, then the other, watched her pink nipples pebble, and sucked them for a while. For as long as I wanted, in fact, because I could. It wasn't like she could get away.

She was moaning again. No more saucy talk. No more scientific explanations. Nothing but surrender.

She watched me unfasten my shirt, finally, one button at a time. Her clothes cut to pieces around her, her arms over her head, her legs still too close together.

That wasn't going to work. I had my hands on my belt, and now, I said, "Spread your legs."

She did it. Slowly. I said, "Farther. Show me," and she closed her eyes, took a breath, and did it. I put a pillow under her hips, and then I put another one there, and oh, yeh, that was a nice look. I took off my trousers, and then I took off my leg, and she had her eyes open again to watch. I said, "If this bed had a footboard, I'd be tying your ankles to it. It doesn't, so I'm going to hold you down instead, and it's going to be a long, long time before I let you come. I hope you're ready to beg, because I'm going to make you ask me for everything. You think you ache now? By the time I'm done with you, you're going to know what aching means."

Twelve hours later, I drank my glass of orange juice, read a book on my phone, since Karen still had her nose in the one she'd stolen from me, and remembered what she'd looked like with her eyes screwed up tight and her mouth open, wailing out her release as her head banged against the bed, her hands pulled frantically to get loose, and she didn't succeed a bit. I also possibly wondered, just a little, whether I'd done all that to distract myself from today.

Probably. It had been hot as hell, though. And then there'd been letting her loose a long time later, after I'd fucked her into another long, slow, rolling orgasm that had rocked her like an earthquake, while she'd still been tied down tight for me. Kissing her wrists, her cheeks, her sweet mouth afterwards, before I'd held her against my chest, stroked my hand over her hair, and told her how beautiful she was, how much she'd pleased me—that had felt like everything. Like tenderness, and like triumph.

And then we bumped and rocked our way down through a rainstorm into the city of my birth, and I set the memory aside, took some deep breaths, and got myself ready to face whatever came my way today.

One step at a time.

39

☆☆

PERSPECTIVE, MAYBE

KAREN

When Jax stopped where he did in the airport carpark, I said, "I feel strangely vindicated."

"Except that you got it wrong." He slung his suitcase and my duffel into the back of the gray Audi SUV. It wasn't raining yet, but the sky was definitely thinking about it, with billowing white clouds doing their best to block out a sun that was still trying to shine. The air was so clean, though, it was like it had been scrubbed.

"Barely." I tossed in my own tote, which was all that he'd let me carry. For a guy with one leg, he was awfully bossy in the "let me do it" department. I was trying to hate that. It wasn't working all that well. "Audi—BMW. Six of one, half dozen of the other. Except that the Audi is probably more reliable. Which you know, because you researched."

I could tell he was trying hard not to smile. He could be that tough guy most of the time, but he couldn't always manage it with me, and I loved knowing it. He said, "Possibly. Could be you aren't the only one who believes in science."

"Ha. I knew it." He opened the passenger door for me like the gentleman he was and wasn't, and I said, "This is also

324

about the cleanest car I've ever seen, except for Hemi's. And, of course, the car you were driving before this. Is there an add-on package you *didn't* get on this thing? Also, please tell me you're not one of those guys who won't let a woman drink coffee in his car in case she spills it. And never mind the horrors of eating."

He laughed before he slammed my door and climbed in on his side, which I was glad of, since that was what I'd been going for. I thought he was nervous about the appointment, which made sense, and nervous about dinner with his parents, too, which didn't. He'd almost died. In *war.* After spending years defusing explosives. In what universe wouldn't your parents just want to hold you tight and tell you how glad they were that you'd lived? Of course, it could be that I was too idealistic, since I didn't actually *have* any parents, but that was how I imagined it would be.

He said, "Nah. You can spill in my car anytime. Leather seats. I told you, my family's in the luxury-car business. But this one, I actually paid for." He turned the car on.

"You say I can spill *now,*" I said, "but how about when the magic's over?"

He'd been about to put the car in gear. Instead, he leaned over, put a hand on my shoulder and edged my frankly gorgeous silk-and-cotton cropped sweater away with his thumb, possibly so he could get to that tender skin again, and brushed his lips over mine. "The magic isn't going to be over," he said. "And I like this dress. Can't believe you hadn't shown it to me yet."

"Because it was my birthday present from Hope," I said. "The dress and the sweater. It's a good thing I *didn't* show it to you, or you'd have cut it off me. But it's not too . . ."

"Too what?"

The dress in question was cotton, and if it had been white, it would have looked like a petticoat, or a corset, or both, and it would definitely not have worked for me. Instead, it was the color of the Pinot Noir we'd drunk last night, which was a whole different story. I hoped. It was sleeveless, made of heavy eyelet lace lined with sheer cotton, and was fitted all the way down to my waist, where it opened into a knee-length skirt. The best parts were the matching silk ribbon that was threaded around the neckline and the waist, and the line of tiny hooks and eyes that ran all the way from neckline to hem.

It wasn't frilly, and it wasn't flowered, but it sure as hell had been inspired by lingerie, and when I'd put it on this morning, I'd felt very, very female. It was a good parent-meeting dress, despite the lingerie thing. Hopefully.

A good Jax-pleasing dress, too, judging by the way he'd taken hold of my hands this morning, said, "My job," and finished fastening the hooks and eyes all the way up to my neckline, not to mention the way he'd held my shoulders and kissed my neck afterwards, which had resulted in us almost missing our flight.

If I hadn't had that IUD, I'd have gotten pregnant for sure, as many times as he'd grabbed me. Eventually, the law of averages *did* tend to win, once you spun the roulette wheel enough times. Good thing I did have it.

I said, "Too sort of . . . I don't know. Girly?"

"Ah," he said. "Do you look stupid in it, you mean. Like you're trying to be something you're not."

Could the guy be a little more perceptive? Expose me a little more? "Well, maybe," I said. "Short hair and all." I'd worked hard on my makeup, but I hadn't regained the weight I'd lost from the whole infection thing, and let's face it. I was still me.

"No," he said. "You look beautiful. And I love your short hair. You look free. Ready for adventure." He smiled at me and brushed his hand over my cheek in that way he had, the one that basically made me want to roll over and tell him I was his. "Ready for anything. My kind of woman."

"We'd better go," I said, in order *not* to beg him to do dirty things to me. "Also, if you cut this one off me, I'm telling."

He laughed. "I don't need to. That's what the hooks and eyes are for. It's like it was made for me. We won't tell your sister."

He'd gone online last night and ordered me a replacement dress and bra on the spot. "A hundred twenty-nine dollars

New Zealand just for the dress," I'd pointed out. "You might want to wait until I'm wearing something cheaper next time."

"Nah. I'd have paid ten times that to cut your clothes off you."

"Which sounds hardly at all like a commercial transaction," I'd said. "Congratulations." He'd laughed, then typed in his address for delivery like that was where I'd be, and I'd tried not to think about any of that too much.

There wasn't any more teasing while we drove the half-hour into Dunedin, because he lapsed into silence. I had the feeling he wasn't even aware he wasn't talking. I knew how it felt to try to be strong when all you felt was scared about what was coming next, so I didn't talk, either. I looked around instead. I'd traveled a fair bit around the country in the course of family vacations, during the few years I'd been involved in them, but I'd never been here, so I might as well pay attention.

If he was nervous about his leg, or about me meeting his parents, he probably didn't need me to point that out. See? Tact.

It was very green outside. Extremely green. Hilly, pastoral, and very New Zealand, like a warmer version of Ireland. Or pictures I'd seen of Ireland, since I'd never been there. I'd never been anywhere, actually, other than here, Australia, and home.

Why hadn't I done that? Why hadn't I backpacked my way around the world for a month or three, during one of those college summers when I'd been sure an internship was more important to my future? Why hadn't I eaten tapas in Seville, and pizza for breakfast in Florence, looking over terracotta-tiled rooftops and the domes of churches, watching swallows wheel and dive through the sky in synchronized perfection? Or Indian street food in Delhi, guessing spices and getting it wrong amid crowds of brightly dressed people and the odd cow? I looked out at puffy white clouds, gentle green hills, and crystal-blue sky, at the kind of scenery that soothed your heart and lulled you to sleep, and wondered why a food person hadn't tasted nearly enough food. Or why somebody who'd almost died hadn't lived nearly enough life.

I'd thought New York was enough. You could get every kind of food there. But could you live every kind of life?

I asked, "Did you like it here? Growing up? I'm trying to imagine, but I can't quite. It's not much like Brooklyn, and it's even less like Manhattan."

"No," Jax said, "I guess it isn't. And, yeh. Not much not to like. I had a pretty easy life."

"Is your parents' house close to the central city?"

"Pretty close. It's at the start of the Otago Peninsula. You'll see." His voice sounded choppy and tense, so I shut up and waited while he headed off the motorway and into the traffic, past an enormous building made of stone and decorated like gingerbread, with a huge clock tower.

"As long as they don't live there," I said, "I guess I'm all right."

I made him smile, at least. "That's the railway station."

We parked in the hospital garage a few blocks farther along, and he didn't say much of anything. Not the thing again about me going to the museum or shopping, and not even a joke about how I'd stolen his book, and now the poor hero was going to be stuck up there, stranded on Mars, in his imagination forevermore. I'd have thought he'd forgotten I was there, except that he took my hand while we walked, threading his fingers through mine like he wanted to touch as much of me as he could hold. Like he needed to hang on to something warm and real, to hold himself right here so his mind couldn't drag him away to a place he couldn't stand to be. And I thought that I knew about that, too.

JAX

I thought about the fact that Karen wasn't talking, and then I forgot about it. It was the same thing as before, the same thing as always. One foot in front of the other.

One artificial foot, and one real one. One step at a time.

This was the next step, that was all. It wasn't a verdict on whether my life was worth living, or whether I still had something to offer the world. Things changed. You could either change with them and find something new to do that mattered, or you could give up, roll over, and die. I hadn't rolled over and died yet. I wasn't going to do it now. All of this had to be for *something.*

I'd tell myself that, because when you told yourself anything enough times, it became your truth.

Inside the building, I gave my name to the woman at the reception desk and sat down beside Karen in the waiting room. She had her book open, but was looking around, taking everything in and storing it away in her furiously agile mind. She looked like a model in that dress, her face all big eyes, cheekbones, and wide mouth, her arms and legs endlessly long and slim, her shining cap of dark hair neat and feathered at the fringes. I wondered how it was that she didn't seem to know it.

I knew—I ought to know—that being beautiful on the outside wasn't the only thing that mattered. It wasn't even in the top three. But I noticed anyway.

There were a few other people waiting. A couple older fellas, missing legs. One who looked like a farmer, sitting with his wife and looking stoical. That would've been an accident, probably. Caught in machinery, something like that. A young blonde bloke I recognized, barely twenty-one, his hair not quite military-short, his arm gone almost from the shoulder. And a girl, maybe six or seven, her arm ending above the elbow, wrapped in a compression bandage. She was with her mum, who was trying not to look worried and sad, and failing. The girl was holding a doll, and she was looking around, too. A bit like Karen, but there was wariness there, too. Fear, surely.

I told Karen, "Be back in a sec," and went over to shake hands with the one-armed fella. Paxton, his name was. It was his right arm he was missing, so I shook the left. Something he'd already be getting used to, or maybe something that was still bothering him.

"How ya goin'?" I asked. "Good to see you. You'll be getting the arm soon, eh."

"Hey, Sarge," he said. "That's what they tell me. Today, I hope. You?"

"Going well. Can't complain."

He glanced at Karen. "That the missus?"

"Not yet," I said. "I'm still working on it."

"I'd say you're lucky," he said, "like always. But maybe not so much, eh."

The leg, he meant. There'd been a grimace, too, when he'd said it. Pain, or something else. I asked, "Something happen?"

He shrugged. "Nah."

"Girlfriend?" I guessed. He'd had a visitor, before. A frequent one, when we'd both been inpatients, me about to leave, and him just coming in. I could've felt some envy, maybe, back then, at the way she'd kissed him. The way she'd seemed like she always would.

"Not anymore." That was all he said, but it was enough.

I put a hand on his shoulder. Sometimes, the hardest thing was not being touched. Or not being touched with love. I remembered that first night, when Karen had touched me, and I'd cried. How mortified I'd been. How grateful, and how scared of it.

Maybe the old man had had it right, when he'd woken up that day and thought about his girl. *I realized that I couldn't think of a day when I wouldn't want to see her face, and I couldn't think of a future that didn't have her in it.*

I wanted to say, "Never mind." I wanted to say, "There'll be somebody better." Instead, I said, "That sucks."

"Yeh."

He swallowed and looked straight ahead, and I gripped his shoulder again and said, "Good luck today. If you need a chat, ring me. Anyplace you've been, I probably have too. Still got my number?"

He nodded once. Too close to tears, and not wanting to show it. I hesitated a minute, then said, "See ya," and headed across the room. Past the little girl, who was watching me.

I thought, *What the hell,* and stopped. The mum looked up,

and I held out a hand and said, "Jax MacGregor."

Her eyes widened. The underwear, or the family. Who knew, in Dunedin. "Moira MacDonald," she said, and took my hand.

"Ah," I said. "Scotland forever."

She laughed, so that was better. Normally, I'd have got down on my haunches, but that wasn't easy anymore. Instead, I stayed where I was and said to the little girl, "My name's Jax. What's yours?"

"Trina," she said. Looking shy, clutching her doll.

"What's your doll's name?"

"Pepper." She waited a moment, then asked, "Do you have a fake leg?"

I'd worn shorts, because I was wearing them every chance I got. Getting used to the looks took exposure, I'd figured, and the sooner I *did* get used to it, the better. "Yeh," I said. "I do."

"Does it work?"

"It does. It's brilliant, actually. I'm still learning to use it, though, and it's weird at night, because I have to take it off when I go to bed. Sometimes I forget I don't have it when I wake up, and I try to stand up like I used to and fall over. That's embarrassing."

She giggled, so that was better, and I said, "I reckon you don't have to fall over as much when you lose your arm. Course, cutting your food's harder."

"And tying your shoelaces," she said. "And buttoning. But maybe my new arm can tie and button, when I get one." Her one hand was clutching her doll tight, holding her to her chest.

"They're doing grand things with hands, I hear," I said. "I think you'll be tying your shoelaces. Playing netball, maybe."

"Or soccer," she said. "You don't need hands for soccer. You're not supposed to use your hands at all, unless you're the goalie."

"There you are, then," I said. "You could be a natural."

"Did you have an accident in a car?" she asked.

"No. I got blown up by a bomb." I touched the scars on

my face. "But they sewed me back up again."

"Oh," she said. "That's lucky. I had an accident in a car. My daddy was in the same one as me. He died."

Her mother gave a choked sound, and I said, "I'm sorry. Bet you miss your dad."

The door behind us opened, and the nurse called out, "Trina MacDonald?" The two of them got to their feet, the mum taking the little girl's remaining hand. Trina turned, though, halfway across the room, and told me, "Maybe they're doing grand things with legs, too. Maybe you can play soccer."

My throat closed up, and I said, "Maybe so," and lifted my hand to her, and she smiled at me, then turned and went through the door with her mum. And I thought, through a wee bit of haze, *Perspective, mate. It's not about what you've lost. It's about what you have.*

Which didn't make it that much easier when the nurse called my name.

40

☆☆

NOT BEING FINE

KAREN

It was two o'clock when we arrived at the Limb Centre. It was nearly three-thirty when Jax came through the door again. After I'd had a chance to think about the look on his face when he'd gripped the shoulder of the guy with no arm, and to wonder what he was saying to him. And, of course, after I'd seen him talk to the little girl with her doll.

That guy—I wanted him. Who wouldn't want him? He was special. Strong and kind.

The guy who came out the door again, though? Not quite so perfect. His face was shut down, and he wasn't looking at me. Not even glancing my way.

Oh. Bad news. And he didn't think I could help, or he didn't think I would. My heart sank. Literally sank in my chest. Well, not literally, because organs don't move like that. Some other physical reaction that felt like that. Sadness. Dread.

Jax went over to the receptionist, spent a while talking to her, then came over at last, still not meeting my gaze, and said, "Ready? Want to get a coffee?" Like he was talking to the . . . coat-check person, handing over his token. Like that.

I said, "Sure," and walked outside with him, where the

clouds were fulfilling their promise and emptying themselves onto Dunedin in the form of soaking, chilling rain.

"Bugger," he said. We were still under cover, because Dunedin, like everyplace else in rainy New Zealand, was Awning Central. "Wait here while I run and get the car. You've got an anorak in one of those duffels, don't you?"

"Yes," I said, "and I'm fine to run with you to get it, and then go for coffee. It's only a couple blocks, and it's too hard to park here."

This time, when he looked at me, his face wasn't blank. It was annoyed. "You don't have to be fine. I'm not asking you to be fine."

"Fine," I said, and he glared at me. Wrong word? Too bad. "But we're running two blocks in the rain to a heated car with, I am very sure, heated seats. *Where* I can get my anorak and warm up, if the experience of getting wet robs me of my strength. Let's go."

He sighed. Being patient. Man, I *really* hated it when a guy was obviously-patient-on-purpose. I was trying my hardest to give him the benefit of the doubt here, to remember that he was under stress—which he hadn't *told* me about—but I wasn't as good as he was at being levelheaded every second of the day. I wanted to get wherever it was that he needed to be before he could talk.

He said, "You don't have to get wet to prove something to me, especially when it's the last thing I want you to prove. Let me try this again. I would prefer to go get the car for you, so you stay dry."

I lifted a hand, then let it drop. "Fine," I said, using the evil word again. "Go get the car. I'm not fighting about this, not right now. I'll fight about it with you later instead. But for the record, you're being really stupid."

He almost smiled. Just not quite. He said, "Wait," and took off. T-shirt, shorts, and hoodie, all of it soaked before he'd gone half a block. And I thought two things.

First: What the hell? And second: Why were men so weird?

☆☆

JAX

That had gone well.

The truth was, I needed the run. Which wasn't two blocks. Typical Karen, to say two blocks when it was four, to tell me she could run it in the rain, and not to see how much I'd rather she didn't.

I drove back, navigating the one-way streets and the traffic around the Octagon at the start of rush hour, and finally rounded the corner and saw her under the awning. She had her arms wrapped around herself against the chill, she was peering in the wrong direction and shifting from foot to foot, and something settled into place inside me.

I knew why I'd needed to keep her dry. And, no, it wasn't just my ego. I was also going to have to tell her everything, even if it ripped its way out of me. I wanted to tell her, and I didn't want to.

When I pulled over, she ran to the car through the squall that had picked up right on cue, hopped in, and said, "Phew. It's pouring. You're soaked. Is that OK to say, or is it still dangerously egalitarian?"

I had to smile. "It's OK to say." I would've kissed her, but I was in a loading zone, and the bloke behind me was hooting, so I pulled out into traffic instead. "Let's start again. Want to go for a coffee?"

"I don't know," she said, saucy again, like you couldn't keep her down. Which you couldn't. "Are you going to explain and let me help with whatever it is?"

"I'm going to try. It may not make much sense."

"Well," she said, "since I'm pretty much the queen of things making no sense right now, or not understanding the sense they make, I could be exactly the right person to receive your confidences. You never know."

Now, I *was* smiling. How could I not? "Right," I said. "Coffee."

"And a snack," she said. "I know we're eating dinner with your parents, but I'm not going to make it until then, unless you think they'd enjoy the sight of me falling onto my dinner like a starved dog."

It took another ten minutes to navigate the few streets back to the Iconic Café, and when I pulled up in front of it, I asked, "Exactly how insulting will it be for me to suggest that you could run in and order us both a coffee while I park?"

"It will be perfectly acceptable," she said serenely, and before I could lean across and kiss her, she was out of the car.

Ten minutes later, I joined her. She was sitting near the black iron stove, in which a fire was burning merrily, with a view of both the windows and the plant-covered brick back wall. She had two coffees in front of her in big white porcelain cups set on saucers, and two meat pies with salad, too. And every bit of it, and of her, looked like everything a man would most want to see.

"Now, you see," I said, sliding into the chair opposite her, "how efficient that was? Also, when I opened the door and saw you sitting here, I was glad." That was putting it mildly. It was more like my heart had leapt. I'd better say that, or at least a bit of it. "Glad you were dry, and looking so beautiful, and glad you were mine. Glad I could keep you that way."

She smiled. All that life in her eyes, all that vitality in her slim body. "Geez, a person could almost think you were sharing. Also, I saved you the chocolate fish."

I picked it up and saluted her with it. "Life is uncertain. Eat dessert first."

She laughed, and I ate her chocolate fish and said, "Right. I apologize for being an arsehole. You were wearing your new dress, looking so pretty, and I felt like I should've told you to bring your anorak, because I could tell it was going to rain."

"And if I had," she said, "you'd still have told me to wait, because you've got some need to be extra-protective right now. It makes you feel better about various things, even though, of course, I'm capable of recognizing rain clouds myself, even with my teeny-weeny girl brain. Also of reading a weather forecast, which I did. I didn't take my anorak with me, though, because I wanted to be cute, so I chanced it. You didn't think about either of us taking one, because you were worried about your appointment. Nobody made a gigantic, horrible, irredeemable mistake. Nobody's lost their manhood.

Nobody even has to feel bad."

You couldn't have stopped me smiling if you'd tried, even though there was still a giant lump in my throat, and too much happening in my chest. I was either coming down with flu, or I was about to get emotional. For right now, I reached across the table, picked up her hand, ran my thumb over the backs of the ringless fingers, and said, "I think you're meant to make it harder than that. Not too flash at fighting, are you."

"Oh, I don't know," she said. "I thought I did OK. Anyway, fighting's either telling the truth, in which case it doesn't have to be horrible, because you're just working things out, or it's being all passive-aggressive and pretending you're actually fighting about something else while you try to control the other person, in which case, why would you want to be together? And I'm being tactful—for me—but I really want to know." Her mobile face changed, got serious, and she gripped my hand and said, "Whatever the doctor said, whatever you heard—you know I love you, right?"

My thumb stopped moving. I wanted to say, "I do?" Or maybe, "You do?" But the words wouldn't come. Everything was rising up in my chest, my throat, and the hand holding hers started to shake.

She said, *"Jax,"* then shifted her chair so she was closer. Shifted it so she had her back to the window. So she was blocking anybody's view of me. "Tell me."

I had a hand over my eyes, like that could hold the tears back. I heaved in a breath, and it felt like the air was having to work to get through. My leg gave a pulsing throb, and I nearly cried out with it. "I'm . . . doing better," I got out. "Leg's doing . . . pretty well. Doc's going to write a letter to my CO. Commanding officer."

"Uh-huh," she said. "Saying what?"

"I'm on track. Maybe two months. Then I can go back. Once I get to full . . . full fitness." I had both hands over my eyes, my elbows on the table. Panicking again, and not, because Karen's arm was around my back, her other hand on my forearm, and that helped.

"But that's good," she said. "Isn't it?"

I shook my head, then nodded. I tried to say something, and couldn't.

"For somebody who hates to cry," she said, "you sure picked a lousy place for it."

The sobs were trying to break through, and I was laughing at the same time. "You were . . . hungry, though. Needed a mocha."

She pressed closer and put her head against my shoulder. "Yeah. And you needed to give me what I want." When I nodded without looking at her, she said, "And to keep me from getting wet. OK. So . . . where do you go? Back to Afghanistan?"

I wiped my eyes with a napkin and focused on taking some breaths. "It's up to the Defence Force, ultimately. I'll most likely be stationed here, though. In New Zealand. I've made enough sacrifice already, is the idea."

"Doing what?" she asked.

"Same thing."

"But . . . explosives?"

"The military's called in when the police need help with that. We're the experts, so they may as well use us. It's a small country. Drink your coffee."

"Oh." She considered that. "All right—first, I'm not drinking my coffee because you told me to, I'm doing it because I can tell you need to get back to normal, since this is embarrassing you horribly. That's also why I'm scooting back to my place, not because *I'm* horrified by your display of unmanly emotion. I'm just saying, in case."

I was smiling again, somehow. "Thank you."

"So you'll probably be staying here," she said. "Someplace here."

"Wellington, Christchurch, or Auckland. The three places where E Squadron is stationed. My unit, explosives specialists. They'll ask me which I want, and try to give it to me. Which would be Christchurch."

"And that's really what you want to do."

"It's all I've hoped for." The words sat out there, bald and unadorned and true.

"Because . . ." she said.

"Because I know how to do it. And it matters." The emotion came straight back again, like it had been lying in wait.

"Then," she said, "that's what you should do."

41

⭐

ON FROM THE PANELBEATERS

KAREN

"Why the hell wouldn't you just stay here?"

The speaker was Jax's dad, Alistair MacGregor. He looked like Jax. Just as tall, and just as gray-eyed. Even more powerful, although in his case, the power wasn't hidden under any easygoing Kiwi-casual façade. Good thing I was Hemi Te Mana's sister-in-law, that was all I had to say. You could say I was familiar with the species.

The place was Jax's parents' house, although "house" wasn't a good enough word to describe it. I knew all about rich people's fancy places, too. See "Hemi Te Mana's sister-in-law," above. Hemi and Hope had moved from the condo he'd owned when they'd been married, because the enormous penthouse of the building on Central Park West wasn't big enough for a family with all those kids. Now, they had *two* apartments, knocked together. Also on Central Park West, with a garden on the terrace where they grew their own vegetables and flowers. And the house on Waihi Beach, of course.

This thing, though, won the square-footage battle. And the "scenery" battle, since it overlooked the harbor, the city

340

skyline across the water, and the wilder lands to the north, and featured winding paths through a whole lot of beachy landscaping. If you looked the other way, you got a sweeping view of the Otago Peninsula, the water dotted with tiny islands and edged by rugged hills, and were reminded of the little blue penguins and fur seals and albatross colony up there, and what you couldn't see—lonely beaches stretching for kilometers, and the wild southern sea. Once their breeding season was over, the albatrosses would be riding the winds from here all the way to Antarctica, to Chile, even all the way around the world, before they came back to nest again.

I hadn't been there, but I'd heard of all of it, and even I knew this was prime real estate. The house itself was absolutely modern, it blended into the landscape, it used wood and glass and curving lines in the most pleasing possible way, and it had absolutely zero view of any neighbors, since it was on about eight acres. That was one way to get privacy—you just bought everything around you. It also had a heated lap pool, a spa tub, a full guest house, a gym, and a media room. I knew that because Alistair had just reminded Jax of that fact, as in, "Why the hell would you be going all the way up to your place, where you can't get physical therapy or massage or even a bag of bloody groceries, never mind being able to swim? Not like we don't have room for you."

We'd barely started dinner. Jax had refused wine, saying, "I'm driving, thanks," resulting in the above discussion. Now, he said, "I'm all good up there. Oamaru's barely half an hour's drive from the house."

Alistair snorted. "Oamaru. You'd barely be driving at all if you stayed here. And Karen, of course." Gee, thanks. That had been heartfelt.

Bethany, Jax's grandmother, a no-nonsense sort of lady with silver hair cut as short as mine, and sticking up more than mine, asked, "Is there a physio in Oamaru, then, Jax?"

"Yeh," Jax said. "There is. Massage, too, and a pool and gym as well. Everything I need. I'll only need to come back for the Limb Centre every few weeks, unless I run into difficulties. Even then, it's only an hour's drive. Anyway, swimming's good, but my fitness is more about running and the gym now. Hill climbing. Pushing it. Getting back to full fitness. Getting serious." As if he hadn't been doing that already, which I guessed he hadn't. Not if your job depended on your body doing what you told it to, no matter how hard that was, or what terrain you had to traverse to get there.

"You'll enjoy the drive back and forth, I'm thinking," his grandmother said. "Calming along the coast, isn't it. Quiet. So many other things to do as well, and to show Karen. Being by the sea could be healing in itself."

Alistair didn't say anything, just pointed out the window. At the harbor, presumably.

Jax's mother, Megan, who was a redhead, like Poppy, and a woman who emitted "calmness" rays like sunshine, explaining where Jax had gotten it, because it sure wasn't from his dad, said, "We don't have waves, though, do we? It's that sound that makes it so special, I think. I bought you a few groceries, Jax. Remind me to give them to you before you leave."

"Oh," Alistair said, "now you want waves."

She didn't say anything, just looked at him, and he said, "Anyway. How did the appointment go today, then? You're moving well."

It was like I wasn't even here. Which, in a way, was good. I also possibly remembered my extended explosion at Hemi, when Jax had sat there and listened. It had been embarrassing having him there, and it had helped, too. It had given me backup. No mixed loyalties. Nothing but support.

Jax said, "The leg's all good. Healing well, and my balance is getting better, too, though I still need to do some work on that, and on my flexibility. Hip flexor muscles, core strength, and so forth. Yoga'd be good, the doc says, so I plan to do that. Another couple months, though, and I should be cleared to go back."

The words dropped into the suddenly-still room like stones into a pool, and then his mother smiled with pure joy. "Darling," she said. "I'm so glad."

"To go back," Alistair said. His eyes had sharpened, and

KIWI RULES

his face had tightened. "You don't mean go back to the squadron."

"Yeh," Jax said. "I do."

I wanted to hold his hand, but I wasn't sure if it would feel like weakness to him to look like he needed it. I tried to send support-waves his way instead, and waited to hear what would happen next.

Alistair said, "They can't make you go back, surely. What, losing your leg isn't enough? How much do they expect you to bleed for them?"

"They're not making me do it," Jax said. "I'm choosing to do it." His voice was absolutely controlled, his gaze absolutely focused. This would be how he looked and sounded when he was neutralizing an explosive. Like he'd gone into some other zone. The Calm Person Zone.

It sure hadn't taken long to get into it. We'd barely started on our grilled salmon, not to mention our forbidden rice/mango/orange salad. It had fresh lime juice and cilantro in it, which Megan had told me she grew in her greenhouse, which was awesome. The salad was absolutely delicious, and I wanted to keep eating it. There was no way right now, though, not with Alistair looking like he actually *was* about to explode. Megan had her hand on his arm, and everybody was holding their breath. Everybody but Jax. He said, "I'll be stationed in New Zealand, most likely. Working with the police some, I'm guessing. Possibly doing some training."

"For what?" his father asked. "Forty thousand a year? Still turning down the chance to be an officer? And the chance of blowing yourself up for good next time you make a mistake?"

I was going to say something. I wasn't going to be able to help it. Except that I couldn't. Shutting up was about the hardest thing I'd ever done, but I did it.

"If you're asking about my salary," Jax said, "It's up to almost seventy-five thousand now. If you're asking about promotion, I want to do the job, not command troops. If you're asking me whether I *will* make that mistake and blow myself or anybody else up—I'll be doing my very best not to. If you're asking why I'd do it at all—because it's what I want

343

to do. And because I can."

"Seventy-five thousand," his dad said. "You're not holidaying in Bali on that. You're not buying a better house on that."

"I don't need a better house," Jax said. "I have a perfectly good house."

"Is a woman going to think so?"

Alistair didn't look at me, but I answered anyway. "If you mean me, I haven't seen it yet, but I don't have to. I'm capable of earning my own living. I'm not hanging around with Jax hoping to strike it rich." Which, no, didn't meet Calm Person Standards, but he was making me seriously mad.

"Are you, now?" Alistair asked. "Are you doing it? Working for your brother-in-law, is that it? Holidaying for him?"

Oh, boy. Jax stood up with a sudden scrape of chair legs. He put his hand out in front of me, too, like he could physically shield me. Which was so sweet, I wanted to cry, although I also still wanted to hit his dad. Very confusing.

Alistair sighed and said, "Sit down. We'll talk."

A long, long moment, and Jax sat down. Somebody in the room would normally have said, "This isn't the time or place," because people always said that, no matter what time and place it was. Fortunately, nobody did say it. As far as I was concerned, it was *exactly* the time and place.

"Everybody," Jax's mother said, "please eat. I'd say I worked hard on this meal, but it was easy. Still—eat. It's a discussion, that's all. It's all of us finding out what Jax wants to do, and celebrating that he's here with us and able to make that choice."

Her voice may have wobbled a little on the final words, and Jax got up again, went around the table, put an arm around her shoulder, and said, "Love you, Mum. You're the best." Which resulted in her leaning her head against his side, wiping her eyes on her napkin, and laughing, and me choking up some, too. My emotions were all over the place.

"Right," Alistair said when Jax was sitting down again. "The Defence Force was something you needed to do. It was better than the modeling, at least. *That* was a waste of bloody time, if you like. That was why I didn't say anything when you switched."

"Well, yeh, Dad," Jax said, but there was a little humor in his voice now. "You did."

Alistair said, "I mentioned that it would be a good time to go into the firm instead, that's all, if you wanted to make a change from modeling, and if you wanted to get serious about your life and your obligations. When you said no, I accepted your decision."

"Again," Jax said, "maybe not so much. I think it was that I'd already enlisted, and I couldn't get out."

"And now," his father went on, "here you are, had a good scare, lost some bits of yourself, but you're alive to tell the tale. Still got the business diploma, and you may not have forgotten everything you learned. Although business is more common sense than anything else, that and judgment and the brains to absorb what you're reading and seeing, and you aren't short of those. Despite the modeling."

"I hope not," Jax said, "if I *don't* want to get myself blown up again. But I don't want to do it, Dad. I know what I want to do, and it's not with the firm."

"After your granddad started it, and built it," his father said. "After I've carried it on all this time. I'm nearly sixty-five. It's time to make the transition."

"You're sixty-two," Jax said.

"Close enough," his father said. "What about your sisters? What about their kids? What about if you want to have some of your own? What kind of life are you offering them?" He wasn't looking at me when he said it, thank goodness. Still—awkward. Either he was implying that Jax was letting down our fictional future children, or he was suggesting that some other lucky woman would be the recipient of the MacGregor seed. And people said *I* wasn't tactful.

"I think my future offspring will be able to struggle by on what I can provide," Jax said. "And that Poppy's will, too, what with Granddad's trust and all. And Heather's past the point of reproducing, surely. That's everybody taken care of."

His father finally shot a look at me. I should be insulted, but I wanted to laugh, too. I said, "If you're worried about me hearing this and getting my gold-digging claws into Jax, I could go into the kitchen while you discuss large numbers, and hum really loudly just to make sure. I'd want to take my plate, though, because this salad is amazing."

Jax said, "No," and took my hand, so there you were. He told his father, "I'm going to tell you again. I'm not interested. I'll never be interested. Poppy isn't interested, either, and you know that if it's less than a thousand years old, it won't even register with Heather." He told me, "She's an art historian, teaching in Melbourne. Does some consulting as well. Specializing in the Tang dynasty. Chinese."

"Oh," I said. "That may not go much better with selling fancy cars and houses than disposing of bombs does, or writing books about hippos." Poppy's bestselling series, it turned out, was about an often-confused blue hippopotamus named Hazel. The bookstore at the Christchurch airport had stocked them, and I'd bought a couple. They were hilarious, which wasn't exactly a surprise. I'd say Poppy had found her niche.

"You should've had another kid, Dad," Jax said. "Fourth time lucky, eh."

"You think it's a joke," his father said. The skin over his cheekbones was darkening, which I was guessing was a bad sign. "It's not a joke. It's forty years of work. Fourteen hours a day. Six days a week."

"Well, seven," his wife said.

"And that's just me," Alistair said. "What *about* your granddad? You can take his money, you can take mine, but you can't give anything back? Do you think selling cars was *my* dream? It wasn't even close. I had a family to think of, though, and so do you. Your granddad had nothing in Scotland. The family had nothing. He came here and *built* this. From nothing. From a panelbeater's shop. He built it, and I carried it on. It's given us everything, and you're ready to throw it away." His voice had risen. He wasn't shouting, but he wasn't *not* shouting, either.

346

Jax got serious again. He wasn't looking at me, but I could see the intention in his body like it was written there. He said, still quietly, "I don't owe you this, Dad. I know you want me to carry on with it. I've always known it, and I'm in the same spot now that I was then. I can't. Selling the firm's going to hurt you, and I know it, but I can't help you. I owe you my loyalty, and you have it. I owe that loyalty to my country, though, too. Put it another way. You could say that New Zealand gave us all of this. Maybe I need to give something back."

Alistair made a dismissive gesture with his hand. An angry gesture, like he could shove that ridiculous idea out of the way. "How much have we paid in taxes? If we owed a debt, it's paid twice over."

"So I should let somebody else do it?" Jax asked. "Somebody who doesn't pay as many taxes?"

"How many other people's livelihoods am I responsible for?" his father asked. "How many taxes do *they* pay? There's more than one way to serve your country."

"You're right," Jax said. "There is. And it turns out that this is my way."

42

☆☆

MOERAKI BOULDERS

KAREN

I woke up early the next morning, but Jax was already gone.

We'd driven north for an hour the night before in the rainy dark, not talking much, after we'd finally finished dinner and Jax had kissed everyone goodbye. Once we were on the highway, I said, "You were awesome, by the way," he said, "Thanks," and that was about it. Shutting down, I guessed, the way you did after a day with too much emotion, when all you wanted was to get home, go to bed, and turn it all off.

A couple minutes after he'd left the highway and headed down a side road in the dark, I got out of the car in a three-bay garage that was as neatly organized as you could possibly imagine, including the two sea kayaks hanging up high via a pulley system, and the mountain bike, road bike, three life vests, and two kinds of skis up on pegs along one wall. I couldn't tell much about the place from that except that Jax was adventurous and neat, which I already knew. I heard rain drumming on a metal roof, and that was about it.

When we crossed under the breezeway to the main house and he opened the front door, I didn't see much else, except that the house wasn't huge, it contained a lot of wood and glass, and the design was modernist. He switched on a few lights, and we crossed through an open great-room space with black metal trusses framing the roofline, and into a bedroom beyond that to the tune of more rain sounds, comforting as a lullaby.

I used the single bathroom, which was done in industrial chic—deep, thick farmhouse sink, poured-concrete counters, huge walk-in shower lined with enormous gray-white tiles, et cetera—all of it exactly what I'd have expected from Jax. Modern. Simple. Efficient. When I came back out to the bedroom, I thought about unpacking my duffels, and didn't, because I wasn't even sure what we were doing next. We hadn't talked about it. I took out my PJs, and that was all.

When Jax came out of the bathroom, I was pulling on my sleep tee. He said, "Want to do me a favor?"

"Sure," I said. "Need me to massage your leg?"

"Well, yeh, if you're offering. I was more thinking—could you take that off? I just want to touch you tonight. I just need to—feel you."

We undressed in silence, and he pulled back the gray duvet on the bed, turned out everything but one bedside light, and started to take off his leg. Once he had, I got lotion from the bathroom, knelt over his lower legs, and did my best to massage the swelling and the pain out of the stump.

He still didn't say anything, just lay back and looked at the ceiling. But when I looked up, his eyes were squeezed shut and the tears were running down his temples. I couldn't hear him crying over the sound of the rain, but I wasn't sure I could have heard it anyway. I knew two things for sure, though. He hated that he was crying, and he needed to do it.

I didn't say anything, just massaged his leg for another few minutes, keeping it slow and easy, until he said, "That's . . . good." After that, I kissed my way up his body, kissed his cheek, his temples, his eyelids, took his tears into my mouth, smoothed my hand over his hair the same way he'd done it so many times, and, finally, kissed his mouth.

He turned out the light.

We made love in the dark to the music of the rain and the

rhythm of our breath. Gentle touches and sweet, slow kisses, hands and mouths and bodies twining together. My lips over his heart, feeling the steady, slow beat of it, my fingers tracing the ragged patterns of the scar tissue on his chest. His hands sliding down my back, holding me at the waist, his thumb touching each of my belly piercings in turn, like he needed to be reminded that they were there, that this was me. His breath in my ear, finally, when he was over me, my legs wrapped around his waist and his fingers threaded through mine.

We made love like my body was his, and his was mine. Like this was our offering, and we needed to give it. Like two people in love.

☆☆

When I woke up, the light in the bedroom was gray and shadowy, and the rain had stopped. I could hear another sound now. Barely. The swish of the surf, and the deeper pulse of it, the thing you felt in your belly and your bones. I pulled shorts, a T-shirt, and a hoodie from my bag, pushed the blinds back, opened the accordion-style doors, and stepped out onto a teak deck that extended out toward the sea like a jetty.

The outside of the house was black corrugated metal, the structure was a simple rectangle, and every wall on the seaward side opened to the dunes and the beach. The air smelled like freshness, like wet grass and salt air, and below me, the horizon was turning pink and the golden sand of the beach curved in a mighty sweep of shoreline. From someplace to my left, there was a noise like gulls crying, or not. Unearthly, but melodic, too.

I followed the sandy path in my bare feet, heading down the slope and onto the beach as the wavy lines of pink began to glow on the horizon. The tide was heading out, and as the light grew, I could see the huge, round, gray boulders, as tall as a person, half-covered by the foaming water that surged, then retreated. I could see, too, the shell-pink and palest blue of the dawn sky reflected in the shine of water on sand, left behind by the receding tide. And I could see a tall figure down the beach, walking, with a hint of stiffness, away from me, past the half-dozen other early arrivals and the photographer with his tripod set up to immortalize dawn on the boulders, like any picture could bring you the touch of the wind, the tang of salt in the air, the gentle majesty of sea and sky, the solitude and the connection, the beating heart of the world.

I caught up slowly, because I didn't want to run. I could hear the sound better now, and I could see a little group of tourists holding up their phones, recording it.

Jax was playing the bagpipes. No tune I recognized. A low note, holding there at the bottom like endurance, and the melody soaring above it, drifting back on the wind. A tune that made you ache, that made you think of sunsets fading into dark, of a bugle playing *The Last Post* over a field of white crosses. Of the sacrifices the brave made, because that was what they'd been asked to do.

He toa taumata rao, Koro would say. Courage has many resting places. In Jax, it had come to stay.

The horizon was yellow and orange now, the clouds above it lit with pink, then purple, the sky slowly turning to azure as the sun broke over the horizon and I caught up with Jax. He was wearing shorts, moving in rhythm to the music, his bare feet leaving footprints in the wet sand. A real foot, and the other one. The one he'd learned to use, when life had given it to him. The one he was walking on with, because it was what he had.

JAX

I played because the sun was coming up over the water. Because I was a New Zealander in my heart, and a Scot in my blood. Because this was the best country in the world, and the beach was the best place to play the pipes, and I was lucky to be here for all of it. Because I had a house that was exactly what I'd always wanted, and last night, I'd had the woman I loved there with me. I played because there was too much emotion in my chest, and it had to come out in my breath and in the music.

And, probably, because it was better than crying again.

I walked past the mountainous boulders, gleaming wet and rough and round in the dawn light, past tourists who immortalized me on their phones and wondered what my story was and what my scars meant. For once, I didn't care what they saw, or what they thought. I knew, and that was enough.

The strains of *Highland Cathedral* drifted back behind me, over the sea, over the beach, taken by the wind, and I took a breath and started in on *Scotland the Brave*. And Karen came up beside me.

I took my mouth off the blowpipe, and the sound gradually faded away. She said, "Don't stop. Not unless you want to. It's beautiful."

"I'd rather talk to you. It's my practice session, that's all. Bagpipes are too loud to play indoors. Sleep well?"

"Yes. I love your house. Tell your dad that if he's worried about it not impressing women, he can stop worrying."

I smiled. Somehow, the things she said always did that for me. "Sorry I'm not wearing the kilt."

She laughed, and I let the pipes rest on their harness, took her hand, and said, "Now I've seen everything beautiful this morning."

"Mm." She rested her head against my shoulder. "Did I mention that I loved you?"

My heart was already too full. Now, it was going to overflow, and I'd already cried twice in the past twenty-four hours. I said, "You may have done. I don't mind hearing it again, though. I could tell you that I love you, too, because it's true."

She sighed. "Yep. It's all right here, isn't it? We're so lucky. Even though you're not wearing a kilt. I'm not sure I can stand the kilt. It could be too much. I could explode from too much manly goodness."

I laughed and turned around. "Coffee, then. Breakfast."

"Sounds good. All right, I've given you lots of recovery time, so I'm just going to ask. Is your dad always a jerk?"

This morning, I could smile when I answered that. "No. He's good to my mum. Good to my sisters. A pretty good boss, from what I know, though he's a tough one. He's disappointed, that's all. Heather wasn't interested in the business. Fair enough. Poppy was a possibility, but she wanted to do her own thing, and now, she wants to do it more. I wondered, for a bit there, if he'd take Max on, but that's not looking like such a good idea."

"No," she said. "I can see that. Something's odd there, I'm guessing. She doesn't seem—quite happy."

"You're right. But there I was, the last chance and the best hope. Not bad at maths, got the diploma and all."

"Business," she said. "Like me."

"Yeh. And then I did the modeling instead of joining him, and that was the biggest disappointment of all."

"Good money, though. You can't tell me he doesn't like money."

"Rich-lister playboy?"

"But it was your own money."

"Not entirely. I got the same amount in trust that my sisters did when I turned twenty-one. Don't tell anyone. You'll be shocked to hear it, but some girls could be attracted to that. He was afraid Granddad had ruined me, because there I was, year after year, wasting my life. Then the military came along. He hit the roof at that one. So you see—three kids, and too much disappointment. And then there's being scared that I'll die, of course."

"You're tolerant."

"I can afford to be." The morning light bathed the boulders and the beach in the kind of glow you couldn't believe was real, the breeze touched the fringes of hair on Karen's forehead and the nape of her neck, and the force of the tide pulled the water out from shore and the doubt from my heart. "I've got what I want."

"Yeah?" She tucked her hand through my arm, and I thought that walking through life with her like that wouldn't be bad at all. "Despite the leg."

"Despite the leg," I said. "Despite everything."

"Then," she said, "could you play me another song?"

So I did. I played *Scotland the Brave*. More people recorded us on their phones, and I looked out at the boulders and the sunrise and the sea, walked on my two legs, and didn't care a bit.

43

☆☆☆

NOBODY CRIES OVER
SAUSAGE

KAREN

That afternoon, I did the thing I hadn't done for two months.
I went to the Prairie Plus website.

I was done being numb. I was feeling life again, and
wanting to feel it more, but there that lump still was, in my
stomach, in my chest, blocking my path. It was time to take
the next step and look, because the alternative was to wall the
past eight years off like they'd never happened. How was I
going to know what to do next if I didn't make some sense of
what had happened before?

To be honest, the walling-off idea was still plenty
appealing. I wanted to think about how Jax and I were going
to spend the next couple weeks instead, but Jax, at least, had
an ending point—or a beginning point, maybe—sitting out
there. We weren't drifting along in a bubble anymore. His
road had a fork in it, and he was going to be heading down it.

I'd started to really enjoy the bubble, though. I wanted my
beautiful bubble. I didn't want to think about the fact that I
needed a job, and I still didn't know what that was going to

look like. I didn't want to think about the company I'd worked so hard to build, and what my former coworkers were doing now. I didn't want to wonder whether Jada was still doing yoga in the aisle, now that she'd moved into the fancy new offices, or whether Byron was still allowed to bring his Italian greyhound, Shazam, to work with him. And I sure didn't want to think for one tiny second about Josh.

I especially didn't want to know who had replaced me. But I needed to know all of it.

My colleagues—former colleagues—had texted me, at first, in shock and support. They hadn't emailed, because my work email wasn't mine anymore, and I had no access to anything in it. That was maybe the most bizarre thing of all. Dozens of emails a day, people writing to me, talking to me, asking my opinion, asking for my decision, just . . . gone, like they'd never been there at all.

I'd thought I was important. I'd thought I was irreplaceable, in fact, which was probably why I'd made Prairie Plus about ninety percent of my life. I'd thought I was giving my time and my attention and *myself* to something bigger than me, something that mattered.

Maybe I had been doing that, though, because what we'd done *had* mattered, surely. We'd made it easy for people to shift the way they ate, at least in one little way, to something better for their bodies and better for the world around them. Plus what Koro had said. I'd helped all those people get jobs and build careers. That was worth something, wasn't it?

I hadn't answered any of those texts, except to say, *Thanks for your support. I'll be fine. Good luck.* I'd copied and pasted that over and over, unable to engage more than that, because thinking about the company, talking about what had happened, had felt like ripping chunks of flesh out of my body.

Now, though, I had distance, right? Almost ten thousand miles and almost two months' worth of distance. I was sitting on a deck on a gorgeous day in New Zealand, looking at the creamy, scalloped crescents of waves washing up gently onto golden sand. I was feeling the touch of a fresh breeze, thinking that in a little while, I was going to take my first run since I'd gotten sick, and I was going to do it on that beach. That tomorrow, I'd go to the gym with Jax, and swimming afterwards, because my arm had healed, and it was time to get back into shape. And that in a week or so, we were going to ride the Alps 2 Ocean cycle trail that ran from Aoraki/Mount Cook all the way to the sea. Training for both of us, and, just maybe, thinking time for me, in the beauty and the quiet of the South Island in late summer.

I mean, we didn't even have to camp. Where else could you take a week-long bike ride through the mountains and the highlands, have your luggage carted ahead for you, and sleep in a bed and have a shower and a beer every night? Clearly, I was the target customer for this glamping deal.

Meanwhile, here I was, knowing that I had to get out of my bubble eventually, so it might as well start now. I wasn't raw hamburger inside anymore. I could text people back now, and I needed to find out which companies were moving and shaking, and where they were doing it. The cobwebs in my brain had been cleared out, surely, which meant that I could shine a light into those dark spaces and start putting something in there. A new plan. A post-breakdown plan. A post-bubble plan.

I needed to know what was going on in the industry, because I needed to present myself to my future employer, whoever that might be, and explain everything I could bring to the table going forward. I wouldn't be a founder anymore, I'd be a cog, and I needed to make myself look like the biggest, shiniest, most functional cog they'd ever seen, so they'd plug me into the machinery at a pivot point, and I could start making a difference again.

My ego didn't matter. Doing something important mattered, and doing it smarter next time *really* mattered. Even if I had to suck it up and take Hemi's advice.

Of course, there was Jax. Oh, boy, was there ever Jax. How could I leave him behind? How could I leave *this* behind? I didn't know, but I was going to have to figure it out.

All of that was why I looked, and possibly why the article

on the *Press* page dropped me like a steer being stunned in the slaughterhouse.

Prairie Plus, Developer of Better Than Beef, Ramps Up Production Under M&P Ownership.

Fine. Even though I was breathing at about twice my normal rate. Ramping up meant more jobs. I didn't want the company to fail. That was the last thing I wanted. The article was from a month ago. I *really* hadn't been looking.

It was the next part that got me.

The company, whose product-development arm is now overseen by Angel Obrigado, hired into the position after the abrupt departure of former VP Karen Sinclair, reported a ten-percent increase in fourth quarter earnings on Friday, surpassing analysts' expectations.

"We're pleased by the growth we've achieved," CEO Josh Ranfeld said, "but we're not standing still. I'm excited to announce that we're moving forward with our new product line, Sizzle. For the first time, people can eat sausage that's both delicious and good for them. No scary mystery meat, and no compromises on taste. We've had amazing feedback from our focus groups, and we're refining the products now, planning to bring them to supermarket shelves later this year."

The article went on to talk about rumblings of competition, particularly from Sunshine Foods, which was reported to be putting together a new division to capitalize on our development of the market, but I only skimmed that. My mind had stayed back there on those first two paragraphs. And if the folds of my brain had started relaxing while I'd been in New Zealand? They'd tightened right back up again, and I got a wave of nausea so strong, I nearly had to dash for the bathroom.

First—Angel Obrigado? My second-in-command in product development, whom I'd fired, five months ago, when I'd found out that she'd shared too much with Sunshine Foods? She'd sworn it was just shop talk, loose lips over wine at a conference, had apologized and made promises, but that wasn't what I'd heard, or what made sense, when I'd pieced together the clues. Emails that she'd forwarded to her personal address, for example, that would be more than useful to a competitor.

I'd been so *mad*. I'd *hired* Angel. I'd trained her and encouraged her and brought her up with me. I hadn't even minded that she was impossibly good-looking, because I didn't judge women on their looks, negatively or otherwise, I wasn't at work to be beautiful, and I wasn't in competition with my colleagues. We were all in it together. We were a *team*.

In the end, we'd done a layoff with severance instead of a termination for cause, because investors and analysts didn't want to hear about internal divisions, but we'd accompanied it with a noncompete agreement that would spike her guns. The same kind of agreement I'd signed when I'd left, the kind that meant I couldn't go to Sunshine Foods now and make M&P—and Josh—sorry.

A noncompete agreement didn't apply, though, if your company hired you back.

Josh had shared my indignation over Angel, or I'd thought he had. Apparently not so much.

And then there was the sausage. My beautiful proposal, the laboriously acquired recipes and techniques I'd been putting together into a presentation on that last day, the product of so many late nights and sudden moments of clarity in the shower after freezing runs in the dark, when I'd dashed out from behind the shower curtain, still soaking wet, to make notes on a legal pad beside my bed, the water from my hair dripping on the paper and smudging the ink.

Now, my proposal, my techniques, my recipes, my research, and all the rest of the fruits of my dreams belonged to Prairie Plus and M&P, like every other bit of my work product. Like the management and the innovation that had resulted in that fourth-quarter earnings number, from a time when I'd made a whole lot of that happen.

Nobody cries over sausage, I told myself when my throat started to close up and the pit of my stomach went icy-cold. *This is done, and it's nothing new. What difference does it make if it's Angel or somebody else? It's the past. What would you want, for the company to go into bankruptcy, just because you don't get to play anymore?* I *didn't* want that, at least in my head I didn't. My heart wasn't so sure. My heart felt one thing. Betrayal.

Part of me wanted to curl up on the bathroom floor again, but it got taken over pretty fast by something else. By the red-hot ball of rage that settled into my chest and had me wanting to pace. Wanting to run. Actually, wanting to hit something, but unfortunately, that wasn't an option.

It was too bad that you'd go to jail for, say, throwing a chair through a conference-room window, because I was really wishing I could go back in time and do it. Imagining it wasn't doing nearly enough for me. All I had was the running thing.

"Screw that," I said aloud when I was doing just that, when I'd put on my shoes and had run off the first, worst flames of rage. I was past the boulders now, and all the tourists taking pictures of them, too, and had moved on to the part of the beach that was empty, where nobody came. Nothing but the birds to hear me, and I was going to yell if I wanted to. Which I did. "Screw all of them," I told the birds. "I'm going to do better. I'm going to do more. Screw all of you."

A voice at my ear. "Hope you don't mean me."

I jumped a mile, and then I laughed, even though the emotion was still roiling around inside me. I kept running, and Jax ran with me. Easily, just like that day on the beach with the kids, even though I could tell from the wet patches on his gray T-shirt that he'd already done plenty during his gym visit.

"Something happen?" he asked.

"Well, *yeah.*"

I explained, and got mad all over again doing it, and he said, "So you went running. You do realize that's why you'll come out on top, right? You realize this is why you'll win?"

"No, but I'd sure love to hear it. That's not exactly at the forefront of my mind right now."

"Sure it is." His footsteps matched mine. In sync. "You have to know it. You're not crying on the bed, you're running on the beach and making vows out loud."

"I cried on the bed at the beginning," I confessed. "Actually, I cried on the floor. Well, I didn't cry. I sort of . . . collapsed on the floor, though. That's why I'm here, in New

Zealand, because Hope and Hemi found me that way, and Hope worries. I'm always skinny, but I'm not usually *this* skinny."

"Mm," he said. "I see."

"You were so sure yesterday," I said. The thing that had kept bothering me, nagging at me like pulling on a loose thread. "You've moved all the way past the anger, all the way to certainty. And I'm still just so *mad*. I'm still so *stuck.*"

"Because it's been five months for me, that's why. How long for you?"

"Almost two months."

Ahead of us, a flock of little water birds on stiltlike legs took off, settling farther up the beach, where we'd disturb them again, and they'd take off again, too, as many times as it took. "At two months in," Jax said, "they fitted me for my leg. It hurt like hell, and I was so weak anyway, I felt like I was dragging it. My skin blistered, and the place where my foot had been burned every night. I couldn't sleep, and I was afraid to take the drugs to help me do it. Afraid to reach for too much comfort, that I'd run away from the pain and the fear and into addiction. The scars on my chest were still lumpy and barely healed—because they'd got infected—and they didn't feel any better than the leg. And I thought—I'm going to be sitting behind a desk, looking at spreadsheets, because I won't be able to do anything else. Anything I know how to do, or anything I want to do. I'm going to be working for my dad. I'm going to be stuck. You can call that panic, if you like. That was how it felt at two months, but I turned out to be tougher than that, in the end. Just like you."

"I always thought I was a badass." I was sweating like crazy, and starting to breathe harder, but I was running the anxiety out, maybe. I could feel it leaving, at least for now. I still had the rage, though. "In an intellectual sense, at least. I was a National Merit Scholar in high school. After my brain tumor. That's a big deal. It's a scholarship thing, except that I didn't get a scholarship, because I had Hemi. I was first in my class at NYU, though. I got it *done*. And I don't know why I'm even telling you this."

"You're not," Jax said. "You're telling yourself. Keep talking."

"It's bragging, though."

"So brag. You've told yourself the negative things. Let's hear you say the positive ones."

"Whoa. What a concept. All right. Here you go. You asked for it. I was one of *Inc.* magazine's 'Faces of Change' two years ago, and I spoke at last year's Biodiversity conference in San Antonio. All right, it's still nerd smarts, but so what? Nerds rule the world. M&P is going to wish they had me back, because Angel isn't half as good as I am, and I'm going to laugh in their faces. Like this. Ha ha ha."

I wasn't exactly convincing myself yet, but maybe I was going where I needed to. I'd thought my cobwebs were swept out, but I could still have some sweeping to do. "I'm not starting over," I said, "or not really, because I'm not starting from the bottom this time. Maybe I wasn't doing too well when I got here, but I'm ready to start figuring it out now. Or if I'm not ready, I'm going to do it anyway. Let's turn around."

We did, and when we were headed back, watching the tide ebb again, being sucked out from the boulders ahead of us, Jax said, "I've been thinking a bit about some of those things myself. One thing in particular."

"I thought you were already there. I thought you'd decided."

"There's that other part, though, isn't there," he said. "Everything I threw away so easily before, because I assumed it would always be there, or I didn't know I needed it."

"Oh," I said. "You mean the love thing." My heart had picked up. You bet it had. That was the thing I *hadn't* said, the other thing I'd thought, when I'd been curled on that bathroom floor. That my sister had been married for about five years by the time she'd been my age. That she'd had two kids by then, and a powerhouse husband who'd have moved heaven and earth for her. I didn't believe in a woman's life being defined by reproduction, but I was realizing that work only felt like half of my equation.

"Yeh," Jax said. "The love thing. I never thought much about it, probably because I assumed I deserved it, the attention and all, and that when I was ready, it would be there. Maybe I mentioned that I was an arsehole. Could be I realized a bit too late that it might not be true, and that the woman I wanted might not look at me now and think, "That's the man for me!" Not in spite of my leg and my face, and not because of it. For the man I am. And then you came along, and you did look at me like that, and here we are."

It was easier to say, maybe, when you were running, not having to look into somebody's eyes. Or maybe it was just that Jax had enough courage for anything. Enough mana to say and do the hard things, and to help the people he loved to say and do them, too.

He'd jumped off the waterfall, leg and all, and it hadn't been easy. I was going to have to follow him in. Kiwi Rules.

Be honest about how you're going and what you're up for, our guide had said. *Help your mate, and if you get into trouble, sing out.*

Or the way Jax had summed it up. *When in doubt, jump.*

I said, "All right. My turn. Here I go. You ready?"

"You know I am."

I took a breath and said it. "I was also lying on the floor because I thought I'd found out for sure that I was too much for a man. Too much snark. Too much competitive drive. Too much energy. Too many brains. I was intimidating, and I was tactless, and I had no boobs. Even a *company* hadn't wanted me, and nobody was ever going to love me. Sounds so stupid. Sounds like giving up. That's how it felt, too."

"Except that it wasn't," Jax said. "It was the bottom of the pit. You climbed out."

My chest was heaving, and not because of the run. I tried to keep going, and I couldn't. I slowed down, and then I stopped. I bent over from the waist, and then I dropped down and crouched there on the sand with the wind blowing and the shorebirds flying and the sea going out, my breath feeling louder than any of it.

Jax got down there with me. Sort of. Finally, he said, "Bugger this leg," sat down on the sand, and pulled me down beside him, making a mess of both of us.

I said, "I want to . . . go places. I want to do things. I want to be alive. I want to have some faith. Not just in work. In my *life*."

"If you let yourself dream it," he said, "you can go after it. The same way you did the first time, but better, because you know more than you did back then."

I wiped my nose with the back of my hand, in yet another display of either badassery or non-femininity, depending on your viewpoint, got to my feet, put a hand out for him, and said, "I notice you didn't say, 'If you dream it, you can do it.'"

He got up himself, and we started to jog again. It felt hard, because my legs had stiffened up, but it felt good, too. "That's because," he said, "it's not necessarily true. You don't know if you can do that thing you dreamt up until you try. And you might not believe in it until you've actually done it. The trick is going forward anyway, into the dark. Maybe you don't make it all the way. No guarantees. Maybe you'll hit a bump and have to start over one more time. Or two. Or five. But you'll be farther down the road when you do. How's that for wise words? They're true, though. You can say that I found them out the hard way."

44

☆☆

PEOPLE IN GLASS HOUSES

JAX

I'd said something, but I hadn't said enough. That was why, four days later, I was lying naked in bed, holding Karen's hand, in a tiny house kilometers from anywhere, in the heart of the dark, because the house was made entirely from glass. Walls, ceiling, floor, everything.

It wasn't actually the dark we were in at that, because the little house was lit with all the stars there ever were. I looked at the Milky Way curving across the sky and thought about the sea stretching below us, and how Karen had walked with me up the track through the bush, turned a corner, and seen a house of glass sitting on the edge of a ridge, all alone. How she'd gasped, and how happy it had made her. I thought about how much she was going to love our cycle trip next week, too, and said, "Of course, there's a place I haven't gone yet."

"Mm?" She kissed my shoulder, sighed, and asked, "Where's that? This is a place I'm glad we went, by the way. Poppy should talk these glass-house-things up more on the website, because this is amazing. Who would know these were even here? I'm telling Hemi that this is so, so much better than camping, and he needs to buy the company. My favorite

365

part was the dinner basket. Well, except for the glass. That's actually my favorite part. This is my idea of a *vacation*. Something you could never do anywhere else. Something you never knew was possible."

"You've only seen two of the sites," I pointed out. "There are nine of them. All sorts of brilliant adventures awaiting the curious traveler."

"Don't care. I'm sold."

"It could be a good thing that Hemi's deciding," I said, "and not you. I think you're too easily influenced by sex and scenery. But seriously, there's a reason I brought you up here instead of going home after the gym, and why we went through Christchurch along the way."

"Oh, yeah? What's that?"

"I wanted to say"—I had to clear my throat for a second here. *Harden up, mate.* "That Christchurch is where I'd ask to be stationed, if I were choosing for myself, so I thought I'd show it to you, and you could see what you thought. It's by the sea, and it's small, which means you can get away easily to places where you can have adventures. That's a selling point, in case I forgot to mention it. But there's also Wellington or Auckland, like we said."

"Uh-huh," she said slowly. "Oh, look. A shooting star." She sighed. "Look how far it went. It really does leave a trail. That's so cool. I'm not sure I've ever seen one, except in movies. It's my first one, and I'm seeing it here, with my Star Sibling. You're supposed to make a wish."

"If you'd shut up," I said, "I'd *tell* you my wish. This is hard enough as it is."

"Oh. OK. I'm listening."

"You don't have to go back to the States at all," I said. "There's such a thing as a work visa. There's such a thing as a skilled migrant visa, too, if we're taking leaps."

The words hung out there like the blazing roof of light overhead. Karen said, "Wow."

"'Wow' isn't much of an answer." My heart was beating like I was about to cut the wire that would either blow me up, or make me safe. Never a comfortable moment.

"That would be . . . *quite* a leap," she said.

"You don't have a job now," I pointed out.

"Geez, thanks. I hadn't noticed." She was trying to scowl at me, but I had my fingers on her pulse, and it was racing as fast as mine was. "So you mean—if it was Auckland or Wellington or Christchurch where I found something, you could ask to be stationed there?"

"That's what I had in mind, yeh. I could ask to be stationed there, and we could live together, to put it fully out there. Or just live close, but if it's up to me—together."

"Huh."

"That's not much better than 'Wow.'"

"I don't know . . . what I'd do, though," she said.

"There are food science jobs here, surely," I said. "Of some sort. I'd say that I'd apply in the States, make this sound more balanced, but they probably aren't looking for Kiwis to join their services, and I don't think I'm the mercenary type. Also, I think you like New Zealand better than I'd like New York."

My joke didn't work, because she was silent for so long, I half-wondered if she'd gone to sleep. This wasn't at all what I'd been hoping for. Not even close.

Maybe I should've gone all the way, with the ring and all. It wasn't that I hadn't thought about it. It was that I'd thought it would scare her off. Maybe that had been just exactly wrong, though. Maybe it was scarier for her to contemplate it *without* the ring.

I waited, realized that having to wait was probably not a good sign, and thought that compared to finding your way through the maze of what-ifs that were human emotions, defusing a bomb was easy.

Finally, she said, "You know how it matters to you so much that you do the explosives thing? The military thing? You know all that stuff you said to your dad, and to me?"

This was even further from my planned outcome. "I do remember that, yeh," I said.

"When you say all that, I think—*Yes.* I want to try to do that. I want to be with you. I think about going home, away

367

from you, and it's . . . it just feels dark, you know? Bleak. I can't imagine it. But it feels that way anyway, to tell you the truth. I have this apartment that I really, really hate. I've realized that, at least. But then, when I think about how bad it would feel to leave, I think—how can I be so sure about you after such a short time? Is this just more questionable judgment? And then I get in this whole . . ." She twirled her hand in the air. "Spiral thing. Because the one thing I know for sure is—it's as important to me to do something that matters, something with food, something *important,* as it is for you. I can't see my way forward yet, but I keep thinking it's right there, just around the corner. I can't quite grab it, but it's *there.*"

"And it's not worth it to you even to try?" I asked.

She'd sat up, now, like she had too much life force to do anything else. In another second, she'd leap from the bed and start to pace. Holding onto her was like holding quicksilver. You'd never manage it, not unless she wanted to be held. *"Yes,"* she said. "Of course it's worth it. I made such a bad choice last time, and I know what everybody else would say, but I can tell—I can *tell*—"She had a fist over her heart, now. "That this isn't a bad choice. That *you* aren't a bad choice. You feel like my . . . my resting place. Like I've been swimming and swimming, fighting off the sharks, for so long, and I don't know how long I can keep it up, and then there's you, and you're this . . . *island.* You're my safe place, where I can rest, where I can breathe, and where I know the sharks will never get me. That's how it feels. And I believe in that. I do. I know that nobody else would believe it, and I don't care, because I know who you are. I feel who you are in my . . . bones, and my bones work with yours. It's like we match, even though we're not the same. It's like we said at the beginning. Our pieces fit, like that piece of the sky in a jigsaw puzzle, the hole where you've tried and tried to make a piece fit, and none of them quite do. And then you finally find it, and it slides into place, just like that, so easily. Which is not a dirty joke, so don't even go there."

I wasn't going to make any joke, dirty or otherwise. "But

you don't feel that enough to move here for it."

"I don't know. It's hard for me to say that," she went on hurriedly, "but it's wrong for me if I don't. I want to ask—couldn't you have wanted something other than the military, been something other than a soldier? How do I know, even if I do move here, that I'll be with you enough? How do I know that you won't . . ." Her hand shook in mine. "Die? I don't. I don't know, and I hate it. It scares me so much, but anybody can die. Anybody I love. Everybody I love. And besides—it's who you are. How can I ask you to be something other than who you are, if I love you?"

I sighed, and then I got both arms around her and pulled her in. What choice did I have? None, that was what. I could walk away, except that it wasn't possible. "You can't," I said. "And neither can I. Bugger."

⭐

The next morning, we drove back to Christchurch, and I took Karen on a run around Hagley Park, along the tree-lined walkway beside the Avon River, and through the botanic gardens, and, once she was sweating and smiling, a few more kilometers to the Black Betty Café for breakfast. We sat at a long wooden table, and she ate a potato cake topped with roast tomato, field mushrooms, wilted spinach, and a poached egg, with a decoration of bacon curls and pesto hollandaise on the side, and said, "One thing about New Zealand—they do savory flavors the best of anybody."

"Mm," I said. "Could be because we have the best meat, and the best veg, too, although that's probably from Queensland. All of it has to do with the soil, and how it's farmed, I hear. We have something better to work with, maybe."

"And you think I don't notice this sales job," she said. "Running through a beautiful park in gorgeous weather, going out for my favorite kind of food, and reminding me that New Zealand has the best meat. *After* the whole bed-under-the-stars thing. I don't like gardens as much as Hope, but that was really pretty. You'd never have torn her away from the roses. She's got a thing for roses."

I said, "You compare yourself to your sister a fair amount. Have you noticed that?"

She stopped cutting through her stack of breakfast. "I do?"

"And yet I'd swear," I said, "that you don't compare me to Hemi."

"That's because you're nothing like him."

I raised my coffee cup to her in a significant sort of way, and she said, "Huh."

"Yeh," I said. "I'm guessing Hope doesn't compare herself to you, other than admiring your strength."

"You think she isn't strong," Karen said. "People always miss that. She's plenty strong. You can't imagine how hard she worked, and how hard it was to keep going. How hard it was to stand up to Hemi, too. You can't *imagine.*"

"I believe it. He loves her to the moon and back, that's easy to see. When a man loves a woman like that, he'll do anything for her, even change. I didn't say she wasn't strong. I said that she admires your strength as well."

"You kind of did," she muttered, still looking narky.

"You fired up just now, for example, because the two of you have that bond. It's the same way a soldier feels about his mates. Absolute loyalty."

"Well, yeah. Of course. She's my *sister.* She's my *family.*"

"Maybe you're enough as you are, though," I said. "Whatever way you're thinking she's better than you—I don't think it's true. At least not the way I see it, and as we know, I'm always right."

I made her laugh, at least. "I never used to be insecure," she said. "I never had *time* to be insecure. I just got it done. I always could, too. That's what gives you confidence."

"You aren't insecure now," I said. "Your world's been shaken up, and you're looking for that way forward. Once you find it, you'll be getting it done again."

She sighed. "Would you quit being so perfect? You're

making this really hard."

I didn't ask what. I knew what.

We drove home, after that. Through southern Canterbury, across the Waitaki River, and on into Otago. Nothing grand about it, not here. Farmland, peaceful and sleepy, but with the sea on one side and the hills rising inland, and the knowledge that the peaks and glacier-carved lakes of the Southern Alps lay just beyond.

I wanted to take Karen to see all of it, and to be slowed along the way by a mob of woolly sheep, nearly ready for shearing, being herded up the highway by a couple of dogs who cut and wove their way expertly through the flock, intent on their job. By a fella on a dirty green all-terrain vehicle driving behind them, a battered yellow "Caution" sign stuck onto the rear. One hand on the wheel, a repertoire of whistles at his command, and the absolute assurance that the hurried travelers around him, with fifteen New Zealand destinations to see in three weeks, would have to stop for sheep, and might be reminded that this was one of the reasons they'd come. I wanted to cycle with her on the Otago Rail Trail, just because the trees were beautiful in autumn, shining gold and red, and you earned every coffee stop and pub dinner along the way. I wanted to take her skiing in Queenstown in winter, and backpacking on the Routeburn Track in summer, across swing bridges with the mist of the waterfalls around you, in the shadow of the Alps, and to watch her delight when she found herself, at the end of the day, in a lodge with a spa tub, eating the food she loved and drinking New Zealand wine. I wanted to show her a place where you could care about your work, but you could care about the rest of your life as well, and you could share it with the people you loved, because everybody agreed that was the most important part. I wanted her to feel her pulse slow and her heart expand, and I wanted her to share that heart with me.

She thought she couldn't have it all. She could. She could have it with me, because I wanted to help her do it. But how was I going to convince her of that?

And then I pulled off Highway 1 and headed up Moeraki

Boulders Road, turned into my driveway, and found a car there. A silver sedan that looked like a rental.

"Huh," Karen said, and I thought the same thing. A mate, maybe, a soldier with a problem. That had happened before. Or Poppy, even though the car was wrong. If this was her, driving a car that wasn't her own, running away, I'd know that the niggles I'd picked up before were real, however breezy she tried to be. Whoever it was, it was likely to be somebody who needed help, which I'd have to give, even though I could all but feel my time with Karen running through the hourglass.

The fella who came around the house could never have been in the services. No possible way. He wasn't even my brother-in-law, Max, much as I'd like to have a fairly serious discussion with Max just now. This bloke was what you'd call "broodingly handsome," if you were in the model-agent business, and was wearing slim-fit jeans, a matching navy button-down shirt that was cut so close to his trim body that he'd clearly done it on purpose, and almost-casual blue suede shoes.

Yes, he was wearing blue suede shoes. I was sure that was meant to be ironic. No man should be wearing clothes that were meant to be ironic. I hated him already. And then Karen said, "Oh, no. *Why?*" and bolted out of the car like she'd been shot out of a cannon, and I thought I knew who he was and hated him even more.

On the other hand—this could end up in a fight. That was cheering.

45

☆☆

THE POWER SEAT

KAREN

My first thought was, "This went differently in my imagination." As in—I'd be getting some award, or coming out of some interview. Possibly wearing an evening gown. I'd see Josh and would pause, one hand resting lightly on a banister, before I picked up my skirt and moved gracefully down the curving staircase, a faint smile on my face.

That had probably come from a movie. Oh, well. It wasn't happening. Here in my real life, Josh was the one who looked dark and elegant, while I was wearing shorts, a grubby T-shirt, and running shoes, and I smelled like a couple hours of running followed by bacon and three hours in the car, during which the sweat had dried. I could also have spinach in my teeth. You never knew.

It didn't matter, not when I jumped out. I was just mad. Jax got out, too, and stood next to me. So he could jump in front of me and take a bullet, probably. The man had been born to protect, and if Josh was cake mix? Jax was four layers of double-coffee chocolate cake with chocolate fudge icing.

Josh's eyes flicked between Jax and me, and I folded my arms and said, "What?"

"I should be the one asking 'What,'" he said. "You never even returned my calls. You never gave me a chance to explain. You never answered me when I *did* explain."

"When did you explain?" I asked. "And what possible explanation could you give?"

"I wrote you an email. I spelled it all out. I left voicemails."

"I hope you enjoyed the exercise, then," I said, "because I blocked you. Of *course* I blocked you. What did you expect?"

"That my fiancée would hear me out? That she'd actually break up with me, not just disappear? That she'd have some guts?"

Oh, boy. If there'd been a window handy, I'd have thrown a chair through it for sure. Or I'd have thrown *Josh* through it. I reminded myself, *No hitting,* waited for the message to get through to my body, and discovered that I'd apparently blocked that, too.

I said, "Your fiancée with no ring and no date, hanging on for nothing. I'm not having this conversation in the middle of a driveway. I have to pee. I need a glass of water. I need to brush my teeth. And you're in my way."

"You haven't changed at all, have you?" Josh asked. Not in an admiring way. He glanced at Jax and asked, "Who's this?"

I said, "None of your business," at the same time Jax said, "Jax MacGregor." He didn't offer to shake hands. His arms were folded, the same way mine were, and probably for the same reason. So he wouldn't hit.

He was about the most controlled guy I'd ever met, and still—he was having as much trouble with that as I was. A helpful thought. I said, "I'm going in the house," and Jax walked past Josh, unlocked the door, glanced back, and said, "If you want to talk to her, wait here. Who knows? Maybe she'll come out again."

When he shut the door behind us, I said, "I really do have to pee," and he said, "Go ahead."

I said, "I don't want to talk to him, and I do. I probably have things to say."

"Fine," Jax said. "I'll take him around back so we can sit.

Come out when you're ready."

"I'm making you violate Kiwi hospitality rules."

"No, you're not," he said. "I'm not doing physical violence. That's close enough."

I didn't have spinach between my teeth, as it turned out. I was sticky and hot, though. I thought about that for about ten seconds, and then I took a fast shower, didn't put on a single bit of makeup, and headed into the bedroom to find something else to wear. Some item of clothing that said, "Fuck you."

I ran into three unfortunate impediments to that plan. First, I didn't have anything printed with that slogan, a sad wardrobe deficiency. Second, my breeziest dress was stuffed into a rubbish bag in a Tauranga landfill, cut in half. And third, the blinds over the bifold doors were up, and when I walked into the bedroom, stark naked, Josh turned his head from where he was sitting on the deck and saw me.

I didn't jump back, or I only did it for a second. After that, I thought, *I've got a body that the hottest man I've ever known can't get enough of, and you don't get to touch it ever again.* And then I went to the closet, took out a stretchy chocolate-brown skirt that I sometimes used as a swim coverup, pulled it up my legs with no hurry at all, and settled it into place. It only came to midthigh, it didn't have the highest waist in the world, and I was just fine with that. After that, I grabbed a blue dress shirt of Jax's, buttoned about three buttons, popped the collar, went over to the door, flicked the lock, shoved it open, and went to sit beside Jax. No underwear, no bra, and plenty of badass.

Jax had seen me in there, too, I was pretty sure, because his intensity level was dialed up to 10. I stretched my legs out in front of me, crossed my bare ankles, and told Josh, "So. You came to talk. Let's hear it."

He didn't say anything for a minute. He was staring at my belly button, because I'd pulled the waistband of my skirt, way, *way* down. I touched the lowest ruby for just a second, then fingered the bow in an absent sort of way and said, "I'm waiting."

"You got new jewelry," he said.

"She got rubies," Jax said. He had his hand on the back of my chair. Not touching me. Just being right there.

Josh cleared his throat and pretty obviously decided not to ask me if they'd been a birthday present from Hope. I thought, *Screw you and your KitchenAid mixer, buddy,* stared at him in what I sincerely hoped was a cool fashion, and said, "You flew a long way to get here. What did you want to say to me?"

"I could say that I wouldn't have thought you'd go for rebound sex," he said, "especially after all the times you told me you didn't want anybody but me. It's been, what, two months? That's some grieving period after eight years. Maybe you thought it was revenge, though. Here's a hint. It just looks tacky."

"Thanks for the tip," I said. "If I cared what you thought, I'm sure it would be useful. What else?"

"I can't talk to you about this with him here," he said, cocking his head at Jax. "Let's go have a drink or something. And seriously? You couldn't find a guy with two legs, at least?"

Before, I'd been sort of . . . angrily triumphant, if that was a thing. Now, I was down to just the "angry" part. I said, "In about two seconds, I'm going to tell you what he's got that you can only dream of. How did you find me? Because I'm going to kill somebody."

He took a breath, and I reminded myself, *You're in the power seat here. And the less you lose your temper, the more powerful you'll be.* I tried to channel Jax. It wasn't easy, but I shut up and stared at Josh until he said, "Jada told me where you were."

"I didn't give her the address." *Not Hope,* I thought. *Please, not Hope.*

"You sent her a link to the house. Do you think we couldn't find it from that? And I don't want you back, not anymore. That's over. This is a business visit."

"Oh, really." I wished I had a drink with a straw in it, so I could sip from it in a cool manner. On the other hand, I wished he'd just leave. The Hope thing had me weak with relief, and something about the tension in Jax's body told me that the second Josh was out of here, I'd discover how Jax wanted to express *his* emotions. I'd much rather hear about that.

"Yes," Josh said. "Really. You're going to be getting an email from M&P tomorrow. It's going to have the official offer in it. They want you back."

My heart hadn't exactly been beating slowly up to this point. Now, though, it started to race so fast, I got a little lightheaded. "What?"

If I'd lost my cool, Josh had found his again. "You're very good at product development. You've been missed."

"So why did you dump me?"

He sighed. Patronizingly. Oh, man, did I ever want to hit him. He said, "I didn't. I told you, it was a corporate decision. You just wouldn't listen. You took it personally."

"Imagine that. So it wasn't you, is what you're saying. It was M&P. They thought—what?"

"That you were too insistent on the One Right Way, too hard to fit into a corporate structure. I fought for you. I just didn't win."

I'd bet he hadn't fought that hard. "Wait," I said. "How would they have figured out how wonderful I was in two months? In comparison with Angel Obrigado, sure. Oh. Wait," I said again. "People have been quitting. Jada said something about that in a text. You didn't get the team you wanted coming on board after all. They didn't move with you. They stayed behind."

"Some did," Josh said. "And since then, there have been a few notices given. Some heavy recruitment. Some jitters."

"Uh-huh. Sunshine Foods. HR's been holding exit interviews, and they've heard my name." Wow, was that good to hear. Something was flooding through me. I thought it was triumph. "Is Angel still there?"

He looked past me. "No."

"Were you sleeping with her?"

His gaze jerked back to my face, then away again. "No."

"Now, see," I said, "I don't believe you. Three months

ago, that would have crushed me. I'd have thought it was me. Now, I don't even care."

"Right," he said. "Because it couldn't possibly have had anything to do with you."

Here came the rage again. I stuffed it down and said, "Yep. Because I care more about what I can do than what I look like. Because I *like* what I look like, and any man who doesn't is a man whose opinion I don't care about. And because all of that makes me better in bed than I'll bet Angel could even imagine. I don't just lie there and figure my job's done by showing up, and aren't you lucky."

Jax made a movement beside me for the first time. I glanced at him and said, "Sorry. If you don't want to hear this, you can go inside. You don't have to . . ."

He said, "Oh, I want to hear it. And you're right. I don't know this Angel, but you're better in bed."

"Get a lot of action, do you?" Josh asked him, and I actually thought, *I hate you.*

Jax didn't say anything, just looked at him like a man with nothing to prove, and I said, "This is stupid. What's the bottom line?"

"The bottom line," Josh said, "is that I'm authorized to offer you six hundred thousand as a signing bonus if you come back. A third of it to be paid upon signing, a third after three months, and final third after six months. Along with a very generous salary and incentive package."

"And I'd work with you again why?" I managed to say it, to sound cool, or at least not blown away. Inside, I was screaming and turning in circles. Not necessarily in a good way. In an I-don't-know-what's-happening-here way.

"Because your leaving wasn't personal," he said. "Because we know how to work together, and because we both know our personal relationship is over. I don't want a woman who walks out on me without discussion."

No, buddy, I thought. *You don't want a woman who doesn't come crawling back no matter what you do to her.* I spread my hand on the table, looked at my nails—for no reason, since they weren't painted—and said, "If M&P wants me back, the price is one-point-two million." And, yes, I was pretending to be Hemi. What did I have to lose?

Josh sighed. "Six hundred is an incredibly generous offer." He pulled his phone out of his pocket, tapped around, and slid it across to me. "Salary. Housing allowance. Bonus potential. Hiring and firing authority. I'm not asking you to decide now. I'm asking you to come back and take a meeting. Question everything. Dig deep. Decide whether you're capable of transitioning to a working relationship with me. I'm less involved with the day-to-day operation now. I'm on the outward-facing side." When I didn't say anything, he added, "It's a hell of an opportunity. It's what you worked for."

"No," I said. "What I worked for was never the money."

"Oh," he said, "I think it was. Partly. The money, and what it represented. Success. Freedom. And the chance to make a difference, to do it right. To do it your way. Well, this is your chance. You'll never have more power than you do right now. You got me all the way out here to ask you. You got to insult me and show me your new boyfriend. You can feel like you won, and now, you can get flown back to New York first class, make your demands, and listen to me having to give up too much to get you back. You've got your chance. All you have to do is take it."

46

⭐

JUST A TAP

JAX

I was a controlled man. That didn't mean it was easy.

There were a few reasons for that. Seeing Karen naked in the bedroom, and knowing that arsehole was seeing her, too. Yes, I knew he'd seen her before. That didn't matter. He was seeing her *now*. Having her come outside not dressed enough, wearing my half-buttoned shirt and nothing under it, and not being sure exactly why she'd done it. The look on his face when she'd touched her rubies, like he didn't even know he was staring. And then there were all the things he'd said. The ones that had made me want to hit him, and the ones that had sent a chill down my back.

On the other hand, *she'd* said some pretty good things in response. You could say that my feelings were mixed.

Now, she was silent, and Ranfeld was starting to talk again, his confidence back. I'd guess it never left him for long. He said, "I'm flying out of Christchurch tomorrow. If you come back with me now, that'd be easiest as far as the hotel and the flight, and then the meeting. I'll wait for you to pack." He glanced at the jewels flashing from her taut belly, the curve of her waist, the length of her slim thighs, and I could read his thoughts like they were written there. He was thinking about that hotel. He didn't care that she was still fragile, and if he knew how much he'd hurt her, that idea was giving him nothing but pleasure. For him, power would always be pleasure. Whatever he said, he wanted her back in his bed, and I knew exactly why.

The rage was burning in my blood, pressing behind my eyes, twisting through my belly and my brain, and I was barely holding myself back. I *was* holding myself back, though.

Karen said, "No." She stood up with a scrape of chair legs, and my heart gave the kind of surge that threw you off balance. That was before she went on to say, "I need to decide."

"You've got three days after tomorrow to meet with the team," Ranfeld said, *not* standing up. "This isn't an open-ended offer. If you don't want it, they'll be going after the next-best option. Jump now, or miss your chance. Come with me, Karen. We're a good team. We can do this together. It matters too much to both of us not to try."

"I've got it," she said. She was almost quivering. She glanced at me, and I read that look as, *I'm about to lose it here. Help me.*

I stood up myself. Ranfeld didn't. "You've delivered your message," I said. "Time to go."

He looked me over, taking in the scars on my face, lingering on my leg. I pulled off my white T-shirt, so I was standing in a pair of rugby shorts and my shoes. "You seem interested," I said, "so here's the full picture. Now get out before I throw you out."

He still didn't stand up. "I don't think so, buddy. I don't scuttle away on command, and I've been practicing Tae Kwon Do for, oh, about ten years now. And, sorry, but you look like the other guy won."

"But you see," I said, "I don't care what you think, or what you practice, and I got tired of you about fifteen minutes ago. Get out."

"Seriously, Josh," Karen said, "you should leave."

He stood up. Slowly. And told me, along the way, "But *you* see—I win."

381

Or, rather, he didn't quite say that. Halfway through, he was taking two careful steps. And on "win," he was starting his kick. With his right leg, the first one he'd used when he'd stood up. The one I'd been expecting. I stepped outside his body as the leg came up, grabbed his ankle with one hand, and struck him hard in the chest with the other one. While he was still snapping back, I got a fistful of his shirt at the shoulder, dumped him onto his side on the ground, and put my knee on his chest.

He was saying something. I wasn't listening. I hauled him to his feet again, grabbed him by the collar and the back of the belt, marched him around the house to his car, shoved him hard against it, and said, "Take out your keys."

He said, "Fuck you." Surprise.

I got hold of his wrist and pulled his arm up behind his back, making him twist to avoid the pain, then reached into his right-hand trouser pocket, found the car key, tossed it to Karen, and hauled him back with enough force that he'd feel it.

"Open the door," I told Karen. "Put the key in the ignition."

She did, then scrambled out again. I shoved Ranfeld into the driver's seat and said, "Go. Or I will fucking kill you." And slammed the door.

He left.

☆☆

KAREN

I was shaking, Jax wasn't even sweating, and Josh's car was disappearing around the curve.

When Jax looked at me, the easygoing mask was gone. I got a blast like a laser from his gray eyes. It nearly knocked me back.

I was expecting something like, "Are you leaving?" Instead, he asked, "Are you OK?" And I just . . . melted.

I nodded. This time, I thought he'd hug me. Instead, he kissed me. Or more like—he grabbed me, and *then* he kissed me. One hand under my butt, pulling me up, the other one around my head, pulling my hair back, and his mouth over mine like he meant it.

I was squeaking, maybe. Saying something. Making some noise, anyway. He took his mouth off mine and asked, "What? No?"

I tried to say something, and couldn't, so I pulled his head down instead. I thought he'd smile. He didn't. He picked me up like that day in the hospital parking lot, except not. He was hefting me under the thighs, all right, but after that?

He tossed me over his shoulder.

I had no words.

I had my palms against his back, bracing myself as he headed fast across the ground, his gait a little jerky, and yanked open the front door. I heard the slam as he kicked it shut behind him, and he had one hand right up under my skirt, on the curve of my butt. If I'd thought he might not have seen me inside, I'd obviously been wrong.

I thought he'd carry me into the bedroom. Instead, he set me on my feet right there. He got one hand on either side of my shirt—his shirt—and when he ripped it open, I heard the buttons hit the floor.

He said, "Take it off. The skirt, too," and when I did it, my hands were shaking. He took off his shoes and socks, then his shorts, his movements jerky and impatient and completely unlike Jax. His chest was rising and falling, and I wanted to say something, but I couldn't think what. *I'm sorry,* maybe, or *Thank you,* but he didn't want to hear either one, because he said, "Turn around and put your hands against the wall."

My safe word was "dolphin." Don't ask me why. Maybe because it was a word I couldn't imagine saying during sex. I looked in his eyes and knew I could say it. I didn't want to say it. He wanted me to do what he said, and so did I.

I turned around and put my hands against the wall.

When he got behind me, took my hands in his, and moved them farther down the wall, I started to shake. When he yanked my legs back, I started to burn. And when he was pinching a nipple with one hand and had the other one between my legs, I started to moan.

He spanked the hell out of me. He made me come three times. He fucked me hard enough that I'd feel it tomorrow. And I shook, called out, moaned his name, and begged him to do it some more.

☆☆

JAX

Maybe not the best way to persuade a woman to stay with you.

By the end of it, we were on the floor, I was sprawled over her, and she was still panting.

I kissed the back of her neck, put a hand over her breast, and asked, "OK?"

She nodded.

"Too rough?"

I felt something in her body. A sort of . . . shaking.

Bloody *hell.* I'd made her cry. Now, the feeling gripping me by the throat was fear. "Karen," I said. "Baby, I'm sorry."

She rolled over, and she was laughing. The relief made me flop over onto my back and put a hand over my heart.

She said, "Hell of a time to ask."

"I should have checked in more," I said. "I got a little . . ." I cleared my throat. "Carried away."

"Mm." She was over me, kissing my mouth, her hand in my hair. "I think I figured that out. Also, if I'm begging you to do it some more, you're probably on safe ground."

"The, uh . . . spanking, though. You weren't begging me then. Just sort of . . . calling out. I should've asked."

"Uh-huh." She took my head in her hands and kissed me again. Slowly, and with plenty of tongue. Whoever this Angel woman was, she wasn't better in bed than Karen. Not possible. When she was done with me, she said, "I'd have told you if I didn't want it. I guess you saw me getting dressed in there."

"Yeh." I had to smile. Too much relief. "I thought I knew why you did it. You didn't want him to win, to make you feel ashamed. You could've put on some undies, though. Possibly not played with your rubies right there in front of him."

"Maybe I wanted him to know that *you* won," she said. "Which I think you just did, all the way around. I'm guessing he left with a pretty good idea of what was about to happen here. Or maybe not, because he's not that discerning. He probably thinks you're a nice guy, and nice guys don't do things like that."

"Well," I said, "there's the fact that I threatened to kill him, of course."

"That's right," she said, sounding absolutely delighted. "I sort of forgot that. That was my favorite part."

Now, I laughed, and smoothed my hand over her bare bum. She wriggled some and said, "Mm. Tingles."

"Seriously, though," I asked, petting her some more there, "too hard?"

"No. Just right." She rubbed her cheek against mine and said, "I'm going to need to massage your leg. All that running, and then fighting."

"That wasn't fighting. That was a tap. But if you want to massage my leg, I won't say no."

"It's hurting you."

"A bit. We'll take a shower first, though. You're clean, and I'm not." I hesitated a minute, then asked, "Are you going?" It was hanging out there, and I needed to pull it down so we could both look at it. So I could know.

"Yes," she said. "I am. I think I have to."

47

NINE THOUSAND MILES

KAREN

Jax didn't argue. That made it harder. If he'd argued, maybe I could have felt like he was a jerk, somehow. Controlling. Pushing too hard, too fast, like those cautionary tales you read about. As it was, I couldn't feel any of that. What he was— was a man who loved me. A man I was hurting.

We talked it over, and he listened while I explained. That I at least had to listen to what M&P had to say, what they were offering. It had been my dream for so many years. I had to find out how closely I'd have to work with Josh, for one thing.

"I could even tell them that they can choose between us," I said. "That if they want me, they have to cut him loose. Nothing to lose, right?" Not that it would happen, not when they'd paid him tens of millions for the company.

"Nothing to lose but a million dollars," Jax said.

"It's not the million dollars," I said. "It's the dream."

We were on the deck again. I was wrapped in a blanket, with my feet up on the seat of the chair, my arms around myself. Jax was sitting back in his own chair, looking at the sea, his crutches leaning against the wall of the house.

He hadn't put his leg back on after his shower, because the stump was too sore. He'd pushed it too hard, had run too far, trying to show me a good time up in Christchurch. I'd massaged it, and then had driven the couple of miles to the Four Square in Hampden and stocked up for him. After that, I cooked dinner for us, almost my first time doing it since I'd come to New Zealand. Almost my first time since that last day at Prairie Plus, come to think of it. That was irony. I was finally getting my mojo back, right when I was leaving.

His kitchen wasn't huge, but it was perfectly outfitted. I made a venison, kumara, and mushroom pie, the filling cooked slowly on the stovetop along with a bottle of Guinness to make the taste richer, rolled out my homemade flaky pastry with a wine bottle on the enormous wooden island, then chilled it and rolled it again, twice over, obsessed, somehow, with wanting to do it right, with making him something delicious this one time.

He didn't stick around to sit on a stool on the other side of the island and keep me company, but went into the other part of the house instead, the work area separated from the great room with sliding barn doors. Which he closed. Reading up on some technical stuff, he said. Reminding himself that he had a future to prepare for apart from me, I thought.

We ate my pie along with a salad out on the deck while the afternoon light faded and the last of the tourists left, with the murmur and roar of the surf as our backdrop. Now, I said, "I never even got to swim in the ocean down here. We don't get to do our bike trip."

He said, "The sea's cold. You won't be swimming here without a good wetsuit." Remotely, like it didn't matter.

I started to say something, then stopped, and he looked at me and asked, "What?"

"I want to talk about this," I said slowly. "But I'm not sure it's OK. If it's just hurting you."

"It's going to hurt me anyway," he said. "Just like it's hurting you. We may as well talk about it."

I raised my head from my knees and said, "I wish I knew. I wish I *knew* what to do, and I just don't, you know? I keep thinking it'll get clear, and it doesn't."

"Never mind," he said. "Sooner or later, you'll know."

He didn't promise anything. He didn't say, *When you do, I'll be here.* That was another thing we didn't know. Another terrible thing. I said, "I'm not going back to him. That's not happening."

"Good," he said, and that was all.

"Can I ask you, something, though?" I asked. "Was he gaslighting me?"

"I never know what that is."

"It's making you believe things that aren't true. Manipulation. Reframing the story so you can't tell whether to trust what you're seeing and hearing, what your mind's telling you, or what *he's* telling you." I shook my head like that would shake the thoughts into place. It didn't work, of course.

"Ah," he said. "Then—yes. That's exactly what he was doing. Saying he hadn't really betrayed you, when it's so obvious he did, in every way. Saying it was your fault, somehow, that he slept with whoever it was."

"Angel Obrigado. She's very beautiful."

"Doesn't matter. You don't get a pass because the person's hot. That's why they call it loyalty."

"Wow," I said.

He didn't answer, but after a minute, he said, "It's not about how they look anyway. It's about being in love."

The tears were rising, the emotion choking me, and I forced it all back. I couldn't make him comfort me for leaving him. That would be unfair, and it would be cruel.

We went to sleep beside each other, not touching, and I wore my pajamas and didn't cry. But when I woke up in the night to find my foot against his shin and his arm across my breasts, like it had happened in his sleep . . . it felt so right, and it hurt so much.

The next day, he drove me to the airport in Dunedin, so I wouldn't have to see Josh. He took me to the terminal, but he didn't come in, just got out of the car at the curb, lifted my two duffels out of the back of the squeaky-clean Audi, and set them onto the luggage trolley I pulled over from the sidewalk.

"Got your passport?" he asked.

"Yes."

He nodded, and I said, "I love you."

He looked at me. Blue scars. Black nerd glasses. Beautiful face, as remote as the moon.

He said, "I know."

I cried all the way to Auckland, looking out the window so nobody would see. I boarded an Air New Zealand flight to Chicago, flying Business Select this time on somebody else's dime, drank three glasses of wine without feeling them, and slept all the way across the Pacific. I drank orange juice and made notes all the way to New York, because I'd chosen to do this, so I had to do it right.

I missed him for nine thousand miles.

48

☆☆

NOT A RACE

KAREN

My plane arrived at La Guardia in the middle of the day, and when I walked out onto the curb from International Arrivals into the February chill, Hemi's driver, Charles, pulled up in Hemi's latest iteration of black Mercedes. Exactly like always, except that the cars were bigger now, because kids. This one was a three-row SUV.

Yes, I could have done something else. I could have had M&P pay for a car. I could have had them pay for a hotel, too. But I hadn't been able to stand it.

Charles got out of the car, wearing the same dark slacks and polo shirt as always. He put my duffels in the back and asked, "Home?"

I said, "Yes, please," and got into the front seat beside him.

He didn't talk to me, because Charles never talked. Usually, I filled the conversational gaps, but today, I didn't have the heart. I got out my laptop instead and looked over my notes, and then I put it away.

New York was busy, and it was noisy. No surprise. Beautiful, in its own way, even on a chilly February day with the snow still lying in patches of gray slush. Especially when

I was stepping out of the elevator and straight into the apartment's foyer, then into the living room, and looking out over Central Park, the Hudson, and the Manhattan skyline. I was carrying one of my duffels, and Charles was carrying the other, not at all happy about not carrying both. Exactly like Jax.

My heart felt like it had been ripped straight in two. It *hurt.* I thought, *It'll get better,* and then Inez, Hemi's housekeeper, came out and hugged me, her arms wiry and strong despite the fact that she only came to my shoulder. I might have dropped my duffel. I also might have teared up.

She got her hands on my shoulders, looked me over, and said, "Too skinny."

I tried to smile. "Missed your cooking, that's all."

She sniffed. "And who taught you everything? If you are not feeding yourself, that is not my problem." And then absolutely contradicted herself by saying, "Charles will put your bags into Maia's room. Come. I have made you pepián."

"I ate on the plane," I said. "About four times."

"Don't be silly," she said. "Come and eat."

She was right, of course. I could somehow manage to choke down a bowl of chicken stew made with tomatillos, peppers, cilantro, lime, and the magical mix of spices that Inez shared with nobody. Nobody but me, that is.

"Why is yours always better, when I follow your recipe exactly?" I asked her, finishing my last bite of pupusas stuffed with red beans and queso Oaxaca and wishing my stomach had room for more.

"Because it is made with love," she said, and I laid my head down on my arm, right there at the kitchen table, and thought, *I can't.*

She asked, "When is this meeting?"

I sat up. "Tomorrow morning at ten. I need to . . . get ready. Go get clothes from my apartment. Can Charles take me?" I was shaking in that way you do when you've been traveling too long, like your body hasn't gotten used to being stationary yet.

"No," she said, and I thought, *Oh. Right. It isn't my house.*

I've never even lived here. And Charles doesn't work for me. She went on, "Hope went to your apartment last night and got clothes for you, of course. Charles says this place you have is terrible. Terrible."

That was a surprise. Charles and Inez waged an ongoing silent war for control, one that Inez always won. Charles didn't normally share anyway, and he shared least of all with Inez.

"Oh," I said. "That's good, then. How are your kids?"

"You do not need to think about that now," she said. "You need a shower, then a swim, and bed."

"Why would you baby me?" I asked. "You shouldn't. So I'm tired. I've still got everything. I'm sitting here." I gestured at the window, which in this case, looked out over the Hudson. "This meeting is about having even more. About getting everything I've ever dreamed of."

Another sniff. "Then you have not dreamed enough. I am making you a mocha. Decaf. You need to sleep."

I would have said that I'd make it myself, but I knew better. I got up instead, leaned against the kitchen island, and watched her absolutely sure motions as she did everything exactly right to make me the best mocha in the world. No chocolate fish, but I didn't even like the chocolate fish. I asked, "Doesn't it ever bother you, that you still work here, and that Hemi and Hope have so much? Don't you ever . . . compare?"

"For a smart person, you can be very stupid." She was frothing milk, paying attention. "Why do you think I still work here?"

"Because you need a job?" Inez had one of those faces where you couldn't read her age. She still looked the same to me as when I'd first met her, fourteen years ago. She'd had grandkids then. How old was she? Sixty? Sixty-five? She'd worked for Hemi forever even then.

She said, "You are wrong. Hemi bought me an apartment long ago. Ten years, at least, when he also began to pay for the other cleaners, although they do not do it well unless I show them what they have missed. He said that I had worried long enough, and it was time not to worry. I also have a pension. That is not why I work." She got a spoon, poured the foamed milk over the coffee into my favorite pistachio-colored mug, drew a fern onto the top with foam, and sprinkled the whole thing with cocoa. "A fern because you will be missing New Zealand."

I was still reeling from the "apartment" thing. "He did?"

"Yes. Because he is a good man. Stupid, sometimes, like you, but good. I am not jealous, no. Everybody has their own life. Mine is good for me. Life is not a race, with only one winner." She handed over my mug. "Take this to the shower with you. I have put your swimsuit and towel on your bed. Now go. I have many things to do."

☆☆

The next morning, I did call for a car. That was because the M&P campus was across the river, in Newark, or maybe it was because I needed to do this myself. I wasn't sixteen anymore, and I wasn't twenty-six, either. I was a grown woman, and a professional. I had ideas, and I had the ability to execute them. Time to believe it.

The kids had all hugged me this morning, and Maia had given me a homemade card made of construction paper and decorated with glitter, which she'd made in Aroha's room with lots of whispering.

The front of it had a picture of two stick figures with dresses. The little one had curly hair and the big one didn't, but they both had huge smiles and hands made out of a circle and five long lines sticking out for fingers.

"We're holding hands," Maia said, wriggling her way onto my lap at the breakfast table. "Except I don't know how to draw holding hands, so you have to imagine."

I kissed the top of her curly head. "I love the holding hands."

"Look inside," she said, and when I didn't open the card quickly enough, she did it for me.

Good Luck Auntie Karen, it said in huge letters. The "L" was backwards, so was the "K," and a shower of silver glitter fell into my lap from where she'd drawn hearts with glue and then sprinkled her shaker with abandon.

"Daddy has lots of meetings," she told me. "But he says meetings can be scary sometimes anyway, so we should say, 'Good luck.' I wrote it for you. Maybe you can take it in your purse, and if your meeting is very scary, you can look in your purse."

Oh, boy. In another minute, I was going to wreck my makeup. Hope said, "OK, everybody. Time to go to school, and let Auntie Karen get her mind ready for her meeting, too. It's lucky that she's very, very smart, so she doesn't have to worry."

"Plus she's good at talking," Aroha said. "All meetings are is talking. That's why Dad's good at them, because he's so scary when he talks."

Now, I stood in a ladies' room of almost aggressive cleanliness, checked out the red turtleneck dress I'd been supposed to wear at the last meeting with these same people, told myself, *Think scary thoughts,* and headed on out and down the corridor. I had a plan, and Aroha was right. I was good at talking. Time to prove it.

The windows in this conference room didn't open, the air was much more climate-controlled than in our converted warehouse in Philadelphia, and the furniture was better. Otherwise, though, it was the same. Deborah Delaney and David Glass sat on one side of the table, and Josh was beside me.

Deborah shook my hand and said, "It's good to see you again, Karen," like she meant it. Well, I guess I *had* been entertaining. I'd bet she hadn't had many meetings end in exactly the way that one had.

Josh had a new fountain pen. It was black with silver ribs,

and probably much more expensive than the first one. Probably the Rolls-Royce of fountain pens, the one he'd always coveted. I would've bet a hundred dollars that the nib was eighteen-carat gold, and that those stripes were something like platinum.

I wanted to throw it out of the window so badly.

Deborah said, "Well. Let's get started, shall we?"

I said, "Fine. I'd like to do that without Josh, please."

Everybody froze. Deborah looked at David, then uttered a completely unconvincing laugh and said, "I think we all know that isn't possible. Josh is the CEO of Prairie Plus. The only way we can move forward is if the two of you can work together. If you can't do that, I'm afraid we've all wasted each other's time."

I opened my spiral notebook. The cover was an abstract design in pink and blue watercolor, with white printing that said, "Think Positive. Be Positive." It had cost $9.99. I was moving up in the world myself, it seemed.

"But you see," I told them, "I have another idea."

49

☆☆

VALENTINE'S DAY

JAX

Karen had been gone more than two weeks.

She'd texted every day, but she hadn't told me as much as I'd expected, or nearly as much as I wanted. She was having meetings, she told me, and that was about it. I tried to hope that she was getting what she needed, achieving the dream and the life she'd longed for. I couldn't quite do it. I couldn't shake the idea that the life she needed was with me.

She sent photos. Of herself with the kids, mostly. Standing at the edge of a pool, wearing her gray-camo bikini like the first time I'd seen her, with her arms around her youngest niece. Decorating heart-shaped cookies, messy creations of icing and candy hearts, with all three of the kids, because it was nearly Valentine's Day. She was wearing an apron in that one, black polka dots outlined in a red heart shape over her breasts, with red straps and a red ruffle on the full skirt, tied with a big red bow around the waist. That was for Valentine's Day, too, I guessed, or maybe just for driving a man crazy. She looked happy, and she looked adorable. Another snap of her alone, lying on the ground beside a sled, covered with snow from her beanie to her boots, with a text that said, *It snowed! And I guess sledding's not like riding a bike, because I seem to have forgotten how.*

All of it could have been posted on her Facebook page, if she'd had one. None of it said, *I'm missing you too much, and I can't stand it. I'm coming back, because you're what home means to me.*

I wasn't used to being helpless. I wasn't enjoying it.

Clearly, I should have tried harder. I should have bought the ring and said the words, and never mind scaring her off.

After four days of working out in the Oamaru gym until my entire body was shaking, of fast, hard swims in the pool followed by running the loop of the South Hill and Skyline walkways until my stump was reddened and burning, I went up to Mount Maunganui again for almost a week, where I ran the hard track to the top of the mountain, swam in the sea, sat in the hot pools, and thought about a plan. After that, I flew home again and went where I wouldn't be looking at my phone, on the cycle trip Karen and I had planned. The Alps 2 Ocean, done my way. Four days of hard grind, seventy-five off-road kilometers every day under the great granite peaks of the Southern Alps, traveling light and camping without a tent.

The track started off in the shadow of the towering mountains, still snow-capped even in February, the alpine grasses on the high plain gold with late-summer color. I rode beside Lake Pukaki, saw the jagged, icy peaks and ridges reflected on the turquoise surface, then took off the leg and jumped in, just for the jolt to my heart from the ice-cold water, and the way it numbed the pain. I swam hard, then climbed out, pulled my clothes on again, and shivered until the sun warmed me. I slept on the ground under the stars on a night without moonlight, and was awakened by a glow in the sky. Pink and gold, green and purple, shimmering and pulsing. The Aurora Australis, putting on a show just for me.

I rode through the gentle green hills above Kurow, across vineyards and paddocks, stopped at the River-T cellar door, risked cycling disaster by tasting their offerings, and headed off again with a bottle of Pinot Noir and another of Chardonnay in my saddlebags. I rode across the bridge, looked down at the winding braids of the Waitaki River making its way to the Pacific, and reminded myself that I'd lived alone for all my adult life, and during the last few of them, I'd learned how to live better. I stopped, on my last day, at the weird and wonderful limestone formations of the Elephant Rocks, tried my hand—and my feet—at bouldering, and quickly found that I had more work to do. I could drive up from Oamaru, though, another time, and do it again with the right shoes. Good for the flexibility and the strength, and I still had a month or more to go before I was back at work. If I were stationed in Christchurch, I'd have heaps of chances to try rock climbing.

It was time to try all sorts of things. Time to put my life and my faith to the test. You could roll over and give up, or you could keep trying.

By the time I turned off the highway onto my road in the late evening with my bike on the back of the car, I was sore, I was dirty, I was tired, and I was cold. The weather was changing, the wind freshening, a late-summer storm blowing up from Antarctica. Nice of it to have held off during my ride, and I'd enjoy watching the show tomorrow as the wind lashed the waves into a frenzy. No two days were ever exactly alike when you lived by the sea.

There was a car in the driveway again. Another rental sedan.

The last time hadn't worked out too well, but never mind. This time, it was bound to be a mate.

She came around the corner of the house, her arms wrapped around herself again like that first day, when she'd stood at the window of the condo and looked out at Mauao, and I'd thought she looked wistful. This time, maybe she was just trying to stay warm.

I forgot about being tired and cold. I was out of the car the moment it stopped, and I had her in my arms.

I didn't care why she'd come, or what she meant to say. I was going to say what *I* had to say, and bugger the consequences. This was my chance. Where did you get in life if you didn't seize your chance when you got it?

She was laughing, and I thought she was close to crying.

Wearing jeans and a gray sweater that slipped off one shoulder, showing twin purple ribbons of bra straps. Not a sports bra this time, but a pretty one instead. She looked bloody fantastic. She looked beautiful.

I said, "You came," and then I took her head in my hands and kissed her. She wrapped her arms around me and kissed me back, and it felt like coming home. Because it was.

A gust of wind hit us, and the first drops of rain spattered the ground. I said, "Come inside," and she said, "You're dusty. Why are you dusty?"

"Did that cycle trip," I said, opening the front door.

"Oh," she said, and then the door closed behind us, and she had her hands on my face, was pulling it down again, kissing me some more while she pushed me back against the door. Kissing me like she'd missed me too much, and like she needed me now. "I don't care if you're dusty," she said. "I want to take off your leg."

She'd only managed to say half of that before I had her in my arms and was carrying her into the bathroom. *I* cared if I was dusty. I needed to give her my best.

She took off my leg, and then we got into the shower and she washed it, and all the rest of me, too, while I leaned against the wall and did the same for her. Kissing and touching with lazy, soapy hands, wanting to hurry, because I was so hungry for her, and wanting to slow it down, too, so it would never end. Wishing with everything in me that I could pick her up right here, because I needed it now, and knowing I had to wait. Hopping out, finally, when I couldn't wait any longer, with her arm around my waist to help me into the bedroom, and not caring that she was helping, because it would get us there faster.

She said, "Towels," and went back for them, and then she pushed me onto my back on the bed and dried me off with the kind of slow strokes that were too much to take right now. By the time she got to my abs, I was done. I took the towel from her hand and tossed it, got my own hands on her hips, and lowered her onto me, and my eyes just about rolled back in my head.

When you want to close your eyes, because it feels too good, but you have to keep them open, because you have to watch. When my hands were on her breasts, and her head was back, her own hand going down to touch herself, like she didn't want me to have to work at all for this. Like she wanted to give me everything.

The rain was drumming on the roof by the time I was holding her hips tight and shoving her down hard, and she cried out and started to convulse around me.

"Say my name," I said, and shoved her down again. "Say it."

"Jax," she said. *"Jax.* I love you. I love you."

That was it. I was gone.

☆

KAREN

This hadn't gone anything like I'd planned.

We were lying under the covers now, my back to his front, his arm and leg over me, while the rain came down hard all around us, the same way it had felt inside my body when he'd held me so tight.

He said, "I could've left marks. I'm sorry. I got carried away." He was thinking about the same thing, then.

"You could've," I said, picking up the hand that was on my breast and kissing it. "But I'll forgive you this time. I have something to say, though. Something I came all the way here to say, in fact."

His body went still behind me, and then he said, "Go on and say it."

"I'm nervous," I said.

"There is nothing you can say," he said, "that will make me stop loving you."

I tried not to cry. I didn't manage it. I'd been so sure, flying here. But it mattered so much.

"Why don't you have a . . . box of Kleenex?" I asked him

when I'd gone for a roll of toilet paper and was sitting up in bed beside him, blowing my nose, with his arm around me, while the rain beat against the metal roof and rolled down the glass doors, and the sea breathed outside.

"Because I'm single," he said, "and I'm a soldier. Tell me."

I said, "I am now a consultant. What do you think?" And waited, holding my breath, for him to answer.

"Uh . . ." he said. "Explain."

"Oh. OK." I took a breath and launched into it. The plan I'd come up with while I'd been swimming, that first day, in the pool in Hemi and Hope's building, when I'd been half out of my mind with fatigue and sadness and confusion, and with my stomach full of Inez's pepián and pupusas. "I'd had all these amazing flavors," I told him, "and the food was so filling and so comforting, exactly what I needed. And I thought—pie."

"Uh—pie?"

"What's my favorite thing to eat, every time I come to New Zealand? What always makes me think, 'Why can't I get this? Why don't we have this?' What is so delicious, you can't stand it, and can take any kind of meat, or not meat, any kind of filling?"

"Ah," he said. "Pie."

"Russian salmon pie," I said, "with cabbage and onion and potato. Savory roasted pumpkin and leek pie. Curried chicken pie. Beef and vegetable pie with chili sauce. Bison and mushroom pie. But with good crust, the fish is wild, and the meat comes from grass-fed animals. It's all about sourcing and production and not cutting any corners. I know how to do all of that, and that's just my *first* idea. There's such an untapped market out there, because frozen pizza is still terrible, but that's the kind of thing people want. Food their kids will eat, food that satisfies them. You can freeze savory pies, and they'll bake up so delicious, and if you've got enough vegetables in there, you've got your meal. I'm sure. This is *it*. And ideas like this are what I do. They're what I'm good at. Forecasting tastes, seeing the trend before it happens."

"OK," he said slowly. "So . . ."

"So I said that I didn't want to do Prairie Plus anymore, or to be an employee. That was off the table. I want to consult, to develop products. I told them that the pie idea wasn't covered by my noncompete—and no worries, I didn't explain it in enough detail that they'd have been able to do anything with it—so if they didn't want me, that was fine, and I'd go to Sunshine Foods instead."

"And what did the wanker say?" Jax asked. "Sorry, but I need to know."

"I made them kick him out before I told them anything. He's not going to run Prairie Plus well without me. Food products are about *food,* not the money part, or the marketing. All the marketing in the world won't sell something people don't want to eat. He's going to flounder. They're going to need my ideas, eventually, and I'm going to sell them to them. Maybe even to Josh, but not until I don't care what he thinks or what kind of pen he has."

"Uh . . . pen?"

"Oh. I didn't tell you about that. He has this extremely fancy fountain pen. He had one before, but I threw it into the street, and a UPS truck ran over it. One of the better moments of my life, besides the one where you beat him up. What kind of pen do you use?"

"Is this a test?" he asked. "I use whatever's handy."

"You pass." I wanted to get up and pace, but I needed to stay here, because his body was so warm, and his arm felt so good. "So I'll be doing some traveling, sourcing ingredients, figuring out production, but that's all right, because you'll be doing some traveling, too, and that'll just make it more exciting when we're together again, right? And I told them I'd be based here."

After that, I held my breath.

"Ah," he said, and he was starting to smile. "You told them that."

It was going to be all right. It was going to be all *right.* "Yeah. I did. Non-negotiable. I'd left without seeing Koro, and I'd left without you, and neither of those things works. Anyway, Christchurch is closer to Chile than New York is, I'll tell you that."

"Chile?"

I waved a hand. "Chile for produce. Maybe Australia, too. In winter, when we can't use the organic stuff from the States. Also Argentina, for beef. And Americans don't eat lamb at all, or almost never. I could do a spiced ground lamb pie that would be amazing. Cardamom, ginger, cumin. There you go. New Zealand." I laughed, because I couldn't help it. As usual during a fraught moment with Jax, I needed to pee, but I needed to say this first. "I couldn't believe it. It just bloomed right there out of my head like magic. It just . . . *came,* when I didn't think any ideas ever could. And since then, I'm doing it again. I'm waking up and having to write things down. I'm making cookies with the kids and thinking about pie crust, and how we have to use butter. It's back. I'm *back.*"

He said, "That's awesome. Seriously. Awesome. I'm proud of you."

He was, too, I could tell. Not because of what he could get from me, because he didn't care about that. Not because of how much money I'd make doing it, because he hadn't even asked. But it was going to be a lot. I'd asked for Hemi's help this time, and had negotiated an hourly rate that was about twice what I'd thought I could charge.

Jax went on to say, "I'm not sure why you didn't tell me, though. These past couple weeks have been . . . hard."

Saying that had been hard, too, I could tell. I put my hand on his face and kissed his mouth, loving him so much, it hurt. "I'm sorry. Maybe I didn't quite believe that you felt this as much as I did. I also didn't want to tell you until I was sure it would work out, and it's taken a while. And then I didn't want to call you. I had to see your face. I had to see what you really thought. Also, I think you should marry me, and ask me to have your babies, because I've got good genes—well, other than my dad—and I'll be a good mom, and you'll be such a good father. We should do it. We should try. It'll be an adventure, and we both want to have adventures, right? Maybe not right away, because I'm getting this thing off the ground. But in a year or two, I think we should."

"Karen." He was smiling. "Baby. Give me a chance."

I rested my head against his shoulder. "Sorry. It's a twenty-four-hour trip. I had a lot of time to think."

"Right, then," he said. "My turn."

"OK," I said, "but first—I really have to pee."

JAX

I had so much emotion going on here, I was either going to laugh or cry. In fact, I was already laughing. I was also grabbing my crutches, heading for my desk in the workroom, and opening a drawer. When she came back, I was ready.

I said, "I have a few things to say, too. First, though, I have to kiss you some more. You can't really blame me. I've been waiting two weeks to do it."

When we'd done some more of that, she'd settled down a bit. At any rate, she had her head on my shoulder and her hand in mine when she said, "I know this isn't the way it normally happens, but I was just so *sure*. I've been so unsure, and now, I'm sure."

"Nothing about you is the way it normally happens," I said, "because what *I* know for sure is that you are absolutely and totally unique. That's why I'm grabbing hold of you and hanging on. It's why I tried to do it the first day I met you, when I asked you to come back home with me after the beach. And you didn't come, by the way."

I knew what she meant. The pieces of me that had been rattling around loose since she'd left had settled into place with a *click-click-click,* and the jigsaw puzzle was complete. Rocks, sea, sky, everything. What had been a tableful of miscellaneous parts was a picture now, and it was beautiful.

"I messed up, though," she said, "that first time. I almost drowned Artie."

I had to laugh. "You did, and so did I. I saw all of them, by the way, a week ago. They were on the beach again, and none the worse for wear. I shouted them lunch at the Coffee

Club. I reckoned it was the least I could do."

"You did?" She brightened even more. You didn't need a sunny day if you had Karen. "That's great. Why were you up there?"

"Ah." I rolled over and grabbed the bag I'd put on the other side of the bed. "You see—I did some thinking, too. Got an idea, and took a leap." I pulled the box out of the bag, and for once, she was speechless.

When I opened it, she put her hands to her mouth, looked at what was inside, and stared at me again.

"It's a ruby, baby," I told her, the tenderness rising in me, swamping me like a wave. "And diamonds." I'd had the fella make it. Three diamonds on either side, the sideways-V shape of them flanking the one and a half carats of cushion-cut ruby solitaire of pure, deep red, all of it set in rose gold. It wasn't like anything her sister would have, or anything anybody else would have, either. It was going to be hers alone. I said, "Rubies are for passion, power, courage, and life force. In other words—you. Call it my talisman, maybe. A stone that could bring you back to me."

"Were you going to . . . come?"

"Yeh. I was going to come. I was going to tell you that I didn't want to do this without you, and if you didn't want to do it without me, we should find a way. But you came to me instead."

"It could be the talisman," she said. "And—Jax. It's so beautiful. I don't even know what to say."

I'd done it right, and surely, a heart couldn't hold all of this. "And by the way?" I said. "It's a day later here. Happy Valentine's Day, sweetheart."

"Is it . . ." she said. "Is it . . ."

She needed the words, and I needed to say them. I'd had time to think myself. Hours on a bike, with the Southern Alps at my back and the wind in my face. "I love you, baby," I said. "I want to marry you. I want to stand at the altar and watch your grandfather walk you down the aisle, and know you're coming to me. It's what he said. I can't think of a day when I won't want to see your face, and I can't think of a future that doesn't have you in it. I want you, and, yeh, I want the babies, too. I told you that before, remember?"

"No," she said. "You said you wanted to take out my IUD. If it hadn't been you, it would've been creepy. I'm sorry, but . . . how much money do you *have,* anyway? This . . . this *ring. Jax.* Is it . . . wasn't it too much?"

I was laughing again, and so was she. "We'll let somebody else take the IUD out," I promised. "As long as it happens eventually. And I have about five million dollars at the moment. I told you—I invested. It could be hard work to stay ahead of you, though."

I got serious, then, because these were the words that mattered. The ones I needed to say, and, I hoped, the ones she needed to hear. "I love you, and I can't wait to set the date. Will you marry me?"

"Yes," she said. *"Yes.* I love you, too. I want to marry you so *much."*

She was still crying some, and I didn't have anything but toilet paper to mop it up. Well, that and the towel from before, which was what I used. After I'd slipped my ruby onto her left hand, her heart hand, where it shone like loyalty and courage. Like our hearts' blood. Like forever.

Like a talisman.

50

⭐

TRANSCENDENT

KAREN

On the morning of my wedding, I woke early, then slipped out of bed quietly so as not to wake the girls, pulled on a sports bra and a pair of shorts, closed the bedroom door behind me, and crept down the stairs in the gray light of a winter dawn.

Hemi was there before me, standing in shorts and a T-shirt, looking out at the beach. "Hey," I said quietly. "Could you not sleep either?"

"Not so much. Want to go for a run with me?"

"Yeah. Please."

"Nervous?" he asked.

"Oh, only about a thousand percent," I said, and he smiled and opened the doors to the patio.

We took off barefoot down the beach to where the going was firm, our feet barely sinking into the packed sand at the water's edge. Down toward the village, where, I was sure, Hemi would buy me a coffee and ask if I wanted a treat, like I was fifteen again. Like I was his little sister.

He said, when we were running in sync, because he'd adjusted his stride to mine, "He seems like the right choice to me, but if you're not sure for some reason, you know I'll get you out of it."

"I'm sure," I said. "I'm so sure. He's such a good man."

"Then what is it?"

"Oh . . ." I sighed. "You know. I'm so excited, and I think, what if I . . . I don't know. Throw up. Pee my pants."

He laughed out loud. "Nah. Not happening. You're going to have your whole whanau behind you, remember? Nobody will be there who doesn't love you. You're also going to be beautiful, and you're going to know it."

This was true, because I had the most gorgeous dress in the world. Made of silk satin crepe in a delicate blush like the creamy inside of a conch shell, its low spaghetti-strapped bodice softened by an attached cowl, and the luxurious weight of the skirt draping over my lower body like the dress had been designed specially to flatter a woman who'd always felt too tall and too thin. Which it had been, because Hemi had created it just for me.

The gray light was morphing into a glow of soft pink. Another wonderful sunrise on the Bay of Plenty, the waves high today from last week's storm, and nobody on the beach but us and a lone dog-walker, far off in the distance. It was going to be a beautiful day, the air clear as crystal, the temperature rising above sixty, everything in the world smiling on Jax and me.

I asked Hemi, "Do you ever wonder how your life turned out so good?"

"All the time," he said. "But I don't wonder how yours did."

"Because my sister fortunately met you? Don't rub it in, buddy."

He smiled. "Nah. Because you're more honest than anyone I've ever known, you're a harder worker than anybody I've ever hired, and you have a mind that looks for the truth and won't let you compromise. Because you've got loyalty and courage and mana. I couldn't be prouder of you. So you know."

"Oh, thanks," I said crossly. "Way to make me cry. I don't even have a Kleenex."

He reached in his pocket and handed one over. "Do it now. Before makeup, eh."

By the time we finished our run an hour later, I was sweating, but I was calm. Or—not *calm,* exactly, because I was never going to be calm today, but excited in a good way instead of an I-might-pee-my-pants way. And when we got back to the house, Hope and the kids were up.

"Hey, sweetie," Hope said, coming over to hug me as much as her enormous seven-months fourth-pregnancy belly would allow. "Happy wedding day. Jax brought you something."

"You're kidding," I said. "Shoot. I missed him?"

"You aren't supposed to see him," Aroha informed me. "It's bad luck."

"There's no such thing as bad luck," Tama said. "Just bad planning and chance, and the better you plan, the less you leave to chance."

"Quote unquote from Dad," Aroha said.

"Because Dad's smart," Tama said.

"Because Dad's right," Hope said. "That's the tradition, though. I think it's just to make it more exciting for both people, and more special. Think about it. That's the only day in your life you get special names for yourself. You're the bride and groom, and on that day, you become something bigger than the two of you. You become a family. That's what Karen and Jax are going to do."

"How about when you have kids?" Aroha asked. "That's making something bigger."

"You're right," Hope said. "That's a very good day, too." She kissed her daughter's head, and Aroha, for once, forgot that she was nearly a teenager, leaned into her, and hugged.

"This is all very lovely," I said, "but I think we're forgetting the most important thing here. What did Jax bring me? It had better be a donut. Was he upset that I wasn't here?"

Maybe *he* was nervous. I thought about being nervous myself about that, and then thought—nope. If a man was ever in it for the long haul, it was Jax. It was what I'd told him. He was my resting place. My island, and my home.

I was definitely going to cry again.

I wondered if I should spare some time to think about Josh, and the bullet I'd dodged there. His future wasn't looking too sweet at Prairie Plus, from what I heard. I'd been right—food products were all about the food. He'd land on his feet, though, because he was that kind of guy, and I didn't care. Before, I'd thought winning meant knowing you'd triumphed, that you were in the top spot. Now, I realized that winning meant knowing you didn't care anymore, because you'd moved on.

Plus, there was my present from Jax. Hope was holding a white bag with gold writing, and it didn't look like it had a donut in it. It was the same kind my belly rings had come in. The same kind my engagement ring had come in, and that, I was sure, my wedding ring had come in, too. I hadn't seen that yet, but I knew it would be special. I suspected more diamonds. Jax might wear T-shirts almost every time he wasn't wearing fatigues, but he sure did like giving me pretty things.

Maia was jumping up and down. "What's your present?" she asked. "You're not s'posed to get your present yet, because it's not the wedding yet."

"The bridegroom's gift to the bride is different," Hemi said. "That's what he gives her to tell her how glad he is that he gets to marry her." He glanced at me, a glint of humor in his dark eyes. "So she isn't nervous. Which means Auntie Karen needs to open it."

My heart was beating like a drum, even though there was nothing Jax could give me that I wouldn't want. There was gold tissue paper in the bag, which was no surprise, and a blue velvet box inside that, also no surprise.

I pulled out the box, opened it, and found out. A chunky, organic swirl of rose gold with a diamond embedded in the front of it and three more along its roughly beveled edge, as if the whole thing had been mined that way by magic dwarves. The pendant I'd seen all those months ago, that Jax had remembered. The one that would look incredible with my barely pink wedding gown, like it was meant to be.

"That's gorgeous," Hope said. "It looks exactly like you. Oh, I do like Jax so much."

There was a slip of white paper under it, and I unfolded it. In Jax's angular handwriting, it said, *Look in the bottom of the box.*

I had to sit down, and I had to breathe a little. Hope asked, "What?"

I lifted the velvet topper. Underneath was a key, the Yale kind, and another note. A URL, that was all.

I put my head on the table and said, "Oh, my gosh. I can't."

Hemi could. Of course he could. He had his phone out and was typing the address in. A smile spread over his face, and he handed the phone to Hope.

"Oh," she said. "Oh, that's so sweet."

"Is it a puppy?" Maia demanded.

"No," Aroha said. "That wouldn't be a good wedding present. They're going on a *honeymoon.* You have to housetrain a puppy."

"Maybe it's a horse," Tama said.

Aroha sighed. "It can't be a *horse.* Auntie Karen goes all over the place, and Jax is a soldier. You can't have a horse if you're a soldier. Where would you keep it?"

"They have it in the cavalry," Tama said. "That's the whole thing the cavalry *is.* "

"Not *now,*" Aroha said. "Nobody fights with horses *now.*"

"Quiet," Hemi said. "Let's show Auntie Karen her present."

Auntie Karen was about to expire from curiosity. Auntie Karen was, in fact, about to run screaming in circles.

It was a house. A house set on the foreshore at Tanners Point, to be exact, in the calm waters of Shelly Bay, halfway between Katikati and Waihi Beach. A house down the coast from Hope and Hemi and only minutes away from Koro, with two ovens and a view of palm trees and the sea, a lawn that sloped down to a safe swimming beach, and kayaks on the grass. A house with three bedrooms, because one of these days, we were going to take out that IUD, and a home office off its perfect kitchen for a wife who was a consultant. And with a spa tub on the deck for a husband whose leg got sore, because he was a soldier, and he was a hero.

I was flying upstairs for my own phone, and pressing the button to call him.

411

"Hi, baby," he said. No stress at all in his voice. He sounded like this was the best day of his life.

My knees were shaking, and I slid down the wall to sit on the floor. "Thank you. For my necklace, and . . . and the house. How can you make my life so beautiful? How?"

"I thought you'd want to be closer to your whanau," he said, and I closed my eyes and had to swallow hard. "The apartment's all good"—the little one we rented in Christchurch, where we lived during the week, heading for Moeraki for the weekends—"but I thought about how I'd assumed I'd stay down south, because it's home. And I realized that you'd want the same thing. You need to be near your Koro while you can, because you aren't going to have him forever, and near your sister, too, and all the rest of them. You're going to want to be home, and when we have kids, you're going to want that even more. I may ask for a posting in Auckland, I thought. We can keep the house in Moeraki, or we can sell it. Heaps of time to decide, but this felt important. It felt right. You changed your life so we could be together. Time for me to show you what I'll do for you."

I said, when I could talk again, "It makes my present to you kind of stupid, though."

He was laughing now. "Can't wait. What is it?"

"You're getting it later. OK. I'm . . . I'm overwhelmed. I can't even think. I'm hanging up. I have to get ready, and . . . so many things. I'll see you later. I can't wait, even though I'm really nervous. Oh—and I love you. So much. I do."

He was still laughing when I hung up.

⭐

JAX

Karen thought I was calm, and she was almost right.

I was sure. That might not be calm, but it felt good.

The carpark was filling up when I got there with my best mate. Colin Armsworth was wearing his dress uniform, and I wasn't. He climbed out of the car with me, looked around at lush grass, stately rimu and rata trees, and the wharenui, the meeting house, with its carved red-stained front barge boards. At all the down-home comfort and stateliness of Makahae Marae, in fact, watched over by the mountains of the Hautere Forest. Koro's marae, and Hemi's. And after today, Karen would finally believe, hers.

Colin said, "Nothing like a Maori wedding."

When Karen's grandfather had told her she'd be married at the marae, she'd cried and hugged him. He'd patted her on the back and said, "Of course you are. Of course. Can't have my mokopuna getting married anywhere else, can I," and she'd cried some more. Like she couldn't believe it.

Now, the rest of my family and friends gathered and waited for the karanga, the welcome song from the women. A pulling song for the canoes, Karen had told me, the same one the people of the night had sung to pull Mauao over the land toward the sea. Not a lonely mountain anymore. A beloved mountain, one who'd taken a while to find his place in the world, but who knew now exactly where it was.

When the song was over, we moved forward, taking off our shoes on the benches at the entrance, which was when Poppy decided that she needed to tell me, "The kilt looks a little stupid without shoes."

She was trying her best to be breezy and cheerful, but I could tell it wasn't easy. She'd sold the glamping business to Hemi a couple months ago, and I thought she might have told Max to move out after that, because he didn't seem to have been home in a while, and he wasn't here today. I wasn't sure of the reasons, because she wasn't sharing, and I wasn't sure what would happen next, either. All I knew was that she had circles under her eyes, and her belly was the only substantial part of her.

I kissed her cheek. "Never mind. Karen will still like it." I'd given my bride the choice of my dress uniform or the kilt, and she'd chosen the kilt, to my absolute non-surprise. My dad, and some of the other male guests, were wearing the full regalia as well. The knee-length kilt in the red and green

MacGregor tartan, the short Prince Charlie black coat with its silver buttons, and the waistcoat, white shirt, bow tie, sporran, and knee socks, with the sgian-dubh, the dagger, tucked into the top of the right-hand one. Or the left-hand one, for me. My working hand.

I was a New Zealand soldier and a Highland Scot, marrying an American at a Maori marae.

Worked for me.

I was doing fine when I came out of a side door twenty minutes later with Colin and the celebrant, and when we stood before the congregation. Dress uniforms and more kilts, Maori tattoos hidden under dress shirts, kids and pregnancies and cousins and grandparents and all the spilling-over generations of the whanau that was so much more Karen's than she'd realized. My cousin Verity playing the violin, its soaring strains merging with the sounds that my mate Gordon, who played with the Royal New Zealand Air Force band, was pulling from the bagpipes. The music tugged at me, plaintive and yearning, and made my heart swell even more, but I was fine.

When Karen's youngest niece, Maia, came down the aisle holding hands with my own niece, Olivia, both of them throwing their rose petals with frowning, fierce determination, I smiled, and I was still fine. And when my nephew, Hamish, came marching down in his own red-and-green kilt and bow tie, carefully holding the satin pillow with Karen's and my rings tied with a ribbon on top, I may have choked up, but I didn't cry.

I was fine when Hope walked down the aisle, too, looking serene and lovely in a dress her husband had clearly designed especially and only for somebody as pregnant, and as petite, as she was, and as she smiled at me with a face full of joy, reached up, kissed my cheek, and murmured, "I'm so happy," before turning to stand and wait for her sister.

All right, maybe I wasn't exactly fine, but I wasn't losing it, either.

And then the music changed, the violin picking up the first strains of *Highland Cathedral,* the bagpipes joining in. The congregation stood, turned, and watched as my bride came down the aisle to me on her grandfather's arm. Slowly, because the old man was slow. But he was so proud.

It was the song I'd played on the beach, when I'd had too much emotion in my heart for it to come out any other way. It was the woman who walked to me, her hair feathered around her temples and across her forehead, her whiskey-brown eyes shining, her generous mouth smiling, all of it just for me. Wearing my pendant around her neck, and, under a dress that flowed around her beautiful body like the waves on the sea, my rubies in her belly piercings. Her joy transcendent, her life force filling the room. A strong woman who'd found her voice, a loving woman who'd found her home.

She came to me just like that. Just like everything.

The two of them got to us as the song ended, and Karen turned to her Koro, put a gentle hand on his shoulder, and pressed her forehead and nose to his in a hongi. By the time they were done, the tissues were out in force. Hemi stood and helped his grandfather to his seat, and Karen handed her bouquet to her sister, then took both my hands, leaned in, smiled like all the stars in the sky, and said, "Hi. I love you so much."

I'd done three hard tours in Afghanistan. I'd watched men die, and I'd killed them, too. I'd lain bleeding in the dust and looked at the leg I'd lost. And even after all of that, it was a good thing our vows were the traditional ones, because otherwise, I'd never have kept it together while I said them.

I pledged my heart and hand to her, and she did the same for me, and when that diamond-studded ring I'd bought had slid home to stay on her finger, and the other band was on my own, when we'd walked up the aisle again knowing we were married, I danced with my wife.

I was better at it now. I'd worked at it. You could call it functional fitness, because it was what I needed to do. Tonight, I'd carry her over the threshold, because I needed to do that, too.

My ring was brushed white gold and absolutely plain on the outside, but the inner surface shone with rose gold to match hers. The same way my softness might stay on the inside most of the time, but she knew it was there, and she knew it was hers.

When she was in my arms, and I was looking down at the neck I'd be kissing tonight, I dropped her into a dip and said, "I liked your present. A lot."

The text had come an hour before I'd seen her in her dress, when I'd been fastening the onyx studs into my dress shirt.

The bride's present to the groom, I'd read. And then thirty seconds more when I'd stood there, the black strip of silk that would become my bow tie in my hand, waiting to see what she'd given me.

A photo.

Her hand, with my ruby on it, pulling aside a curtain of palest-pink satin, showing me the prettiest curve of bottom a man could ever hope to see, edged by a strip of white lace. And in my handwriting, down there at the bottom of that curve, where her bikini would ride up, and anybody would be able to see it . . .

Jax.

I'd smiled so hard.

Now, she was the one smiling as I pulled her up and waltzed her in a circle.

"It's not a house," she said, "and it's not a diamond. But it's all yours. Just like me."

Better than a medal.

A KIWI GLOSSARY

A few notes about Maori pronunciation:

- The accent is normally on the first syllable.
- All vowels are pronounced separately.
- All vowels except u have a short vowel sound.
- "wh" is pronounced "f."
- "ng" is pronounced as in "singer," not as in "anger."

across the Ditch: in Australia (across the Tasman Sea). Or, if you're in Australia, in New Zealand!

agro: aggravation

air con: air conditioning

All Blacks: National rugby team.

ambo: paramedic

Aotearoa: New Zealand (the other official name, meaning "The Land of the Long White Cloud" in Maori)

Aussie, Oz: Australia. (An Australian is also an Aussie. Pronounced "Ozzie.")

bach: holiday home (pronounced like "bachelor")

backs: rugby players who aren't in the scrum and do more running, kicking, and ball-carrying—though all players do all jobs and play both offense and defense. Backs tend to be faster, leaner, and more glamorous than forwards.

bench: counter (kitchen bench)

berko: berserk

Big Smoke: the big city (usually Auckland)
bikkies: cookies
billy-o, like billy-o: like crazy. "I paddled like billy-o and just barely made it through that rapid."
bin, rubbish bin: trash can
binned: thrown in the trash
bit of a dag: a comedian, a funny guy
bits and bobs: stuff ("be sure you get all your bits and bobs")
bollocks: rubbish, nonsense
boofhead: fool, jerk
booking: reservation
boots and all: full tilt, no holding back
bot, the bot: flu, a bug
Boxing Day: December 26—a holiday
brekkie: breakfast
brilliant: fantastic
bub: baby, small child
buggered: messed up, exhausted
bull's roar: close. "They never came within a bull's roar of winning."
bunk off: duck out, skip (bunk off school)
bust a gut: do your utmost, make a supreme effort
caravan: travel trailer
cardie: a cardigan sweater
chat up: flirt with
chilly bin: ice chest
chips: French fries. (potato chips are "crisps")
chocolate bits: chocolate chips
chocolate fish: pink or white marshmallow coated with milk chocolate, in the shape of a fish. A common treat/reward for kids (and for adults. You often get a chocolate fish on the saucer when you order a mochaccino—a mocha).
choice: fantastic
chokka: full
chooks: chickens
Chrissy: Christmas
chuck out: throw away
chuffed: pleased

collywobbles: nervous tummy, upset stomach
come a greaser: take a bad fall
cot: crib (for a baby)
crook: ill
cuddle: hug (give a cuddle)
cuppa: a cup of tea (the universal remedy)
CV: resumé
cyclone: hurricane (Southern Hemisphere)
dairy: corner shop (not just for milk!)
dead: very; e.g., "dead sexy."
dill: fool
do your block: lose your temper
dob in: turn in; report to authorities. Frowned upon.
doco: documentary
doddle: easy. "That'll be a doddle."
dodgy: suspect, low-quality
dogbox: The doghouse—in trouble
dole: unemployment.
dole bludger: somebody who doesn't try to get work and
  lives off unemployment (which doesn't have a time limit
  in NZ)
Domain: a good-sized park; often the "official" park of the
  town.
dressing gown: bathrobe
drongo: fool (Australian, but used sometimes in NZ as well)
drop your gear: take off your clothes
duvet: comforter
earbashing: talking-to, one-sided chat
electric jug: electric teakettle to heat water. Every Kiwi
  kitchen has one.
En Zed: Pronunciation of NZ. ("Z" is pronounced "Zed.")
ensuite: master bath (a bath in the bedroom).
eye fillet: premium steak (filet mignon)
fair go: a fair chance. Kiwi ideology: everyone deserves a fair
  go.
fair wound me up: Got me very upset
fantail: small, friendly native bird
farewelled, he'll be farewelled: funeral; he'll have his funeral.

feed, have a feed: meal
fizz, fizzie: soft drink
fizzing: fired up
flaked out: tired
flash: fancy
flat to the boards: at top speed
flat white: most popular NZ coffee. An espresso with milk but no foam.
flattie: roommate
flicks: movies
flying fox: zipline
footpath: sidewalk
footy, football: rugby
forwards: rugby players who make up the scrum and do the most physical battling for position. Tend to be bigger and more heavily muscled than backs.
fossick about: hunt around for something
front up: face the music, show your mettle
garden: yard
get on the piss: get drunk
get stuck in: commit to something
give way: yield
giving him stick, give him some stick about it: teasing, needling
glowworms: larvae of a fly found only in NZ. They shine a light to attract insects. Found in caves or other dark, moist places.
go crook, be crook: go wrong, be ill
go on the turps: get drunk
gobsmacked: astounded
good hiding: beating ("They gave us a good hiding in Dunedin.")
grotty: grungy, badly done up
ground floor: what the U.S. calls the first floor. The "first floor" is one floor up.
gumboots, gummies: knee-high rubber boots. It rains a lot in New Zealand.
gutted: thoroughly upset
Haast's Eagle: (extinct). Huge native NZ eagle. Ate moa.

haere mai: welcome (Maori; but used commonly)

haka: ceremonial Maori challenge—done before every All Blacks game

hang on a tick: wait a minute

hard man: the tough guy, the enforcer

hard yakka: hard work (from Australian)

harden up: toughen up. Standard NZ (male) response to (male) complaints: "Harden the f*** up!"

have a bit on: I have placed a bet on [whatever]. Sports gambling and prostitution are both legal in New Zealand.

have a go: try

have a nosy for... : look around for

head: principal (headmaster)

head down: or head down, bum up. Put your head down. Work hard.

heaps: lots. "Give it heaps."

hei toki: pendant (Maori)

holiday: vacation

honesty box: a small stand put up just off the road with bags of fruit and vegetables and a cash box. Very common in New Zealand.

hooker: rugby position (forward)

hooning around: driving fast, wannabe tough-guy behavior (typically young men)

hoovering: vacuuming (after the brand of vacuum cleaner)

ice block: popsicle

I'll see you right: I'll help you out

in form: performing well (athletically)

it's not on: It's not all right

iwi: tribe (Maori)

jabs: immunizations, shots

jandals: flip-flops. (This word is only used in New Zealand. Jandals and gumboots are the iconic Kiwi footwear.)

jersey: a rugby shirt, or a pullover sweater

joker: a guy. "A good Kiwi joker": a regular guy; a good guy.

journo: journalist

jumper: a heavy pullover sweater

ka pai: going smoothly (Maori).

kapa haka: school singing group (Maori songs/performances. Any student can join, not just Maori.)

karanga: Maori song of welcome (done by a woman)

keeping his/your head down: working hard

kia ora: hello (Maori, but used commonly)

kilojoules: like calories—measure of food energy

kindy: kindergarten (this is 3- and 4-year-olds)

kit, get your kit off: clothes, take off your clothes

Kiwi: New Zealander OR the bird. If the person, it's capitalized. Not the fruit.

kiwifruit: the fruit. (Never called simply a "kiwi.")

knackered: exhausted

knockout rounds: playoff rounds (quarterfinals, semifinals, final)

koru: ubiquitous spiral Maori symbol of new beginnings, hope

kumara: Maori sweet potato.

littlies: young kids

lock: rugby position (forward)

lollies: candy

lolly: candy or money

lounge: living room

mad as a meat axe: crazy

maintenance: child support

major: "a major." A big deal, a big event

mana: prestige, earned respect, spiritual power

Maori: native people of NZ—though even they arrived relatively recently from elsewhere in Polynesia

marae: Maori meeting house

Marmite: Savory Kiwi yeast-based spread for toast. An acquired taste. (Kiwis swear it tastes different from Vegemite, the Aussie version.)

mate: friend. And yes, fathers call their sons "mate."

metal road: gravel road

Milo: cocoa substitute; hot drink mix

mince: ground beef

mind: take care of, babysit

moa: (extinct) Any of several species of huge flightless NZ birds. All eaten by the Maori before Europeans arrived.

moko: Maori tattoo
mokopuna: grandchildren
motorway: freeway
mozzie: mosquito; OR a Maori Australian (Maori + Aussie = Mozzie)
muesli: like granola, but unbaked
munted: broken
naff: stupid, unsuitable. "Did you get any naff Chrissy pressies this year?"
nappy: diaper
narked, narky: annoyed
netball: Down-Under version of basketball for women. Played like basketball, but the hoop is a bit narrower, the players wear skirts, and they don't dribble and can't contact each other. It can look fairly tame to an American eye. There are professional netball teams, and it's televised and taken quite seriously.
New World: One of the two major NZ supermarket chains
nibbles: snacks
nick, in good nick: doing well
niggle, niggly: small injury, ache or soreness
no worries: no problem. The Kiwi mantra.
not very flash: not feeling well
Nurofen: brand of ibuprofen
nutted out: worked out
OE: Overseas Experience—young people taking a year or two overseas, before or after University.
offload: pass (rugby)
oldies: older people. (or for the elderly, "wrinklies!")
on the front foot: Having the advantage. Vs. on the back foot—at a disadvantage. From rugby.
op shop: charity shop, secondhand shop
out on the razzle: out drinking too much, getting crazy
paddock: field (often used for rugby—"out on the paddock")
Pakeha: European-ancestry people (as opposed to Polynesians)
Panadol: over-the-counter painkiller
partner: romantic partner, married or not
patu: Maori club

paua, paua shell: NZ abalone
pavlova (pav): Classic Kiwi Christmas (summer) dessert. Meringue, fresh fruit (often kiwifruit and strawberries) and whipped cream.
pavement: sidewalk (generally on wider city streets)
pear-shaped, going pear-shaped: messed up, when it all goes to Hell
penny dropped: light dawned (figured it out)
people mover: minivan
perve: stare sexually
phone's engaged: phone's busy
piece of piss: easy
pike out: give up, wimp out
piss awful: very bad
piss up: drinking (noun) a piss-up
pissed: drunk
pissed as a fart: very drunk. And yes, this is an actual expression.
play up: act up
playing out of his skin: playing very well
plunger: French Press coffeemaker
PMT: PMS
pohutukawa: native tree; called the "New Zealand Christmas Tree" for its beautiful red blossoms at Christmastime (high summer)
poi: balls of flax on strings that are swung around the head, often to the accompaniment of singing and/or dancing by women. They make rhythmic patterns in the air, and it's very beautiful.
Pom, Pommie: English person
pong: bad smell
pop: pop over, pop back, pop into the oven, pop out, pop in
possie: position (rugby). Pronounced "pozzie."
postie: mail carrier
pot plants: potted plants (not what you thought, huh?)
pounamu: greenstone (jade)
prang: accident (with the car)
pressie: present
puckaroo: broken (from Maori)

pudding: dessert

pull your head in: calm down, quit being rowdy

Pumas: Argentina's national rugby team

pushchair: baby stroller

put your hand up: volunteer

put your head down: work hard

rapt: thrilled

rattle your dags: hurry up. From the sound that dried excrement on a sheep's backside makes, when the sheep is running!

red card: penalty for highly dangerous play. The player is sent off for the rest of the game, and the team plays with 14 men.

rellies: relatives

rimu: a New Zealand tree. The wood used to be used for building and flooring, but like all native NZ trees, it was over-logged. Older houses, though, often have rimu floors, and they're beautiful.

root: have sex (you DON'T root for a team!)

ropeable: very angry

ropey: off, damaged ("a bit ropey")

rort: ripoff

rough as guts: uncouth

rubbish bin: garbage can

rugged up: dressed warmly

ruru: native owl

Safa: South Africa. Abbreviation only used in NZ.

sammie: sandwich

scoff, scoffing: eating, like "snarfing"

serviette: napkin

shag: have sex with. A little rude, but not too bad.

shattered: exhausted

sheds: locker room (rugby)

she'll be right: See "no worries." Everything will work out. The other Kiwi mantra.

shift house: move (house)

shonky: shady (person). "a bit shonky"

shout, your shout, my shout, shout somebody a coffee: buy a round, treat somebody

sickie, throw a sickie: call in sick
sink the boot in: kick you when you're down
skint: broke (poor)
slag off: speak disparagingly of; disrespect
smack: spank. Smacking kids is illegal in NZ.
smoko: coffee break
snog: kiss; make out with
sorted: taken care of
spa, spa pool: hot tub
sparrow fart: the crack of dawn
speedo: Not the swimsuit! Speedometer. (the swimsuit is called a budgie smuggler—a budgie is a parakeet, LOL.)
spew: vomit
spit the dummy: have a tantrum. (A dummy is a pacifier)
sportsman: athlete
sporty: liking sports
spot on: absolutely correct. "That's spot on. You're spot on."
squiz: look. "I was just having a squiz round." "Giz a squiz": Give me a look at that.
stickybeak: nosy person, busybody
stonkered: drunk—a bit stonkered—or exhausted
stoush: bar fight, fight
straight away: right away
strength of it: the truth, the facts. "What's the strength of that?" = "What's the true story on that?"
stroppy: prickly, taking offense easily
stuffed up: messed up
supporter: fan (Do NOT say "root for." "To root" is to have (rude) sex!)
suss out: figure out
sweet: dessert
sweet as: great. (also: choice as, angry as, lame as ... Meaning "very" whatever. "Mum was angry as that we ate up all the pudding before tea with Nana.")
takahe: ground-dwelling native bird. Like a giant parrot.
takeaway: takeout (food)

tall poppy: arrogant person who puts himself forward or sets himself above others. It is every Kiwi's duty to cut down tall poppies, a job they undertake enthusiastically.

Tangata Whenua: Maori (people of the land)

tapu: sacred (Maori)

Te Papa: the National Museum, in Wellington

tea: dinner (casual meal at home)

tea towel: dishtowel

throw a wobbly: have a tantrum

tick off: cross off (tick off a list)

ticker: heart. "The boys showed a lot of ticker out there today."

togs: swimsuit (male or female)

torch: flashlight

touch wood: knock on wood (for luck)

track: trail

trainers: athletic shoes

tramping: hiking

trolley: shopping cart

tucker: food

tui: Native bird

turn to custard: go south, deteriorate

turps, go on the turps: get drunk

Uni: University—or school uniform

up the duff: pregnant. A bit vulgar (like "knocked up")

ute: pickup or SUV

vet: check out

waiata: Maori song

wairua: spirit, soul (Maori). Very important concept.

waka: canoe (Maori)

Warrant of Fitness: certificate of a car's fitness to drive

wedding tackle: the family jewels; a man's genitals

Weet-Bix: ubiquitous breakfast cereal

whaddarya?: I am dubious about your masculinity (meaning "Whaddarya ... pussy?")

whakapapa: genealogy (Maori). A critical concept.

whanau: family (Maori). Big whanau: extended family. Small whanau: nuclear family.

wheelie bin: rubbish bin (garbage can) with wheels.

whinge: whine. Contemptuous! Kiwis dislike whingeing. Harden up!

White Ribbon: campaign against domestic violence

wind up: upset (perhaps purposefully). "Their comments were bound to wind him up."

wing: rugby position (back)

wobbly; threw a wobbly: a tantrum; had a tantrum

Yank: American. Not pejorative.

yonks: ages. "It's been going on for yonks."

LINKS

Never miss a new release or a sale—and receive a free book when you sign up for my **mailing list.**
Find out what's new at the **ROSALIND JAMES WEBSITE - http://www.rosalindjames.com/.**
Got a comment or a question? I'd love to hear! You can email me at **Rosalind@rosalindjames.com**

ALSO BY ROSALIND JAMES

The *Escape to New Zealand* series
Reka & Hemi's story: JUST FOR YOU
Hannah & Drew's story: JUST THIS ONCE
Kate & Koti's story: JUST GOOD FRIENDS
Jenna & Finn's story: JUST FOR NOW
Emma & Nic's story: JUST FOR FUN
Ally & Nate's/Kristen & Liam's stories: JUST MY LUCK
Josie & Hugh's story: JUST NOT MINE
Hannah & Drew's story again/Reunion: JUST ONCE MORE
Faith & Will's story: JUST IN TIME
Nina & Iain's story: JUST STOP ME
Chloe & Kevin's story: JUST SAY YES
Nyree & Marko's story: JUST SAY (HELL) NO
Zora & Rhys's story: JUST COME OVER

The *Sinful, Montana,* series
Paige's & Jace's story: GUILTY AS SIN
Lily & Rafe's story: TEMPTING AS SIN
Willow & Brett's story: SEXY AS SIN

The *Portland Devils* series
Dakota & Blake's story: SILVER-TONGUED DEVIL
Beth & Evan's story: NO KIND OF HERO

The *Not Quite a Billionaire* series (Hope & Hemi's story)
FIERCE
FRACTURED
FOUND

The *Paradise, Idaho* series (Montlake Romance)
Zoe & Cal's story: CARRY ME HOME
Kayla & Luke's story: HOLD ME CLOSE
Rochelle & Travis's story: TURN ME LOOSE
Hallie & Jim's story: TAKE ME BACK

The *Kincaids* series
Mira and Gabe's story: WELCOME TO PARADISE
Desiree and Alec's story: NOTHING PERSONAL
Alyssa and Joe's story: ASKING FOR TROUBLE

ACKNOWLEDGMENTS

Thanks to my alpha read duo, Kathy Harward and Mary Guidry, for their advice and inspiration as they read along with this book, and to Mary for her assistance with other author business so I could write.

Thanks to Richard Vian for his help with corporate ownership and financing questions.

Thanks to my husband, Rick Nolting, for reading along, and to my sister, Erika Iiams, for talking with me about the characters. Thanks as well to my son, James Nolting, for giving me my first view of the Moeraki Boulders at sunrise. True magic.

Thank you to New Zealand for being itself.

And finally, one big giant thank-you to my wonderful readers. I appreciate you.

Manufactured by Amazon.ca
Bolton, ON